THE SPELLBINDERS

The SPELLBINDERS

Aleardo Zanghellini

Lethe Press
Amherst, MA

Published by LETHE PRESS
lethepressbooks.com

ISBN: 978-1-59021-696-5

Library of Congress Cataloging-in-Publication Data
available on request

Cover art
by VILELA VALENTIN

Cover and Interior design
by INKSPIRAL DESIGN

One

THE NEW QUEEN

February 1308.

The winter wind mercilessly drove the white sand of Wissant into her eyes, caring nothing for that all-important principle: that Queens' bodies were hallowed, things of consequence, not to be trifled with. Curiously, the powerful tang from the ocean, assaulting her nose since they came in sight of the port, had seemed easier to excuse. In point of fact, she had felt like yielding to the briny pungency with abandon, dilating her nostrils, even readying her windpipes.

Queens' bodies were hallowed, things of consequence, not to be trifled with: even – perhaps, especially – a twelve-year-old Queen's body. Her husband made it apparent on their wedding night, a fortnight ago. She had spent weeks steeling herself against the prospect of consummation. On their wedding day, she sighed with relief when she realised that King Edward of England, whom she was to lose her virginity to, was tall and blond with broad shoulders, a broad forehead, and clear blue eyes. Unlike other men, he was also easy to talk to; suddenly, the whole thing seemed rather less dreadful. At night, when they kissed, his body responded in the way her women had told her a man would when intimate with a pretty girl. (It looked queer, fantastically so, but she had managed not to giggle. Thank God.) But he held back. He told her he wouldn't dream of touching her while she was still a child: his sister, Lady Elizabeth, Countess of Hereford, had commanded him to spare his young bride until she started having her menses. Besides, twelve was too young for that sort of thing, and he didn't mind waiting. So he said.

It must be for the best. Still, she was curious about what it would feel like. Her women had told her the pain would soon change into something quite different, if her husband had the right skills. She was almost sure he was possessed of considerable amatory manoeuvres, at least if his kisses were anything to go by. Were all grown up men – he was ten years her senior – capable of such formidable feats with their lips? Admittedly, her experience, until now, was limited to the time a few weeks ago when she had conscripted her younger brother Robert into trying out a bit of pecking in preparation for her wedding. A pitiful affair, that – enough to make one blush at the recollection of it. She had made Robert swear upon the Virgin's soul that he wouldn't mention it to anyone.

They were sailing to Dover on separate ships, she with her retinue and Edward with his. She composed a mental picture of her husband. He was unarguably handsome. On their way from Boulogne, where they had married a fortnight ago, to Wissant, the King's countenance had lit up when he told her how much he looked forward to introducing her to his friend Sir Piers Gaveston, Earl of Cornwall. He said that the Earl was excessively good-looking, that he had more charm and wit in his little finger than the rest of the English nobility put together, and that she was bound to fall for him. It shouldn't alarm her, he said, for everyone fell for him – except those who didn't, he supposed, of whom there were increasing numbers of late, for they resented the fact that the King loved the Earl better than them. And how could he not, when they were all so stodgy and lifeless, and the Earl so spunky, sparkling, buoyant? But she would see for herself, her husband told her. And Lord Gaveston, he added, would simply idolise her, for he was a lover of all things beautiful, and she was as comely as any Queen of Europe.

He had made his Earl sound like a dream.

+

At Dover port the white cliffs stretched sideways, left and right, gleaming in the chill sunshine like so many frozen waterfalls, whiter even than the white sand of Wissant. No sooner did she set foot on land than the Earl of Cornwall advanced to greet her. Her husband had not exaggerated his good looks. Kneeling on one knee before her, the Earl looked up to her face and said that the reputation that preceded her was well-deserved. Remembering Edward saying that the Earl abhorred flattery, she felt a thrill.

'Ravishing,' the Earl said as he stood up. His eyes were still fixed on her, but Isabella felt that he was really speaking to himself, almost as if she were out of earshot. There was, too, something queer in the way in which he said it: a hint of alarm, perhaps.

Her husband looked delighted and stamped a kiss on the Earl's lips. It seemed the most natural thing, but for reasons she could scarcely fathom, the kiss seemed to cause a minor commotion. Some of the nobles who had gathered to greet them frowned, and a couple of them whispered into each other's ears. Jealousy, she supposed. The French nobility would have known better than to show their pettiness so openly.

Later, after she had more opportunities to study her husband and his friend, she realised there was something ineffable about the two of them together. It had to do with their physical differences. Her husband: fair, strapping, each of his movements deliberate. The Earl: dark-haired, less brawny than sinewy, ample-shouldered but slender-hipped, a cat-like suppleness in his bearing. It was...as if each gave off a glow that illumined the other.

After their procession through the streets of London, all decked out and draped in gold to welcome her arrival from France, they stayed for several days at the Tower, waiting for the day of the coronation at Westminster. Edward was anxious that she should enjoy every comfort. She didn't have the heart to tell him that, despite the new tapestries on the walls and the crackling braziers, her rooms in the Tower were little more than a pale imitation of her apartment at the French Court.

The procession from the Palace to the Abbey was a little anti-climatic. Her husband, in green and black, looked like a knight out of a romance. She was sure that in her outfit, sewn to match his, she must look quite fetching too. But it was hard to feel dignified in one's bare feet, as a preposterous tradition required. As to the magnates of the Realm carrying the Royal insignia, they were attired in expensive cloth-of-gold, but the cut of their tunics wouldn't have impressed anyone at the French Court. Besides, as the Earl of Cornwall whispered in her ear, the Peers, with the possible exception of Sir Roger Mortimer, simply didn't have the looks to do justice to the precious material. Lest anyone think the Earl of Cornwall a mere mortal baron among many, the King had insisted that he should array himself in pearl-studded purple silk. As a result, Lord Gaveston, with his commanding looks, effortlessly strutting right before the King and her as he carried the crown, looked for all the world as if he himself were born to Royalty.

In the Abbey, she made an effort to get into the mood of things but felt absolutely no change descending upon her during the rituals of the consecration, unction, and coronation. As long as she kept quiet, no one would ever be aware of it; however, the lack of mystique bothered her a little. Then they returned to the Palace: the Earl of Cornwall himself had made arrangements for a reception in the Great Hall.

And here she was now, wearing the jewels her father had sent from France, and a gorgeous gown embroidered with motifs of ivy, oak leaves, and butterflies. She might be young, but she knew she could live up to the expectations of poise the guests demanded of the Queen of England. Daughter to a King and wife to another: quite enough to go to one's head. Sitting next to her husband, she felt all eyes on them. They were the centre of attention, would be the centre of Court life – well-nigh the centre of the world, for that matter. But these were idle thoughts. For now, she simply wished to enjoy the moment. The hall looked suitably grand. Everything was perfect. *Everything*. Well, everything except the food. She had been warned not to expect the same delicacies that were the order of the day at the French Court, but how could the cooks get it quite so wrong?

'Edward, do you think the swan is a little on the dry side?' she asked, making sure not to be overheard by the guests. He would appreciate her discretion.

'My dear, the whole menu was rather poorly executed... And it took so long for us to be served. I expect the Earl is mortified. I wonder what could have caused it. When he entertains me with feasts and banquets, his arrangements are always flawless.'

'It is strange.... Keep smiling, Edward, you don't want the guests to think anything is amiss. Do you think it's deliberate?'

'Why, no, Isabella – what reason could the Earl of Cornwall have to want to offend us? You know he's the truest of my friends.' Despite his obvious displeasure, he had managed not to raise his voice.

'Dear husband, keep smiling, please... You misunderstand me. I meant that someone is sabotaging the Earl's efforts. It happens all the time at home – sorry, I mean at the French Court.'

Edward regarded her with surprise. 'You've more acumen than you have any right to possess at your age, my dear!'

She tried not to look too pleased. 'In that case, hadn't you better go to the Earl?'

'Would you mind very much if I did?' Edward had already started pushing his chair back.

'Edward, wait,' Isabella whispered. *Upon my word, don't heirs apparent receive any coaching for Kingship on this island?* 'Please remember not to look perturbed.'

He kissed her lips, then her hand, and walked over to the table at which the Earl was sitting with his wife, Lady Margaret, and her close family relations, the De Clares. As the King approached, they stood up to receive him.

+

'I'M SORRY.' PIERS mouthed the words without emitting a sound as soon as he caught Edward's eye.

But as Edward approached, he realised the thick lashes failed to mask the uneasiness in Piers' eyes. He immediately sought his lips, as much out of habit as a desire to put an immediate end to his anxiety.

'Sorry for what?' he whispered.

Piers shook his head. 'When troubles come, they arrive in military formation. First the tapestries, and now –'

'Piers, smile; don't look *perturbed*.' Piers opened his mouth as if to speak, but Edward cut him short. 'There, for once my social graces are more alert than your own.' He grinned. 'Tapestries, you say? What could possibly be wrong with the tapestries?'

'You seriously mean you haven't noticed? It quite defies belief that the weavers could get *my* arms mixed up with the Queen's...'

'Hold on, Piers, we can't keep standing here, whispering like this.' Edward turned to Piers' wife. He raised her hand to his lips. 'My dear niece: Madame Isabella the Queen is very anxious to get to know you better. Would you do me the favour of following me?'

Margaret bowed her head and let her uncle lead her to the Queen.

'CHIN UP,' EDWARD said as he returned to Piers. He took the seat vacated by Margaret. 'I mean literally, Piers: raise your chin, you know, ever so slightly.... And don't fear to lower your lids a little; God knows you show off your lashes to perfection when you do that. To say nothing of how wonderfully condescending you look.' He winked. 'Now, at the tender age of twelve, the Queen is equipped with more intelligence and kingcraft than the King her husband. Do you know what she told me? She said you were being sabotaged.'

Piers narrowed his eyes. 'Sabotaged?' He was as struck by the idea as the fact that it hadn't occurred to him.

'The poorly cooked food *and* the haphazard service...it can't be a coincidence.'

Piers felt a knot inside his stomach loosen: discovering that one's arrangements had been interfered with was, after all, infinitely less concerning than doubting one's own competence in executing them.

Edward picked the end of a parsnip off Piers' plate and pushed it into his own mouth. 'I wonder who exactly we have to thank for attempting to discredit you.'

His eyes started scanning the room, but Piers put a hand on his forearm. 'We'll never find out unless you have recourse to violence, Edward; and I forbid you to taint the memory of this day with it.'

Edward shrugged. Piers wondered what faces the guests would pull if they overheard Lord Gaveston issuing prohibitions to the King. He pursed his lips to suppress a smile.

'In any case,' said Edward, 'in respect of the tapestries, you're quite wrong. No one got the arms mixed up, either accidentally or by design. The weavers executed the design just as I commissioned it. I thought having your arms next to mine was rather a nice touch.'

Disbelief, amusement, sheer delight: even Piers didn't quite know which he felt most. 'A *nice* touch?'

Edward frowned. 'Why, is it so strange? We're sworn brothers, are we not? Brothers-in-arms share common heraldic patterns – what could be so wrong with our arms appearing next to each other on the tapestries?'

Piers regarded his lover quizzically: could Edward be serious? He shook his head, even as he felt a rush of warmth for the King suddenly wash over him. 'On the occasion of yours and your newly-wed Queen's coronation banquet, I'd say there's rather a lot that's wrong with it...'

But Edward brushed his protest aside with a wave of the hand. 'Pour me some wine, Piers, let's celebrate! I love you so – tonight it seems to me more than ever. Kiss me now, Perrot, and don't rush it – make it last.'

+

WHEN EDWARD HAD gone back to the Earl, Isabella ordered one of the attendants to fetch a stool, and, patting the seat with her hand, invited Lady Margaret to sit down.

'Everyone at this table is positively ancient,' she whispered in the Countess of Cornwall's ear.

Lady Margaret smiled. Dimples appeared on her cheeks and chin. Isabella took an instinctive liking to her husband's buxom niece. She admired her sky-blue dress, with velvet trimmings the same purple as the Earl's outfit.

The, returning her gaze to Margaret's face. She said, 'Why, you look nothing like the King.'

Lady Margaret shrugged. 'I don't take after my mother's side of the family.'

Isabella smiled. She turned to look idly at Edward and the Earl. 'Do you think we secured the most handsome husbands in the Kingdom?'

Margaret drew her veil over her breast. 'Everyone thinks so, I daresay.'

'But not you?'

'Oh yes, My Lady, of course I do.'

'Do you also find that something happens to them when they associate?'

'Yes, My Lady. The Earl glows in the King's presence. It's quite impossible to miss, is it not?'

'That's what I thought. My husband the King is always quite full of life, from what I can judge – but never so much as when he's with the Earl.' She returned her eyes to the two men. 'What's the Earl like at home?'

'Charming, of course. But he rather keeps to himself.' Isabella gave Lady Margaret a quizzical look; the latter smiled timidly. 'Lord Gaveston has been the King's right hand for almost as long as I have lived. I can hardly expect him to pay much attention to me. Not right away, I mean. We've only been married a few short months.'

As she spoke, her hands were joined before her, resting on the table: they too were dimpled. Isabella reached out to cover them with her own. She turned once again to look at her husband. Just then, the Earl slowly reached towards the King, holding Edward's eyes, until their mouths made contact. Isabella quickly realised that this kiss was unlike that which the men had exchanged on her arrival in Dover. This time, the Earl's mouth lingered on the King's just long enough to make it dubitable that this was the kind of pressing of lips customarily exchanged between good friends or political allies. The sight had her bewitched. She remembered how good Edward's kisses felt and wondered if they tasted as sweet on the Earl's lips.

Two

BANISHED

It was a stroke of good luck, really, that the Earl of Lancaster's Royal cousin and his Gascon favourite took it into their heads to make a public spectacle of themselves at the coronation banquet. This considerably simplified Lancaster's task. But he must take care not to give himself away. When he suggested that the Earls should meet formally to discuss the matter of Sir Piers Gaveston, Earl of Cornwall, he took care to make the others feel as if the source of the idea lay elsewhere.

'Perhaps there is something,' he said innocuously at the coronation banquet to the Earl of Lincoln, 'to the suggestion one of us made – was it Warwick, or Pembroke? – that the matter should be discussed at a general meeting of the Earls. What do you think, Lincoln?'

And, lo and behold, a couple of days later, the meeting was already underway. Lincoln was an old bore; his noble, disinterested concern with the dignity and stability of the Crown could be quite sickening. Heavens, he even *looked* like a bore, with his paunch and thinning hair, and the washed-out blue of his eyes! But Lancaster had to grant he was efficient, if nothing else.

It was a dull day towards the end of February. As he made his way to the meeting room, Lancaster mentally rehearsed his lines. The other Earls were already assembled when he arrived. Lancaster greeted them, and their responses ranged from half-hearted to gruff. No one seemed particularly interested in being there, and for good reason: it was cold and miserable. The time of year and a leaden sky diminished the amount of natural light admitted into the hall – never abundant at the best of times – to the point of ludicrousness. He ordered one of his attendants to see to the torches on the wall and sent two others out to fetch ale and cups from a nearby inn. He couldn't very well have his plans scuttled by uncooperative weather.

Opening the discussion, Lincoln went straight to the point: Lord Gaveston posed a threat to the good management of public affairs.

'But how?' asked Lancaster, seizing his chance to provoke the others to express their opposition to Gaveston in the clearest of terms. 'I'm still not clear *in what way* the Earl of Cornwall's presence interferes with the country's good government.'

'By being Earl of Cornwall, for a start,' said Sir Aymer de Valence, Earl of Pembroke.

Pembroke, Lancaster reflected, was very much like a junior version of Lincoln: virtuous, dependable, and sincerely convinced, apparently, of the royalist rubbish that was apt to escape his mouth. In looks, however, they couldn't have been more different: Pembroke was dark, distinguished in a haggard sort of way, and curiously un-English in appearance, with sharp features that included a rather prominent nose.

Lancaster said, 'If I'm not mistaken, Pembroke, you yourself attested the charter granting Lord Gaveston the Earldom. And didn't Lincoln confirm that it could be done and had been done before – that the Earldom of Cornwall was not inseparable from the Crown?'

'But don't you see,' said Pembroke, 'the point is that it was done *for* Lord Gaveston. It may not have been completely unprecedented, but it was an unusual step. In hindsight, it's obvious the King wouldn't have taken it for anyone else.'

Lancaster affected mild impatience. 'So King Edward has favourites? What of it? There's nothing unusual about a King having especially trusted counsellors and desiring to advance them.'

The Earl of Hereford crossed his arms. 'A place that perhaps you yourself aspire to occupy one day, Lancaster?'

Lancaster had expected the charge. It came as no surprise, either, that it should issue from Hereford's lips. Like everyone else, Hereford aspired to be the King's chief counsellor; but unlike the others, he thought he had a special claim to it as the King's brother-in-law. Self-entitlement grounded in the natural rights of kinship made perfect sense to Lancaster: after all, he was the King's cousin. But he disliked and mistrusted Hereford's smooth ways, that polish that made you forget the man's asymmetrical facial features just as easily as the ambitions he secretly nursed.

'Don't all present here today have precisely the same aspiration?' he asked.

'Whether or not we do,' said Lincoln, 'under the circumstances, it's only honourable for us to be concerned. Lord Gaveston is not qualified to occupy such a position of trust.'

Good. The conversation had been steered away from the question of Lancaster's own motives and back to the matter of the Earl of Cornwall; Lancaster's next move would make sure it stayed there.

'You still haven't explained,' he said, '*why* Cornwall is so little qualified. Doesn't he have as distinguished a military record as any of us? Didn't the deceased King himself place him in the household of the Prince of Wales?'

The Earl of Richmond hesitated a moment before saying, 'But he subsequently removed him from that placement by shipping him off to his native country.'

As Lancaster turned towards Richmond, he concealed his distaste by forcing his face to assume a neutral expression. Everything about Richmond was contemptible. Nothing in his looks could ever be described as commanding; much worse, however, was the maddening indecisiveness that made Richmond look at an issue from every possible side. Would anyone take any notice of what the ineffectual man had just said?

Smoothening the front of his surcoat with a hand, the Elder Despenser said, 'We don't know the circumstances of Lord Gaveston's banishment. Was it even an exile properly-so-called? The late King's order only mentioned "certain reasons" why Lord Gaveston should leave the country, but it was never clear what the King's intentions were. The terms of the banishment order seemed to imply the late King would eventually recall him. We can't really know, My Lords, on what grounds the late King objected to Lord Gaveston, if at all.'

Despenser had spoken with studied equanimity, so completely incongruous with the roguish looks he shared with his son the Younger Despenser – looks that, Lancaster always thought, must permanently condemn their line to an air of parvenu. Despenser's defence of Gaveston was not surprising to Lancaster. The current balance of power was serving Despenser, a baron without an Earldom, better than he had any right to expect. He wouldn't want to risk upsetting it by sending Gaveston away.

'What more do we need to know,' said the Earl of Warwick, 'beyond that which is plainly before everyone's eyes? We were all able to determine the *exact* nature of the present King's regard for Gaveston at the coronation banquet!'

Good boy. Warwick could always be trusted to bring things to a head: for all his learning, he had always retained something fundamentally uncouth and animalistic about him. He brought it out in others, too. His remark elicited general grunts of approval; someone muttered that the tapestries had been a disgrace, and another claimed that the Earl of Cornwall should have never returned from exile.

'My Lords, Lord Gaveston has *never* acted dishonourably,' said Despenser. 'How many would have shown the same restraint, when he was appointed Keeper of the Realm during the time of the King's wedding in France? Wouldn't a man given to abuse have exploited the vast powers he was granted then?'

Warwick's diminutive, close-set eyes seemed to disappear completely behind a frown. 'Why would he need to do that, when he has the King at his beck and call?'

'Are you implying,' said Lancaster, 'that the Earl of Cornwall has induced the King to advance his interests and those of his protégés in ways unwarranted by their relationship of mutual trust?'

'Why, don't *you* think so, Lancaster?' asked Hereford with boyish, exaggerated surprise.

'But where is the evidence?'

'Really, Lancaster,' said Pembroke with his usual level-headedness, 'royal purple and pearls.... Aren't they evidence enough?'

The remark was met with a chorus of 'Ayes,' and, as the meeting drew to a close, Lancaster said to himself that all had gone according to plan. The Earls had bit the bait, and united in demanding from the King a redress of their grievances against Gaveston. At the same time, the Elder Despenser, as genuinely devoted to the current King as to the former, was sure to report to the King that his cousin Lancaster had spoken in Gaveston's defence. And once Gaveston was out of the way – Lancaster had little doubt that this was now the fate awaiting the Gascon – the King would naturally gravitate back to him, Lancaster, as his only trusted friend among the Earls.

It was frustrating to think that, having been his cousin's closest friend many years ago, Thomas of Lancaster had subsequently forfeited that position, never to regain it – particularly now that, with the Crown sitting on Edward's head, it would have made all the difference to Lancaster's fortunes. When they were children, Edward had used to look up to him like an older brother. Then, seemingly overnight, Edward had grown taller and heavier, started acting as if he had a mind of his own, and generally taken it into his head to behave like a fool. Scoffing at tournaments, going swimming, treating the word of stable grooms on a par with that of men of rank. Lancaster's cousin had always been peculiar, but what could be dismissed as whimsical in childhood became intolerable in a youth. To make things worse, Gaveston had turned up, out of that God-forsaken country of his, and had appropriated the lion's share of his cousin's regard, leaving only scraps for everyone else.

Yet, despite the distance that had grown between the cousins in the last decade or so, it wouldn't do to deny the history that had once been between Edward and him. It was on this that Lancaster now banked when he predicted that, with Gaveston gone, his cousin would turn to him for support and advice. Edward himself would be much better off for being freed of the presumptuous Gascon – yes, even if some deception was required to make this come to pass. It would be to the King's advantage to re-kindle his former closeness with his much more deserving cousin. For he *did* deserve power, financial gains, and influence. Wasn't his lineage as flawless as anyone's?

+

When Edward learnt about the Earls' meeting from the Elder Despenser, rather than summoning Piers, he immediately went out to find him.

'Backstabbing, conniving pack of traitors, the lot of them!' he shouted as he stormed into Piers' chamber, scarcely noticing his lover had re-decorated it with the tapestries from the coronation banquet. Piers had a hard time trying to calm the King down; it didn't help that his own failure to see all this coming unsettled him deeply.

'It's all so illogical,' Margaret said after Edward had finally left. She asked Piers what sorts of men the Earls were. Supposing it was true that the King didn't have them in his confidence and favour – why did they begrudge Lord Gaveston the trust and favours the King accorded *him*? Wasn't envy a capital sin? And how did her husband's counsel prevent *them* from counselling the King as well? Did the favours the King bestowed on him stop them from seeking favour with the King?

'I don't know, my dear,' said Piers. 'Perhaps the King and I *are* partly to blame. We could've been more cautious, I suppose. Men are flawed creatures. One is well-advised to adjust one's conduct to other men's vices. Instead, your uncle and I.... We didn't really do that. Having sensed their jealousy, we provoked it further. We responded to their envy with vices of our own, I'm afraid.' He sighed.

Margaret considered this briefly. 'Hubris, you mean?'

Piers nodded. Of course, provoking the Earls every now and again had felt exhilarating. But Piers kept quiet about that, lest he spoil the impromptu moral lecture he had just visited upon this child that Edward had insisted he marry. When Margaret said she still couldn't see why the Earls thought *they* had a right to resent his closeness to the King, when she herself, Piers' own wife, did not mind it, he regarded her almost as if he had seen her for the first time. *You're a beast, Piers Gaveston,* he said to himself. *Have I neglected you horribly, child?*

He extended an arm toward her. 'Come here.'

She obeyed. He was sitting close to the brazier. He sat her in his lap, her back pressing against his chest. He pushed her veil out of the way and rested his chin on her shoulder. He felt her control the impulse to squirm, as the stubble on his cheek teased her neck – agreeably, he hoped. They stayed like that for a long while, without speaking. It was the most physically intimate he had ever been with her.

+

Westminster, late April 1308.

THE TREES HAD finally leafed out, and the sunlight spilling through the small window of the King's chamber had a greenish cast, making the room look vaguely otherworldly. Or perhaps it was just Piers' anticipation, as if he sensed the unreality that was about to claim the world he had known for nearly a decade. A blackbird's song reached his ear, flute-like. He wished he could lose himself in the spell of the soothing, liquid notes. He inhaled deeply, bracing himself for what was to come.

'What are their demands?' he asked.

Edward looked suddenly exhausted. He sat down at the table, elbow on it, hand on his forehead, eyes closed. 'That you be stripped of the Earldom of Cornwall.' His voice was barely audible.

Piers exhaled a long sigh. 'You must accept their demand, Edward.'

'They hate that a foreigner should have it. And they expect me to live under the pretence that they're your equals! *Peers,* they call themselves.' Edward stood. 'Whose Peers? Not mine! I've only contempt for the lot of them.'

'Still, you must accede to their requests,' Piers said calmly, but louder this time. He stood upright, holding his elbows, face turned towards the window.

'But they also want you banned, Piers – exiled, don't you see?'

They turned to look into each other's eyes in perfect unison. Edward's were brimming with tears.

Piers felt a tear run down his own cheek, but he managed to control his voice. 'Then promise you'll allow me to go. You can't put on me the responsibility of bringing civil war upon you. I could never live with myself.'

'Piers, I beg you, don't –'

'They're up in arms in the Abbey as we speak. In arms against *you*, because of *me*! Your kingship is your birthright – you must let me go.'

Edward dried his face with the sleeve of his tunic. His eyes returned to Piers, entreatingly. 'Was it so obvious – did I make it obvious that they were nothing to me, that you are everything?'

Piers' arms reached out behind Edward's back and drew him close. 'Hush now. I'll find a way to return to you. I promise.'

The birdsong had ceased, but Piers only realised it after Edward had disengaged himself from his arms.

+

The Tower of London, 1308, before the middle of May.

When Edward went to the Queen's chamber, she was sitting on a stool. The white linen of her night shift, embroidered with tiny rosettes, made her look like a young girl – which, of course, was just what she was, even if he sometimes forgot. One of her women was combing her hair: it draped neatly down her back, all the way to the end of her spine. In the candlelight, it lacked the lustre it showed in the sunshine. It was a pity, Edward thought, that women should go about with their hair covered.

After Isabella sent her women away, he knelt down in front of her and took her hands in his. The smell of lavender hung about her. He swallowed; then he broke the news of Piers' exile.

'But you can't let him go! It's impossible!'

Edward sighed. As if banishing his own lover was not harrowing enough; as if he needed his girl-bride's dismay to weaken his already shaky resolve...

It was an effort to keep his voice from breaking. 'I've already promised him that I'll allow him to go, Isabella. I can't force him to stay.'

Isabella shook her head, nose and lips quivering. 'But why, Edward? Don't you love him?'

'Please don't torture me, my dear... There's no other way.' He looked away. 'My officials have already prepared the writ of banishment. I shall have to sign it before long.'

'Why do they hate him, Edward?'

'Because he's better than them, and a foreigner. And because I love him.'

'Will they start hating me, next?'

'Isabella...'

'Can't we keep him here, in the Tower? He'd be safe if –'

'My dear, do you wish to confine him to the Tower for the rest of his life, like an immured nun?'

She lifted her eyes to his, tears thickening her lashes, looking like the distraught child that she was, and breaking his heart once over.

Disengaging her hands from his, she turned abruptly away. 'Oh, I *hate* them with all my heart! Why must they subject him to such indignity! Will he ever be able to come back? Come back to you, Edward?'

He felt his heart melt as he fought back the tears. 'He promised he shall find a way. He promised.'

Three

THE CUNNING MAN

THE WRIT OF banishment provided that Sir Piers Gaveston should depart no later than 25 June 1308, and that on that day, the lands associated with the Earldom of Cornwall would revert to the King's hands. Edward had managed to negotiate with the Peers that Piers should not, however, be stripped of the title of Earl itself.

In late June, Edward set off from Windsor with Piers and Lady Margaret. He would see them off at Bristol port; from there, the earl and his wife would sail to Ireland. Once they reached Reading, their route followed the course of the river Kennet westwards, all the way to Marlborough. Less than an hour after leaving Reading behind, they crossed a wooden bridge to the southern side of the river. A decade earlier, squabbles about who was financially responsible for repairing it had nearly thrown Edward's father, then King, into a seizure. On any other day, the recollection would have been cause for mirth. But this was no ordinary day. Or wasn't it? Hadn't Piers been exiled once before? Before then, hadn't Edward's father taken Piers from his household? Edward turned to look at his lover, riding upright without stiffness, eyes fixed ahead, the very paragon of knighthood, and sighed. Enforced separation from the man dearest to his heart seemed an inevitable occurrence in Edward's life.

It was after midday, and they soon came in sight of a mill. Its grounds made for an ideal stop; in proximity of the building, the river branched out attractively into three separate streams, forming two islands – one long, thin and inaccessible, and the other much smaller, right behind the mill. A footbridge led to the smaller island. Edward instructed Piers' men and his own escort to rest at the front of the building, guarding access to the footbridge. He and Piers would retire to the island and enjoy some privacy before resuming the journey. He didn't have the heart to ask his niece Margaret to wait with the soldiers by the mill. Instead, he offered her his hand and led her onto the bridge. No sooner were they on the other side, however, than Margaret excused herself and retired to the farthest corner of the island.

+

MARGARET MADE HER way through the meadow, her advance greeted by a multitude of small, winged things taking off from the wildflowers on either side of her. Some of them appeared intent on landing in the ash-coloured cloud of curls that had expanded over her shoulders as soon as she had removed her linen veil. She let them be: there was enough of her billowy hair to spare some for the use of damselflies.

She was following a well-trodden path amongst the weeds. They came all the way up to her elbows, though this was hardly an impressive scale, for she was barely fourteen and late in developing. *Chances are I am as tall now as I ever will be.* The thought was dispiriting, but only very mildly so. She was learning to be content with her looks. Finding a log, she tested it with her hand. It appeared solid and no water seeped out of the mossy lining when she squished it, so she sat down.

It was her husband that had done it – made her increasingly comfortable about herself, that is. He may not have had a great deal of time for her, which was hardly unusual for husbands, let alone if they were the King's favourites. But she had received more compliments from him in less than a year as husband and wife than from the world at large throughout the entire course of her life.

The magnitude of the change that this had wrought in her struck her quite suddenly. Wondrously, too, her husband must be honest, for she was at a loss to ascribe his amiability to any ulterior motives. He had no reason to flatter her with an eye to her fortunes, for they were already his. And since he didn't seem especially anxious to require uxorial services of her, his compliments couldn't be a ruse to mellow her and have his way with her body under the bed-sheets.

In fact, her husband would have been at perfect liberty to take no notice of her whatsoever, if he had been only half-minded to. For, notoriously, in the eyes of her uncle the King, Sir Piers Gaveston could not put a foot wrong. This made it all the more extravagant that her husband should say to her, in the queerest, off-handed way, the most extraordinary things, the likes of which she had never known a man to express to a woman in real life, let alone husbands to their wives. Apparently, she was possessed of beautifully tapered fingers and a remarkable smoothness of nail (fancy that); her ash-coloured curls were 'an exceedingly scarce commodity.' Best of all, her plumpness suited her and, growing up, she must take care not to lose her rotundity.

To think that she had looked upon this marriage with some apprehension, imagining it would mean trading the interference of her family for the tyranny of a husband! (Though, in fairness, she supposed that her lot as the second daughter of the Earl of Hetford hadn't actually been the bondage it had sometimes seemed to her.) But it turned out her uncle the King had chosen for her a consort who left her free to think her thoughts and dream her dreams at leisure – one that, adding to the bargain, wasn't half-bad to look at, and proved pleasurable company on those occasions when their paths crossed for more than a few minute in a row.

Was it really any wonder that, when confronted with the alternative to follow him in his exile to Ireland or stay put, she would choose the former?

+

THEY SAT ON the grass, under one of the ash trees, close to the reeds growing by the water edge. The air was warm and still, the sky blanched; hundreds of diminutive damselflies, enamelled turquoise and black, hovered among a frothy overabundance of pignut flowers.

'She could have chosen to stay in England, you know,' Piers told Edward, looking in the direction in which Margaret had walked off. She was no longer in sight. He was sure the reason she had excused herself, just now, was for his and Edward's sake – she had sensed they would appreciate some time alone. He had learnt something of his young wife's perceptive nature since their marriage a few months before.

'It's at least a small comfort to know my niece at your side, Perrot. Take good care of her.'

'She's only a child. Much too young for all this.'

Edward squeezed his hand. 'I wish I could make time stand still.'

'I'll come back to you. I promise.'

'I wouldn't be letting you go if I weren't sure of it.' Edward looked briefly away. Then he squeezed Piers' hand again, almost as if to make sure that it was still in his. 'My blandishments are already starting to work. Your brother-in-law, the Earl of Gloucester, is already back into the fold; it's only a matter of time until the others follow suit. Even better, four of the Earls have endorsed your appointment as Lieutenant of Ireland – and none of the others have actively hindered it.'

Piers smiled at Edward in an effort to reassure him. 'That's something, considering.' Even as he uttered them, he realised his words were implying that he hadn't been fooled by Edward's efforts to suppress his misgivings. Too late now. 'You'll be proud of my lieutenancy in Ireland. I know how much it means to you to send me off in an honourable position.'

'To me and the Queen. I don't know that it wasn't Isabella herself who put into my head the idea of appointing you Lieutenant of Ireland. Since I had to send you away from me anyway.'

They were silent for a while. No sound or stirring came from Margaret's direction. *Asleep*, Piers reflected. *She was on edge all day and night yesterday.*

Edward moved closer. Piers' hands drew the King's face to his own, slowly. His lips sought out the King's, then moved over Edward's cheekbone, jaw and neck. He stopped briefly to contemplate the face of his lover, now kissed by faint sunshine.

'Your eyes… like two damselflies,' he whispered in Edward's ear. 'You taste salty,' he added inconsequently. He returned his lips to Edward's neck, grazing about his Adam's apple. He reached his hand into the King's hose and cupped his cock and balls. Edward was still soft. The warmth and feel of him was reassuring, but there was also something heartbreakingly vulnerable – pitiful, even – about the lump of flesh that weighed in Piers' palm. A hair away from tears, he abruptly pulled Edward's hose down and buried his face between his lover's thighs, trying to think only of the body he knew and loved so well – its texture, taste, and scent. He kissed Edward's cock, and slipped its length, still soft, into his mouth. He held his breath as it started pulsing with life against his tongue, inching its way, with slow deliberation, deeper into his mouth... Then, lost in lovemaking, they consigned the anguish of the past few months to temporary oblivion. And, afterwards, they fell asleep.

Piers emerged from his slumber with the feeling, ever unnerving, of a pair of eyes fixed upon him. *Margaret*, he thought to himself. Without opening his lids, he discreetly removed his hand from whichever part of Edward's body it was presently resting on (mercifully, it seemed to be somewhere over, rather than inside, the King's hose). Finally opening his eyes, Piers winced: the hoary tangle of hair and beard standing above them was not his wife – not to mention the putrid odour reeking from it. Piers felt he might throw up.

Edward awoke, and the man spoke, an accusatory finger pointing at them. 'This closeness of yours invites uncleanness!'

Piers suppressed an urge to give the old scarecrow a good thrashing. 'Piss off.'

'Uncleanness? Do you mean this?' Edward placed a hand over Piers' thigh, and grinned. It was just like Edward, Piers thought, to engage an eccentric in conversation. 'I'm afraid it's a little late for your warning, old man. We've been unclean for the past decade or so.'

'Uncleanness and death! You court death!'

'Watch your tongue, imbecile,' Piers said. 'I'm not above ripping it out.'

Edward gestured to him to hold back. 'Explain yourself, philosopher.'

'Make it end,' said the man. 'He,' – pointing at Piers – 'he'll be your ruin.'

'My ruin?' echoed Edward.

The man crossed himself. 'You'll never be rid of him. Watch out, or you'll never be rid of him!'

'But don't you see, old fool, that's just my most ardent desire: never to be rid of him.'

Edward turned towards Piers, and Piers could read it all in the King's eyes: how he was still rapt with Piers' own beauty; how, almost a decade after their first meeting, it still struck the King as unequalled.

'Be off now,' Edward said.

The man hesitated but cowered as soon as Piers stirred to stand. Muttering to himself, he scuttled towards the footbridge and out of sight. The air clarified, Piers inhaled deeply. He and Edward looked at each other and burst into a nervous laugh.

'Where on earth did he spring from? Didn't you give instructions to guard access to the island?'

'He must've already been here before we arrived.'

The realisation came to them simultaneously, striking panic in both their hearts.

'Margaret!' they shouted in unison, dashing towards the spot where they supposed Piers' young wife had been lying asleep.

'Margaret!' Piers said again when they reached her, and he took her in his arms. 'Are you all right, child?'

'I…think so. Why? What's the matter?' She looked bemused, but not alarmed. Both men sighed with relief.

'Nothing,' Edward said. 'An old fool, posing as a cunning man, had been hiding on the island…. But he's gone now. We thought he could have...that he might have…. Never mind. Forget about him. We should leave.'

Piers and Edward resolved to put the incident out of their mind and spent the rest of the journey to Bristol reassuring each other of Piers' timely return from exile. They rehearsed the progress Edward had already made to convert the other Earls; in due course, Lincoln himself would have to come around to Edward's wish to recall Piers. For, after all, Lincoln had always believed in the primacy of Royal power.

On the voyage to Ireland, however, there was little that Margaret could do to take Piers' concerned mind off Edward. Piers could picture it all with uncanny clarity: Edward returning alone to Windsor, overwhelmed by melancholy as he reminisced about the first time they had met, in Canterbury, almost a decade before.

Four

AS FATE WOULD HAVE IT

Late February 1299.

EDWARD'S FATHER, THE First Edward, had travelled to Canterbury to perform offerings at the Cathedral. The King was courting St Thomas' intercession in a bid to propitiate Celestial Powers for the upcoming campaign in Scotland. Halfway through the service, fourteen-year-old Edward sidled out of the choir towards one of the side chapels. Here, he deftly disrobed his splendidly embroidered cape, revealing a tunic made of comparatively more modest material. Having entrusted the cape to one of his grooms, he summoned a stray altar boy, who, flashing a toothy smile, showed him an inconspicuous side exit.

Outside the sacred building, Edward took a deep breath and wondered what was wrong with him: it was unlike him to feel light-headed. A few rays of sunshine helped relieve the chill from the February air. Hardly a soul was in sight; pilgrims and burghers were either inside the Cathedral with the monks or crammed around its main entrance on the western side of the building. He started walking eastwards, skirting the southern wall of the Cathedral. Not far from the easternmost point of the sacred building, the wall encircling the monastic complex bent sharply, forming a corner. In its shelter stood a clump of trees, English yews, judging by their evergreen fronds. God be his witness, he sorely needed a leak, and wasn't that just the spot for it? Judging from the tang of urine quickening his nostrils as he approached the thicket, the same idea had occurred to dozens before him.

Still pleased with how he had managed, despite his tallness, to slip out of the Cathedral unnoticed, or so he believed, he turned around to look at it. The flying buttresses, spaced at regular intervals, made the Cathedral look like the rib cage of a gigantic beast, a carcass picked clean by birds. Even the pale limestone was the colour of bone. He shivered.

As he turned towards the thicket again, a young man emerged from the trees, still in the process of adjusting his hose. He stared Edward squarely in the face; the man's own expression bore a grin, exposing a neat row of white teeth. Incongruously, the man's apparent geniality gave Edward a queer feeling of clandestinity. Timidly, he smiled back, a quick, noncommittal affair, studiously avoiding the man's eyes, and hurried past the stranger and into the ticket. While emptying his bladder, the vague queasiness that had troubled him inside the Cathedral returned. If nothing else, it had the advantage of taking his mind off his dismal lack of aplomb a moment ago.

Stepping back out of the trees, the sight of the same man threw him a little. His eyes swiftly took in the remarkably handsome face – how did he manage not to notice it before? – and the well-cut robe hugging his slim, athletic figure. Suddenly feeling the burden of his teenage years before the riper manliness of the other, Edward stopped in his tracks. *Judas, have I been staring?*

'Someone's been pushing bucketfuls of ale on you too, eh?' The stranger's friendly address checked his escalating agitation, only to make his mind go blank. Luckily, the muscles in his face seemed impelled by a knowledge that required no great presence of mind. Obligingly, they lifted the corners of his mouth in what surely must pass for a smile.

'What's with all the fuss?' the stranger asked.

Edward cleared his throat. *He thinks me a dolt.* 'Nothing, I just…it's just...'

He interrupted himself, aware of his blunder. The stranger's question had not been about him: good breeding would have prevented the man from drawing attention to Edward's lapse in social graces, even if the stranger had noticed it (of course he had).

Edward got a hold of himself. 'You mean the commotion at the other end of the Cathedral, right? Why, it's the King. The people are astir because the King is here, with his new wife, Queen Marguerite and…the King's son of course, Edward of Caernarfon.' He made sure to utter the last part with distinct emphasis. 'They're here to make offerings in preparation for the military expedition to Scotland. To put down the rebellion, you know.'

'I had been wondering where all the Brothers disappeared,' said the man. He took a folded piece of cloth out of a travelling purse. 'I was hoping the monks would be able to offer me accommodation in their guest quarters…. But not much chance of that happening now if the Royal family's in town. Oh well.' He unwrapped the parcel to reveal a flat, square confection, translucent but darkish, and started chewing on it. '*Pâte de coing*. Would you care to try some? From home.'

Without waiting for a reply, he took a second piece of the confection and raised it to Edward's mouth. *Like Holy Bread from a Priest's hands*, Edward thought to himself, struggling to suppress a giggle. Grinning, the man gently pushed the slightly sticky confection into his mouth. The finger momentarily brushing against Edward's lower lip took his breath away, but the acidic taste of the confection quickly overrode any other sensation. His queasiness suddenly seemed a distant memory.

'And where's home?' he asked, emboldened.

'Gascony's home. I arrived in Dover yesterday. As a matter of fact, we sailed here in view of the Scottish campaign you've just mentioned.'

'You a soldier?'

'My father's a banneret. We owe King Edward military service, what with the King of England also being Lord of Aquitaine. Except, of course, that King Philip of France disputes that.'

'Frenchmen fighting for King Edward of England.'

'In his service almost continuously for the last several years. My father is unaccountably devoted to King Edward.'

Unaccountably? If the stranger's loquacity had seemed to suggest that he must have had a drink or two, that conviction was now confirmed in

Edward's mind by the indiscretion that had just escaped the Gascon's (rather fetching) lips. Edward looked away, hoping the man would take the cue and change subject. Despite the unconditional loyalty he reasoned he owed his Royal parent, Edward could not say that the Gascon's ambivalence towards King Edward was enough to make him, the King's son, dislike his new acquaintance. Altogether, it was best if he, Edward, was not put to the test on that point.

'And,' the Gascon said, 'you are –'

'Following King Edward's Court,' Edward said quickly.

'A retainer?'

'Of sorts, yes. Is this your first time in England, then?' Surely later he would be able to work out why he felt a sudden impulse to conceal his identity.

'My first time was actually...let me see...' He started finger-counting. 'Three years ago. Though I sailed back to the Continent almost immediately, to fight in the Flanders. Then I was back for the Scottish campaign of 1298. Then back to the Continent. Now here again. Back and forth.' He shrugged. 'Anyway, it keeps me busy. And well-fed.'

He smiled briefly, then dropped his eyes to the ground, revealing eyelashes so impossibly long that Edward couldn't help wondering if it was all a ruse to show them off. When the Gascon returned his gaze to Edward's face, it was less amiably than before; more searchingly. Edward instinctively looked away, but soon plucked up his courage and stared back – only to discover that the Gascon was busy surveying, of all things, his lips! His heart started racing like a colt, and he worried the pounding must be visible through his tunic. Edward swallowed. Slowly but surely, the stranger's hand reached for Edward's jaw, and the boy's entire body froze. Except his cheeks: *they* were smouldering. Then, the Gascon's thumb skimmed across his lower lip, from one corner of Edward's mouth to the other, and a sudden feebleness swished from Edward's belly down to his knees. The man pulled his hand back and briefly held his thumb suspended before Edward's eyes: a small piece of the confection was stuck to it.

'*Pâte de coing* can be a little messy.'

He grinned, and, lifting the thumb to his own lips, he sucked it clean. Edward felt deflated.

'But you're shaking,' the foreigner said, frowning.

Edward himself couldn't tell if he was shivering because of the chilly air or trembling with...with whatever it was that he was feeling.

'Why are you not wearing a surcoat in this ghastly weather?' asked the Gascon.

Edward laughed. 'It's not as bad as all that...for February.'

The pulse in his temples faintly hurt.

The Gascon lifted his eyes to the sky. 'The sun's gone. Shall I –'

They were interrupted by the sound of approaching footsteps. Edward gasped at the sight of his attendant, even as he realised that this feeling of being caught red-handed was uncalled for, really quite absurd.

'At last, My Lord. I've been looking for you everywhere. It's time for Communion. The King will make a terrible scene when he realises you're not there.'

The Gascon's eyes widened as he realised the exalted status of him to whom he had spoken so freely. 'Confound it,' he whispered between his teeth.

Edward sighed, feeling overwhelmed by a feeling of regret – though at what exactly, he was not sure.

The next moment, the Gascon was on his knee, head limp, dark curls tumbling over chiselled cheekbones and jaw. 'Forgive my idle talk, My Lord. I don't always mean what I say.'

Seeing him so abashed, Edward felt a strange thrill, mixed with the urge to tell him it was of no consequence. If only his attendant... Edward sighed.

'Please, My Lord, be so good as to follow me back inside,' the attendant said. 'You look pale, My Lord. It's most unusual.'

Taking him gently by the arm, he started leading Edward toward the Cathedral. Edward allowed him to do so at first, but after twenty or so steps he suddenly wrenched himself free. He turned to look in the direction of the Gascon. The soldier was no longer on his knee, but standing still, straight as a lance, his gaze following Edward's retreat.

'*Pâte de coing!* Fit for a King,' Edward wanted to shout, inconsequently, to the young Gascon. He did not. Instead, turning around again and quickening his pace, he plunged through the doorway into the Cathedral. Inside, as he looked up at the rib vaulting, he almost felt as if the Cathedral had swallowed him whole, a King's son trapped inside the beast's belly, away from the Gascon soldier who, God-like, made his home out there, in the open. He was brought back to reality by the sight of the attendant, suddenly appearing in the doorway he himself had crossed only moments ago.

Five

MISGIVINGS

THE KING'S MEANDERING progress to the North involved numerous more prayers and alms offerings at sacred places. The Prince's Court followed the King's.

Edward quickly recovered from his physical ailment, but he felt unsettled. The accidental tryst with the soldier in Canterbury had sensitised a rawness, induced a queer languor of the mind. A bittersweet longing held sway over his whole being: an alloy of promise, regret, expectancy, disquiet. Were these the symptoms of lovesickness? His tutor Guy Ferre had once instructed him about them. Curiously, he experienced the condition as vaguely addictive: for the first several weeks at least, he felt no definite urge to be cured.

He longed for Langley, his favourite residence, and to see his sister Elizabeth. He could hardly commit to paper the story of his lovesickness for a nameless, dark-haired stranger, but wouldn't it be wonderful to tell her face-to-face? They could have had a good laugh at his absurdity, and at picturing their father's antics if he caught wind of Edward's inexplicably intense feelings for a stranger he had briefly chatted with on a winter day;

moreover, when he had been rather feeble-headed, and the stranger rather tipsy...

The Gascon had said he was due to join the Scottish campaign upon which Edward himself would be embarking in a few months' time. The prospect was vaguely intoxicating; it had even reconciled Edward with the thought of going to war. Sometime after Easter, through some casually phrased enquiries, Edward was able to ascertain that the troops of a Gascon banneret by the name of Arnaud de Gaveston were among the portion of the Royal army that would accompany the King northwards. When the Gascon contingent finally joined the Royal party, however, weeks went by without Edward ever catching sight of the banneret's son among the soldiers.

There was still a chance, Edward supposed, that the man would be making his progress northwards independently and join his father on 24 June, the date on which the King had summoned all his troops to meet in Carlisle. But the Gascon might well try to avoid Edward. His comments about the King, after all, had bordered on the treasonable. If the foreigner had worried that Edward would report him to his father the King, he may even have thought it prudent to make his way back to the Continent, abandoning the plan of joining the Scottish campaign altogether. When Edward considered this possibility, he felt as if happiness would now elude him forever. When that kind of despair crept over him, telling himself that this was all self-inflicted foolishness brought him no solace, and his friends, the wards of the King, would find him unusually taciturn and even morose.

+

THE KING AND his following reached the city of Carlisle on the appointed date, at the beginning of June's last quarter. By this time, Edward had determined that he must put his infatuation to rest. He would act like the King's son, like his father's son, like an adult. If he wasn't quite an adult yet, he'd make sure to grow into one presently. Of course, upon their arrival in Carlisle it did cross his mind that he might finally chance upon the Gascon soldier again. Putting a hand to his chest, he found his heart to be beating at much the same rate as usual. *Good*, he told himself. *That's good, is it not?*

Much of the army was already gathered in the city, but it had been decided that the campaign would not start for another week or so. During this time, Royal officials would survey the King's forces and relay necessary information to the leaders of the different units. This lapse of time would also give the soldiers who had been delayed en route an opportunity to reach the city.

It was the time of the year when the sun was at its zenith and the days in the northern counties fabulously long. The camp was abuzz with the drone of bees feeding on the wildflowers, the chatter of soldiers with inquisitive townsfolk, and the distant sound of singing and dancing from the city: impending war or not, it was the Feast of the Nativity of St John. Everything seemed to beckon to Edward, the air no less rife with possibilities than with the heady smell of horses and men. But he resisted the urge to wander about camp. He told himself he really had no reason to do so, for after all it should not matter whether the Gascon soldier was there or not.

Instead, he decided to spend the evening at the Castle, questioning the aging John de St John, his instructor in martial arts, about the background to the impending conflict. From what Edward could make out, it sounded like his father had exploited an accident in the Scottish line of succession as a pretext to claim English control over Scotland, sorely trying the Scots' patience in the process – though Sir John certainly did not put it in these terms, and surely Edward was missing something crucial. For didn't everyone, including Sir John, think his father splendid at handling the whole thing?

Having given proof to himself and others of his ability to get both involved and interested in grown-up concerns, the Prince of Wales retired for the night to the privacy (did grooms count?) of his chamber. There, he had a momentary lapse into youthful immaturity, though he decided not to be too hard on himself for it. After all, if he hadn't coaxed the seed out, it would have spilt by itself overnight and made a sticky mess of his bedclothes – and what would have been the good of that? And if the Gascon's face had flashed through his mind a couple of times while he was pleasuring himself – well, everyone knew one's mind had a mind of one's own at such times and was prone to wander...

+

It wasn't, however, possible for Edward to remain shut up in the Castle for the rest of the week. When not busy attending to his father, training, or exploring the city and its inns with different members of his household, Edward naturally found himself filling the hours wandering about camp. Equally naturally, during such outings, he was always irresistibly drawn to that part of the heathland at the edge of the camp, where Sir Arnaud de Gaveston's contingent was encamped; though he would keep at a considerable distance from their tents, lest he give himself away.

On the third day, having again stopped in sight of the Gascon encampment, Edward was standing by the stream that tumbled over rocks and peaty ground in the heathland. Some nearby soldiers had identified him as the King's son despite his inconspicuous choice of clothing, and they now came to pay their respects. The Prince was only half-listening to the discussion that was taking place between them and his attendants when he caught sight of Sir Arnaud de Gaveston's son. His heart skipped a beat. The Gascon was no more than about forty feet away from the Prince, engrossed in conversation with another soldier. Even while leisurely linking arms with his companion, he bore himself like a knight.

Apparently quite by accident, Sir Arnaud de Gaveston's son turned his head in Edward's direction, and their eyes met. The Gascon seemed to stop halfway through a sentence, but it took him only a fraction of an instant to recover. He lightly nodded at the King's son, rather austerely, and returned to attending to his interlocutor. A feeling of unreality washed over Edward. He was not sure what he had expected, but everything – even the Gascon pretending not to see him at all – would have been better than this. He took some moments to collect himself; when he was almost sure his voice would not betray his agitation, he told his companions that they would go back to the Castle.

The next couple of days, he returned to that part of camp alone, his attire chosen even more carefully so that he would not be easily recognised as the King's son. He ventured a little closer to the tents of the Gascon troops than he had dared previously, and on both days, he caught a glimpse of the dark-haired man he had failed so miserably to get out of his head. Although he couldn't muster the determination to approach him, on both days, he lingered by the stream long enough, so he thought, to give the other an opportunity to seek him out. Nothing came of it.

Hopelessness and foreboding now flocked, raven-like, into his mind. His infatuation was obviously unrequited: the Gascon's distance made this apparent. Clearly, he had attached far too much significance to the way in which the other had appeared to dally with him in Canterbury. It had all been meaningless – why had he ever allowed himself to think otherwise? Edward couldn't even confront the man to either confirm the worst or dispel his misgivings. He was the King's son: no one could freely refuse him if he as much as intimated that he fancied them. Others' honesty, he knew, was the one luxury that would always elude him.

It was a blessing, really, that the campaign was not due to start for a few days yet, for he didn't know, given the circumstances, how he could manage on the field. Then again, perhaps some fighting would shake him out of all this pointless brooding.

Six

AT LAST

Edward returned to the stream by the Gascon encampment on the sixth day. The day after tomorrow, the army was due to set off for the Scottish border. What on earth did he think he was trying to achieve?

It was the hottest day they had had in Carlisle yet. Sweat trickled from his armpits down his ribs. Horseflies were pursuing him with a vengeance, the blasted things. The bellow of a cow reached him from somewhere beyond camp, on the other side of the stream. It sounded derisive, the more so because shrubs of gorse and blackthorn concealed the animal from view. Impatient with himself at the inanity of the things he went about fancying, Edward knelt down by the edge of the stream. Filling his cupped hands with the cold water, he splashed and rubbed his face.

Perhaps one-hundred feet downstream, half-a-dozen knights were bathing where the brook widened to form a small natural pool. His eye was irresistibly drawn to their nakedness. Suddenly, he felt unhinged: did he catch a glimpse of Sir Arnaud de Gaveston's son among the bathing men, or was he imagining it? He quickly turned away, drawing back from the edge of the water, and retraced his steps in the direction of the oak thicket where he had tied his horse. Breathing heavily, he made a conscious effort not to run.

About to untie the horse, he saw Sir Arnaud de Gaveston's son stepping out from behind a tree. He stood right next to him, his curls distended with dripping water, shirt and hose clinging to his wet skin.

'My Lord. Can I speak to you, please?'

His deliberateness was infectious. Edward felt unaccountably calm.

'Here?'

'No.' The man's chin jerked towards the open moor.

Edward searched his eyes briefly, then, with the Gascon at his heels, started walking towards the wide expanse of heathland without a word, leaving the camp behind. The moor was flooded with late afternoon sunshine and alive with the trills of skylarks ascending from the bracken and diving back into it. Edward was aware of them in the same way as he was aware of what was happening to him: something observed, rather than experienced. It was an odd sensation, both unusual to him and one he didn't like. Feeling that he must shake it off, his pace steadily gained speed. As he was about to break into a run, the other, from behind, put a hand on his shoulder.

'Here will do.'

The Gascon lay down on a patch of bracken, his back to the ground, hands clasped behind his head, eyes to the sky. Edward studied him. He knew it was a breach of etiquette for the other to lie down while he, the King's son, was still standing; he knew he should be bothered by it, but he wasn't.

'Won't you lie down, My Lord?' the soldier said.

And so Edward did. They remained still for a minute or so, faces to the sky, shoulder touching shoulder. Before long, Edward started feeling the wetness from the older man's shirt working its way through the cloth of his own. He put his hand on the other's thigh: the hose that covered it felt clammy.

'What's your name, Arnaud de Gaveston's son?'

'Piers Gaveston, My Lord. Your servant.'

'You're soaking wet, Sir Piers Gaveston.'

'I didn't have time to dry myself before putting my clothes back on.' Piers Gaveston's hand took hold of the one that Edward had left resting on his thigh. 'At the stream.... Why did you run away, My Lord?'

'I didn't flee.'

Edward knew he said it much too defensively, almost as if he had added:

Don't flatter yourself. He saw Piers Gaveston turn his head away, hoping to conceal a smile. It was irritating.

'And why did you follow?' he asked, disengaging his hand from the man's own.

'I don't know. Tomorrow may be too late. The day after tomorrow we'll be at war.'

'Are you saying we're going to die, Sir Piers?'

'No. The Scots will not let themselves be drawn into battle easily. We'll have to winnow them out. And we'll probably fail.'

'But even then, we could die, couldn't we?'

'I suppose so. Theoretically.'

Edward turned towards him, propping himself on his elbow. 'How does one theoretically die?'

The Gascon smiled. '*Touché.*'

Edward regarded the whole length of him. 'Take your shirt off, Sir Piers. You'll catch a cold.'

'As My Lord wishes.'

They both sat up, and Piers slipped the shirt over his head. His skin, Edward thought, was extraordinary: finely textured – as you are more apt to see on women than on men – and luminous, but underlaid with a duskiness, like plums. He could see the darker colour undiluted in his nipples.

Piers followed the direction of Edward's gaze and ended up with his chin against his collarbone, eyes fixed on his own torso. He raised his head to face Edward and smiled. His hand reached out to take Edward's by the wrist and pressed the boy's palm to his own chest. Edward stroked his midriff.

'You are beautiful,' he said, softly, as he caught his breath.

Piers' hand reached out to pull Edward's face close to his, gently. Edward saw small lines forming at the corners of Piers Gaveston's eyes as he smiled. Did the man ever stop smiling? Gaveston pressed his mouth against Edward's own, his hand on Edward's nape, holding him close – not so hard as to prevent Edward from pulling back, but enough to make it clear pulling back was distinctly discouraged. When Edward parted his lips, Piers didn't slip his tongue into his mouth, as Edward half-expected him to. Instead, he took to nibbling his lower lip and then sucked on it, softly at first, then hard. Edward felt his cock pulling under his clothes, and pushed the hose just past it, down to his thighs.

Piers made him lie down, and Edward's whole shaft was suddenly enveloped in warm wetness. In a matter of seconds, he was spending himself in the Gascon's mouth. When Edward's body stopped convulsing, and his breathing quietened, Piers lay down next to him.

'Your first time like this, My Lord?'

The flush that the fading had left on Edward's cheeks deepened. He nodded.

'After a few times it won't be so unbearably intense. You'll last longer.' Piers raised himself on an elbow and kissed him. He was beaming.

'I'll bring you off, now,' Edward said.

'Another time.'

Edward felt confused.

'There will be another time, will there, My Lord?'

Edward nodded, but continued to wonder why the Gascon didn't want him to return the favour.

'Trust me, My Lord, it wouldn't be much fun for you now, after your *petite mort*. When you bring me off, I'd like you to enjoy it as well.'

Edward nodded.

'I'll take care of myself now, if only you'd be so kind as to remove your shirt, My Lord.'

Edward complied, and Piers started kissing his neck and ears and mouth. He spent himself on Edward's belly, his tongue thrust deep into Edward's mouth all through the fading. Then he rolled on his back.

His eyes closed, Edward inhaled deeply the smell of pleasure spent and crushed heather, luxuriating in the feeling of enervation that follows lovemaking. Then he lifted himself on his elbows and regarded with fascination the liquid sin pooling around his belly button. He dipped a finger into it and brought it to his mouth.

'You taste different from me,' he said, and it didn't matter that he had just revealed that once or twice he had tasted himself.

Piers sat up and took hold of his own cock, no longer hard but still enlarged. He milked out the last droplets of seed into the palm of his other hand. Then he raised the hand to his mouth and, sticking his tongue out, licked the liquid off.

Piers knitted his brows. 'I suppose you're right...rather bitter.' He pulled a face.

Edward laughed, and the peal belonged in the heathland, kindred to the calls of skylarks and meadow pipits.

+

PIERS HAD SLIPPED into a light sleep. He was lying on one side, his mouth no more than four or five inches from Edward's ear. Every time Piers exhaled, moist warmth radiated on Edward's earlobe, the softest hiss blending with the whirring of the denizens of the moor.

Edward lifted a hand to chase a fly from his nose. A light musky scent gently invaded his nostrils. *His smell – on my fingers. This is it. This is... perfect.* Piers stirred and opened his eyes – *Dark brown agate? Obsidian?* – riveting them to Edward's own. *His smile.* Edward swallowed. He was happy, surely happier than he had ever been, so why did he feel like crying?

'You seemed so distant,' he said to Piers.

'People do when they're asleep.' Yet another smile. 'But the sun's hardly moved. Surely I drifted off for only an instant.'

They both sat up.

'I didn't mean just *now*,' Edward said, unsure if Piers was serious. 'You were distant these past few days.'

'What would you've had me do, My Lord? You were dreadfully aloof yourself. You ran away from me, not one hour ago.'

'I didn't run.'

'As you wish, My Lord.'

'What I *wish* is that you explained to me why this sudden change now. The war, you said. Did you want to fuck the King's son before dying?' It sounded worse than Edward meant it.

'My Lord, I fought several wars already, and in all honesty, I don't particularly intend to die in this one. Besides, who was fucking whom? I really don't think the matter is very clear-cut.'

His grin. They were both quiet for a while.

Then Piers asked, 'Why can't you simply believe me, My Lord?' He looked genuinely perplexed.

'Believe what, Sir Piers?'

'That I wish to be at your side. Is it so difficult to see?'

Edward regarded him, thinking exactly at what point he was supposed to have worked out that this was the Gascon's intention.

'I don't mean just like any other Knight at your Court,' Piers said. Then he looked briefly away and continued in a more hushed tone. 'At your side as the man closest to your heart, My Lord.'

Edward took a deep breath. 'Why...do you wish that, Sir Piers?' he asked, as calmly as he could. He wanted to seek the other's eyes, but something – fear that he might detect in them the other's insincerity? – stopped him.

'Why shouldn't I?' Piers answered with defiance.

'Is it because I'm the King's son?'

'I had no idea of your station in Canterbury, My Lord: didn't I make my interest clear then?'

'I hardly think so. I spent months agonizing over whether or not you cared for me at all.'

'My Lord –'

'In any case,' Edward said with sudden mirth, 'are you trying to tell me that when you pick up a boy under such circumstances as those of our meeting in Canterbury, your intent is to be the man *closest to his heart*?'

'You're hardly a *boy*.'

'I'm fifteen, Sir.'

Gaveston lifted an eyebrow. 'Oh,' he said.

He didn't say King Edward could have given his son two or three more years before dragging him to the battlefield.

'But you don't look fifteen, My Lord. I mean, you're better built than most knights I know, and taller than me, and more...substantial.'

Gaveston's lips curled. Edward blushed.

'As for Canterbury...I *was* taken by your looks, yes. Do you hold that against me?'

Edward looked away. 'Is it the blood that runs through my veins?'

'Your *blood*? What about it?'

'My blood qualifies me for Kingship, Sir Piers – so I'm told. Is it also what qualifies me for your attachment?'

'I'm not in the habit of courting every heir apparent I cross paths with, if that's what you mean.' There was just the faintest shadow of exasperation in Piers' voice.

'That's reassuring,' said Edward.

Piers sighed, and Edward knew the Gascon thought he was being sarcastic. Edward didn't know whether or not he had been.

'You're the King's son, My Lord. I cannot shut my eyes to that fact. You cannot undo it. And why should we?'

'But how can I trust you, Sir Piers? You said...in Canterbury you said you don't always mean what you say.'

'But I was lying!' said Piers cheerfully.

Edward knit his brows. 'If you were lying, then it means you always mean what you say.... But if you always mean what you say, how could you have been lying? Which is it, Sir Piers?'

The Gascon shook his head. 'I.... What do you want me to say, My Lord?'

'Answer this, then, truthfully: when you implied you disliked my father the King, in Canterbury, did you mean it? Or didn't you?'

'I was hoping I didn't quite imply anything as strong as dislike.' He sighed. 'It's true, My Lord. I don't particularly like the King. King Edward used my father twice as a hostage in the past. The King uses people. I'm loyal to your father – but I cannot say I approve of his ways, let alone that I like him. Sorry if my words pain you, My Lord. I-I think I'd better go.'

+

PIERS GOT UP, readying himself to leave, but before he could do so he was checked by the sound of Edward's words: serious, deliberate.

'I accept you, Sir Piers Gaveston. As the man closest to my heart.'

Had he heard properly? He sat down again. Edward now pressed his lips together and looked away. Dropping on one side, he cradled his head in Piers' lap. Piers raised his hand over Edward's head and hesitated for a moment, keeping it suspended in mid-air. Then, he laid it gently on the other's head, passing his fingers through the flaxen strands of hair.

'I'll find a way to make it happen,' Edward said, his voice trembling. The tip of his index finger traced the trail of black hairs that framed Piers' belly button and, plunging downwards, disappeared into his hose. 'I shall always keep you at my side, Sir Piers. I swear it upon God's soul.'

Piers pulled Edward's head towards his face and pressed his mouth against the lips from which the fatal words had just escaped. Clutching each other, they tumbled on the bracken.

+

THEY WERE SITTING with their legs crossed, facing the sun, which, now quite low, turned the horizon into a burnished firmament gleaming here and there with the gold of broom and gorse.

'How do you propose to prevent us both from getting killed on the battlefield, Piers?'

The Gascon shrugged. 'I haven't been knighted yet, but knighted or not, I'll be sure to have your back. Try to arrange with your father that I be assigned to your unit.' He paused to ponder. 'I hope the King doesn't plan to send you to the front line?'

'So what, even if he does? Sir John says I fight well.'

Edward started pulling up some blades of grass and collecting them in the palm of his hand.

'Your instructor is right,' said Piers. 'I saw you training in the evenings. When Sir John *made* you, that is.'

Edward, still occupied with the grass, looked up to meet his eyes.

'What?' Piers arched his eyebrows. 'Are you surprised I've been stalking you? If you want to know, this whole week I've hardly been able to take my eyes off you. A regular lecher, I've been.'

Edward laughed and threw his handful of grass at him.

'How old are you, Piers?'

'Twenty-three.'

'It's a little old.'

'It is, I suppose, but how was I to divine you were only fifteen?'

'I mean that I may be able to persuade the King to make you one of his wards despite your age. Then you'd naturally be assigned to fight alongside me. And you'd belong to my household, even after the campaign is over.'

'King's wards? What are they?'

'Just that. There are ten at my Court. They're supposed to be roughly my contemporaries – and scions of the higher nobility. But there are precedents to admit into their ranks members of lesser status. You are valiant, well-bred, gallant...'

Piers grinned. 'Don't hold back, My Lord.'

'The King will be open to being convinced that you'd be a good influence. Does the King know your age? Do others?'

'I don't think my age is a matter of common knowledge in England, My Lord.'

'Even if your father told mine, it's just the sort of detail the King would take no notice of. Talk to your father – Sir Arnaud, is it? – tonight. Tell him you may be able to join my Court, but that age may be an objection. If the King, or anyone else, should ask him your age, you are...nineteen.'

'Nineteen: will I get away with it?'

'Just about,' said Edward regarding him critically. 'My God, you *are* beautiful.'

'You'd better not say that too often, My Lord. I'm notorious for my vanity.' Delight radiated from Piers' face. He looked at their lengthening shadows. 'Time to head back, don't you think?'

'Yes, we should.'

'Shall we go separately?'

'Whatever for? Isn't the King's son allowed to befriend the men fighting for England?'

'As long as you don't befriend them all the way you befriended me.'

'We'll return together, Piers.'

'There will be talk, My Lord.'

'Let them!' said Edward.

Several centuries' worth of rumours, he thought, would be a small price to pay for the thrill of seeing that gratified look on the Gascon's face.

Seven

BONDS CEMENTED

PIERS HAD BEEN right in prognosticating that the war in Scotland would drag on. After a lull in 1302, hostilities resumed in 1303. The King's forces were still in Scotland in the winter of 1303-1304. With the King based in Dumferline, Edward, Prince of Wales, now of age, over-wintered with his household in Perth. It was a period of relative military inactivity. One evening after Christmas, he and Piers, having retired early to the Prince's chamber, were sipping wine in bed. The French woollen tapestries that, at Piers' instigation, had been hung to line the room's walls failed to mitigate the cold. The Gascon got out of bed to revive the fire in the braziers.

'This is just atrocious. The damp. The cold. Exactly how many hours of daylight have we seen today? Can it even be called *light* – that lurid dimness fighting a losing battle against the thick blanket of clouds?'

'Come here, Perrot! Drink this nectar – it'll warm you up!' Edward lifted his hands, each holding a cup half-full of wine. 'Drink *my* nectar, too!' With a grin, he kicked off the blanket, exposing the full expanse of his naked body to the chilly air.

'I wish your nectar could pass some of that northern constitution on to me… How can you not be freezing?' Piers jumped back in bed, none too carefully, and pulled up the blankets on his side of the bed. The minor commotion made Edward spill some of the wine. The drops started rolling down his chest, slowly.

'Better fix that.' Piers took to licking the tracks of ruby-red liquid off his lover's midriff and ribs.

Edward laughed. 'It tickles! Was there even any on my nipples?'

'Hard to tell. But I'm always thorough.'

'Say, Piers – I've a wonderful idea.'

'Yes, I caught your drift a moment ago. Your nectar, and what not.'

'No! I mean *yes*, that too. But later, as a way of celebrating.' Piers looked at the Prince quizzically. Edward stared back, smiling. 'Dress up, let's go!'

'Where to, Edward? It's freezing outside!'

'It's freezing in here, you just said so – so what difference does it make? We're going to fetch the Priest!'

'Whatever for? He'll be asleep!'

'He'll have to wake up. This is the day he will officiate at our brotherhood compact. Quick!'

Piers' lips curled in delight. 'You want us to undergo an enfraternisation ceremony? You want us to be sworn brothers?'

'We've been acting like brothers for more than three years now. It seems only fitting. Besides, if there's any chance of me passing my northern constitution, as you call it, on to you, surely it must be through a compact of sworn brotherhood!'

'Acting like brothers?' Piers was taking Edward's points one at a time. 'Have we? Do brothers…offer each other their nectars?' He raised a dubious eyebrow.

'You are nitpicking. Quick now!'

+

THE PRIEST HAD indeed been sleeping, but promptly responded to the Prince's summon and appeared to consider it rather a special honour to witness the compact between the Prince of Wales and the man who was rapidly becoming known as his 'Companion'. In the Chapel he lit a candle, as well as a generous number of rush-lights. Their glow produced a deceptive impression of warmth. In actual fact, the Chapel was fully as glacial as Piers had expected it to be; he was glad for the wolf pelt he had wrapped himself in, even if it rather offended his sense of propriety. The occasion surely demanded Italian velvet and brocade from Byzantium. Then again, even if he had had them at hand, they would have been out of place in this dismal little chapel bereft of marble, silver, stained glass, and all the things that, to his mind, must make the life of holy men and the duties of altar boys just about bearable.

'How should we proceed, Father?' asked Edward.

'You will take turns to make the compact. You must spell out what each of you commits to and pledges in the interest of your sworn brother. I shall witness it all and administer to you the Holy Host and the Blood of our Lord Jesus Christ.' Piers, at one time fascinated and repelled by the man's bushy eyebrows and luxurious beard – which made it look rather as if a beaver, tail and all, were suspended from his ears – hadn't been paying much attention, until the words 'blood of our Lord' caught his ear.

'Wine?' he asked.

'Yes, Sir Piers, what else?'

'Is it...*quality* wine, Father?' Edward's elbow nudged him between the hip and the last rib, but Piers continued, undeterred. 'Bad wine gives me the most awful headaches. I would be very happy to send my attendant to fetch some from my personal supply. The occasion demands for the best we can provide, don't you think?' He flashed one of his most seductive smiles.

'It's blessed wine, Sir Piers. It's simply *impossible* that you should suffer any ill-effect as a result of drinking it. Unless your mind is not suitably disposed to receiving it as a *sacrament*, of course.'

'The Sacristy's wine will suit *both of us* just fine, Father,' said Edward. 'We are very honoured that you should share it with us. Are we *not*, Sir Piers?'

Piers looked at Edward askance and sighed. 'Quivering in anticipation at the very thought of drinking it, Father – now that I think of it. Practically quivering.'

'Shall we proceed?' said Edward, eager for this spell to bind them both.

The Priest fetched the Host and the wine and placed them on the altar, with much formality.

'Please draw closer to the altar, My Lord – you too, Sir Piers. Yes, like this, facing me.' The Priest opened his hands in prayer. 'Our Lord, we presume to call You to be our witness to this pledge. The Prince of Wales and the Prince's Companion, Sir Piers Gaveston, are here to be united in sworn brotherhood. They make their pledges before you, that they may forever be bound by them till death do them part. Make your pledges now, My Lord, Sir Piers.'

'I swear to take Sir Piers Gaveston as my sworn brother.' Edward turned towards Piers. 'I take *you*, Piers Gaveston, as my sworn brother. My first commitment to you is that I shall never have another. I shall be true to you until the last of my days. Also, I shall love you more than anyone else – much more. Let's see…I shall raise you above all others, that they may see how great my love is for you. I shall support you and defend you, always. I shall always take your side. And I shall always keep you by my side.'

'Your turn now, Sir Piers,' said the Priest.

'I take you, Edward of Caernarfon, in all humility, as my sworn brother. I shall serve you to the best of my ability, to the end of my days. I shall never deny my support and assistance to you…. And I shall return your love thrice-fold, till the end of my days. In fact, I'll gladly die for you should the moment demand, if it is God's will. Until then, I shall never leave your side. If I am forced to, I shall always come back for you. I swear.'

'Good,' said the Priest. 'Now you'll both partake in the sacrament of the Holy Communion.'

The Priest lifted the Host above his head before breaking it into two and raising one half to the Prince's mouth. After taking it, Edward crossed himself. Then, it was Piers' turn to do the same. The Priest's hands then took hold of the vessel with the wine. Again, he lifted it over his head before offering it to the Prince.

'Only half, My Lord, if you please. The rest is for Sir Piers.' Edward drank and handed the cup back to the Priest, who – a small linen cloth at the ready – was about to wipe the cup's rim before handing the vessel over to Piers.

'That will be unnecessary, Father,' said Piers putting a hand on the cleric's forearm and pointing with his head at the cloth.

The Priest was slightly taken aback.

'The chalice, if you please, Father.'

The Priest handed over the pewter cup. Piers took it and made a point of drinking from the place in the rim where a faint ring indicated Edward's lips had touched it. The taste wasn't nearly as bad as he had feared. When he was done, he handed the cup back to the Priest.

'You should seal your pledge with a kiss,' said the Priest next.

Edward stepped forward and, a very serious expression on his face, pressed his lips against Piers'.

'I now declare you, Edward of Caernarfon, and you, Sir Piers Gaveston, sworn brothers.'

Piers looked at Edward – so young, so unsullied – and thought how easy it would be to keep his pledge. He would never let anyone or anything come between them.

+

BACK IN THE comparative warmth of the Prince's chamber (they had instructed a valet to keep the fire going), Edward took off his clothes and slipped under the blankets and furs. Piers, still wrapped up in his wolf pelt, busied himself with the braziers for a few minutes; then he joined his lover.

'The fire was perfectly tended to, Piers. I know you've simply been waiting for me to warm the bed for you.'

'My new brother promised to always support me and defend me. He has successfully defended me from the icy bedding. Test passed.'

'Always at your service, dear brother.' Edward leant his head on Piers' shoulder and knitted his brows. 'When you did that thing, with the cup, towards the end of the ceremony – before the Priest declared us sworn brothers…'

'What of it?' asked Piers.

'It was unnecessary – we kissed, afterwards.'

'All the best things in life are utterly unnecessary. And anyway, how was I to divine that that incontinent Priest would later command that we should kiss?'

Edward laughed. He pointed with his eyes at the bedclothes bulging between his thighs.

Piers grinned. 'Oh, my courtship of the holy vessel was entirely calculated to have that effect on you, Your Grace. Do you think it aroused the Priest's interest too? I bet he thought we looked indecently handsome side by side.'

Edward laughed again. He pushed Piers on his side, facing away from him, and patted his buttocks. 'Now let's see if anything can be done to toughen up that constitution of yours – softened by too much southern sunshine. On all fours, brother.'

Piers obliged. He felt a generous mouthful of spit from Edward's lips drop at the base of his spine and coat the crack between his buttocks. Then the head of Edward's prick nudged the soft ring of muscles, and his insides shifted in anticipation. Let the Prince of Wales enter what was, as of today, rightfully and officially his.

Eight

TROUBLE AFOOT

It was the beginning of that lustiest of months, May, in the year 1305. In a clearing in the forest on the Langley estate, Piers and Edward were standing by their horses, admiring the swathes of bluebells carpeting the beech woodland.

'You know,' said Piers 'on a day like this, even without bright sunshine, there is something perfectly glorious about the countryside here. Bluebells never bloom in such abundance on the Continent.'

'No bluebells in the woods in April and May?'

'Hardly any. It's the poet's daffodils that blanket the mountain pastures at home this time of year. One day, God willing, I'll show them to you. Their scent will make you swoon.'

'Bluebells are scented,' said the Prince.

Piers cocked a dubious eyebrow. Then, inhaling deeply, he became aware of a barely perceptible odour in the air. 'Very well, perhaps a faint sweetness.'

'A little like yours.' Before Piers could protest, Edward went on to say, 'Not quite, though. Yours is more like the musk of the apothecary's rose.'

'*Musk*? Are you saying I *stink*, My Lord?'

'I'm saying you smell good, Perrot. I thought so the very first time.'

'I was *smelly* when you first saw me in Canterbury?' Piers asked, with unadulterated horror.

Edward shook his head. 'I realised you had a nice musky scent when we first made love.'

Piers wondered if his body was giving off any odour right now. He resisted the urge to bow his head and sniff his armpits. Altogether better to change the subject. Better still if in doing so he managed to pay back his dear Prince.

'You know, Edward, you're no longer the rawboned lad of five years ago.'

'I thought you said then that I was "better built" than most grown men.'

Piers shrugged. 'You were young and impressionable. In need of reassurance.'

'Look to yourself, Lord Gaveston,' shouted the Prince, as he started chasing his lover around the meadow. He grabbed Piers by one leg, and they tumbled on the grass. The Prince then drew close and whispered something in Piers' ear.

'Now?' asked Piers.

'Why not? Not that I'm keeping a record, but we've never had another tryst *en plein air* since our first time together.'

'Rather remiss of us.' He grinned. 'You planned this all along, didn't you? This is why you insisted today on the two of us going out on a horse-ride alone, instead of joining the May Day festivities you so lavishly paid for.'

'I thought lovemaking in the woods might be a nice way to celebrate the advent of spring.'

+

PIERS STEPPED NIMBLY to the edge of the meadow, where it met the woodland. He threw his back against the smooth, columnar trunk of the nearest beech tree and let his hose drop and bunch around his ankles. Then he beckoned Edward to approach.

'On your knees, My Lord, if you don't mind very much.'

'Ha!' Edward felt ecstatic as he dropped before Piers and, lovingly, he studied the appendage thrusting from between his legs: its root nestled in a sprouting of diminutive dark curls; the well-proportioned shaft was laced with amethystine veins, and the lustrous head had the silkiness of a juicy plum. He took hold of Piers' erect cock and, closing his eyes, pressed it against his cheek. He loved all of Piers in this warm cock of his – all of him – and the thought occurred to him that if God struck him dead right now, he would have no regrets; it would be a beautiful way to die.

'Are you still with me?' The voice came from above, sportive, and it wasn't God's; rather, it was his own personal god's.

Edward opened his eyes. 'Such impatience calls for chastening.'

He stuck out his tongue and determined to tease Piers with it for the next several minutes, without giving him the satisfaction of taking his cock into his mouth. He began with the balls, soft velvet overlaid with bristling roughness. Was there any other detail in a man's anatomy more agreeably a man's than his nuts? Of course, all sorts of things could go wrong with the way a man's balls turned out, but when they turned out right – and Piers' were, of course, just perfect – what other part of the body could be so yielding and yet so tenacious? Abandoning his resolve to only use his tongue, Edward slipped his lover's twin globes into his mouth, gently tugging at the sack. Then Piers started waving his hand vigorously.

'Wah-iji?' Edward asked.

'Pardon?'

Edward freed his mouth. 'What is it?' He could hear the impatience in his voice. He felt silly.

'It's nothing. Don't turn. Someone's been enjoying the show.'

'Where?'

'Don't turn. From between the trees at the other end of the meadow. I think it might be Sir Walter Lan-*goat*.'

'Not Langton? Fie on the old rake! Why are you greeting him?'

'What else is there to do? Under the circumstances, you know?'

Edward sighed. 'Are you sure it's he?'

'Fairly sure. Yes, it's he.'

'The Devil take him. If you can recognise him, he must be close enough to have identified *us*.'

'Me perhaps, but he can't be sure about you – as long as you don't turn. Which has the not inconsiderable benefit of leaving you free to resume attending to me.'

'What's he doing now?'

'Let me see...I must've scared him off. He's gone. Departed. For good.'

Edward turned. His eyes scanned the edge of the woodland enclosing the meadow, from left to right.

Then Piers said, 'I remain reliant on the benefactions you were so generously conferring upon me only a moment ago, My Lord.'

Edward turned to him. Piers had a playful expression as his glance travelled back and forth from the Prince's eyes to his own expectant – if slightly diminished – prick. Edward smiled and drew close to kiss his lover.

+

Langley, a few weeks later.

'LET ME DO it, Edward. I may not be as foul-tempered as you, but I'm sure I can work myself into a suitably vile mood. I shall then be almost as effective.'

They were both looking up at the sky, the sunshine forcing them to screw their eyes. Their heads performed the same circular movements as they followed the dark silhouette swoop and dive into the meadow.

'That's a boy!' shouted Edward as the falcon began flying back towards them, clutching a rabbit in its claws.

He turned to Piers. 'Piers, I'm simply dying to give the bastard a good thrashing!'

'I know, and fully sympathise, but beating the Treasurer-cum-Bishop-of-Lichfield would not go down very well with the King, would it? You know Lan-*goat* is the apple of your father's eye. I mean, if good old King Edward ever had something remotely approaching what exists between you and me, it would be bound to be with Lan-*goat*. I know, I know – the thought is enough to make one a little queasy, but I am speaking hypothetically.'

Edward frowned, even as his lips curled up at the corners. 'Be serious, Piers.'

'I *am* being serious. On the assumption that Langton could not identify you with certainty as the angel that was bringing me rapture on May Day, it's safer for you to stay out of it altogether. Let me go to him. I shall be unsparing. I'll tell him that, unlike me, he has not earned himself the right to have the run of the princely preserves. I'll say you would be extremely aggrieved if you knew of his trespass. And that I'll be sure to immediately inform you of a repeat of his offence. It'll work.'

'I have to do this myself, Piers. Unless I make Langton cower, he's bound to tell my father what he saw at the next available opportunity. God only knows what the King would be capable of doing then. I won't admit to having been there – I'll simply say to Langton you and your companion had no choice but to detail his transgression to me, as I require you to report all trespasses upon what's mine.'

Piers sighed. 'If you think it best, Edward.'

+

Midhurst, 14 June 1305.

EDWARD WONDERED WHETHER the reason why he had been so peremptorily summoned before the King, on the day after they had spent an amicable Whitsunday together, might have something to do with the May Day incident. Could the Treasurer be so devious as to have waited until Edward's arrival at his father's Court from Langley before informing the King of what he had seen? He wondered if his recent attempt to intimidate Langton into silence had backfired and perhaps even caused the Treasurer to speak to the King when Langton might otherwise have kept the news of his and Piers' indiscretion to himself. There was no doubt in Edward's mind that the Treasurer deserved whatever castigation he had got from him; but he supposed it was possible his rebukes could have been a *little* politer. Piers, who had been listening to the exchange between the Prince and the Treasurer from the next room, had been both charmed and astounded by some of the insults Edward had thrown at Langton. But even so, Piers had added that he could see all this coming, and that he should have insisted on doing the chiding himself...

Edward entered the Spartan, sparsely furnished room where his father conducted his business – a place he hated, nearly as forbidding as its principal occupant. There was a mustiness in the air; Edward wondered how his father – a soldier and, like himself, a man of the outdoors – failed to see that the room badly needed airing. The windows were still sealed with waxed linen, as in the heart of winter. He almost went to rip the canvas off himself, but he reconsidered after casting a glance at his father.

The King's frown made his fury perfectly obvious. Edward had seen this often enough and had fully expected it upon approaching him. What he had not been prepared for was his father to suddenly look so old – the sagging cheeks, the dullness of his colouring. The must-coloured material of the King's tunic did little to mitigate the effect.

'You wanted to see me, Sire.'

'Are you out of your accursed mind, Edward?'

Well, that at least settled the matter of whether or not he should sit down.

'The Treasurer is the worthiest of the Royal officials and my most trusted friend! How *dare* you insult him so brutally?'

Edward was conscious of standing quite stiffly, with his feet apart, arms hanging at his sides, and his chest pushed out. But, in his father's presence, assuming anything other than a martial attitude seemed out of the question. 'Sire, he trespassed upon my woods.'

'Upon your rendezvous with that Gascon dog, rather!'

'But you have always approved of Piers.'

'Do you expect me to approve of him for making a whore out of the heir to the throne of England?'

Edward blushed.

'Gaveston may have charmed his way into your Court, and beguiled even my graces – but I shall not stand by while you allow him to abuse the body of the King's son...my own flesh, Edward!'

'Father, you have no right...'

'No right? *You* have no greater claim than Me or the people of this country over your body! The body of the future King!'

Edward kept that supposed object of public ownership very still, except for clenching his jaw and looking away.

'My orders have already been issued,' the King said more coolly. 'As of today, all your sources of income are suspended, for lack of restraint in dealing with a high-ranking Royal official. Furthermore, Gaveston and Sir Gilbert de Clare will immediately remove themselves from your Court – never to return to it.'

Edward's eyes widened. 'Why?'

'For conduct unfitting of their station as familiars of the Prince of Wales, Edward! Is it so difficult to understand?'

'Unfitting?' Edward's dismay did not prevent him from noticing the incongruity, as he saw it, of his father's orders. 'But what does Sir Gilbert have to do with all this?'

'Your hair, My Lord!'

Had the King gone cuckoo? 'Please don't speak to me in riddles. What do you mean "your hair"?'

'Do you really think Lord Langton would dare approach me to deliver the news that Piers Gaveston was befouling the mouth of the *Prince of Wales*?'

The blush lingering on Edward's cheeks now veered to scarlet. 'So the Treasurer said it was *Sir Gilbert*?'

'The Treasurer, Edward, reported to me that you had ill-used him in a way out of all proportion to his transgression! Only then did he recount what he had seen during his involuntary trespass on your grounds! He had chanced, he said, upon Sir Piers being publicly fellated by a "tall, well-built, flaxen-haired man"! His very words! Of course, I asked Lord Langton to find out who, among the *knights* and *grooms* in your Court, came close to that description! Have I spelt it out sufficiently clearly now?'

'But it wasn't Sir Gilbert! It was –'

He couldn't finish. His father walked up to him and violently struck him on the cheek. Edward was speechless, though less through intimidation than incredulity and revulsion. His hand instinctively went to his smarting cheekbone, but just as quickly he removed it, not wishing to give his father the satisfaction of thinking he had been hurt.

'What you think you know is, as of now, a *lie,* My Lord! You will *never* admit, either publicly or to my face, to your goings on with the Gascon – do you hear? If ever I hear word of you two being intimate again, I swear I shall pull out that *flaxen* hair of yours with my own hands, strand by strand! Go now and don't dare return to my Court until further notice!'

Edward marched out of the room, feeling he must be more disgusted with his father than the King had been with him. He knew King Edward's choleric nature too well to try to reason with him. His mind, rather, was racing to hatch a plan that might thwart the execution of his father's orders. As soon as he reached his lodgings, one of his attendants, a young boy of twelve or thirteen, rushed to meet him, tears streaming down his cheeks.

'They came to ban Sir Piers from Court!'

Edward bent down to hug the boy for a few seconds, then he gently pushed him away by the shoulders, and held him at arm's length. 'Where?'

'No one knows.' The boy kept sobbing. 'He gave me this, My Lord.'

From his sleeve, he produced a creased strip of paper. Edward instantly recognised the material as coming from Piers' personal stock, imported directly from the Continent – everyone else at his Court used parchment. Piers had evidently scribbled the message in comparative hurry:

"My dear, We did not play this well. Do not do anything rash, please, & do not seek Us out. We shall let You have news as soon as possible. Comply with Your Father's orders & show Him You remain a humble & devoted Son. Do not despair. Your Father has always shown Us favour. Let the waters calm down, then ask Our noble Lady, Your Father's Consort, to intercede. She loves Us dearly and She has His ear. We are confident this can be undone. We shall not long be separated from You. We shall never break Our promise to You. We commit You to God, may He have You in His keeping until such time as He pleases to return custody of Your Lordship to Us."

No sooner had Edward finished reading the note than his favourite greyhound was let out of his chamber and rushed to greet him excitedly, oblivious to his master's grief – or had the animal known to distract him from it? Edward's despair relented a little. He gave orders to be left alone and bent down to kiss the animal.

Nine

THE FIRST BANISHMENT

23 May 1306, the Feast of the Pentecost.
The Prince's chamber, near London.

PARTICLES OF DUST danced around a shaft of late morning sunshine filtering through the window. Edward was lying on his back. Piers scrambled over the Prince and, facing him, straddled his lover's hips. His gaze dwelt on Edward's flat stomach, rounded shoulders, substantial arms. Edward's prick reflexively expanded, rose, and lodged itself between Piers' buttocks.

'You can stop that,' said Piers.

'Stop what?'

'You needn't particularly grow any larger.'

'Sorry,' Edward replied, and, as he said so, his hips thrusted mischievously.

'I didn't mean *that*. Down there, you can grow all you like. I was referring to your body size. It's more than adequate now.'

Edward lightly tossed his head to clear his eye from a stray lock of hair. 'I thought you liked my stature, and that I was "filling out".'

'I may have said that. But I don't particularly care for getting crushed during lovemaking.'

Edward swatted him with the pillow. 'You aren't so small yourself.'

'A good half-foot shorter than you,' said Piers, recovering the pillow and putting it under Edward's head. 'And considerably lighter. Do you think we're well-assorted? A good match, pleasing to the eye?'

'Didn't you once say we are "indecently handsome"?'

'Do you keep records of everything I say? In any case, that was before you threw sense to the wind and outgrew all reasonable proportions.'

'Your insults will only make me worship your litheness more. You're very much like him.' Edward's toe nudged the greyhound curled up at the other end of the mattress.

'Are you comparing me to that mangy thing?' asked Piers. The lustrous brindle of the hound's well-groomed coat proved the lie in his description.

'You have all sorts of reasons to be devoted to my hound.'

'I'm letting him sleep on *our* bed, aren't I? Anyway, why *should* I be devoted to him?'

'He was the only one with the power to cheer me up when you were taken away from me,' Edward said. 'This reminds me: remember that note you left for me when my father banned you from my Court a year ago? Wait – I'm sure I kept it.'

Edward pushed Piers aside and got up. He started rummaging through the contents of a coffer in a corner of the room and emerged with a book – a French Romance – out of which he extracted a slightly creased slip of paper. He handed it over to Piers and sat next to him on the bed. Piers read through it quickly.

'It's rather a nicely crafted message, is it not, considering I was practically thrown out of your household with no notice at all.' He handed the paper back to Edward.

'Well-crafted or not, does it not strike you as a little immodest?'

Piers looked baffled. 'In what way?'

'Let me see.' Edward scratched his chin. 'In a vaguely *profane* sort of way?'

Piers knitted his brows. He snatched the slip of paper back from Edward's hand and perused it again. 'For the life of me, I know not what you might mean. I'm sure I'm rather nice to God in my message. I speak of

Him entirely amicably.'

'But that's exactly it, Perrot. You speak of God as if He's something of a mate. All this business about Him handing custody of me over to you. Isn't that a bit presumptuous?'

'I'm sure I don't know what you're talking about. Perhaps God has delegated your safe-keeping to me. Perhaps He has put me here – and returned me to you – for that very purpose. So what if we strike deals, God and I? Have little secret arrangements, like good mates? I'm sure He trusts I'm good for you, far better than anyone else.'

Edward looked at him seriously. 'In that case, what shall I do if you're taken from me again?'

Piers stroked Edward's hand, resting limply in his lap. 'I'll come back. Last time it worked, didn't it?'

'And what if something happens to you?'

'What is to happen to me? Nothing will happen as long as I stand by your side.'

Piers kissed his shoulder, but Edward sighed.

'Don't be gloomy, Edward. One year ago, everything seemed lost, and look at you now. Everything restored to you: your avails, your Court, your father's trust, and…me. We really are indebted to Queen Marguerite. Without her goodwill…'

'And dear Elizabeth's.' Edward lifted his feet on the bed and crossed his legs, his hands holding his ankles.

'Of course. It's a shame your sister couldn't attend our knighting ceremony yesterday.'

'It's a blessing, Piers. Don't forget two knights died in the crush.'

'Yes, how awful, poor devils. Yet it was beautiful, Edward: you looked the part if anyone ever did. And when you knighted me –'

'And two-hundred-and-fifty-eight others…'

'Yes, that was rather a bore, I suppose.'

'Do you feel like going on this new Scottish expedition, Piers?'

Piers became suddenly serious. 'I'm a trained soldier. The rebellion in Scotland and the King's attempts at crushing it have been permanent fixtures in my life. I accept them as such. We can't let Robert the Bruce get away with his provocations. In any case, the King has put the entire campaign under your command this time – it does make the idea of going to war more appealing than usual.'

Edward smiled. 'Freshly knighted, and with you by my side, I rather feel as if I could take on the world, Perrot.'

'You could start, perhaps, by taking *me* on,' said Piers with a wink. 'What do you say?'

'I say you'd better cajole that mangy thing off the bed first.'

As if on cue, the dog jumped off. They looked at each other and laughed. Piers pushed Edward back on the mattress and, as before, straddled his hips. Edward grabbed Piers' buttocks, digging his fingers into the muscular flesh. Piers grinned, and Edward gasped with surprise when three fingers pushed into his mouth. Piers removed them just before they touched the back of his throat, and though he had feared he might gag, for a moment Edward found himself wishing – without quite knowing why – that Piers had probed deeper. He spread Piers' buttocks apart, allowing his lover's fingers to smear the cleft with Edward's own spit. With his cock throbbing and poised to squeeze in, he wondered how many of the young men he knighted yesterday were filling their hours of leisure as fruitfully as Piers and him.

+

December 1306.

THE BRAZIER KEPT the Prince's chamber surprisingly warm – unpleasantly so, thought Edward. He almost missed the bracing cold of the Scottish Lowlands. He made for the window, intending to remove from it the waxed linen, affixed last month as protection from the chilly winter air.

'Are you out of your mind?' asked Piers as soon as he guessed Edward's purpose. Edward snorted, but desisted.

In his black woollen doublet Piers was more sober-looking than usual – or would have been, if the black of the fabric didn't set off quite so magnificently the cloisonné pectoral cross he was wearing.

Piers resumed the conversation Edward's movement had interrupted. 'I suppose we asked for it – Gilbert de Clare, Roger Mortimer, and the rest of us.'

'Don't be ridiculous.' Edward sat on the bed and stretched his arms. 'What could the harm possibly be in your attending the tournament? No one could have suspected the King would look upon it as desertion, much less that he'd punish you by confiscating all your goods and lands.'

Piers sighed.

'Why,' Edward said, 'except for the fall of Kildrummy in September, there's scarcely been any action worth speaking of during this campaign. If I hadn't been in command, I might well have joined you.'

'I thought you found tournaments tedious.' He flicked a speck of something off his shoulder.

'That's beside the point. You know, it's just that my father's mettle, which is rotten on a good day, gets absolutely putrid if he feels even slightly challenged.'

'Says the man notorious for his equanimity of spirit...'

'That proves my point – aren't I living proof of the King's cantankerousness? Who do you think I got it from?' Edward crossed one calf over the other leg's thigh and started massaging it.

Piers made him lie down on the bed and started kneading his legs. 'You're a better man than your father. Don't let his shadow define who you can be.' He paused his speech to concentrate on the task at hand. 'Oh well.'

Edward sat up. 'It's not *well*, Piers. Punishing you so harshly – as if you were no different from any of the others. There's a clear message for me, you know, in the confiscation order against you. My father's saying in the clearest of terms that I must drop you. He wants to deny your status as Companion of the Prince of Wales.'

'Aren't you reading too much into it? Your father has never particularly minded me. I still think he likes me.'

'Your insistence that everyone likes you, Piers, maintained even in the face of your knowledge that a great many people don't, has always perplexed me.'

Piers appeared to consider this for a moment, then made a dismissive gesture with his hand. 'You overcomplicate things.' He stood and walked to the window.

Edward stared at his tapered back in silence for some moments; then an inspiration came to him. 'Say, I just had a wonderful idea, Perrot!'

Piers turned, crossed his arms and looked at Edward askance. 'When you say that, it tends to portend trouble.'

'Nonsense. When I'm King...which, given my father's health, may be sooner rather than later...'

'Yes?'

'My first act will be to make you Count of Ponthieu.'

'Didn't you inherit Ponthieu from Queen Eleanor? Why would you want to give me your mother's lands? You were Count of Ponthieu even before you became Prince of Wales, and –'

Edward had walked up to him and was fingering the large cross hanging from Piers' neck, sparkling with colours like a butterfly's wings. 'Can't you see?' He let go of the jewel and both his hands went to Piers' cheeks. 'That's precisely why I want *you* to have Ponthieu.'

'You don't have to give me Ponthieu. Keep me by your side, always, as we have promised, and I'll not want anything.'

Edward's thumbs moved across Piers' cheeks towards the corners of his lips, forcing them into a pout, resembling nothing so much as a diminutive bleeding heart. He kissed it. 'You will not want anything, and you will have everything. It's a promise.'

Piers regarded him doubtfully, but Edward's mind was made up. His father was confiscating Piers' lands on account of Piers' offence – grievous indeed – of attending a tournament: so be it. Not only would he undo this affront to his lover when the King was no longer around to interfere, but he'd make up to him for it many times over.

+

It seemed to be one of King Edward's foibles that he should make his personal living quarters as unpleasant as a rich man possibly could without completely losing his peers' respect. The King's chamber was invariably the least welcoming room in each of the King's many residences. Now, take this one for example, thought the Treasurer, Sir Walter Langton: the rug and hangings old-fashioned and all but threadbare; the fire out, as often as not; the linen tablecloth unadorned; and no cushions to soften the wooden hardness of the chairs.

'And when did this pledge or undertaking concerning Ponthieu take place, Lord Langton?' asked the King. Uncharacteristically, there was less anger than weariness in his voice.

The Treasurer, shifting his ample backside with some discomfort on the bare wood, thought that the King might not last past the year's end. 'My informant couldn't be sure – he is only a young groom, Your Grace – but at some point before Christmas, apparently.'

'I see. We shall have to get rid of the Gascon once and for all. And that only weeks after pardoning him his latest infraction. But there's no avoiding it. Unfortunately, my son cannot be trusted around him. It is a shame, rather. Lord Gaveston is a man of many qualities.'

'Your Grace.'

'But I must find a way of arranging it without aggravating the situation. If I have Gaveston imprisoned or executed, my son will never forgive me. I shall lose him for good, and God only knows, with his temper, how he may retaliate.'

'Besides, Sire, the Gascon has some supporters at Court.'

'Yes, it wouldn't be prudent at all. The alternative is to banish him from the country for good and forbid him ever to return. But then I would need a convincing pretext to do so. I could hardly state that the reason is that the Prince of Wales forgets himself in the man's presence. That would call into question my son's suitability to succeed me to the throne. Besides, banishment orders can be broken, and this one most certainly would. And an order of permanent exile would alienate the Prince of Wales from me almost as effectively as his Companion's execution...'

'Sire, I've given it some thought – with your permission – and I believe I may have devised rather a fitting and effective solution.'

'Well, speak then: does it look to you like I have time to kill?'

Langton thought that, with his long body stretched on the four-poster bed and his hands twined over his stomach, the King didn't, at that moment, look absolutely overwhelmed with business. 'Sire, we should – pardon me, *you could*, Your Grace, order that the Gascon should depart from the country and return to his birthplace until recalled. The world at large need not know why Lord Gaveston is leaving – the order can be suitably vague, but we could put about rumours that you require him to attend to important matters concerning Aquitaine. I suggest, however, that you should be open with both the Prince and Lord Gaveston himself about your reasons for sending him away – though not so open as to mention your knowledge of the Prince's undertaking to give Ponthieu away. Inform them that you are worried about the sway Sir Piers has over the Prince of Wales and tell them that Lord Gaveston will be recalled soon enough, once the Prince has, after a period of healthy separation, shown signs of having recovered full command over his own mind. Be indulgent, Your Grace: it is of the essence that you should show no animosity towards the Gascon. Fix a generous term for Lord Gaveston's departure: one or two months, Sire. Provide him with an ample allowance. Do not forbid your son to see him while he does remain in the country.'

'I'm afraid you're far too sanguine about my son's prospects of recovering self-mastery, Lord Langton!' The King roared with laughter, looking for a moment like his bellowing former self; but then, he was shaken by a violent fit of coughs. When he recovered, he said, 'We could probably get my son to comply with such terms. But even assuming that putting some distance between the men would clear up my son's mind, his wits would be sure to get clouded again directly after I recall Gaveston to England.'

'This is why, Sire, an accident could befall the Gascon en route to his homeland. A push overboard, Your Grace, secretly administered by one of the boatmen while the vessel is high at sea. If you were agreeable, of course. I don't make the suggestion lightly, Sire. But we must do what's in our power to help the Prince fit himself for the Godly mandate of ruling upon the English people when he succeeds you – may God our Father delay that day for many years yet, Sire.'

The King gestured impatiently for Langton to conclude the exposition of his plan.

'I fear, Sire, the Prince of Wales won't be ready to rule unless he is delivered from Lord Gaveston as soon as possible. If I am right, God will choose not to stay the hand of our man on the boat. In the event, however, that He sees fit to spare Lord Gaveston's life, I would take it upon myself to arrange for some trusted men to secretly meet the vessel when it docks on the Continent. Purely as a precautionary measure, Your Grace: if the Gascon is on board and alive, my men would take him discreetly into custody until you decide what to do with him.'

'The devil take you, Lord Langton.'

The Treasurer, who was also Bishop of Lichfield, chose to take the King's remark figuratively rather than literally.

'Very well,' said the King. 'I'll decree that Gaveston must leave for Gascony by the end of the month of April, for unspecified reasons. And you, Lord Langton, shall oblige me by attending to all other details.'

'I live to serve you, Sire.' Langton rose from his chair, reading himself to bow and retire.

'Another thing, Langton.'

'Sire?'

'Promise me that, whatever happens, after my death you will support my son unconditionally, as you have supported me. Promise it by all the Saints in Heaven.'

Langton hesitated only for the fraction of an instant. 'But of course, Sire, you have my word.'

Langton knew the Prince of Wales could scarcely suffer the sight of him. He had few illusions that he would be able to retain his position of power when the Crown sat on the young Edward's head. But Langton would now have to stand by the new King's side, no matter what.

+

EDWARD AND PIERS reached Dover on 5 May 1307, five days later than the date by which Piers had been ordered to leave the country. The ship due to take him to Gascony had been patiently waiting for him, ready to lift anchor. Even so, Edward and Piers managed to escape for a couple of hours for a walk over the white cliffs. Edward gave strict instructions that no one should begin loading Piers' belongings on the ship until their return, and that no one must follow them.

They scrambled among brambles and sickly sweet-scented gorse up a hillside that afforded quick access to the top of the cliffs. The views were spectacular and ever-changing: the sunshine alternated in rapid succession with the mist soaring from the sea over the chalky cliff-face. Facing the horizon, they inhaled deeply the pungent sea-air. Then Piers turned to kiss Edward's mouth – a prolonged kiss that left Edward gasping for breath.

'Sorry, Edward.'

'What for, Piers? For making me delirious with love?'

They sat down facing the sea, side by side on the thread-like tussocks of grass, interspersed with clove-scented gillyflowers and wild cabbage, its foliage flushed purple. Edward took his lover's fingers in his hand and marvelled anew at their silkiness, which was only enhanced by the hardened skin of his palm – the skin of a soldier's hand.

+

EDWARD SAID, 'I'VE something important to tell you.' He hesitated briefly. 'There's another ship secretly waiting for you. I took the initiative to arrange it all.'

Piers showed no surprise.

'If you choose to board it,' Edward went on to say, 'it will take you to Crécy, in Ponthieu. I know that you long to visit your homeland, Piers, but Gascony is dreadfully far. Whereas if you choose *my* ship – if you choose Ponthieu, Piers, I could easily arrange to visit you. Besides – '

'Besides, something's off.'

'Did you smell it too?'

'The ship's crew. Something not quite right with it.'

'Do you suppose –'

'Hiding something? A conspiracy to get rid of me? Possibly.'

'Just what I feared. The very thought makes me sick! Surely my father couldn't be so callous…'

'Well, it's just possible that we're getting carried away. You know, you and I are occasionally prone to exaggerating my importance.' Piers smiled, and stroked Edward's jaw, looking deep into his eyes. 'Then again, I've been thinking about it, and the King's attitude in this whole affair has been rather mystifying. This reasonableness of his, this liberality…they are all quite unlike him, are they not?'

'Completely unlike him.' Edward stood up and turned away. 'And we... taken in by it, all keen to appease him!'

Piers knew that if there had been an object lying around to kick, Edward's foot would have dispatched it all the way to Calais.

'Never mind that now,' he said, and he too got to his feet. 'It's not as if I have to agonise over this decision. Ponthieu it is.'

Edward turned around. 'Are you sure?' he asked tentatively.

Without waiting for a reply, he threw his arms around Piers' shoulders, holding him fast against his chest.

I'd choose the drab northern skies of Ponthieu one-hundred times over my Pyrenees and their poet's daffodils, if that means proximity to you, Edward – even if I suspected no treachery on the Gascony-bound vessel. But that would sound overdramatic.

Instead, Piers said, 'Considering what passes for the warm season at northern latitudes, I find your decision to send along with me all those buckram quilts – not to mention the sixteen tapestries – a bit less extravagant.' He paused briefly. 'All the same, I'm sure I'll manage my voyage better with my bones intact.'

Edward laughed and unlocked his arms. Then, frowning, he said, 'If the King recalls you from Ponthieu, it will be safer if you find reasons to delay until I myself recall you. That won't be until after the King's death...but the time can't be far off now. You've seen how ill he's been looking, of late.'

Piers considered if Edward had just wished for his father's death. How far-removed was that thought from patricide itself? Should he advise him to disclose it as a sin of thought to his confessor?

'You're my life, Perrot,' said Edward. 'All of it. I wish I could board this ship with you and leave this accursed Kingdom behind.'

'Your Kingdom is your birthright. Don't let anyone take it from you. Not your father, nor any lesser man than him. Nor any better man, for that matter.'

'A birthright, Piers? Or a burden? I feel it's the latter. And I can only bear it as long as you're by my side. None of it is worth it, without you.'

Piers said nothing, but he drew Edward close, and this time, it was he who fastened his arms around the Prince. Edward's bulk felt so natural, so undeniable in his embrace, that it seemed almost unfathomable to him that his arms, so accustomed to that particular assemblage of flesh and bone, should soon be empty of it for God knew how long.

Ten

THE TIDE TURNS

AT DOVER, WHILST Piers' coffers were being loaded onto the Ponthieu-bound ship, Edward questioned the crew of the vessel that would have taken his lover to Gascony. With the necessary persuasion, one of the crew confessed he was taking money to facilitate Lord Gaveston's arrest upon landing in Gascony, but no more. The man denied, however, knowing where the money was coming from; all he knew was that he had seen the emissary that very morning.

As it turned out, his description of this man matched the one person, among those that Edward secretly had his men follow from Dover port, whose eventual destination was none other than the main residence of the Treasurer and Bishop of Lichfield, Sir Walter Langton. Apart from the discovery of Langton's involvement, however, there was little else that Edward's investigations could produce. He could hardly take it upon himself to hurt men who were in his father's or Langton's pay in order to extract confessions, let alone hurt Langton himself.

As Edward expected, the King refused to give him an audience. Filial duty to the King must be unconditional: the heir apparent had no more right than a regular subject to question the King's authority by interfering with his plans – murderous or not.

Edward's fall from grace resulted in the King decreeing that he himself, rather than the Prince of Wales, would be in command of the upcoming campaign in Scotland. What was worse, Edward was kept wholly in the dark about what role he was expected to play in the war. But at the very least, by thwarting the King and Langton's plans, Edward had shown his father that he was endowed with more *savoir-faire* than the King had ever given him credit for. Besides, Piers was safe. Everything else was of secondary importance.

+

IN CRÉCY, PIERS kept himself occupied as best he could. Edward kept sending him extravagant gifts – jousting outfits, money, even horses. The Castle was well-provisioned, with victuals worthy of a King: Piers had never had swan and heron quite so often as he did during the weeks he spent in Ponthieu. The Castle garrison was numerous enough to make him feel entirely safe, and he would even go on excursions in the surrounding countryside and forest – with a bigger escort than usually accompanied his outings with Edward in England. To kill the long hours of leisure, he trained, played chess, wrote letters. A couple of times he even tried his hand at catching fish in the Maye – on both occasions wondering why Edward found fishing so engrossing.

If he felt that, when busying himself in these activities, he was going through the motions, rather than genuinely enjoying himself, he knew the problem was not in the nature of his occupations, but in the apprehensions he seemed unable to shrug off. How was Edward faring in England by himself? He was still so young, barely older than Piers was when they first met, and green – much more so, it seemed to Piers, than he had been at Edward's age. Had he, unwittingly, held Edward back – being always by his side, counselling him, sparing him some of the tedium of official business, sometimes even making his decisions for him? Now that Edward was estranged from his own father, how would he cope without Piers' support?

Piers had sensed, in recent months, a growing antipathy directed at them both. The Earls resented him for being closer to Edward than they ever were or would be. This, he supposed, was entirely to be expected. At times, however, Piers also became dimly aware – and the realisation always hit him with a pang – that the English nobility targeted their displeasure at the Prince himself... He reasoned that the Earls would be forced to outgrow the meanness of their hearts once Edward became King; but he also feared that, for the time being, Edward, deprived as he was of his father's favour, remained vulnerable to their scheming.

As June progressed, each new sunny day Piers spent in Crécy was clouded by an ever more oppressive feeling of foreboding. Something was bound to happen very soon, and Piers' mind, given his anxieties about Edward, couldn't help casting this as yet undefined occurrence in all manner of sinister moulds. If only they could see him now! Many an English acquaintance of his would then have felt compelled to revise their mental picture of Lord Gaveston, a blithe spirit fabled to be all but immune to despondency.

Then, sometime after the middle of July, he received a brief letter from Edward. It required Piers to return immediately, informing him that the King was dead, *God rest His Soul*, and indicated that by the time Piers caught up with him, Edward would be across the Scottish border with the English army. Although the letter ended with a customary expression, Piers had little doubt about just how literally Edward meant it: *The Holy Spirit save You & keep You*.

August 1307, the King's chamber in Dumfries Castle.

EDWARD AND PIERS were sitting side by side on the four-poster bed. Piers approved of the sage-green hue the wood had been painted in. It contrasted beautifully with the ochre colour of the quilt. He didn't approve of himself – dirty and smelly from his journey – sitting on it, but Edward had laughed off his concerns and pulled him down next to him.

'When I saw the body I felt nothing, Perrot.'

'You think you didn't. Such reactions are not unusual upon disturbances of the spirit. Give yourself time.'

'Piers, I really didn't feel anything. As if a stranger had passed away.'

'Your father was not an easy man to love. Unlike you.'

Piers looked around for his robe – where had he deposited it? – but then caught sight of a large piece of woollen cloth folded on the bed and wrapped himself in it. Having cooled down from his ride, the final segment of the long journey that had taken him to Scotland and Edward, the chill inside the stone castle, even at the height of summer, felt suddenly very uncomfortable. Ponthieu had seemed positively Mediterranean by comparison.

Edward said, 'I wish the Scottish magnates found me so easily lovable. I wonder how many of them will show up to pay homage in the next few days.'

Piers sighed. 'English-Scottish relationships may be the least manageable of all the legacies your father bequeathed you.'

'He stirred up trouble, plunged us all into the midst of it, and made his exit.'

'Where, exactly?'

'Not far from Carlisle – on his way to give Robert the Bruce a lesson. Only he didn't even start, this time.'

'And where's the body?'

'On its way south. I went part of the way; but with the army assembled and ready to move, I was forced to turn back. We crossed the border into Scotland the last day of July. I intend to make short shrift of my affairs here, though. I can't see how my being here...or how this whole campaign, for that matter, should be treated as any kind of priority. Not when I have the helm of the Realm to take over. I shouldn't have forced you to come all the way up here if I myself am not likely to linger long. But I was practically dying to see you.'

'I wouldn't have had it any other way,' said Piers.

+

PIERS STOOD AND busied himself by lighting a fire. Edward thought it rather idiosyncratic in August, but he said nothing. After all, wasn't the show of his lover's foibles proof that Piers was here, truly before him, flesh and bone, and not just a washed-out recollection conjured up by his own mind?

'Piers,' Edward said, 'amongst the affairs I've had to attend to in the last few days, two are of great consequence. I require your assistance in carrying out at least one of them.'

'I want nothing better. I hated knowing you were on this side of the Channel, your access to the King cut off, your situation precarious – and I confined to Ponthieu, an object of your cosseting, worse than useless.'

'Well, now, does that mean you resent the gifts I sent to make your stay in Ponthieu bearable? Because if that's the case, you might not welcome the first of the important news I have to break to you. You were made Earl of Cornwall, you see. On 6 August, to be precise. It occurred to me you might like *Earl of Cornwall* better than Count of Ponthieu.'

Piers dropped the woollen cloth off his shoulders and returned to the bed, standing facing the King. Then, all of a sudden, Edward found his lips engulfed into his lover's mouth.

At last Piers released him and asked, 'Is it prudent, though? Wasn't the Earldom of Cornwall destined to your half-brother?'

'To hell with prudence. Aren't I King? I shan't have anyone interfere with my desire to honour the worthiest man –'

Piers' lips returned to his, preventing him from speaking any further. Edward gently pushed him away.

'I haven't quite finished, Perrot.'

'Yes?' Piers returned to the fire, which was crackling in earnest now.

'I've also made arrangements for your marriage.'

Piers looked at him from across the room. 'Oh.'

'I myself am soon to marry, Piers.'

'I know that. You are King. You must produce legitimate heirs. Consolidate political alliances. All that... You *must* marry.'

'And so do you, Piers, if the world is to take you seriously. I've given it much thought over the last few months.'

'I daresay you have.'

'Listen, Piers. You must be supported not only by titles and lands, but by the security of family bonds. Only marriage will bring you that.'

'Either marriage, or being your Companion, I would have thought.'

'No one will ever give you your due as my Companion. You've been

Companion of the Prince of Wales for the last four years. That status ceased to exist the moment I became King. No one but his Queen has ever been *companion* to a King. There's no precedent for it. Besides, unless you forge an independent existence, you will always be obscured by my shadow. I can't allow it. You must shine, Piers. I want your glare to be blinding.'

'And what about us?'

Edward sensed this was as close as Piers would ever get to making a scene – something good breeding forbade him. He had anticipated Piers' opposition, of course, only he hadn't expected it to be grounded in anxiety about the preservation of their relationship. Had he forgotten they were sworn brothers?

'I'm never going to give you up! I'm only giving up the privilege of having you in my household at all times and being with you whenever the whim takes me. The privilege of claiming an exclusive right to your lips. If there were any other way… But there's no alternative. Not if you want me to remain King.'

They were both silent.

Piers sighed. 'And who am I to marry?'

'Margaret de Clare.'

'The *child* Margaret?'

'I'm sure she worships you. All girls do.'

'Good Lord – but she's your niece!'

'Of course, it must be someone that will embed you into the Royal family. Say you will go ahead with it, please.'

'All right, all right,' said Piers, sounding too much, Edward thought, like a man who resolves to have an aching tooth pulled out on the spot, the sooner to put pain and worry behind him.

'Bother…I suppose if I am to marry anyone it might as well be your niece.'

'Don't you like her, Piers?'

Piers rubbed his hands by the fire. 'She is rather…short.'

'That she is. But she is still practically a child.'

'And when am I to marry her?'

'On November 1.'

'This very year! Oh, very well. I suppose you mean well. Can we change subject now?'

'As you wish.'

'Well, then, what do you say if, with my newly-found fortune as Earl of Cornwall, I hold a great Royal feast for the King? To cheer him up in this infernal place, where even high summer is as dreary as midwinter?'

'The King would think that very nice of the Earl of Cornwall.'

'A week from now? It's settled then... But marriage, Edward, and to that child.'

'You're a good man, Perrot. I would swap places with Margaret de Clare here and now, if only I could.'

'Oh, I don't know.' Piers pulled down his hose and began walking across the room towards Edward. Thanks to the heat from the fire, the blood now flushed his extremities, and his prick and balls dangled agreeably with every step. 'I'm positive Margaret is destined never to see quite as much of my *love* as Your Grace.'

'One last thing,' said Edward.

Piers sat down on the bed next to him. 'What now?'

'Langton.'

At the mention of Langton's name, Piers stopped stroking his cock. In fact, he proceeded to put it back inside his hose. 'What about him?'

'As one of the Royal executors, he has been in Burgh-in-Sands, where the King, my father, fell, and is now on his way to Westminster to make arrangements for the funeral – though that of course won't take place for a few months still.'

'Arrest the bastard,' Piers said, in a tone which indicated that doing anything else with the Treasurer would have been completely implausible.

'I see we are of one and the same mind.'

'As always. Well, nearly always. Whenever Margaret de Clare is not concerned.'

'Leave wee Margaret out of it. Now, as Earl of Cornwall, you have just inherited Wallingford Castle, which happens to be conveniently located to serve as Langton's prison – if Langton is intercepted where I think he will be, assuming I give the order to arrest him later today.'

'Wallingford is at your disposal, Your Grace. Its illustrious history will be augmented for serving as noble a purpose as imprisoning the Goat.'

'Thank you. Some of Langton's treasure may come in handy to cover the expenses of my coronation ceremony in a few months' time...I'm thinking there should be enough left to transfer to the Earl of Cornwall.' Edward grinned. 'In recognition of his assistance in ridding the world of that scoundrel.'

'The Earl is grateful to the King for His liberality. But I have it on good authority that just at this moment, Lan-goat's treasure weighs rather less heavily on the Earl's mind than do King Edward's Crown jewels.'

Piers thrust his hand into Edward's hose. Edward's grin widened. He hastily tore off his clothes before assisting Piers with his – his notion of 'assistance' consisting more or less of ripping the buttons off Piers' tunic one by one. He cursed his own impatient, large-handed clumsiness; Piers laughed.

Lying on top of Piers, their cocks trapped between their stomachs, Edward kissed his lover's face – every chiselled bone in it, every inch of bristling cheek. Then, Edward's mouth went down to the plum-coloured nipples, the dark-skinned cock, and as he inhaled Piers' scent, he felt this would be a repeat of the first time they made love, when his fading had happened embarrassingly quick.

Eleven

MANLY PURSUITS

Early January 1308, at the Manor House, in Wye.

EDWARD AND PIERS, freshly returned from a horse ride, were sipping hot cider in the Royal chamber, sitting side by side on the bed. For once, the temperature pleased Piers. The Abbot of St Martin's Abbey ran the place splendidly. The Abbey itself had been renovated not long ago, and it seemed obvious that he had seen fit to spare some labour and money to update the Manor too. The Royal chamber had been made especially comfortable for the King's visit: well-seasoned cherry wood burned fragrantly in the brazier; four matching woollen rugs covered the floor; and trestles of exquisite craftsmanship had been placed at regular intervals around the room's perimeter, supporting dozens of candles, which threw their glow on the battle scenes embroidered on the wall hangings.

'There's hare's blood all over him.' Piers jerked his chin towards Edward's hound, lying blissfully weary on the rug by the bed.

'Vicious beast. Vicious and beautiful,' said Edward, dotingly. 'And how is your wife Margaret doing?'

Piers set his cup down and leant backwards on the bed, reclining on his elbows, his knees still bent over the edge of the mattress, feet still on the floor. 'Splendidly. I hope. I don't get to spend a great deal of time with her. She is preposterously young. What were you thinking? She also appears to be the only member of the female sex completely immune to my charms. Not that I've tried very hard, admittedly – what with her being practically an infant. In any case, our lack of interest in each other is perfectly symmetrical. So there's that at least.'

'She looked pleased enough a few weeks ago, when you held the tournament in Wallingford in her honour.'

'That was *your* idea.'

'It was a very *good* idea. You keep throwing *me* celebrations. You must think of her too.'

'I do. I think of her so much, that I make myself ill.'

Edward patted Piers' thigh. 'Come off it, you've only been married two months. You'll find married life suits you, once she's grown up a little… or once *you* have.'

'Well, I sure hope marriage will suit *you*, Your Grace. One more month, isn't it?'

'Hardly as long as that. I expect I shall be away for two or three weeks, while you take care of everything.'

'I accepted the position of Keeper of the Realm only because I can't think of a better way to spite those pompous, opinionated Earls.'

'I trust no one else, Piers. But I grant that vexing your detractors will be an especially gratifying *incidental* outcome of putting the Kingdom in your hands during my absence.'

Piers grinned. He stood and went to the table: small bunches of dried lavender were neatly arranged in a basket sitting on the table-top. He took one, held it briefly to his nose, then tossed it into the fire. A delightful aroma filled the room. Edward drew in a breath and then exhaled slowly, groaning blissfully.

'And what about your coronation?' asked Piers. 'I'll need some notice if I'm to organise a banquet worthy of the occasion.'

'Around the feast of St Valentine, I suppose, or more likely a little later. As soon as practical after I have returned from France with the Queen.'

'She's not your Queen yet.'

'Unlike you, I make an effort to adjust to the idea. Do I detect a spot of jealousy?'

'You can count on that. She's supposed to be extremely pretty.'

'Is extremely pretty any match for furiously handsome?'

'It'll be up to you to judge.'

'I made that judgment seven years ago, Perrot. It's not up for revision.' Edward, still sitting on the bed, extended his arm. Piers came back, standing before him. 'Take it off,' said Edward, pointing at his lover's shirt, sporting a motif of stags embroidered in red on a white linen base. Piers had specifically chosen to wear it today on account of its rustic charm.

He deposited the shirt neatly on the leather and wooden seat nearby and Edward drew him close. The King started kissing Piers' navel, his stomach, his hip-bones. Then he turned his lover around, and, pulling down his hose, let his lips travel around his buttocks, before abruptly stopping.

'Something the matter?' asked Piers. 'I was warming up.'

'You know, Piers, the French King – whom I shall soon have to call father... The French King has been having the Knights Templar arrested, tortured, and tried, ostensibly for doing to each other just what I'm doing now.'

'Meaning?'

'"Triple indecent kissing – of the lips, navel, and base of the spine."'

'Kissing the "base of the spine"? Do the pious soldiers lip one another's arseholes? In that case we qualify for honorary membership in the Order, I dare say.'

'Don't jest, Piers.'

'I only hope that the good Knights have the sense of having a bath first.' He grinned.

'This is serious, Perrot. As if King Philip's actions weren't enough, the Pope has been pressuring me to prosecute the members of the Order here in England – in the name of the Church, that is.'

'In other words, if anyone must enrich themselves at the Templars' expense, Pope Clement thinks it might as well be him: determined to get in there first, he is – before *you* hit on the idea of emulating King Philip. The old devil pre-empts the move he thinks *you*'re about to make by downgrading you to one of his agents. Cunning of him.'

‘I wrote to the Pope and to the other European Kings whose services he’s trying to enlist. I told them that this is madness...that I cannot believe the charges.’

‘Can’t you, though?’

‘Not as they are presented – as part of an initiation ritual. King Philip is dressing up a bit of harmless fun as some kind of heretical cult, simply because it happens to be expedient for his coffers. The whole business is horrid.’

Piers nodded and readjusted his hose, still in disarray from Edward’s ministrations. He sat down next to the King, having quite lost his lust for the time being. They kept sitting silently, side by side, absently watching the wood as it was slowly consumed by the flames in the brazier. Then Piers shuddered: burning at the stake might well be the fate awaiting the Knights if the charges were proved.

‘Thank you,’ he said, putting a hand on Edward’s thigh.

Edward turned to look at him. ‘What for, Perrot?’

‘For foisting the little runt upon me. You’re protecting me in more ways than one.’

‘Piers, that’s barbaric! My niece is perfectly pleasant to look at.’

‘Whatever you say, Edward. But thank you all the same.’

Piers knew full well that Margaret was pretty, but he also knew he could get away with saying absolutely anything to the King – and, sometimes, he enjoyed taking full advantage of that fact.

+

And so it came to pass that in early 1308, Edward went off to Boulogne to marry Isabella of France, daughter of King Philip the Fair, and upon their return, they were anointed King and Queen of England. But Edward had underestimated the hatred of the Earls, and Piers’ fate was sealed at the coronation banquet. Gossipers said that the attentions King Edward had lavished upon the Earl of Cornwall at the banquet had been an affront to the Queen (a stance which would have surprised Isabella herself). The Earls took those attentions as ultimate proof of the King’s willingness to open his heart and his ears to one man only – a foreigner at that, and until recently, a member of the *lesser* nobility. Rank, or a lack thereof, wasn't Gaveston's only fault in the Earls' eyes: he was also too dashing and well-dressed, and, for that very reason, highly suspicious and generally unfit for the trust and favour of a King. Especially when the King happened to be surrounded by such paragons of wisdom and nobility as themselves, for, after all, they were the Peers of the Realm for a reason. Thereby, through combining forces and threatening civil war, by the middle of 1308, the Earls succeeded in having Sir Piers Gaveston exiled a second time.

However, as usual, Edward thwarted their plans. Through his and Isabella's ingenuity, Piers was instead honourably dispatched to the post of Lieutenant of Ireland – a move that lessened the blow considerably.

On his return from his journey to Bristol, where he had seen the Gavestons off on their voyage to Ireland, Edward couldn't stop thinking about the queer incident involving the cunning man on the small island by the mill on the river Kennet. The old man's words kept echoing eerily in his ears: *You'll never be rid of him, you'll never be rid of him.* When he rode again by the mill, Edward crossed himself and, under his breath, said, 'Never be rid of him: In nomine Dei, Amen.' In the name of God, make it so.

Sometime after the King and Queen were reunited, Isabella learnt that Archbishop Winchelsey had prohibited the Earl of Cornwall's return from Ireland upon pain of excommunication. She was in disbelief: the Earl had never confessed to any guilt, she said to Edward, nor had he been tried in any way! How could the Archbishop commit himself to such baseness, such treachery – and after Edward had reinstated him into the Archbishopric (Edward's father had taken it from him), and picked him specifically to officiate at their coronation?

Edward realised he had miscalculated. The fact that Winchelsey and he shared a loathing for Lord Langton apparently hadn't been enough to reconcile the Archbishop to monarchical authority. But Pope Clement had the power to undo whatever Winchelsey did, and he probably also had the inclination to use it. The Archbishop had an insalubrious penchant for causing trouble: the Pope couldn't very well be pleased with the constant threat of insubordination he posed. Still, Edward had to think of what he might offer Pope Clement in order to persuade him to rescind Winchelsey's excommunication sentence...

Twelve

A KING'S WOES

ONE YEAR WAS a long time. It might not seem like it, perhaps, if you'd been around for as long as the Earl of Lincoln. Then, Edward supposed, with almost six decades behind you, and, surely, not much time left of this mortal life of yours, you might take the view that one year was nothing, that it would be over before you knew it. That's just what Lincoln had said: 'It will be over before you know it, Your Grace'. Only, it wasn't true. The year of his separation from Piers – and he was only a few months into it – was proving interminable, longer-drawn than any Edward had ever known.

Lincoln said that Edward should wait twelve months, that it was quite unthinkable to recall Piers any sooner than that. Edward's material incentives, he said, may have the power to bring about the miracle of changing the Earls' minds about Lord Gaveston, but not at the cost of their self-respect. Demanding their acquiescence to Piers' return before a year had gone by amounted to asking them to utterly humble themselves, it was akin to rubbing their faces in the dirt. They would never consent to that, said Lincoln; and even if they did, buying their agreement on those terms wouldn't be a solid basis on which to build a reconciled Kingdom. In any case, Edward shouldn't ask it of them.

Edward was supposed to understand all that. Only he didn't. The Earls, as far as he could see, had foregone their self-respect the moment they had allowed him to *buy* their agreement to Piers' recall. Some had given their consent even before Lincoln had let himself be persuaded of the unfairness of Piers' exile, of the dangerous precedent it set to the integrity of Royal power, and of Edward's own intention to behave more guardedly henceforth. Why should the timing of Piers' return now make any difference? But Edward had given his word to Lincoln – almost the only one left among the Earls whom he still trusted – and now he'd have to keep it.

+

IN NOVEMBER 1308, Thomas of Lancaster sought special audience with the King. Lancaster's exultation at Piers' banishment had been overshadowed, over the last few months, by his growing dismay at the apparent success of Edward's ongoing efforts to convert Piers' opponents. Lancaster had witnessed just how well the King's tactic was paying off – a strategy centred as much on material inducements, as on making the Peers feel that he was willing to let them into his confidence.

There was much that was alarming about this development. Before he knew it, Lancaster might find Gaveston restored to his place at Court – with the difference that, this time, the King would make sure to retain the loyalty of the other Earls by readily according them favours. This threatened Lancaster's hopes to augment his status, wealth, and power at Court: as far as he was concerned, there were, quite simply, not enough of these commodities at the King's disposal to satisfy everyone. And their supply was bound to decrease significantly if Gaveston returned.

Lancaster did not care to be merely one among many competitors vying for Royal favour. Besides, even if the King's supply of political and material benefits had been unlimited, everyone knew power and riches tasted less sweet the less exclusive their possession. Indeed, weren't power and riches wholly relative matters? Whatever one's power and influence amounted to, they ceased being power and influence the moment everyone possessed them. As to wealth, it presupposed a distinction between those who had it and those who didn't. A man couldn't be 'rich' in a world where there were no 'poor'; and he couldn't be 'really rich' unless he kept *the rest* of the well-to-do from rising above *moderate* wealth.

It was therefore essential to prevent the Gascon exile from ever coming back. If the impossibility of his return could be impressed upon the King's mind once and for all, the King's newly-found liberality towards the other Earls would cease too, for he would no longer have any incentive to appease them.

Gaveston's return would also dash Lancaster's hopes of re-establishing the former rapport existing between the King and him – a rapport whose loss Lancaster had never really gotten over, although he could scarcely admit this to himself. Indeed, these days Lancaster tended to take the cynical view that, in his desire to keep the King and Gaveston apart and to regain the King's full confidence, he was actuated purely or primarily by his political and material ambitions. It would never do – now that the prospect of his plan's success was uncertain to say the least – for Lancaster openly to acknowledge that he was jealous – that he desired Edward's confidence in and of itself. It was quite inconceivable to admit that he yearned to once more taste something approaching the sweetness of his younger cousin's veneration for him when they had both been children. Yet, in his most honest and lucid moments, Lancaster knew that these particular desires were *precisely* the reason why Gaveston's return loomed larger for him than it did for any of the other Earls.

+

HAVING CONSENTED TO give Lancaster special audience, Edward braced himself for something deeply unpleasant. God knew he had had many of these moments in the past few months, but not generally at the hands of his cousin Lancaster. *Tu quoque, Brute.*

Edward knew what would happen: at the first mention of Piers, he would – as it had now become his habit when discussing him with anyone other than Isabella – withdraw inside an invisible armour. Lancaster could then be his guest, let it all out, and go on all he liked: just as long as he didn't expect his words to make any difference.

Was he being close-minded? Edward made no apologies to himself. Piers was his own life, and he didn't need to justify his desire to live: it asserted itself and was its own justification.

+

'THOMAS,' HIS COUSIN said as Lancaster entered the King's chamber.

The King was sitting at the table and gestured to his cousin to take the seat facing him. A small, sable cow-hide, supple and beautifully soft to the touch, was draped over the seat Lancaster took. An identical one covered the seat occupied by the King, and a third was in use as a table cloth. *Irish hides of the highest quality: no doubt gifts sent from that ingratiating Gascon dog*. The King himself was attired in the kind of *recherché* manner that had become characteristic of him ever since he had fallen under Gaveston's spell. Today, a vermillion pattern of two herons facing each other stood out on the shimmering grey front of his silken surcoat, their gemstone eyes picked out by the light reflecting on them. Lancaster was as fond of luxurious furnishings as any self-respecting nobleman, but he found that personal adornment betrayed excessive vanity and a discreditable levity of character.

Lancaster took a deep breath through his nostrils and prepared to launch his offensive. 'Sire, I know you and love you too well not to be absolutely honest with you. Blunt, where needed.'

'You know I expect and demand no less of my friends.'

'It concerns the Earl of Cornwall, Your Grace.' He paused briefly to check his cousin's reaction, but the King betrayed no emotion. 'I know how much you're exerting yourself to bring about a revocation of Cornwall's exile, Sire.'

'As is my prerogative,' said the King.

'Indeed, Sire. But I have your interest at heart when I advise you not expend your energies on a mission that must ultimately prove...futile, if you don't mind my saying so.'

'Futile, Thomas? Says *who*?'

'Sire, you must know that the Peers of the Realm have no real intention to allow Lord Gaveston back, still less to allow you to restore him to his position at Court if he were to return. You deceive yourself if you think otherwise. I'm concerned that you are allowing yourself to be manipulated.'

Lancaster realised he'd been speaking to a spot on the wall right above his cousin's left shoulder. Something – a spider? – had been crawling, half-heartedly, over it. He now made a deliberate effort to seek the King's eye. His cousin stared back, in silence, but the vein running conspicuously down the middle of his forehead and the faintly flaring nostrils were eloquent enough.

The King exhaled. 'You have made yourself perfectly clear. Was there anything else?'

It hadn't worked. *Stubborn mule of a cousin.* Lancaster had to think quickly. 'Sire, I think you underestimate –'

'I assure you I'm not underestimating anything, although it strikes me that all this time I may have been *over*estimating *your* loyalty to *me*.'

Lancaster steepled his fingers. 'Sire, you shouldn't wilfully seal your ears to the voice of reason –'

'There is no *reason*!' shouted the King. 'No reason to keep the Earl out of the country and away from me! Pretexts, made-up grievances, invented abuses...and now prophecies of doom, coming from your very mouth, Thomas – you who profess to be my friend! Why should I bow to jealousy, pettiness, and greed *masquerading* as reasons? And since when have you joined the ranks of the paltry creatures that fear, rather than admire, excellence? Those whose actions belie their claim to be *my* Peers – let alone the Earl of Cornwall's!'

Lancaster had closed his eyes. Intertwining his fingers, he opened them again and said, 'Sire, I've nothing but your interests at heart. You do me an injustice if you take any other view of the matter.'

The King said nothing; folding his arms, he looked to the floor. It was clear, then: Lancaster had, *in finis*, less than a speckle of influence over the King. It made him feel foolish, and it hurt. What was worse, he was faintly aware of the fact that it hurt him unreasonably – in much the same way that a rebuff hurts a scorned lover. It hurt him, that is, with that peculiar kind of insanity that afflicts someone who claims a right to having their feelings reciprocated by the object of their desire, labouring under the delusion that their fancy makes them automatically deserving. As his cousin kept his counsel, Lancaster felt his anger mount – anger at the King's obstinacy; at himself for destroying, possibly for good, the progress made in months of carefully planned work; and at Gaveston for effortlessly succeeding in securing the King's trust that, he now realised, the King had in fact been withholding from him, Lancaster, all along.

'All I'm asking is that you make a King's choice, Sire,' he said with some violence. 'This bondage you feel for *Gaveston*,' – try as he might, just now he couldn't speak the man's name without disgust – 'this self-imposed obligation of fidelity to such a man...they are unworthy of you.'

'*Bondage*?' asked the King, staring straight into his cousin's eyes.

Did the shadow of a sneer fleet across the King's face as he said it? How incongruous, how utterly infuriating.

'What do you know, Thomas? What do you *think* you know? You're hardly fit to speak to me of my bond with the Earl! Do you think it's as easy as putting the injustice and affront already suffered by the Earl on one plate of the scales and then balance it against all the hatred for him – all the antipathy of lesser men – and all the nefarious acts that they will be intent on orchestrating if he is to return? You know nothing. Can you balance the love of a King against the hatred of his *subjects*?'

He didn't say *Peers*. That was deliberate, Lancaster knew it, and calculated to offend.

'Can you balance the love of a King against the practicalities of well-ordered rule? The mind revolts just thinking about it, Thomas! Do you realise what you're asking? How can I look at this as anything but a betrayal?'

Lancaster felt the right side of his face twitch. 'I've always defended you and that Gascon adventurer against the ill-will of others,' he said between his teeth.

'Oh, you missed no opportunity to impress upon Us just how much the *other* Earls detest him: and have We not always shown gratitude for your *support*, as We, in Our blindness, have regarded it until now? Let it be very clear, Lancaster: *if* and for as long as you've been on Our side, and made it your business to defend Us, you've been doing no less, but certainly no more, than is required by loyalty to your King. Be gone now!'

Lancaster hesitated: should he attempt a last appeal?

Then his cousin leant across the table and shouted, 'Leave, or I'll have you thrown out!'

With his open hand, the King struck him on the chest, sending his seat tottering, and Lancaster himself into a perfect rage. His tongue cursing, he marched out the door, which slammed shut behind him. And, having reached his lodgings in the Royal Palace, Lancaster made arrangements to leave the Court at once.

+

PIERS WAS DOING his part, ensuring that his military record as Lieutenant of Ireland would be distinguished enough to make it very awkward for the Peers to oppose his return when the time was ripe.

Meanwhile, this side of the Irish Sea, Edward – who, since his break with Lancaster, mistrusted the Earls more than ever – resolved to enlist the assistance of forces not only temporal, but also spiritual. This he did by founding a Dominican Priory at his favourite residence in Langley and liberally providing for its future financial needs. He did not presume to offer this to God as *quid pro quo* – the Priory in exchange for Piers' return. But surely the foundation of the Priory could not hurt his endeavour? He also sought spiritual direction from the Black Friars – his favourite appellative for the Dominicans – concerning his relationship with Piers.

'Can a King love too much, Brother?' he asked a learned member of the order one unusually hot afternoon in April.

The Friar, who was seeing to the organisation of what would become the Priory's physic garden, asked Edward permission to sit down on a nearby low wall. Drying the sweat from his brow, he answered that it was impossible for a King to love too much, for Christ was our King and His Love was boundless, and how could Christ be at fault? The greater the King's love, the more it resembled the love of God.

Edward said that the Love of Christ was a different matter altogether; why, Christ, even loved his enemies, whereas he, the King, couldn't help resenting them, for they hated his friend. Our limited capacity for love, answered the Friar, was a consequence of the Fall, but the King should keep trying, and with God's help, he may yet come to love his enemies. Their hatred for his friend was a mortal sin, of course, but Edward's charity, 'through prayers and good works', especially his forgiveness, could assist in moving his enemies to repent for such a sin. In buying his enemies the graces of God that would move them to repent, Edward's forgiveness would indirectly also be buying his friend the love of his enemies, for they couldn't truly repent until they stopped hating his friend. Edward suspected the logic of this was a little tortuous, let alone circular, but took the Brother's word that it wasn't.

Having put to rest the question of whether one man can love another too much, Edward asked the Brother whether a man can love another 'in the wrong way'. The Friar looked bemused. There was no wrong way to love, he said. Love did not admit of being right or wrong. If it was wrong, it had ceased to be love, or it had never been love in the first place. This pleased Edward, for he had not the slightest doubt his love for Piers was a genuine case of love.

Edward took one more step in the spiritual domain to help along his lover's speedy return. In a bid to get Pope Clement to lift Archbishop Winchelsey's excommunication sentence against Piers, he wrote to the Pope that henceforth he would be more accommodating in the prosecution of the Templars, which so far he had resisted. As his scribe penned the words the King dictated, Edward remembered Piers' censorious words about the First Edward many years ago: *The King uses people.* He feared he was becoming like his father, but with Piers by his side, he knew he could justify it. Piers wouldn't even have to comfort him, he wouldn't have to say anything at all: his presence alone would be enough to cleanse him of all shame and guilt – to remind him that whatever he had done, he had done for good reason.

THE BLEAK WINTER months, with their mournful skies and long-drawn nights, had been the worst. Edward's despondency then grew to such proportions that even Isabella – always so ready to see the best in him – must have found his company barely endurable. He felt a distance coming between them, and the worst thing was that he felt powerless to do anything to bridge it. He knew that, with Piers the other side of the Irish Sea, he had every reason to seek her company and rely on her support. Her youth didn't matter: he was sure that she was willing – more than that, desirous – to comfort and encourage him. But his sullenness made it all but impossible for her to reach out to him; and every grey winter day plunged him more deeply into despair, and unable to open his heart to her. What if Piers should die during this year in Ireland? What if an accident befell him, or he found himself locked in mortal combat with one of the local Lords he was trying to subdue?

The advent of spring relieved the most oppressive of these thoughts. As the days grew longer, and the constant winter wet gave way to sunny spells and fitful showers, it seemed impossible – almost obdurate – not to be affected. With so many memories of springtime delights shared with Piers, and the anticipation of many more to come, how could Edward be insensitive to swelling buds, bursting catkins, and returning swallows?

But as summer approached, bringing with it, more definite than ever, the promise of Piers' return, Edward's growing joy could be suddenly obliterated by the recurring misgiving that something fatal was going to happen to his lover after all, in these, the *very last* days of their enforced separation. Panic would then seize him. If it came to pass – if Edward was to lose him – he'd spend the rest of his life cursing Lincoln for persuading him not to recall Piers earlier. And every new morning he'd greet the day with a curse on himself, too, for failing to clasp his lover to his chest long enough when he bade him his last farewell at Bristol port.

These fears, however, turned out to be unfounded. Edward couldn't be quite sure exactly which of his many efforts should be credited with bearing fruit, but Piers and Margaret returned to England on the twenty-seventh day of June of the year of our Lord 1309.

Thirteen

CHRISTMAS AT LANGLEY

THAT YEAR, 1309, the Royal couple spent the Christmas season at Langley with the Earl and the Countess of Cornwall.

One morning, the four of them were taking a stroll in the grounds of the estate, linking arms. The two women were in the middle, with Piers on the Queen's side and Edward on his niece's. Blades of grass, sheathed in frost, crunched agreeably under their feet.

'We hardly ever see you these days, Earl,' said Isabella. 'The last time we were all four of us united under the same roof was in September, was it not?'

Piers cast a furtive glance at the Queen, who had spoken with her eyes fixed ahead of her on the frosty landscape. Was this young woman full of poise really the child bride Edward had brought over from Boulogne less than two years ago? He had thought her remarkable even then: but the beauty, the correct bearing, the carefully controlled speech – vaguely incongruous, even unnerving, in the young girl – had now blended to produce a wondrous effect of natural grace and self-assurance.

'My Lady, I wish I had fewer demands upon my time and could visit you and the King more often.'

'He's been trying to reform his ways, my dear!' said Edward turning towards his wife, his breath condensing in great clouds of white steam over Margaret's head.

'Only too true, My Lady. I've been spending more time than I care to recall consorting with the Earls – those who don't shun me, that is. Truth be said, I secretly hope more of them had the nerve to avoid me. I can never be sure whether the ones who stoop to associating with me do so purely to conciliate the King. And even supposing they genuinely desire my company, I can't say I desire theirs, exactly.'

'Are the Earls behaving uncivilly to you, Lord Gaveston?' She turned to look at him. 'It's the prerogative of my station and my sex to signify displeasure in myriad subtle ways, and I intend to make use of this as circumstances demand.'

Piers smiled. 'You may see fit to spare Lincoln, Surrey, Richmond, and Gloucester, Lady Isabella. They've been gracious enough.'

'Note taken,' said Isabella. 'In any event, returning to the matter of your absenteeism, I concede that in the last few days you have been making up for it by associating with my dear husband at every opportunity. *He*, no doubt, appreciates it.'

'I'm so sorry, my dear,' Edward said. 'Have we been neglecting you and Lady Margaret very badly?'

'Don't be sorry, Your Grace!' said Margaret. 'Your intimacy with my husband, even if it deprives me of his company at Christmastime, is a small price to pay for my peace of mind. During our year in Ireland, the Earl gave ample public evidence of his statesmanship skills, but he also proved to me – privately – how unremittingly he can mope when he is separated from you.'

Piers feigned a scowl. 'You naughty –'

'I'm no longer a child, dear husband,' Margaret said, triumphant.

'You're hardly taller than one. But, truth be told,' Piers said, turning to the others, 'she's also as bonny as any.'

Edward and Isabella exchanged a conspiratorial smile.

'Don't worry, my dear Earl,' said Isabella, 'your wife and I both know you and the King were simply made for each other. My husband worked tirelessly to bring you back. It still eludes me how he could manage to persuade Lincoln – the most resolute of your detractors, I thought – to plead with the others for the revocation of your exile. When the King accomplished that, I knew that the restoration of the lands of Cornwall to you must follow soon.'

'And yet, Isabella my dear, don't forget the Earls are all fractious again now… We seem to be doomed never to have any peace.' Edward sighed. 'Lancaster's betrayal has hit me worst.'

'Wasn't he an earnest advocate for us?' Margaret asked.

Piers responded with a shrug; Edward by looking dispirited.

'The sincerity of my uncle's erstwhile support is very much in question,' said Isabella. 'He seemed to have presumed that being a cousin of the King's entitled him to more favours than even the King's generosity showed him. What perfectly unbearable arrogance. As if the King didn't have enough on his hands trying to pacify the rest of them. Your efforts accomplished more than any of us had any right to hope for, Edward. Upon my word, Earl, you bring out the best in him.'

Piers' laugh was a little strained. 'That's an unconventional way of looking at my influence on the King, Lady Isabella.'

Margaret pointed at two large colourful birds, with yellow crests and long tails, strutting about the aviary. 'What are those, Your Grace?'

They arrested their stroll and unlinked arms.

'They originate from the East,' Edward answered abstractedly.

'A few years ago,' said Piers, 'the King used to keep all sorts of exotic creatures here at Langley, Margaret – did you ever see them? It was quite a collection. A lion used to accompany him to war, you know.'

'I loved my pets,' said Edward, his voice tinged with melancholy, as he drew Isabella's mohair cape, appliquéd with a wreath of holly and ivy leaves, more snugly around her. 'You never even saw most of them, Piers.'

'True,' Piers said, winking at both women, 'I think I may have missed the *camel*.'

'A camel,' gasped Isabella. 'What's to love about a camel, my dear husband?'

Edward shrugged. 'She had a soft snout. I used to ride her, too, sometimes.'

Isabella pinched her nose. 'Did she also offer delights of the olfactory variety?'

Edward swept his right foot left and right over the frosty grass before him, leaving a bow-shaped mark. 'That's always been Piers' prerogative,' he said, seemingly without giving much conscious thought to it.

At once Piers knew he had turned red. 'When we were young,' he hastened to say, 'the King had this fancy that I – this is so embarrassing – that I had…a *nice* smell about me, Lady Isabella. I admit I was never quite able to accept it as a compliment.'

Margaret chuckled, and Piers felt his blush deepen.

'Oh, come here, Earl!' Isabella turned to put an arm around Piers, who hid his face on her shoulder. 'Edward, you're a perfect beast.'

Piers realised that the shattering of his self-possession was a good whose scarcity increased its entertainment value for all present. He played along until the shadows lifted from Edward's face.

Fourteen

TO WATCH, TO FEEL

Approximately one year later, a few days before Christmas 1310. On the Scottish border, in the Castle of Berwick-upon-Tweed.

ISABELLA HAD RETIRED to her room after the midday repast, to dictate some letters. She had then felt suddenly tired. Having asked her attendants to leave her alone, she had lain on her bed, under the furs, intending to have a brief sleep. One of the resident cats – the red-tabby one – had snuggled up next to her...

Unsure of how long she had been asleep, Isabella awoke just in time to see the cat jump off the bed. One of the doors on the wall-to-wall cupboard was ajar, and the cat disappeared behind it. She stretched and got up, surveying the motif of oak leaves carved on the oaken cupboard doors: the idea was a happily conceived one, but the execution was no better than you'd expect *this* far north on *this* side of the Channel. Never mind. She pulled the cupboard door open wide, so as to let the cat out. *How odd*. Where could she have gone? She turned around to check the room. The animal was nowhere to be seen.

She shivered. The fire was still burning, but it had lost its battle against the winter chill coming through the small window. She wrapped around her shoulders the largest of the furs that were lying on the bed, lit a candle at the fire, and returned to the cupboard. She inspected the inside more closely. A narrow, half-height door was ajar in the back of the cupboard. She crouched down, pulled the door open and lifted the candle. Not, as she initially thought, a concealed compartment, but what looked like...*a secret passage!*

Another shiver went down her spine – the sensation, this time, too delicious to be a response to the cold. Still huddling in her fur, she set down the candle, standing in its little clay dish, and pushed it ahead of her into the passage. Then she made her way through the secret door on all fours. Past the half-height door, the passage itself turned out to be high enough to allow her to stand. She picked up the candle, and carefully advanced through the narrow stone corridor. Alas, it was only a few steps long. At the end of it was a low doorway, the same height as the door she had just crossed at the other end.

The cat was sitting in the doorway, for all the world looking like she'd been waiting for the Queen, her eyes reflecting the light of the candle in the slightly unsettling way cats' eyes do. She came towards her and rubbed herself on her gown a couple of times, before disappearing in the direction Isabella had emerged from.

The Queen crouched before the second doorway and sneaked through, emerging into what looked like a wall cavity. At her back was the stone wall through whose doorway she had just passed, and less than two steps ahead of her was a wall made of wooden panels, which, she guessed, must look like wainscoting from the other side. She moved the candle around to find the door that, she assumed, would give her admission into the room on the other side of the panelling, but she failed to find one. Good thing she was not prone to panicking in dark, enclosed spaces.

A little light was filtering through a slight crack in the panelling, at eye level. She laid the candle on the floor, a little way from her feet, to make sure she wouldn't inadvertently knock it over, and drew close to the crack to peer through. The small windows on the outer wall of the medium-sized room she was looking into admitted just enough natural light to identify it as the King's chamber. The First Edward had had the Castle rebuilt not long ago: did he envisage the room she had just come from to be the Queen's chamber, or was it originally intended to serve another purpose – and, if so, why should it secretly connect to the King's chamber?

She was about to pick up the candle and retrace her steps back to her room to report her discovery to Edward, when the door to the King's bedchamber creaked open. She returned her eye to the crack in the panelling and saw her husband and Lord Gaveston entering the room, the Earl carrying a chess board, and Edward a burning rush-light and an abundance of unlit beeswax candles.

The Earl of Cornwall set his hand to lighting the fire in the hearth (a modern luxury, Edward had told her, installed when the Castle had been rebuilt), while Edward sealed the small windows with their wooden shutters. Edward then placed the candles in small groups on different items of furniture around the room and used the rush light to light them all, including the ones already stuck in the two candelabra at each side of the bed. She shook her head: it was just like her husband to attend to such tasks himself, and conscript the Earl into their execution, instead of having it done for him by one of his valets. She caught her breath to stop from giggling.

'Did you say anything, Edward?' asked the Earl. It made her want to giggle even harder.

'No, nothing, Piers.... Now, this is much better.' Edward looked satisfied about the room, now enveloped in a warm glow.

The Earl sat down at the table where he had previously laid the chessboard. Edward joined him and made the first move. Isabella was about to call out to them, but wouldn't it be much more amusing to emit an eerie-sounding noise and observe their reaction? Except that it would probably be un-lady-like, and certainly unbecoming of a Queen. *Bother*. She raised her hand to tap the panelling, but the Earl's voice made her stop.

'We've been seeing far too little of each other, Edward. Don't get me wrong, I enjoy being in command of my own contingent. But I've missed you.'

'Me too, Piers. The journey from Roxburgh to Berwick never takes more than four hours. I don't know what our excuses have been for not making a more regular habit of it.'

'How about the ghastly Scottish winter? Anyway, it's nice finally to be visiting. The Queen is getting more and more beautiful.'

Isabella smiled and bit her lip. No question of tapping the panelling now: she would listen just a little longer, and then retreat.

'Like father, like daughter: Philip the Fair, and Isabella the Fair. I keep thinking, too, how much shrewder she is than me at her age.'

'Was it really she and not you who hit on the idea that you should resume the Scottish campaign while the.... What do the eight Earls and their prelate friends call themselves these days?'

'"Lord Ordainers". Pretentious wankers. In any case, yes, the idea came from her. "If the Lord Ordainers have the audacity to think they're good enough to lead you, you must show everyone their conceit: subdue Scotland without them, while they make it their business to meddle with the King's own affairs in England." That's what she said. She can be awfully eloquent.'

'And shall we manage to subdue Bruce?' asked the Earl. 'We haven't accomplished a great deal so far.'

'You know I've little appetite for violence if there's a chance to get what we want peacefully. No need to kill Bruce, if we can – if *you* can, rather, get him to pay me homage and acknowledge the English King as Scotland's feudal overlord. You did yourself much credit in Ireland, Piers. If there's anyone who can pull off this diplomatic mission, it's you.'

'Bruce is proud. He won't be easily persuaded.'

'We'll go to war in earnest if Bruce really asks for it. But we should hold out until circumstances are propitious for reaching an agreement. I'm in no particular hurry to return south. As long as I stay up here, it means I'm unavailable to hear the Lord Ordainers' recommendations about my household.'

The Earl considered his next move on the chessboard. 'Can we afford being away for much longer, though? The Scots are notorious for dragging conflicts out indefinitely... How long will the Earl of Lincoln last as Regent? I hear his health is failing him. Without his moderating influence, who knows to what level of presumptuousness the other Earls may rise.'

'If Lincoln dies, the Regency in the South will have to fall upon your brother-in-law. There's hardly anyone else left that we can trust. That's why I'm sending young Gloucester de Clare with you, to parley with Bruce – he can do with all the experience of statesmanship he can get.'

The room was warming up. They both stood and removed their robes.

'Edward,' said Piers, after they sat down again, 'I know you don't like to talk about it, but don't you think it might have been a mistake to accede to the barons' demands that they be granted the power to govern your household? I worry that your agreement emboldened them.'

'I don't like having the Lord Ordainers interfering with my affairs any more than you do, Piers. I didn't agree with a light heart. Don't forget that I insisted that the appointment of the Lord Ordainers should not be treated as a precedent. And I made it clear that I gave my assent only as a matter of courtesy... But really, Piers, what choice did I have?'

What indeed, thought Isabella? The Earls had been in arms at the February Parliament, even Pembroke – level-headed Pembroke – and Edward's brother-in-law, Hereford. They had threatened to depose the King unless he agreed to their demands. Edward might have risked refusing them – he *should* have, perhaps; but he didn't, because of Lord Gaveston. It was the threat to the Earl's life that made Edward capitulate. Faced with the same choice, she would have done the same. Probably.

The Earl sighed. 'Is there no end to the discord, the humiliation you must endure… Can it be right for you to concede so much in order to protect me?'

Isabella had always assumed the Earl's self-assurance and *amour propre* to be virtually without cracks. Yet here he was, implying he was not worthy of Edward's love and concern.

'I've never felt humiliated, Piers! Do you think their accusations of recklessness can touch me?' Edward's mouth twisted in a strange grin. 'Why should I care, even if they claim I'm ill-advised – that I cannot keep my own affairs in order? Do they not claim I lost Scotland, when my father never gained it to begin with? They twist the truth to suit their prejudices… Let them believe what they will. Let them convince themselves of their accusations, let them take whatever measures they please. So what, even if I lose some of my prerogatives, as long as I can keep you safe and by my side? Let them feel in control, let them *be* in control! They won't then be able to say so easily that I'm ruled by you. We'll be left in peace once and for all.'

Isabella turned away from the panelling and dabbed the corner of her eyes with her sleeve. She couldn't really relate to Edward's professed forbearance at parting from the prerogatives of Royal power; but she marvelled anew at her husband's surpassing love for the Earl. She felt it was unfair to intrude any further and was about to leave, when a sudden commotion in the bedchamber – a thump, and a noise like a lapful of walnut shells dropping on a hard floor – drew her eye once again to the crack in the panelling. She saw her husband reclining over the table, and the Earl – *trapped?* – under him, his back to the wooden tabletop, the chess pieces scattered all about him and on the floor. The two men were face to face, Edward's hips – *forced?* – between the Earl's knees, his hands gripping the Earl's shoulders, pinning him down against the table top. The Earl looked helpless, dwarfed by Edward's brawn...

Is he out of his mind? What's the meaning of this – why has he suddenly turned against the man he loves most, moments after that display of absolute devotion? Horrified, she almost gave out a cry, but something at the back of her mind arrested the movements of her lips and throat, just in time. *Could it be?*

The Earl stretched his neck and drew his face closer to Edward's. Their mouths stopped just short of making contact: instead, the Earl's tongue reared between the pink sheath of his lips and its tip reached out to touch Edward's own. Edward pulled back. He removed the Earl's tunic and shirt, as well as his own, then returned his mouth briefly to the Earl's lips, before proceeding to trace a trail with the tip of his tongue across his lover's neck, chest and stomach, down to the belly button, and then beyond, between the Earl's thighs...

The sight had Isabella entranced, short of breath, all but stupefied. And yet, as she witnessed this most fantastical, most incredible of sights, everything seemed to fall into place – not only her husband's devotion to the Earl, but also what, up to now, had seemed to her the most ineffable quality of their bond: the way the company of each always seemed to transfigure the other. Her own response to all this finally became fully intelligible to her, too: she could now explain the thrill she invariably experienced in their joint presence ever since she had seen them kiss at the Coronation banquet. She had not known, exactly; yet, part of her had always known.

She no longer worried about her own indiscretion, now. Of course, third parties had no business in the tryst between the King and the Earl, but, equally, as a matter of course, she was no third party. After all, she and Edward had been joined in holy matrimony. But even more than Edward she *was* the Earl: she was his litheness against the King's fleshier muscularity, his skin – which was neither fair nor dusky, or, rather, both at the same time – contrasting against the ruddier cast of the King's own; she was the Earl's tongue searching the familiar sweetness of Edward's lips; and she shared the Earl's desire that Edward should flare with desire for him, and with it, singe every last region of his own body.

She kept watching until the two men moved from the table to the bed, and Edward knelt on the mattress, sitting on his heels, and the Earl sat straddling his thighs, and, chest to chest, Edward eased himself into the Earl, slow, slow, sending the muscles on the Earl's back quivering, like folded wings. For a wild moment, it occurred to her that the Earl might be half woman – how else could Edward find a way into him? – and it seemed to explain the riddle of his beauty, for everybody knew the Earl's fair features put many maidens to shame. Then, intuition – perhaps assisted by a closer glimpse – let her into the mystery of exactly *how* Edward's flesh had joined the Earl's, and her hand went to her mouth. With his arms and legs wrapped around Edward, and Edward's fingers buried in the lustrous black curls on the back of his head, the Earl started rocking his hips back and forth. The movement, in which Edward partook as much as the Earl, brought home to Isabella that it truly was possible for two to become *one* flesh...

Twain once more, they lay down side by side, their backs propped on cushions against the headboard, one arm of each around the other's shoulders. Each man – for, looking at him now, from this angle, facing her with his legs splayed apart, it seemed clear to Isabella that, if the Earl wasn't a man, then nobody could possibly be – each man used his free hand to grab his own shaft, and took to sliding the fingers vigorously up and down it. After a while, and nearly at the same time, their chests became soaked (their necks too, because the Earl's seed leapt further than Edward's, and scattered left and right). Then, when ecstatic groans escaped their mouths, she understood that this curious hand movement – by far the most peculiar of their amorous diversions – had finally brought them to the fading. And there was a strange smell seeping through the crack, like the flowers on some plants, but which?

After the heaving of their chests had decreased, the Earl said, 'Edward: did I ever mention that I once called the Earl of Warwick "dog"?'

'Once? You've been regularly referring to him as the Black Hound of Arden for over a year, haven't you?'

'I believe I might have.' The Earl grinned. 'But I meant that I called him a dog... *to his face.*'

Edward smiled, delighted. 'Are you out of your mind?'

'I was drunk, Your Grace. I must have been, I'm sure.'

'It's not the sort of thing that helps our cause, exactly...'

'No, Sire, I suppose it isn't.' They burst out laughing, and the Earl looked even more irresistible than usual.

By the time Isabella had left her station by the panelled wall, the length of her candle had halved. As she stooped to go through the low doorways in the secret passage, she felt a little foolish. But later, as she was getting ready for supper, the anticipation at sharing the table with Edward and the Earl almost made her want to dance around the room.

When, later, she retired for the night, she imagined the two men lying down on either side of her, their breath warm on her cheeks, their hands extended to meet over her stomach. She was still awake when the shift in the rhythm of her maids' breathing gave the signal that they had entered into the territory of dreams. Her longing for her husband by then had become keener. The tips of her middle and ring fingers went to her lips, and she kissed them, making believe they were Edward's lips. As they reached just behind her lower lip, her tongue extended to touch them. Slick with slaver, they backed out of her mouth, fondled her chin, zig-zagged over the smoothness of her neck and, tickling her gently heaving body, traced over mounds and depressions the same path that Edward's mouth had followed along the Earl's torso and stomach only a few hours ago.

Isabella was no stranger to the feeling that enveloped her lower belly, radiating inward and upwards, when, all alone, the fancy might take her to cross her feet and squeeze the bedclothes bunched up between her thighs – pressing and releasing, pressing and releasing. Now, for the first time, her hand came to know of its ability to evoke the same thrilling sensation, when her fingertips reached past her hip-bone to caress the down between her thighs.

She took a deep breath as she gave herself up to that feeling, wallowing in its miraculous, luxurious quality. Only by digging her teeth into her lower lip could she keep herself from whimpering. And she made believe that the teeth biting her lip were Edward's; and the tongue parting her lips down below – and burrowing its way deep inside her, and marvelling at her warmth, and at her softness – was the Earl of Cornwall's.

The following morning, the Earl noticed a small cut and asked her how she had injured her lip.

She shrugged. 'Edward,' she answered.

It made the Earl arch his brows.

Fifteen

THRICE BANISHED

A mild, misty morning less than a year later, in early November 1311.

THE GROUNDS OF the Royal Manor in Sheen, upon the river Thames. After more than a decade in England, Piers was still not used to the way in which an English autumn mist could persist throughout the entire day, not so much blocking out light as imparting to it a certain density, a milkiness that lent everything it enveloped a quality of unreality. The moisture in the air collected on leaves and, dripping off, produced a thin steady shower under the canopy of trees. A multitude of tiny droplets crowded on Edward's eyebrows, turning them thick and hoary, making him look like an incongruously smooth-skinned elder. Piers worried about the same effect on him: his own impersonation of old age must be much more convincing, what with the creases at the corner of his eyes, which, for the last year or so, had refused to disappear even after a good night's sleep. His hand went to his brow to wipe the moisture away.

'This is madness, Edward,' he said.

Edward pushed back the hood of his brown woollen cape, revealing hair whose wave had spoilt a little in the moisture. The sight added to Piers' melancholy.

'How so?' asked Edward.

'You can't just drop everything to come to see me off.'

'Are you saying I'm reckless, Piers? That I don't take the job of governing seriously? Because that makes you sound very much like one of my mortal foes.'

'Edward...'

'Perhaps I *am* reckless! Perhaps this misery I brought upon us is well-deserved! What would you have me do?'

Piers sighed and lowered his gaze. A film of moisture covered the velvet of his doublet, turning its blue to slate-grey. 'I simply worry about you.'

'You needn't,' Edward said, cross, his fist covering his mouth, the knuckles touching his lips. 'It's just for a few hours. I told the Elder Despenser to keep an eye on things.'

'You could at least have brought a small escort with you.'

'It's only fifteen miles back to Windsor. With this cape on, I could be anyone. I'll be back by evening, and no one will even have noticed I left. I told my valets to say I'm indisposed.'

Piers shook his head. 'You're never indisposed...'

'Piers – I couldn't bear to have other men interfere with us in these last few hours together! It's bad enough to have *your* men sitting there.' Edward's chin jerked in the direction where Piers' escort had been making ready. 'When's your boat due to leave?'

'Whenever we give the order.' Piers' gaze became lost in the distance. Then, dewy-eyed, but hoping that Edward saw no more than the mist gathering on his long lashes, he said, 'Thank you for making the time to see me off.'

Edward smiled. 'That's daft. I'm not here to do you a favour.'

'No, I know. It's just... I've been missing you. Since you left Scotland, I –'

'I wish I hadn't felt compelled to leave you with Lady Vescy in Bamburgh –'

'I know, Edward, I'm not saying it could've been avoided –'

'I *had* to keep you safely away from the August Parliament –'

'I know...'

They had been talking over each other.

Edward seized Piers by the shoulders. 'I had to keep you away from the Parliament. Considering last year's experience, I...' His voice trailed off. 'I thought I'd learnt to expect the worst of these gatherings of the magnates, but this time, the Lord Ordainers managed to exceed even my worst expectations.'

The vein throbbing on Edward's forehead reminded Piers of other parts of Edward's anatomy, where veins throbbed to an altogether different effect. He brushed these thoughts aside as inopportune. He wondered how Edward would cope without him.

'We've already discussed it,' he said, lifting each of his hands to the corresponding shoulder, covering Edward's hands with his own. 'A coalition of the Earls would easily outnumber our supporters. For the time being we're at their mercy. We must do as they say.'

Edward turned away to kick a stone lying on the path. 'If only I could outwit them! You say you missed me, and of course you have – we've hardly seen each other since I recalled you to London last month, busy as I've been *failing* to figure out a way of reversing your banishment.'

Piers's hand went to Edward's arm and made him turn around to face him. He took hold of the sides of Edward's cloak at chest height. 'You haven't failed me, Edward – you got the Duchess of Brabant to offer me refuge on the Continent, and –'

'She's my *sister*! Faced with your third exile, all I managed to do is get my sister to do me a small favour. Meanwhile the Ordinance providing for your banishment remains intact, and here we both are, ready to give effect to it.' Piers exhaled. 'Don't sigh. If that's not a failure, what is it? Hasn't the last decade been a damning record of my complete inability to keep my promise to always have you by my side?'

'We held out as long as we could.' One of his hands let go of the cloak, slipped under it, and stroked the breast of Edward's tunic. 'We gave in only when there were no other options. And it was the right thing to do. You know I'd never want you to risk civil war on my account. How would getting killed or losing your Crown help us stay together?'

'But how shall I manage to bring you back this time, Piers? Banished not just from this cursed island, but from Gascony, Ponthieu, Ireland... "forever and without return"!' Edward's eyes filled with tears. 'Banished "as a public enemy of the King and Kingdom".'

'Edward.' Piers took Edward's hands in his own. 'I'll find a way to come back to you.' He had no idea how, but simply saying it made him believe it. 'This time, too. And the next, if necessary.'

'Then swear it on God's soul.'

'I shall always come back to you. I swear it on God's soul.'

Piers brought one of Edward's hands to his lips. It didn't stop Edward's sobs.

'How's my niece?' Edward asked at length, wiping his eyes on his sleeve.

'Well enough, considering.'

'How callous to exile you when your wife is due to give birth any moment now.'

'At least they allowed her to retain Wallingford.'

'Her brother Gloucester was completely ineffectual at curbing the Ordainers when I appointed him Regent. Lincoln had been doing a far better job of it. Why did he have to die?'

'Gloucester is still young. Give him time. He may yet prove himself one of your best allies.'

Edward sighed. 'Piers, I didn't travel incognito all the way from Windsor simply to discuss Gloucester. Shall we?' Edward's head jerked in the direction of a small cottage on the grounds of the Royal Manor. It was invisible through the mist, but they were both well acquainted with it.

Piers nodded and they started walking in the direction of the lodge. But he felt uneasy – almost as if making love now, before his departure, amounted to accepting that it might be for the last time. In the end, all they did was hold each other, Edward's head nestled on Pier's chest, breathing in his lover's sweet, musky scent, and Piers stroking the King's cheekbone, and braiding the flaxen strands of his hair into thin plaits that came undone before taking shape.

+

AROUND THE TIME the Earl left, Isabella thought it best to remove herself to Eltham and the Kentish countryside for a few weeks. The immediate aftermath of the Earl's departure was bound to be troublesome. She had learnt from the Earl's second exile that there was little she or other humans could do to help her husband cope (dogs, hawks and horses tended to be more effective); still, she found her uselessness difficult to accept. Even more difficult to accept, for the first time in their relationship, she felt a growing resentment for her husband in his failure to acknowledge her efforts to help.

When she judged that the pain of the Earl's departure had become a little less raw, she rejoined Edward. As soon as she reached Windsor, she went to the King's chamber. He wasn't there.

'Out hunting, My Lady', a groom said.

The room was damp and chilly; she instructed a valet to light a fire. She sat at the table, waiting for her husband to return. But she felt tired, and after a while, she stretched out on his bed, over the quilt, and fell asleep.

+

WHEN EDWARD CAME back, he took her in his arms and lay down on the bed next to her, her head resting on his shoulder, his hands twined over her own. He must smell of horse and the physical exertion from the hunt, and was glad she showed no sign of minding it. For a while, neither he nor she said anything.

'You'd think by now I had gotten used to forced separations from the Earl,' he said at last. 'But it's driving me insane, worse than ever. The barons and prelates are so dead-set against his return – now even insisting on banishing his friends.'

Isabella sighed. 'Do you know where he is now?'

'In the Flanders, in readiness to be admitted to the Duchess of Brabant's household, as soon as her official response arrives. Or so I understand. I'm rather disappointed in my sister.'

'Let me know as soon as you have news. I'll write to Lady Margaret. She must be in much distress, even if she keeps her grief private.'

Edward nodded. He had trouble understanding how any person of feeling could keep such grief 'private'. But then he thought of Margaret's pregnancy, and he felt that Piers must come back as soon as possible, as much for the sake of his wife and the baby's, as his own sanity.

Sixteen

REUNIONS

MARGARET SAT WATCHING the flooded meadows and brown river, swollen by the winter rains. Almost everyone in her household had taken it upon themselves to point out that it was no good leaving the comfort of the Castle in her condition. Well, she was the Countess, and if she wished to get some air, even in winter, she would. It wasn't as if she was planning to go far, either. Wallingford Castle was built by the river, and all she wanted was to leave the fortified walls and look at the water. They probably simply resented having to escort her.

She watched a pair of swans glide over the river. Two of their chicks followed, old enough to be of mature size, but still donning the plumage – smudged grey and brown – that gave them away as unfinished work. Unfinished work: she felt like that too, even if her pregnant belly was proof to the contrary. Perhaps some people reached maturity without ever convincingly looking the part. And was it such a bad thing? The cygnets, for all their failure to have attained the white splendour of adult swans – perhaps *because* of it – looked more at home than their parents in the muddy waters of the Thames.

She caught her breath. Still not entirely used to the sensation, she put a hand where the baby had kicked. She had mixed feelings about this pregnancy. It went without saying that the Earl and Countess of Cornwall should produce an heir. In any case, after she had started bleeding, she had desired her husband to make love to her, and so she couldn't very well resent the outcome too much, she supposed. She worried, however, that it was not unknown for women to die in childbirth. That was putting it mildly, of course. And although the baby's kicks were not painful, they always gave her a strange feeling of being at its mercy. She wondered how her sister Eleanor felt about her numerous pregnancies and thought that she, Margaret, should have made time to chat about it with her, properly, in person. Perhaps she should write to Eleanor right now and ask her to receive her. It would do her good to spend a few days with her family.

Then again, she was the wife of Lord Gaveston, the disgraced exile. Would it be fair on her sister if Margaret asked to be received? Could she really rule out the possibility that Eleanor would see it as an imposition? The truth was, she couldn't. They hadn't seen enough of each other in the last few years for Margaret to be able to say with complete confidence that she still really knew Eleanor's thoughts. True, Eleanor was daughter-in-law to the Elder Despenser, whose loyalty to the King was beyond doubt. Still.

Margaret shrugged. *Disgraced.* That's what her husband, supposedly, was. It was difficult to fathom. She only associated – when she did associate at all – with her husband's retainers these days, and they no doubt took great (and unnecessary) care to shelter her from any ugliness that might come her way. Her husband's disgrace seemed to her rather an abstraction, his absence being the only concrete marker of it.

She missed him; she wondered what the future would bring. He had told her that she should not dream of going with him this time; that she was in no condition to travel; that his position abroad was still uncertain; that he wouldn't believe the Duchess of Brabant's undertaking to admit him to her Court until he was actually settled there – though Margaret should take care not to tell the King about his scepticism. Only then, he said, only when he was settled, should they consider her joining him. But he also took the view that she shouldn't relinquish England; by staying on, she would ensure the baby could, in due course, assume its own position in the Court, which was their son's – or daughter's – rightful place. (She was glad he did not assume the baby would be a boy.) She saw merit in these arguments. Nonetheless, she rather felt that she might decide to go to him as soon as she felt up for travel – whether or not he thought it best.

It wasn't that life would be inconceivable away from him. She couldn't think of anyone at all who, should they be removed from her, would make her life unbearable. But the fact was she really liked him. Of reserved temperament and retiring habits, she set great stock in the quality of her relationships with those in her immediate circle. Her husband had earned his place in her heart not through the formality of their marriage bond, but through daily acts showing his consideration, his willingness to confide in her (at least on some matters), and his visible pleasure at amusing her.

How lucky that Eleanor had already been married by the time their uncle, the King, decided to marry Sir Piers Gaveston off to one of the De Clare sisters! She was pretty sure the King would have chosen Eleanor for the Earl of Cornwall if she had still been available. She had a feeling her uncle favoured Eleanor – and no wonder, for Eleanor was older, always sensible, easy to like, not reserved, and prone to spells of sullenness like herself. Now imagine if she, Margaret, had ended up having the Younger Despenser foisted upon her as husband! She shuddered. Nobody liked the Younger Despenser. Except her own sister, that is, and that was the main reason why she couldn't be sure she knew or understood Eleanor at all these days.

The Younger Despenser was universally disliked, yet it was her own husband that was an exile, not Lord Despenser. She supposed her husband was also disliked. But the reasons why the two men were unpopular were very different. The Earl of Cornwall was disliked because her uncle the King loved him above all others. The Younger Despenser, on the other hand, could claim full credit for people's antipathy. It was a dislike for the kind of person that he was widely thought to be: unkind, unaccommodating, indifferent to the fate of others, and quite implacable. Not very fetching either, if she had to be honest, but then, it was easy for her to speak, having bagged the most handsome man in the Court. But what was the good of having bagged him, if all she had left was the idea of him?

It was a testament to the pettiness of her fellow countrymen, and to their warped moral compass, that her husband should suffer the consequences of their dislike, and the Younger Despenser tolerated to go about scot-free.

+

A FEW DAYS later, at the beginning of January 1312, Edward sent a messenger from Windsor, instructing her to make immediate arrangements for a long journey. Margaret imagined the worst. Were the Earls now going to ferret her out of her home? Hadn't it been formally agreed that she would keep Wallingford Castle?

The King arrived the next day with a relatively limited convoy. He burst into the hall, looking so radiant that, with his fair hair and tall stature, Margaret thought he could have been the Archangel Gabriel bringing the happy news to the Virgin Mary.

'He's back, Countess,' he shouted, as soon as he saw her.

'*He* is back? How can it be, Your Grace? So soon? Why? When?'

'I don't know the details – he's in Yorkshire. We must go to him at once!'

Her uncle looked with some apprehension at the bulge beneath her breasts, larger than he had reckoned, presumably. Having nearly reached the full term of her pregnancy, she knew she was quite an extraordinary sight. Her hands instinctively went to her belly.

'Can you travel, Lady Margaret?'

'Of course. The Earl must see the baby. Is the Lady Isabella accompanying you, Your Grace?'

'She will join us later in York. Her household travels slowly.'

'Of course. All is ready. Let's depart at once.'

+

EDWARD HAD GRANTED Piers his present sanctuary, Knaresborough Castle, five years before. When Piers sighted, from the fortified wall, the King's small convoy approach the rocky outcrop on which the Castle stood, his heart leapt with joy. Yet, he hesitated a moment before going out to meet the King: he wondered if he looked gaunt or, God forbid, sallow. The chest ailment that had been troubling him since the previous April – when he had been in Roxburgh for Edward's Scottish campaign – was taking its toll. Would Edward think him aged?

Edward jumped off his horse and rushed to him, the emerald green of his velvet surcoat and the black of his hose bespattered with mud from the ride. Piers felt the King's arms lock around him in an embrace so tight, so long, that for a moment, he wondered if Edward would ever let him go. When he was finally released, he realised the King had been weeping. He took Edward's head, one hand on each of the King's cheeks, and stood on the balls of his feet to reach up and kiss his lips.

He led the King inside the small hall in the Castle. It was more modest than Piers' living quarters generally were, but a fire was burning heartily in the brazier, and the wall hangings, of heathered wool, kept out some of the winter chill. Earlier, he had given instructions to his attendants about the King's reception: immediately some food and wine were brought in. Edward, however, showed little interest in them. He made Piers sit down next to him on the bench closest to the fire. Then he placed his arm around his lover's shoulders, his other hand on the Earl's thigh, and reclined his head so that his closed lids were touching the socket of Piers' neck. Neither of them spoke for some time.

'Your smell, Piers. As sweet as ever.'

Piers experienced the sensation, familiar to him in moments of close intimacy with Edward, of falling apart under the pressure of the King's love.

'And your looks: do I ever take your beauty for granted? It always seems to me you are even more beautiful whenever you return.'

Well, that at least settled the matter of whether he looked gaunt. 'I'm sure I could do with being banished a few more times, just to hear your flattery.'

At Edward's initiative, they changed their position so that they were both straddling the bench, facing each other.

Edward smiled. 'I can't believe you've already come back to me. But I couldn't have borne it any longer. Not even one more day, I swear upon God's soul. I felt this time I might die. How did you know?'

'I...felt the same, Edward.'

There was more literal truth in this than Piers wished to convey or than

Edward could suspect. Since autumn turned into winter, Piers had been feeling increasingly weak. The coughing was bad, prone to make his chest rattle. He'd suddenly feel short of breath; sometimes panic would seize him as he gasped for air and an intense pain gripped his ribcage. Despite his relatively young age, and although he couldn't be sure, Piers started wondering whether his end might be near. Inexplicably, the thought didn't trouble him. Perhaps, he felt that he had had more than his fair share of life's delights. This novel awareness of life's transience, however, seemed to bring new clarity to him: it made at least relative physical proximity to Edward an immediate imperative, as much for his own as the King's sake. He didn't mention any of this to Edward.

'You came because you couldn't bear being apart from me, Perrot?'

'Yes, Edward. If I can't be the Prince's Companion as in the old days, I must at least be permitted to share the same Kingdom as my King.'

Edward leant over and kissed his forehead. 'I'll raise an army if they drive me to it. I'll give up everything if I must. Nothing else matters.'

The King took Piers' hands in his. He had always loved looking at Edward's hands clasping his own: the different cast of their skins, the equally long fingers, and the veins, as prominent on the back of Edwards' hands as on his own. The veins, especially, delighted him: they gave away, unmistakably, the sex of the hands' owners. It was like looking at their two cocks pressing against each other.

'You know, Piers, over the last two months I'd sometimes feel oppressed by the thought that we might gradually grow apart, the memory of each slowly fading from the other's mind. Finding life bearable without each other: wouldn't that be ghastly? You understand me Perrot? You don't think I'm crazy?'

'No, Edward. You said it yourself. Nothing else matters. Besides, we promised. Never apart. Never again.'

Edward flexed his knees and stood. He faced Piers, his legs still straddling the bench. Piers reached out to touch the erection visible through the King's hose. Closing his eyes and throwing his head back, Edward pulled his cock out. The tight grip he held around the shaft made its head go turgid and glow ruddy. Piers took it in his mouth, and he knew it was silly, really, but the feeling was so right and satisfying – like a glove that fits perfectly, like a duty fulfilled, like coming home. Edward was in his prime, so gorgeous it was almost intimidating. Piers' own huskiness might be on the wane, but it didn't matter. For here was the King's cock – lush, sleek, glistening, and outright glorious – and Piers could still pay tribute to it better than anyone else.

+

His shirt back on, but his hose still lying on the stone floor, Edward walked up to the table where a servant had earlier deposited the food and drink. Piers, reclining on an elbow, was still lying on the furs they had removed from the benches and used to cover an area of the floor.

'You know,' he said, 'every time I see your arse like this, peeping out from under your shirt – which seems designed specifically with the intent of letting your arse peep out from under it – I always feel like giving it a bite.'

Edward pivoted on his hips to look at him. 'What's to stop you?' he asked, between one chew and the next.

A pang of sadness went through Piers at the thought that all of this – contemplating Edward's hose-less beauty after lovemaking – would one day have to end. But he forced himself to snap out of his morbid brooding. He got up, and walked to the King, standing by the table. He lifted the back hem of Edward's shirt, and his teeth gripped the portion of flesh where Edward's buttock met the back of his thigh. Edward let him do it; then he turned around, slowly, until his prick was hovering right before Piers' eyes. It had started expanding anew.

'Again, Your Grace? Well, I suppose we've almost two-and-a-half months of unwilling abstinence to make up for.'

Edward frowned. 'Actually, we shouldn't.'

'Something's the matter?' Piers flicked Edward's prick with his thumb and got to his feet.

'I've been selfish, Piers. Forgive me. We should go to your wife at once. I left her – *them,* actually – in York.'

'The Lady Isabella is there too?'

'No, not yet,' Edward grinned. 'But your daughter is!'

'Margaret has given birth?' Piers' mouth forgot to close; Edward's grin widened.

'Yesterday! Both of them are fine! Let's hurry, and you'll see for yourself.'

'I hate leaving a job half-done, Your Grace.' Piers cast a regretful glance at Edward's prick. Then he looked up and smiled. 'But I adduce in my defence the birth of my daughter!'

'As long as the Earl promises to finish what he started at his earliest convenience, We give him permission to go to her.'

They dressed hastily and exchanged idiotically delighted grins. Yes, he had done the right thing coming back.

+

Mid-January 1312. York.

'SHE TAKES AFTER you,' said Margaret.

'What, that little runt? I hardly think so,' said Piers. 'My wet nurse always assured me I was an exceptionally good-looking infant. The same can't very well be said of...'

He cast a glance at the baby sleeping in the crib. Her tiny body was all wrapped up in linen bandages. He checked the back of her neck: frightfully hairy, but no doubt she would moult, in due course. How about her complexion, though?

'I suppose she's all right. A bit blotchy perhaps.'

Margaret gave him a warning look.

'No matter,' he said quickly. 'She'll grow out of it.'

+

EDWARD OPENED THE door and walked into the room.

'Lady Margaret, Piers – sorry to interrupt.'

'Don't mention it, Your Grace,' said Margaret amiably.

'You look well, Lady Margaret. Piers, I've thought about it – if we are serious that...' He cast a quick glance at the infant. 'Might little Joan's complexion be a little on the blotchy side?' he asked.

'Oh, for the love of God,' said Margaret. 'There is nothing wrong with her complexion! She's perfectly normal!'

Piers gave Margaret a Didn't-I-say-so? look; Edward gave Piers a What's-the-matter-with-her? one.

'Of course, Lady Margaret,' said Edward. 'I'm sure you must be right. She'll grow out of it, in any case.'

Margaret turned the other way. Extraordinary, really, the things women could get themselves worked up about, thought Edward.

'Now, to return to us, Piers, if we are serious about you staying for good, I must undo what the Ordinances have decreed – in relation to your banishment, that is, and in respect of anything else that is unjustly prejudicial to me. We must make your return publicly known, and I must officially declare you good and loyal and decree that you were unjustly and unlawfully exiled. Nothing short of that will do. If I make it clear that you are here lawfully… If we firmly abide by that truth, we may avoid the worst.'

'And what is your case for declaring my exile unlawful, Your Grace?' asked Piers formally.

Edward waved the scroll he had been holding in his hand. 'First, it is highly doubtful that the Lords had the constitutional power to make the Ordinances at all.'

'But they'll say your agreement to the Ordinances validated that power, or vested it in them.'

'And I shall respond that that would be so only if my agreement had been freely given. But how could I *freely* consent to giving the Lord Ordainers *carte blanche* to utterly control me and my government? My arm was twisted.'

Piers put his hands on his narrow hips. 'I doubt the magnates will accept the argument.'

'That's why there's a back-up one. Now listen to this: even if my consent had been freely given, no one can validly bind oneself to suffering the kind of far-reaching, intrusive powers that the Lord Ordainers claim they are entitled to exercise. And even if one, hypothetically, could validly bind oneself to the Ordainers' power, not even my consent could validate a blatantly unjust exercise of that power. That is to say – if you want to know, Piers – that even if the Ordainers lawfully held the power to make the Ordinances, – and I concede it only for the sake of argument – the lawfulness of their power was dependent on its good exercise. And your banishment was not such an exercise – in fact, it was an abuse of power, because it runs counter to the just laws and customs of the Realm, which my coronation oath binds me to defend. *Voilà.*' Edward sat down at the table where Margaret was examining some letters sent to congratulate the Gavestons on Joan's birth.

Piers said, 'You speak like a King, Your Grace.'

'I am one, and I'm determined that the Earls should know it. I have already noted all the finer points of our defence here.' He tapped the scroll. 'I shall write the writs annulling your banishment myself, if I have to. And I'll have all the lands of the Earldom of Cornwall restored to their rightful owner.'

Margaret looked up from her letters. 'Thank you for all you're doing for my husband, Your Grace.'

Extraordinary, really, how quickly women could get over the things they got themselves worked up about, thought Edward.

'When little Joan grows up,' Margaret said 'she will learn of the great love her great-uncle, King Edward, bore her father. Your kindness will make her weep, Your Grace.'

The infant started wailing.

'Clearly, I've an unusually precocious daughter,' said Piers.

He leant over the crib, took her in his arms and walked over to the window. Nothing could be seen through the oiled pig-bladder stretched over it to seal it, but the light was much better there. He inspected the baby. All the crying had turned her vermillion. He raised her and snuggled his face against her tiny body. Then, holding her at arms' length, he looked at her again, and smiled rather dotingly.

York, before February's last quarter.
An unusually balmy day for the time of year.

EDWARD AND ISABELLA were strolling in the grounds of St Mary's Abbey. The snowdrops, grown in great quantities by the monks for medicinal purposes, were in full bloom – swathe upon mounding swathe of nodding white and green corollas. By a happy coincidence, Isabella was wearing a white tunic with green trimmings on the wrists and waist, and green gemstones set around the neckline. She hoped, inconsequently, that her husband would be both conscious of her looking like she belonged to their beautiful surroundings, and mystified about the reason why.

'It's so nice to finally have you with us,' said Edward.

'Yes, my dear, we haven't spent time together with the Gavestons in what seems like ages.' She linked arms with him.

'Pity you just missed Lady Margaret's churching.'

'The journey took longer than I anticipated. With all the rains, the roads were a perfect nightmare.'

'How did you find her?' Edward asked.

'The countess or the baby-girl? Both look in very good health. The baby particularly: she is very ruddy, don't you think?'

Edward looked faintly amused. 'That's one way of putting it.'

Isabella wondered at this, but she did not pursue the matter. 'Is the Earl a little wasted, though?'

He sought her eyes. 'Do you really think so? He always gives me the feeling of being the lustiest man alive – but it's been a trying time for all of us, despite the joy at having him back.'

'I hope we shan't face a rebellion. But you did what had to be done, Edward. I took it upon myself to write to Lancaster and some of the others – I hope you don't mind. I told Lancaster that you always think fondly of the intimacy formerly existing between the two of you, and that you grieve at the distance that has come between you. I added that in any case we trust him to be as loyal as ever. Do you think he will see my implication?'

'That we expect him to endorse my rescission of the Ordinances? Of course, he will.'

'I sent him and his Countess some tokens of our regard.'

He patted the hand she had slipped under his arm. 'It was very well done, Isabella.' They stopped, and he turned towards her. 'What would I do without you?'

He picked a snowdrop and tucked it behind her ear. Then he locked his arms around her waist and their eyes met. The King looked radiant; it pleased her. She drew closer to him.

'You're very beautiful, my Queen. You look all grown-up.'

Close as she was to him now, she became aware of his arousal. 'Grown-up, you say. It may have something to do with...'

'Have you started bleeding, my dear?'

She performed a curtsy. 'I have indeed, Sire.'

'Isabella!'

He kissed her mouth softly, then hard.

That night they consummated their marriage, four years after it had been contracted. His mouth teased her for so long that by the time he was ready to enter into her, every inch of her body tingled with unendurable keenness. In the end, the pain wasn't nearly as bad as she had been told it would be, and the pleasure from his thrusts and rebounds had a queerly familiar quality about it. Later, she wondered if she was meant to enjoy love-making quite that much. Then it occurred to her that it was Lent, and they weren't supposed to have had intercourse at all, let alone enjoyed it! Oh well.

+

St Paul's, London, 13 March 1312.

THE EARL OF Gloucester, Margaret's brother – young and baby-faced, for all his thinning blond hair – lifted his large, sky-blue eyes to the Cathedral's stained-glass windows, and from there to the wooden rib vaulting sweeping overhead. What an incongruous place for the business at hand. He furtively crossed himself and asked God forgiveness for what was to come.

'If the Lord Ordainers cannot agree as Lord Ordainers to raise arms against the King,' said Lancaster, 'it falls upon the best among them to break down the King's obstinacy and restore legality.'

'The "best" among them,' repeated the Earl of Arundel, a little dubiously. 'Do you mean us, Lancaster?'

Gloucester met Arundel's grey eyes with a feeling of gratitude. *Not an absolute nest of vipers, then.*

'Who else?' asked Lancaster

‘I’ll never participate in any act of coercion against the King,’ said Gloucester with emphasis. *Not, at any rate, on account of a completely innocuous, if admittedly impolitic, infatuation my uncle may have for my brother-in-law.*

‘I don’t ask you to participate in any act of coercion, Gloucester,’ said Lancaster. ‘Lord Gaveston is your sister’s husband after all. But I remind you that, like the rest of us, you owe allegiance and homage to the office of the Crown, not to the person of the King. So, I expect you not to interfere if others choose to shoulder the burden you’re unwilling to bear.’

‘The Earl of Surrey, like me, will never agree to take up arms against the King,’ said Gloucester, though he was far from sure it was true.

‘It’s unclear whether he would – that’s why he wasn’t invited,’ said the Earl of Hereford with his usual weasel smile.

‘I wish you had left me out of it too,’ said Gloucester, his eyes involuntarily fixing on Hereford’s off-centre nasal bone. He felt for his uncle: how unfair that this man, his brother-in-law, should be conspiring against him.

Hereford patted his back. ‘Too late for that, Gloucester. Rather: I wonder why the King has allowed the Ordainers to meet, when he had initially instructed his sheriffs to bar all barons and prelates from gaining access to the towns of the Kingdom.’

‘Because,’ said the Earl of Pembroke, ‘albeit sometimes misled, the King is not, after all, nearly as unreasonable as some of you gathered here make him out to be.’

Well done, Sir Aymer de Valence: put them in their place. Gloucester envied Pembroke his aristocratic looks. People only had to look at his dark, intense eyes, the commanding, hooked nose – and they’d know he meant business.

‘You really think we exaggerate the King’s unreasonableness, Pembroke?’ asked Warwick. ‘Has King Edward not reinstated Lord Langton to the Treasury? Is there anyone more inimical to the barons than Lord Langton?’

Warwick: the learned, the devout, the pig-faced, the viper. ‘That was taken care of when we met with the other Lord Ordainers,’ Gloucester said. ‘With or without Langton, the King can draw no monies from the Treasury’s coffers until he gives up Lord Gaveston.’

Lancaster said, 'Yet, Warwick is right that the King's reinstatement of Lord Langton is profoundly telling. The King had been keeping Langton prisoner since his father's death – he could hardly stand the sight of the man. And now, of a sudden, he elevates him to the position of Treasurer. Why do you think, Gloucester?'

Gloucester sought Pembroke's eyes, then said, 'Lord Langton is a very experienced statesman, and the King was short of options. It's not as if he has many friends left – as this secret meeting proves all too clearly.' He had spoken too quickly, but at least he had said it.

'The most notable thing about Lord Langton, as far as I'm concerned, is that he thinks he can make the magnates of the Realm cower before him,' said Warwick. 'His appointment is an overt provocation of us all – an act of war.'

Gloucester snorted. Was it denseness, or bad faith? Did Warwick realise his own absurdity?

'I have a proposal,' said Pembroke. 'Lord Gaveston must be captured. Very well, let us do it. I volunteer to be in charge of his arrest.'

'Why you?' asked Warwick.

'Because I trust myself better than I trust any of you, except Gloucester, and Gloucester will not do it. Lord Gaveston will be judged by his Peers. He remains a nobleman, not a common criminal. There must be no execution without a proper judgement of whether and why he broke the Ordinance providing for his exile, and of whether the Ordinance was constitutionally valid in the first place.'

'I've no objection,' said Lancaster, affecting (Gloucester was sure it was affectation) a benevolent smile. 'It will give me great pleasure to hunt down the minion. But I shan't lay a finger upon either him or the King. I'll let Pembroke proceed to the actual capture of the Earl. It's an arrest we are after, not an execution. Arundel, Warwick, Hereford – are you with us?'

The Earls nodded their assent.

'And you Gloucester: do you promise not to interfere?'

'Only if all is carried out as you have just set out – without harming King Edward or the Earl, or any member of his household. Only if Pembroke is in charge.'

'You have my word, Gloucester,' said Pembroke, putting a hand on Gloucester's forearm.

'Well then, it's settled,' said Lancaster. 'The plan must remain secret. Our knights will move northwards at different times, under the pretext of attending tournaments. Meanwhile, we must leave enough forces in our lands to secure the country in the event that the King starts gathering an army. You can agree to that Gloucester, can't you? You can agree to defend the South if need be?'

'Of course I'll defend my lands in case of aggression, but the King is not going – '

'And I'll defend the West,' said Warwick, cutting him short.

'And I, the East,' said Hereford.

Lancaster nodded. 'We shall also need the support of the Warden of the March, Lord Clifford. If the King attempts to cross the border to seek the Scots' assistance against us, or to leave Lord Gaveston there under Bruce's protection, Lord Clifford must stop him.'

'I trust I'll be able to secure Lord Clifford's support,' said Pembroke.

'Very good,' said Lancaster. The way in which he stroked his chin sent a chill down Gloucester's spine.

When the other Earls left the Cathedral, Gloucester stayed behind. Kneeling down, he prayed that nothing untoward should happen to his sister, his uncle, or his brother-in-law. He did so in one of the chapels, out of sight, self-conscious that his devotions might make him appear even more cherubic.

Seventeen

SEPERATIONS

York, 31 March 1312.

Edward and Piers were having the midday repast privately, in the King's chamber. Edward downed a cup of wine. 'I'm going to make the custody of Scarborough Castle over to you.'

'Sir Henry de Percy won't be much pleased at us taking it away from him.'

Piers put a morsel of bread in his mouth, and for an instant, his teeth flashed white. He rubbed them daily, with a devotion that verged on fanaticism, either with fresh sage leaves, or a piece of muslin dipped in a mixture of ash and an aromatic oil he procured at extravagant expense from Al-Andalus. He even brushed them with well-chewed ends of liquorice sticks – a trick learnt from a merchant from West Africa. Edward had always been vaguely jealous of this fabled merchant from Piers' past, with skin the colour of raisins, and muscles that glistened when they caught the sunshine. The King suspected he and Piers had been lovers.

Edward said, 'Lord Percy must have prepared himself for something like this, since my visit to Scarborough in late February. He must have known what was on my mind. Why else would I send you over to the Castle to check all defences, let alone post a garrison there?'

'Well, he may have suspected you wanted to *borrow* the Castle from him to keep me safe there. Our taking it away may still come as a shock.'

'I'll find a way of making it up to him. It's much safer if the Castle becomes yours, than our hoping for Lord Percy's good-will when the day arrives when we have need of his hospitality.'

They both turned to the food. The frumenty soup was delicious, and Edward was the first to finish. He spilt some on his woollen hose, just missing the silk and goldthread trim that ran down the length of the outer side of the leg. Before he could proceed to smear it into the cloth by attempting to remove it, Piers had stood up and, using a piece of bread, soaked the drops of thick liquid off Edward's thigh.

'Thank you,' Edward said as Piers resumed his seat. He sighed. 'It's so frustrating that all we can do is sit and wait for a possible attack and make plans.'

'We must make what we can of the situation. You couldn't very well raise a large army and keep it indefinitely on stand-by, waiting for the Earls to perform an act of aggression which may never be forthcoming. Nor can you precipitate civil war by being the one launching an offensive against the Earls.'

'I know.'

Edward pushed the knife into the baked apple. It was pulpier than he had expected. A clear brown syrup oozed out of the cut, and a whiff of spices tingled his nose agreeably.

He said, 'Going to Newcastle at least will make for a welcome distraction.'

Piers clucked his tongue. 'If you can call the purpose of our visit a *distraction*.'

Edward and Piers' visit to Newcastle-upon-Tyne was intended to give them a better understanding of exactly what was happening along the border with Scotland. The latest reports from further north were that Lord Clifford, Warden of the March, entrusted with protecting England from Scottish incursions, was keeping his forces stationary all along the border despite the fact that the self-proclaimed King of Scotland, Robert the Bruce, was mobilising his army towards the port of Berwick-upon-Tweed – which remained strategically vital for the English. If it was so, as Piers and Edward reasoned, this might well be a sign that Lord Clifford had decided to side with the Earls and against them: believing that the King and the Earl of Cornwall intended to seek refuge in Scotland, Lord Clifford apparently sought to prevent them from crossing the border, at the cost of letting Berwick fall to the Scots.

'How much do you think I should tell Isabella of our misgivings?' asked Edward.

'Everything,' said Piers, straightening the opal ring Edward had given him a few weeks ago. It was a little loose for his slender fingers. 'She has a right to know.'

Edward called out to one of his grooms and asked him to fetch the Queen.

Several days later, Edward sent out some of his trusted men on reconnaissance from Newcastle. When they returned with news confirming Lord Clifford's defection, the blow was scarcely lessened by the fact that Edward had fully expected it. When his father had died, Clifford was appointed his counsellor, alongside Lincoln, Pembroke, and Warwick. Lincoln and Edward had their differences, but Lincoln had been faithful to the last. Had Edward been naive in expecting the same of Clifford and taking his loyalty for granted? He could only assume that Lord Clifford resented the fact that he, Edward, had never put his advice before Piers'. But Piers was as seasoned a warrior as Clifford, and hardly younger than him. Lord Clifford should have swallowed his pride.

SPRING ARRIVED LATE in the northern counties – in Newcastle even later than York. Towards the beginning of April's last quarter, when the weather had only just started noticeably warming up, Piers fell seriously ill.

By that time, Isabella had moved to Newcastle with her Court, and as soon as she heard the news, she rushed to her husband. He was shut up in his room, having given instructions to be left alone.

He turned towards her as she entered, a haunted look in his eyes; then he returned his gaze towards the open window. She shut the door behind her and stood with her back to it. Birdsong – unmistakably a robin's – came through the window, filling the silence between them with a mocking serenity.

'It's not the first time,' said Edward, without looking at her. 'He was ill for two whole months in the winter following the Scottish campaign of 1300. Seriously ill. I thought I might lose him. We had only just met.'

She walked to him and took his hands, forcing him to look at her. 'But what's wrong with him *this time*, Edward?'

'He's weak, short of breath. He says a pain grips his chest. He can't breathe.' Again, he looked away.

'What did the men of medicine say?'

'They are useless.' He disengaged his hands from hers and threw himself on the bed. 'They put poultices on his chest and gave him herbal infusions, and who knows whether they are doing any good! All last night, he was groaning and in cold sweats.'

'Has he been washed? Did you have someone wipe him?'

'I did it myself.'

'Has he been eating?'

'Hardly anything since the day before yesterday.'

'He must eat, Edward, even if you have to force the food down his throat.'

He turned on his side, facing the wall.

'Do you understand?'

'Yes, Isabella.'

'I'll have my apples delivered to his quarters. The last batch from last year's crop. Wizened, but still good – apples are in short supply at this time of year. Make him eat those today, to start with, then gradually build his appetite up to something more substantial.'

'I'm going to lose him, Isabella, aren't I?'

'No!' She walked to the chair by the window and sat down, arranging the veil on her chest so as to protect it from the breeze. 'It wouldn't make any sense. I refuse to entertain the notion.' She paused. 'Edward.'

'Isabella.'

'I wish I could break this news to you under more auspicious circumstances.'

He rolled on his other side, looking at her. She fingered a bunch of cowslips pinned to her breast. The sunshine enlivened the green of her gown. She felt more alive than she thought she had any right to be, given the Earl's predicament. 'I'm pregnant.'

He jumped off the bed and knelt by her side. 'Isabella!'

He took her hands.

'This is why I can't visit the Earl. You understand. Under the circumstances, it's best if I retire somewhere else.' She couldn't bring herself to say: in case the Earl's sickness is infectious and fatal.

'Of course, my dear, I know just the place – Tynemouth Priory. It's well-fortified and, as you know, very beautiful. I shall send a messenger immediately, to warn them of your imminent arrival.'

'Tynemouth is ideal. Stay by the Earl day and night. He needs you. I'll have prayers said for his recovery at the Priory.'

She kissed him and left the room, thinking that she should never forgive him if he let the Earl die.

+

Tynemouth Priory, 5 May 1312.

'I MADE UP my mind, Edward.'

He should have gotten used to it by now, but the King was always amazed at how his young wife could keep a cool head even in the direst of straits. She was looking out to the wide expanse of the sea, the colour of slate, and her veil flapped in the wind. Her intentness made her look older than her sixteen years and added fierceness to her beauty. It made him feel proud, even as it unnerved him.

'I'll return to York by land. Lancaster has no quarrel with me. I shall be perfectly safe. It would be a waste of his time to run after me. And he wouldn't. In his tediousness, he got it into his head I am the hard done-by wife: I can tell from his letters. I'm not in danger.'

He put his arm around her shoulders, grateful and relieved. A journey by boat wouldn't have been good either for her or the baby she was carrying

– not the way the weather was looking.

'In that case, Piers and I shall set sail for Scarborough today. It can't be long now before Lancaster's army is upon us. It's been two days since he very nearly ambushed us in Newcastle. It's taking him longer than I thought to work out where we fled to.'

'Those formerly close to one, once estranged, always make for one's worst enemies. But Lancaster will pay for this, if not in this life, then the next.' He saw her jaw clench. 'He'll seize the goods in your convoy, won't he?'

'That looks inevitable,' he answered.

Seagulls were floating over their heads, their cries plaintive, as if keening. She shuddered.

'The Earl looks better,' she said.

'He got some respite in the last couple of days. We're grateful for your prayers.'

'A journey to Scarborough on a small fishing boat when he has only just started recovering – hardly ideal. I suppose there's no alternative.' She sighed. 'How long will it take you?'

'Less than a week, I think.'

She frowned at the plummy grey clouds darkening the horizon. 'Try not to drown, will you? Neither I nor Lady Margaret are ready for widowhood yet.'

He didn't try to explain to her that sinking to the bottom of the sea, clutching Piers to his heart, seemed far more desirable to him than any number of alternative fates likely to await them if Lancaster and the others had their way. He pressed his lips to her head. The linen of her veil smelt new – a little like sweet-scented bedstraw – and it reminded him of the night he had made love to her.

'I'll do my best,' he said.

+

When the boat finally reached Scarborough, Edward – for all his fondness for water, swimming and rowing – had never been so glad to feel the steadiness of land under his feet. They avoided the port and decided to scramble up the cliff-side, in the event that an ambush was awaiting them along the main road up to the Castle. Having reached the cliff-top, they followed the walls to the entrance of the stronghold, where they alerted the guards to a possibly imminent attack and gave the necessary orders.

In the main tower, they ate, drank, and quickly washed – the water miserably cold, there being no time to have it heated. They even managed a change of clothes, Piers having had a few of the less desirable items from his and Edward's wardrobes transferred to Scarborough some weeks ago, when Edward had made him keeper of the Castle. The pink tunic was hardly Edward's most dashing, but it didn't seem to matter when the fresh linen of the clean shirt brought him such untold comfort.

As they performed a round of the fortress, it became apparent that something was amiss: there was no indication that the orders they had given, prior to their departure, to replenish the fortress' stocks had been executed. The men in charge of the task explained how, over the last month, two major convoys carrying provisions had been intercepted on their way to the Castle and robbed by well-organised forces. It had been impossible to make alternative arrangements – unless the King had expected them to plunder the surrounding countryside, that is.

'Sir Henry de Percy,' said Piers. 'He's the only one who could have suspected with some certainty about our intention to use the stronghold as a refuge.'

The former keeper of the Castle too had joined forces with his cousin Lancaster, then. *Confound him.*

Edward seized Piers' forearm. 'There's not a minute to spare. I must gather my forces and raise an army against Lancaster, Clifford, Percy and the other traitors. The men we left in Newcastle and Tynemouth will have reached York and Knaresborough by now; I'll also send messengers to the Lords who are still loyal to me. But you, Piers, must stay put.'

Piers opened his mouth to protest, but Edward shook his head.

'Let's just pray our enemies won't start their siege before I manage to have a convoy of provisions reach you here at the Castle. Make it clear to the garrison that they must use whatever provisions you have left sparingly. I'll come to relieve the siege as soon as I have assembled an army that's up to task.'

Piers nodded. Edward knew his lover was a consummate soldier who had more experience of sieges than most, and certainly more than he himself did. But Piers must see that he could keep a cool head and rise to the occasion.

He squared his shoulders. 'Piers, do not, for any reason, leave the Castle. It's *you* they're after. This is a war you can't afford to take on as a warrior – not until you have an army at your command. You must stay holed up in here. As the Castle's keeper, you are sworn not to surrender it to anyone but me, and then only if I am not brought here a prisoner. Don't forget it!'

Piers nodded again. There was nothing left to say. Edward had horses brought to him. Having selected a few men to accompany him, he hugged Piers in much the same way he did on routine occasions, for this wouldn't – couldn't – be the end. His jaw set, he mounted his horse, and disappeared behind the first set of gates of the fortress.

FOR A MOMENT, Piers felt dazed, struggling to re-establish his hold on reality, trying to make what he *knew* to be the truth *feel* like the truth: *This is not something you are witnessing. It's happening; it's happening to you.* Then it sank in, and the reality he had just reconnected to – the Piers-and-Edward reality, whose intensity made any other possible experience opaque, its depths unfathomable – started falling to pieces; and the shards must have started plunging into his lungs, because suddenly he couldn't breathe. It wasn't his ailment – for there was no coughing, no painful rattling, no blood-stained spittle, only his lungs and his throat becoming still, turning to bone, and the terrifying thought, like a premonition: *What if I shan't see him again?*

He gulped: air, laced with the smell of horse dung, poured into his windpipes. *Horses – of course! Quick: dart after the man who brought the King his mount – jump on the mare Edward passed over – bareback, yes, no time for a saddle – and shout, for the love of God, shout to the top of your lungs:*

'Open the gate!'

The drawbridge had not yet been lifted since the King's passage – it clattered under the horse's frantic hooves. A further sprint… But the mare had to halt: the outer gate barred her way.

Through the iron lattice Piers could just about make out the tail of the King's small party. He shouted Edward's name so hard that his voice cracked. His lungs were in agony. But the King couldn't possibly hear him.

He had known it all along.

Piers got off the horse, walked to the gate and, gripping the bars, watched the Royal convoy shrink away from view.

'Edward,' he whispered.

The mare, unaware of his anxiety, paced about, snorting around his ears. He stood a long time with his eyes fixed into the distance, until the tears dried.

Eighteen

SURRENDER

He didn't have enough men. Lancaster's forces were stationed all the way between York, where he was, and Scarborough, where Piers was confined. Their numbers increased daily. And he, the King, didn't have enough men to face them. In fact, he was outnumbered to such an extent that even attempting to re-provision Scarborough Castle, let alone lift the siege, was inconceivable.

He had asked Isabella to sleep in his bed that night. He needed her to give him strength. With her by his side – her and the baby inside her – he had no option but to forget his own misgivings, be decisive, competent, self-assured. The anxiety-ridden wreck who feared for his lover, who could hardly sleep at night, and who rose with black circles around his eyes in the mornings, would be banished.

Isabella asked, 'But how could Surrey end up conniving with the others to besiege the Castle? And what's in it for Lord Percy and Lord Clifford? It quite defies belief.'

Edward thought of Surrey, so bland, so innocuous-looking. He shook his head.

She sighed, and put her hand in his, the other resting on her belly. 'What are the conditions you negotiated?'

'The Earl will surrender to Pembroke, Surrey, Lord Clifford, and Lord Percy if his physical safety is guaranteed at all times. He will be escorted to Wallingford, where he is to remain under house arrest, but undisturbed, until I reach a further agreement with the magnates in Parliament. If no agreement is reached by 1 August, the Earl will be restored to Scarborough. If in the meantime the Earls break the truce, again he must be permitted to return to Scarborough Castle.'

'Can you trust Pembroke? Will he abide by the terms?'

'I'm sure of it.' As sure as he could be of anything given the circumstances, at any rate. 'His letter gave me to understand that he very much sees his involvement in the Earl's capture as a matter of containing the damage.'

She looked dubious.

'He's jealous of the Earl of Cornwall, Isabella – I don't deny that – but he's a man of integrity. I think him quite incapable of breaking the law and customs of the Realm, the courtesies of war, or his word to me. I trust him as much as I could trust any man but Piers himself.'

'But what if...' She paused to swallow. 'What if Parliament condemns the Earl?'

'The arrangement buys me time to secure the military support of my vassals in Aquitaine. Perhaps even of your father.'

Isabella tucked the bed covers under her chin and was silent. Edward guessed what was going through her mind: she would try her best to intercede with King Philip, all the while knowing that it was highly unlikely that her father would move a finger to support them.

'I shall ask the Grey Friars to pray for the Earl's safety,' she said, as if to confirm he had read the sequence of her thoughts correctly. 'I'll also inform Lady Margaret. No doubt she'll want to leave for Wallingford at once.' She yawned. 'Let's try to get some sleep now.'

She clasped his hand under the bedcovers. In truth, what alternative was there but for Piers to leave the safety of Scarborough Castle? Provisions were already in short supply, and the siege was causing more and more damage. Piers had been right: taking Scarborough Castle from Lord Percy would make an enemy of him, and thanks to Percy's knowledge of the fortress's weakest points, the siege engines were proving themselves doubly effective. A breach was inevitable sooner or later. In any case, Piers would be safer in Wallingford: it would be much easier for Edward to gather his men – whether many or few, he didn't know – in the South.

He rubbed his thumb on the back of her hand. It was silky smooth, like Piers'. He loved her. His wife. She was beautiful, frighteningly clever. She carried his baby. He did love her. But she wasn't Piers.

+

PIERS GAVE HIMSELF up on 19 May. One week later, his four captors – Pembroke, Surrey, Clifford and Percy – met with the King in the Benedectine Abbey of St Mary, in York, to firm up the details of the arrangement negotiated by Edward, which Piers had agreed to in writing upon his surrender.

Edward insisted on the face-to-face meeting at St Mary's. There was much in it that left Edward hopeful. Surrey, the most recent defector from the Royalist side, showed himself considerably abashed in the King's presence. He was obviously willing to defer to Pembroke's judgment. And Pembroke was second only, in the trust Edward accorded to the Earls, to the now defunct Earl of Lincoln (Gloucester having forfeited that position to Pembroke last year, by reason of his general uselessness in managing the Ordainers). Edward felt especially reassured when Pembroke solemnly promised to keep Lord Gaveston in his personal custody and to ensure his safety.

As the meeting drew to a close, he asked to be shown the prisoner.

'But, Your Grace,' said Pembroke, 'we agreed that you should attempt neither to make direct contact with Lord Gaveston nor deliver him from Wallingford until he appears before Parliament.'

'I have every intention to respect the agreement, Pembroke, as soon as you take him into your *personal* custody to lead him south; but no sooner.'

'You don't trust us, then, Your Grace?' asked Clifford. 'You don't believe that Lord Gaveston is alive?'

Extraordinary, really, that Piers was about the same age as this man, who, with his sparse hair and sagging jowls, could easily pass for his father.

'If I didn't believe Cornwall is alive, Lord Clifford, you wouldn't have had a chance of asking the question in the first place – seeing as your head would be hanging limp from your broken neck.'

Running through him with his sword wouldn't have been an option, as they had left their weapons at the door before entering the meeting room.

'Then, Your Grace,' asked Percy, 'why do you need to see the felon Gaveston?'

Felon indeed: he, whom Lord Percy was hardly even worthy of being pissed on by. He would have to break their necks after all. Could he take on all four? He tightened his fist.

'You're forgetting yourself, Lord Percy,' said Pembroke, forbidding behind his frown and in his customary black velvet. 'The King, as the King, needs no reason to desire to see Lord Gaveston.'

Percy looked down. Edward exhaled and unclenched his fist. He should really have made a habit of seeking Pembroke's assistance long ago.

'I shall lead the King to Lord Gaveston, if no one objects,' said Surrey quickly.

Pembroke nodded. As they walked out of the meeting room, Edward cast a sideways glance at his escort. Surrey's shoulders were hunched, as usual, the neck sticking out of them at an awkward angle. Edward remembered Piers once joking that the man lacked, quite literally, backbone.

'Where is he being kept?' asked Edward when they were outside.

'In a room in the vicinity of the infirmary,' Surrey answered.

'Let's go through the physic garden.'

'There's a more direct route, Your Grace. But whatever pleases you.'

He moved with brisk deliberateness among the aromatic plants in the cloistered garden, until he found what he was looking for: a bush of the apothecary's rose. It was the rarer, striped variety, and it had only just started to flower. He picked one of only two buds that had expanded into blooms. The sunshine was bringing out the sweet perfume.

'Take me to him now, quickly,' he said to Surrey.

They could access the room in which Piers was being kept directly from the grounds. As they approached it, Edward saw that the entrance was barred by an iron gate.

'Do you have the keys?'

'Pembroke has them, Your Grace.'

Edward was irked that Pembroke had not offered him the keys, though, on second thought, it was probably for the best: he couldn't be sure that, if he had been able to unlock the gate, he wouldn't have knocked Surrey unconscious and attempted a doomed escape with Piers.

'Please retire around the corner until I call you.'

Surrey bowed and did as he was told. Edward walked the forty or so steps that still separated him from the gate and looked into the room. As his eyes adjusted to the dark, he winced. He had expected to see Piers either standing, or sitting erect, in the sort of effortless, dignified grace that was so characteristic of him, and which, under the circumstances, would have said: 'I may be beaten, but do not think for a moment that I'm broken.' Instead, his lover was slumped on a bench against the wall, clearly oblivious to Edward's approach.

Edward felt a swell of rage surge within him. What indignities had they already subjected him to? Was this the reason why they hadn't wanted him to see Piers? He swore it upon God's soul, he would go back to that room and... But Piers was simply sleeping: Edward started breathing again, relief and weariness washing all over him in equal parts. His lover, asleep, was so achingly beautiful that he was frightened to call out his name and break the spell.

+

PIERS HAD A hunch. *Someone is watching you. But no need to worry.* Slowly, he turned his head towards the gated doorway. Against the light flooding into the room through the iron latticework, he recognised Edward's unmistakable outline. No one else was that tall and had shoulders quite that broad; no one else's hair, backlit, glowed, halo-like, in quite the same way about their head.

'Hello there, Your Grace,' he said, softly. He stood and walked to the gate. He smiled.

'Piers. I-I can't see you well, Piers,' Edward said, his Adam's apple bobbing up and down. He rubbed both eyes with the back of his hand.

'If you stopped weeping, Edward, you might stand a better chance.'

Smile, Piers Gaveston, damn you – even with pity yanking at your heart.

He mustn't know.

'Sorry, Piers.'

'They're treating me well. Really.' *Speak softly, reassuringly.* 'Pembroke and Surrey are seeing to it. Please don't worry, Edward.'

Edward's hands grasped the latticework of the iron gate. Piers came closer and kissed the King's fingers. There was a French rose, the *versicolor* type, crushed between the King's hand and the metal of the gate.

'Is this for me?' He put his nose to it and inhaled. 'It smells good. Sweet and musky. Wait, let me guess: like me?'

'Take it.'

Why do you make it sound like an imploration? Are you not my King?

'I can't, Edward. My hands are tied, you see.'

Edward looked at him uncomprehendingly.

'I mean literally, Edward. Look.' His torso pivoted on his hips, then back again.

'They tied your hands behind your back,' Edward said, half-stupefied, and he sounded like a child. Then he caught his breath. 'Piers: this is not the end. I shall set you free, Piers, I promise I shall!'

'I know, Edward, I'll come back to you. Nothing can keep us apart. Not for very long, anyway.'

Edward let go of the metal bars and thrust his arms through the grid, drawing Piers to him. The rosebud fell on the flagstones as Edward shook with sobs, his body pressing as close to Piers as the metal barrier between them allowed.

'Kiss me, Piers. Please.'

'Then bend your knees a little.' *That's right. Softly, say it softly.* 'I haven't grown any taller in the last three weeks or so.'

Their lips managed to make contact. With the cold iron pressing against his cheekbone, Edward's lips felt scorching on his own. The King released him.

'I love you, Piers.'

'I love you too, Edward. I thought I might not see you again.'

'What do you mean?'

So much alarm in your voice, Edward. Sorry. You're a pathetic weakling, Piers Gaveston. Did you have *to give in to self-pity? Smile, for the Love of God, he needs to see your smile.*

'It was only for a moment. A moment of weakness, when you left Scarborough. Not important.'

'I should've stayed with you.'

Piers shrugged. 'You will set me free.'

'If it's the last thing I do, Perrot. I can't let you go.'

Piers looked at Edward's arms, still firmly wrapped around him. 'So it seems.'

He grinned. Edward smiled back, between the tears.

'But, you know, I like it that way. Never let go of me.'

'Piers, can I touch you?'

Now, that would be amusing. 'Go ahead, Your Grace. I don't recall we have ever made it a habit to ask for each other's permission.'

Edward let go of him, and his hands sought some more congenial spaces between the criss-crossing metal. When they reached inside Piers' hose, his body responded immediately.

Piers gasped. 'I...somehow I don't think ...that we're going to get away with this...right here, right now!'

Edward's cheeks were still wet, but he had stopped weeping. 'Oh yes?'

With his cock worked by the King's well-schooled touch, Piers' pleasure built up fast, and before he knew it, he was spending himself in Edward's hand. Edward's eyes were laughing, brimming with joy: almost as if those spasms that, only moments ago, had convulsed Piers' body also released the King from his agony of worry. What was it about love – the love of the flesh – that could draw two men so close, leave them ecstatic, make them feel that they alone, and nothing else, mattered? Edward pulled his hand out of his hose, grinned at him, and flicked the seed on the floor. It glistened in the late May sunshine, rather as if a sprinkling of opal cabochons had been set, incongruously, in the flagstones.

Piers grinned. 'I believe that was somewhat unseemly of us. Even by my standards.' His cheeks felt hot. *Good: flushed, I probably look a little more youthful.*

'The monks at St Mary's have quite a reputation, actually,' said Edward.

'Do they?'

'They're notorious!'

They both laughed, and when they stopped the silence seemed almost frightening. But then Edward looked into his eyes, his lips still curling, ever so slightly, at the corners, and Piers knew that the King's heart was still light.

'You should go now, Edward.'

'Yes. The sooner I do, the sooner you will reach the safety and comfort of Wallingford.'

'Hold out your hand, please.'

Edward put his hand though the grid. Piers closed his eyes and placed his lips on the knuckles. He knew the kiss lasted a little longer than it should have, and he hoped Edward didn't notice.

'Go now. And please don't turn back, Your Grace.'

Under the wide brow, Edward's eyes pierced, damselfly blue, into his own.

'Piers...'

Smile at him now. Yes, like that.

'As you wish, Perrot.'

The King turned on his heels and called the Earl of Surrey. Piers' eyes followed their backs – one square-shouldered, one hunched – as they quickly strode off. A short distance from his feet, on the other side of the gate, the apothecary's rose lay on the flagstones, sweet-smelling and dishevelled.

Nineteen

BETRAYAL

Deddington, 9 June 1312.

THE BEDCLOTHES FELT coarse and smelt musty. He could put up with all manner of discomforts while on campaign, but he wasn't on campaign: couldn't the monks have done a little better by the Earl of Cornwall, the closest man to King Edward's heart? He supposed his Earldom and Edward's favour were exactly the reasons they hadn't tried harder to make him comfortable. He sighed.

All right, so perhaps he wasn't going to die of disease after all. He had been able to breathe normally for the last week or so. As they moved southwards and June advanced, warmer temperatures began to set in, and that seemed to work wonders. Assuming his chest was actually on the mend, and he had many years to live still, should he have stayed on the Continent, a guest of Edward's sister, the Duchess of Brabant? Should he have built a new life there, and be content with seeing Edward, and Margaret, and his daughter Joan, on those occasions when they could spare the time and expense to visit him? Edward wouldn't have been free to visit him as often as he liked, because, according to the Ordinances, the King could not leave the Kingdom without the consent of the barons in Parliament. But he might still have managed a visit, say, every other year...

But no, actually – no. Whether or not his ailment was deadly made no difference. He had returned because he wanted to be with Edward before it was *too late*. But 'too late' did not mean only that he might die soon. '*Before it's too late' also means, as Edward pointed out, before we grow apart; it means before heart-rending regret sets in; before I reach the point in my life when I look back and realise that, deprived of the King's companionship, I have only half-lived. Coming back 'before it's too late' means returning to him before bowing to the inevitability of breaking the promise I made to be by his side, always.*

So, whether or not he was going to die soon of natural causes, coming back had been imperative. It was the only way to be honourable to Edward, and the only way for him, Piers, to make his life the best it could be. In any event, if he was not so sick after all, and was not going to die shortly of a natural death, it still seemed more than possible that he would die soon from the political wrangle.

He knew that Edward's agreement with his captors at St Mary's Abbey had really been intended to buy him time; the King could then summon foreign help to put down Lancaster's superior forces and allies. But what if Edward's plan failed – what if no foreign help were forthcoming by the date of his trial before Parliament? Surely, in that case, Parliament would condemn him to death. True, he could always attempt an escape with Edward, leaving the Kingdom behind, for good. He had always maintained that Kingship was Edward's birthright and that he should never give it up, but Edward would be far happier to be on the run with him than rule a Kingdom without him – let alone rule a Kingdom with him dead. When the alternative was put as starkly as that, he had to grant that, for his own part too, being on the run was preferable to being dead.

He brushed the sweat off his brow with the back of his hand. Was it that hot, or had he been wrong thinking his night sweats were over? Or was it anxiety over his fate, or excitement at the prospect of fleeing with Edward? 'Fleeing with Edward': he was being ridiculous. The prospect, given the turn that events had taken tonight, seemed speculative at best. All thanks to Joseph the Jew. (If he did go on living, he really must stop calling Pembroke

'Joseph the Jew'. Unfortunately, the nickname fit him like a glove.)

What could Pembroke have been thinking? Was seeing his wife so urgent as to warrant breaking his word to the King? Deddington Rectory was a place easily vulnerable to attacks, and Pembroke had left behind only a meagre garrison to guard him. Wasn't it more than possible – wasn't it likely even, that his enemies (those who, unlike Pembroke, put their grudges before knightly gentility) would attempt to capture him that very night? What would that mean for him then, unarmed as he was? Considering he might die that very night, it was a little premature to fantasise about fleeing the Kingdom with Edward.

He couldn't see how Pembroke's desertion could possibly square with his promise to Edward that he would have Piers in his personal custody until he was safely delivered to Wallingford. Perhaps Pembroke really was yearning to visit his wife in Bampton, as he had claimed. He supposed that if Pembroke's bond with his wife was as fast as his own with Edward, he could forgive Pembroke. Still, it wasn't as if *they* – Sir Aymer de Valance and his wife Lady Beatrice – had been forcibly separated four times, first by the former King, then by the magnates, and last upon pain of excommunication. No, upon reflection, there was little excuse for Pembroke's conduct.

Their process south from York had been everything but inconspicuous. Was Pembroke graciously stepping aside to give someone more dangerous, more impervious to moral qualms, the opportunity to do what needed to be done? Gone were the days when Edward could accuse Piers of being under a delusion that the whole world liked him. He knew that by now virtually everyone – including Pembroke – must think it would all be so much easier if the Kingdom could be freed from Lord Gaveston's inconvenient presence.

He shuddered. He felt cold now, but he was loath to pull up the bedcovers. Rough as they were, and drenched in sweat as he was now, they'd be sure to send him into an agony of itchiness. God, but he stank. 'Sweet muskiness', indeed. Apothecary's rose, indeed!

Dear God, if I'm to meet my death tonight, then help me make peace with it. But if You can spare me, then please allow me to keep my promise to the King that I'll always go back to him. Thy Will be done. In nomine Patris, et Filii, et Spiritus Sancti.

+

Earlier on the same day, in Howden, south of York.

ISABELLA REARRANGED HER pale blue veil to keep the sun out of her eyes and said, 'I'm told the western front of the Minster, with the four pinnacles, was completed only last year. Have you ever seen anything like it, Edward? The masons who have been working on it are French, of course.'

He attempted to take an interest in the building's restrained ornamentation – a carved fretwork of interlacing trefoil patterns around the windows. The early afternoon sun made the stone glow a shade lighter than the mellow colour of heathland honey.

She smiled. 'Aren't you glad you came, now?'

'It's lovely, my dear.'

He was aware that, when she had insisted on this pilgrimage to Howden – complete with river cruise, swimming, and fishing, for she knew everything about his love of boats – she wanted to take his mind off Piers' arrest. That's what she was trying to do even now – and he loved her for it. He knew he should try harder to make her believe she had relieved his anxiety. But he also knew he could never fool her.

'Are you very worried, Edward?'

He sighed. 'I'm sorry, Isabella. Anxious – I'm anxious. Not at his current condition – he said at St Mary's that he was being treated with all due respect, and you know I trust Pembroke. But I worry about what is to come later. What if my efforts to raise an army against Lancaster within less than two months prove fruitless? What will happen to the Earl then?'

There was no answer to this, and she attempted none. 'That must be the tomb of John of Howden,' she said. Her arm pointed out to Edward the destination of their pilgrimage. 'Let's go and pray the Saint, that he may watch over the Earl.'

He really should try harder. She must think him a rather ungrateful husband.

+

Piers woke up. He had been fretting so much last night that he must have only had a couple of hours' sleep. It must have still been very early – the June sun rose in the small hours of the morning, and it was still fairly low on the horizon. The night had passed. The misgivings that had made him so apprehensive hadn't come true. *Thank God.* Meanwhile, the daylight invited hopefulness. Presumably, Joseph the Jew – that is, Pembroke – and the men he had taken with him would be back before the midday repast. Then, they would all make it to Wallingford by evening. He sat on his bed, his feet resting on the rushes strewn across the floor. He exhaled, and it was as if in a single breath he released all the tautness of his body. He bet if he lay down again now, he might actually get some proper sleep.

Suddenly, his ears caught the signs of a commotion outside – shouting, neighing, thuds. He shook his head. *Here we are.* Funny: now that the time had come, he felt no panic. He walked – did not run – to the window. There he was. The Black Hound: Sir Guy Beauchamp, Earl of Warwick – surrounded by a large contingent of men, against which the inadequate number of guards left by Pembroke could scarcely offer any protection. He quickly crossed himself. *I'm finally done for, Edward. The Dog hates me with a vengeance. Sorry I couldn't keep my promise.*

He left the window to put on his hose and shirt, then went back, cupped his hands around his mouth, and, with the most defiant voice he could muster, shouted, 'If it's not the Black Hound of Arden!' He grinned, so that Warwick could be left in no doubt about his contempt. 'Stalking me, are you? Here for my flesh and blood, are you – like the good dog that you are! Well, help yourself! Feast on it!'

He turned around, shutting his ears to Warwick's response: the man was utterly bereft of wit, and couldn't be trusted not to spoil the moment. Still in his bare feet, he made for the exit out of the barren room in which he had spent this – his last – night. He fully intended to walk out and meet his death then and there. But before he had a chance to open the door, Warwick's guards crashed through it and seized him. He didn't tell them it was unnecessary; it wouldn't have stopped them from roughing him up. He let them do it. What did they think, that just because he was the King's favourite, he had never experienced hardship? Why, he had been a soldier for longer than he cared to remember.

They took him outside, where the Dog, the Black Hound of Arden, ordered that they should tie his wrists with a rope. They tied it tighter than they had to, and the Dog didn't stop them. Piers expected no less. Only then did he favour Warwick – whom he had studiously avoided acknowledging up to this point, for this was no intercourse between equals – with a smirk of disdain. It wasn't difficult – the Dog had always disgusted him, from his pretences at scholarship, to his narrow-eyed prying.

He was led on foot to the village – the end of the rope that tied his wrists held by one of the guards riding a horse, forcing him to scamper and run to avoid being dragged behind the animal like a plough. His lungs obliged, and he managed, but why had he forgotten his shoes, idiot that he was? He chose not to look at the blood that, by the feel of it, must be collecting around a couple of his toenails.

A crowd of villagers gathered as he was paraded through the street of Deddington. He walked, looking straight ahead, even when they spat. Their bestiality only increased his poise and sangfroid. If they only knew: few things in life had more power to reassure Sir Piers Gaveston in his *amour propre* than witnessing the herd instincts of an uncomprehending crowd.

Their taunts grew louder, and, he supposed, crueller when they learnt who he was. It was strange having those words thrown at him as insults. *Cocksucker. Arse-licker.* He *was* a cocksucker – sucking cock came to him as easily as breathing, and as gladly. And just as willingly, he had licked Edward's arse: the very first time he had done so, a few years into their relationship, his lust had overpowered him so much that the seed had spontaneously shot out of him, and Edward had laughed.

But he suspected his persecutors intended the insult in its less literal meaning. *The King's whore*: they shouted that at him, too. 'Whore', unlike 'arse-licker', he had been metaphorically rather than literally: for he had been wanton with Edward, and Edward wanton with him. Praise the Lord for that.

When his captors made him mount a horse – or rather the wreck of one – he noticed, in the crowd, a Dominican Friar crossing himself and then raising a hand in his direction, performing a quick blessing. He nodded in response to the Brother's charity, to signal his appreciation rather than his gratitude. Gratitude, after all, was the disposition of the undeserving.

He suspected that they might be directed to Warwick Castle, which he believed to be about thirty miles north of Deddington. *Oh, the irony: thirty miles in the opposite direction lies Wallingford.* It quickly became obvious, however, that they were heading west rather than north, and they kept that orientation for several hours. The company was as dull and sullen as one imagined Warwick's hand-picked group to be. At least they mostly ignored him. Only when he fell asleep would one of them intervene and decide to poke him awake – in the ribs, or in his flank – and then his escort would produce a pointless grunt of triumph as his head jerked and eyes opened. Warwick rode behind him, saying virtually nothing for the whole journey. A couple of times, he wondered if the Dog was still even with them, but never turned to check.

His horse stank badly. Then again, so did he in the clothes he had been unable to change or have washed since leaving York, and it was odd why he should care. Everything was different from what he expected. He had always imagined that if he knew he was about to be imprisoned and then die, he'd treasure every instant on his way to his cell, concentrating on every sight, mindful of every feeling it elicited. His awareness of the world around him would be sharpened by his knowledge that this was his last chance to savour it all, and he would make a conscious effort to engrave it all in his memory. But it wasn't like that at all. He found he had lost all interest in the reality immediately surrounding him. He scarcely knew if they were riding through forest or farmland, in dull or bright weather. All he cared about was in his own mind, already engraved with beauty through the years, and it had a name that summed it all up: Edward. That was all he cared about. That and the stink – quite unbearable – and who knew which was worse – the animal's or his?

Eventually, they reached Elmley Castle. It had been the traditional demesne of the Beauchamps until they had inherited the Warwick Earldom and had moved their primary residence to Warwick Castle. Edward was bound to find out sooner or later that he had been taken prisoner by Warwick; but his captor's choice to take him to the secondary residence of Elmley would, at least for a time, throw anyone attempting to rescue him off track. As Piers saw it, it seemed that Warwick was buying himself time with this decision. If that was the case, it seemed to suggest, too, that

Warwick hadn't yet decided how and when to seal his fate. Nonetheless, he was sure that death of some kind would soon be forthcoming. There was no doubt that the Dog wanted him dead. If he tarried, if his own execution was being delayed, presumably it was only until the Dog secured the prior endorsement of the Churl, otherwise known as the Earl of Lancaster, who, since inheriting the possessions of the late Earl of Lincoln, had become by far the most powerful man in England.

Upon reaching Elmley Castle, they locked him in the keep, the most secure part of the timber and earthwork construction, and chained him for good measure. His wrists smarted where the rope had cut through the skin. He craved water: his mouth was parched, and he was desperate to wipe off the sweat and dust from the road. But none was brought, and, exhausted, he fell asleep on the dirt floor.

+

EDWARD. HAS JOSEPH the Jew informed you of my capture yet? Somehow, I'm convinced he hasn't: he's dawdling to give the Dog time for his dirty work. Mind you, Edward, Pembroke needn't be doing all this deliberately… It seems more in character for him to be finding pretexts not to tell you – for, after all, you would be angry at the news, and Pembroke will be fooling himself that he may yet be able to free me, that he wishes *to free me, before he is forced to tell you about his blunder.*

Pembroke is probably exerting himself on his way here right now – ineffectually, of course. Admittedly, since he pledged his lands to you in the case he should fail to guarantee my safety, he does have some incentive to come to my rescue. But don't you think that secretly – though he can scarcely admit it even to himself – he is pleased at the turn that events have taken? Am I too cynical in thinking that he is tying his own hands, as it were, so that when I'm done for, he can sigh with relief at my demise, while being able to disclaim any complicity in it – not only before you, but before the tribunal of his own conscience?

And what's the Dog waiting for? I've been kept prisoner for days now. Why won't he simply get on with it? I made my peace with it: I know I'll not survive this. Damp and lack of sunshine have been making me sick again. Being reminded that my health is failing makes it easier to reconcile myself with the thought that I'll soon be put to death.

I suppose if the Churl… Churl or Fiddler, Edward? I should really decide once and for all which one suits Lancaster best; I'm leaning towards Churl… I suppose if the Churl is still in the North, it must have taken some time for one of the Dog's dogs to summon him; and it will take yet more time for the Churl himself to make it down here. That probably accounts for why my head happens still to be sitting on my shoulders.

That's assuming, of course, that when they do get around to it, they will give me a knight's death by decapitation, rather than hang me like a commoner and a traitor. It doesn't terribly matter. Regardless of the kind of death they decide to administer, it's not as if you've ever left anyone, least of all me, in any doubt about how exalted my status is. In fact, if they do hang me, it may even play in our favour – showing them to the whole Kingdom for the beasts that they are. Let them hang me if they wish, by all means.

I know you will take care of Margaret and Joan. You loved Margaret before I did. But she did grow on me: I want you to know that. I'm more worried about you than my wife. She will pull through. She had already steeled herself to the prospect of living husbandless when I was last exiled, I think. I left then knowing she would make it. I'll leave now, for good, secure in the very same knowledge. But what about you, Edward? Will you simply break down, without me?

Are there others like us? Will there be? Men whose lives are twisted together like the yarns in a two-strand rope… Unwind one strand from the other, and the yarn in each will itself unravel into individual plies – too insubstantial to carry the weight of a human life, let alone a Kingdom. But you have unyielding support in Isabella. You can carry the weight of the Kingdom with her. Don't give her up.

+

19 June 1312, Warwick Castle.

THEY FINALLY TOOK me to Warwick, Edward. I've been here for a few days – I lose count. I suspect the Black Hound must have felt time was up – and decided to speed things up by sparing the Churl one further day of travelling southward.

The Churl did arrive here two or three days ago – I saw him from the window. And others too. They've been parleying, no doubt deciding what to do with me. What could they possibly be debating? I suspect it's for the sake of form. So they can tell themselves it was all lawfully done and by the consensus of the magnates. You know how their hypocrisy has always disgusted me. But I have too little time left to occupy my thoughts with lesser men.

It's only you I want to think of now. Remember the moor, Edward, the heath where we first made love – the larks and bees all around us? You were so young, and handsome, and took my breath away... And the island by the mill on the river Kennet, pignut flowers as white as the sky, and your eyes blue and black like damselflies... And the bluebells carpeting the beech wood at Langley – remember them? Isn't that when all our troubles began? But how could it have been otherwise? Haven't we lived all the more fiercely because of them – our troubles, our woes? How could anyone know love like ours, if nothing ever stood in its way? I look back at it now, Edward, and realise what I've known all along: that it's all been unalloyed gold.

+

TIME'S FINALLY UP, Edward – my time. One of the Dog's dogs just came to tell me to look to myself, for today I will die my death. There was much delight on his ugly snout. (Why are many men so painfully ugly, Edward? I shall die without knowing.) I replied to him that soon, then, I shall stink as bad as his decay-ridden, festering mouth. (Not that I have been smelling very fresh myself, since the day of my capture in Deddington.) He grunted and spat at me. He missed, of course. Chained or not, I'm still nimbler than any of them.

+

Later on, the same day, outside the walls of Warwick Castle.

THE SUN SEEMED blazingly hot, almost like being transported back to the summers of Gascony – though the effect was no doubt magnified by his spending too many days in dankness and dark.

He looked at the men that had assembled, apparently waiting for him. 'Sir Humphrey de Bohun, Earl of Hereford and brother-in-law to the King; Sir Richard Fitzalan, Earl of Arundel; even the King's own cousin, Sir Thomas, Earl of Lancaster! *Comrades in arms* of our King Edward since the Scottish campaign of 1301, if I remember well. *Trusted friends* of our good King, who have always had his best interests at heart, and are going to prove it today. I daresay your wife, Lady Elizabeth, won't be much pleased about this, Hereford. The King assures me his sister has always had a soft spot for me.'

Hereford clenched his jaw and looked away. Piers grinned.

'So, where might we be going?' Piers asked.

'*You* are going to hell, Lord Gaveston,' said Lancaster. He spewed this so violently that Piers fancied the words were at one with the spittle he involuntarily propelled out of his mouth as he spoke.

'Yes, I was informed of that earlier today. Yet the Black Hound has decided he wants nothing to do with it. He takes things this far, practically single-handedly, and then loses his nerve. It does explain the dallying of the last ten or twelve days. Let me guess: isn't your own Kenilworth estate just a few miles up the road, Lancaster? That's where I'm to be dispatched to my fate, then. Dear me, everyone agrees that treachery is required to get rid of the Earl of Cornwall, but it takes a *Churl* to bring it to pass, doesn't it?'

'Go on, Gaveston, lash your tongue away while you can,' said Lancaster. 'Soon enough it will be made stiff for good. You've done enough damage with it, and words are the least of it.'

Lancaster stroked his beard, and Piers tried to imagine him without it. Any resemblance between Edward and his cousin was only passing, thank God. He knew it shouldn't matter either way, but, stupidly, he found he couldn't have borne it if his persecutor had looked like his lover. Lancaster's innuendo about his own tongue gave him a perverse pleasure. That such men as these should fail or pretend not to understand the joy and thrill of his physical intimacy with the King made his and Edward's love all the more precious to him. The official grievance against him was that he was a bad counsellor to the King, who supposedly heeded him exclusively, but Piers fancied that the magnates' resentment at being excluded also resembled the jealousy of shunned suitors. Did these men have a love life? He wondered if his crime was chiefly that of reminding them of their own unslaked, wilting lust.

As he walked up the road to Kenilworth, the sunshine felt startingly hot on his neck. How wondrous the life of the body, even a body that had recently started to fail him. How much pleasure his own flesh had given him; how much more pleasure it had exchanged with Edward's. He mouthed his thanks to God for it all. But he must keep alert. He was resigned to death, but he did not wish it to take him by surprise. They walked for no more than a couple of miles north of Warwick Castle. He was faintly aware of the tapestry of farmland and copses around him. Under different circumstances, he might have delighted in the scenery; but he couldn't feel it today, and it didn't seem to matter.

Lancaster gave the order to stop. They must have crossed the boundary between Warwick's land and Lancaster's estate. So, this was it. He could now be safely sent to His Creator, while the Dog who had abducted him would not have to take any responsibility. Piers spat, while his eyes remained riveted on the two swordsmen who were clearly going to be his executioners.

'Now, let's be done with it,' Lancaster said.

The way the Churl gave the order made it seem he regarded Piers' execution as a minor inconvenience. No doubt he did, and Piers knew better than to care for it. The Earls stood aside, moving outside Piers' periphery, presumably retiring to the road verge. Piers stood, with his hands tied behind him and his legs wide apart, feet placed firmly in the middle of the road, and he faced his executioners. Sweat trickled copiously down his brow and stung his eyes, complicating the task of following the swordsmen's movement. There was mercy in the heat, though: it made it natural for him to perspire, and impossible for others to tell that, now that the time had come, he was, after all, afraid – that the sweat was due as much to his fear as the sun's hot rays.

The swordsmen had a brief exchange in a foreign tongue.

'How appropriate,' Piers said, 'that the man who began his career as the Companion of the Prince of Wales should end it at the hand of two Welshmen.'

The men looked at him. '*Bydd yn ofalus, cymar Tywysog Cymru,*' said one. Be ready then, Companion of the Prince of Wales.

As the man advanced towards him, Piers' lips drew apart to show a row of ivory teeth, half-way between a grin and a snarl. The Welshman lifted his sword. Piers' eyes shut; his jaw tightened; the muscles in his belly hardened; but he didn't flinch. The swordsman thrust his weapon forward, and the blade ran clean through Piers' stomach, missing his spine, and the point emerged on the other side. Pain: piercing, startling, but not unbearable. The swordsman quickly pulled it out, and Piers' body bent into two and collapsed, his eyes opening as soon as he hit the ground.

On his side, bent into two, his cheek stuck in the mud. A pair of feet – the swordsman's – planted on the ground before his eyes. Then, a whizzing sound, blood bursting from him, his flank blooming with pain. Pain that was piercing, but not unbearable. His tied hands were unable to press on the wound, and blood threw it unchecked. His blood smelled raw, like wild animals.

'I...forgive you,' he managed to say to the swordsman, hoping the Earls did not presume he meant them. Where were they, anyway?

The pain... Piercing, but not unbearable. Not yet... He ground his teeth and closed his eyes. His head felt lighter and lighter. And lighter... He thought he might be losing consciousness.

Something pressing against his palate. *Edward*? Edward's prick. He sucked on it, then opened his eyes. Oh yes, he was dying. That piercing pain in his flank, almost unbearable. And that object in his mouth – his own tongue.

He closed his eyes again and saw the cunning man on the small island by the mill – Annus Domini 1308 – warning Edward that he would never be rid of Piers. *If only*. *If only*. He tried to take a deep breath, but his windpipe rattled against his will. And the pain – at some point, it had become unbearable. Oblivion was approaching. *Lord have mercy on me... Admit a sinner to Your Presence...*

'Do it now!' A voice – a *churlish*, *fiddling* voice – issuing an order to someone, forcing Piers briefly back into consciousness. Long-lashed lids opening one last time; eyes not quite glazing over; a sudden flash of inspiration in them.

On second thought, God, please don't take me, not yet – I've yet to show Edward the poet's daffodils! He closed his eyes. A broad swathe of flowers bloomed across his eyelids – six-petalled, dazzling in their whiteness, dancing in the breeze of a mountain meadow. In its midst, two men: one tall and fair, the other dark and lithe. Two men; one carnal embrace.

The second executioner approached Piers from behind. Piers did not see him lift the sword that, with a single, clean stroke, severed his head and sent it bounding a couple of feet away from his body. A body that had been admired by friends and foes alike, but whose portents had been known, for the better part of his adult life, to Edward alone.

Twenty

MERCY

THE LAD, LITTLE more than a boy, didn't reply right away. The Dominican Friar – the same one that blessed Piers in Deddington ten days before – felt the youth's eyes on him. God had seen fit to favour the Brother with generous hips, smooth cheeks, and a relatively high-pitched voice: it always put strangers on their guard, and while his cassock mitigated the problem, it didn't eliminate it.

'Aye, Brother,' said the lad at last, 'he was taken to Warwick Castle three or four days ago. But they took him away again this morning.'

The Friar sighed, his gaze moving from the copper of the lad's sunburnt skin to the Castle walls and donjon, rising yellow in sunshine and green in the shade, from the reflections of the motte's grassy banks. On an overcast day it would have been uniformly grey.

'And are you sure it's the same man I described to you?'

The lad squinted as sweat trickled from his forehead into his eyes – piercingly blue against the tan of his skin. He brushed the sweat away with his forearm. Hay-making under the June sunshine was hard work.

'Aye Brother, 'tis him. Thin, well-made, black hair. Foreign-looking.'

'And which way did they take him today?'

'The road to Kenilworth.'

'Which way is that?'

The lad pointed out the direction.

'Thank you.' The Friar dismissed the farmer with a faint smile and turned to the Brother who was accompanying him. 'It sounds like the Earl of Lancaster has taken the Earl of Cornwall into his custody. Let's hurry. Kenilworth should be only about four or five miles from Warwick.'

He turned his back on the Castle and his unimpressed travelling companion and started walking briskly in the direction of Lancaster's estate.

'It's beyond me why we had to get mixed up in this at all,' the second Friar moaned, struggling to keep up with the zealous pace of the other. 'This is exactly what happened in Elmley – it took us three days of walking to reach it from Oxford, only to be told, once we got there, that the prisoner had been removed. No doubt once we get to Kenilworth we'll be told he has been taken somewhere else again.'

'Brother, we Dominicans are a mendicant order – why does travel vex you so much?'

The other shook his head impatiently. 'Why did you have to tell the Prior you saw Lord Gaveston taken prisoner in Deddington? And why does the Prior care so much about him?'

'You must know our good King Edward has always favoured our order. The least we can do is –' the Friar suddenly stopped.

'What is it?' asked the other.

A small group of workmen were advancing towards them, in the direction of Warwick Castle. As the workmen approached, the Brothers realised that they were carrying a ladder, held parallel to the ground. On it was lying the headless body of a man, his shirt and hose soiled and bloodied. The head itself had been wedged between the legs, presumably to stop it from rolling off the ladder. The Brothers looked at each other and crossed themselves.

'Who are you?' asked the Friar. 'What are you doing?' His voice had been trembling, and there was nothing he could do about it: he had recognised the Earl of Cornwall in the corpse the workmen were carrying.

The man at the head of the party glanced the Friar over before answering. 'We're cobblers, Brother. We found this poor devil up the road, at Blacklow Hill. The Earl of Warwick is a pious man – he's sure to give the gentleman a proper burying. Move along, Brothers. He may look light, but he's heavier than you'd think – a gentleman born and bred, for sure, well-practiced in battle and tournaments.'

They stood aside, let the cobblers hurry past, and sat down at the edge of the road. They were silent for a while.

'Well, it was only a matter of time. We did our best. Now let's head back to Oxford and report this to the Prior.'

The Friar who had addressed the cobblers paused to think. 'Not so fast. Let's go back to the Castle.'

'Warwick Castle? Again? What for? Those nice men are taking care of it. The Earl will see to it that the remains –'

'The Earl is the one who got him killed, you dunce!' He stopped, briefly, to ask God (but not his travelling companion) forgiveness for the insult that had escaped his lips. 'Let's go to the Castle, I tell you.'

He got up. His companion sighed. In the proximity of the Castle's outer gates, they detected the small party of cobblers once again, advancing back towards them. They were still carrying the ladder with Gaveston's body. The Friars looked quizzically at the man who had spoken to them earlier.

'The Earl of Warwick says he wants nothing to do with it,' said the cobbler. 'We are to return the body exactly where we found it. *Exactly*, he said. Move along, Brothers.'

'But –'

'The Earl says the man died excommunicated, and that he wants the body nowhere near his land. We do as the Earl commands. If you want to pick up the body after we deposit it, it's all yours.'

The Friars parted to let the men through, and then kept at their heels. At Blacklow Hill, the cobblers stopped and set the makeshift bier on the ground. The Friar who had seen Gaveston alive in Deddington hurried to collect the severed head from the ladder. The cobblers then shifted the body next to the pool of blood that had drained from it at the time of the execution a few hours earlier. It had soaked into the earth and was, by now, mostly dry.

When the cobblers were gone, the Friar, still holding on to Piers' head, instructed his companion that he should immediately return to Warwick

Castle and seek out the lad who had been hay-making. They required the use of his cart, and he would be paid handsomely for it, if he cared to come to Blacklow Hill and help them haul the body onto the cart and escort them to Oxford.

When, unable to arrive at a reasonable excuse, his companion left for Warwick Castle to fetch the lad and his cart, the Brother set down Piers' head on the road verge and dragged the corpse away from the dirt. It surprised him how very heavy and unwieldy dead bodies always were. He arranged the body neatly on the grass in a supine position. Then, he stripped a pad of wet moss off the turf and used it to thoroughly wipe the mud and blood off the head of Piers Gaveston. When he was done, he sat cross-legged and held the skull cradled in his lap.

'We shan't be able to inter you in sacred ground, if you died excommunicated, Lord Gaveston. But don't worry, we shall embalm you and keep you above ground, somewhere in the Priory, and you'll hardly know the difference. We'll remove what's inside and drain the blood and wash you with spirits and fill you with all manner of sweet herbs and spices. I'll douse your skin with chamomile and rose water myself, and I don't think I'll have any trouble convincing the Prior to let me procure some balsam – the King's recompenses will far outstrip any expense. Nothing works quite as well as balsam. Then we shall wrap you in waxed cloth – to exclude the air, you know. And we shall put more sweet herbs, lavender and rosemary, all around you. You will stay as fresh as the Trojan hero, I promise.' The Friar realised he was speaking as much to comfort himself as the soul of the murdered man. 'I'll stitch your head back myself, Lord Gaveston. For your own sake, as well as the King's. I stitch very neatly, you know. I have a woman's hands, you see... And a woman's heart, perhaps, Lord Gaveston. I must, or else I don't see why the sight of you should affect me so.'

His hand lightly caressed the corpse's bearded cheek, then wiped away the tears that, having just run from his eyes, had wetted Gaveston's forehead. As his fingers closed the eyelids trimmed with injudiciously long lashes – curved, and the colour of obsidian – the Friar wept no less at the brutality of men than at the waste of so much beauty.

Twenty-One

A KING'S HAUNTING

EMPTINESS. THE COMFORT of tears, his need to be ravaged by grief at his lover's death, anger at Warwick and Lancaster: these were denied him. In their stead, a hollowness, a kind of dumb stupefaction took residence within him.

Edward learnt about Piers' death almost exactly a month after he last saw him in St Mary's Abbey in York. He immediately started attending to the business consequent to the news, arranging his own prompt return to the South. But it was as if all this was being performed by a competent third party, whose lucidity and efficiency felt entirely alien.

It was very late when he retired to his chamber that day. Helped by his attendants, he performed his nightly routine mechanically. Then, he instructed his valets to sleep outside his bedroom for the night: he needed badly to be alone. In bed, he stared into the cave-like darkness of the chamber for a long time, unable to make sense of it all, to imagine life without Piers. When he finally closed his eyelids, the queer feeling of an inward split continued. He could *see* himself lying on the bed in the pitch-dark, hair dishevelled about his head, eyebrows knitted. Was his soul hovering above his body, ready to depart for good and join Piers? Was he dying? But no, he could *feel* his body, the taut weariness of every fibre in it...

And now, he was slowly drifting to sleep, consumed by a uniform, unbroken darkness. No, not 'uniform': for something both familiar and disturbing dwelled within it; something that filled him with longing even as it made his flesh crawl. He could sense its presence first, then he saw it. The allure of it was so dreadful that the ground suddenly gave way beneath his feet, though he hadn't been standing at all, and he snapped out of sleep, despite never quite falling asleep in the first place; his heart was pounding, and the hair at the back of his neck was standing, and droplets of sweat were beading on his temples.

Eyes wide open, not staring into the darkness, but searching it. *Piers?*

'Piers,' he repeated, and the word came out of his mouth this time. The sound wrestled the darkness briefly before being swallowed. He closed his eyes again and found that, in this state, he was able to conjure up the vision that had intruded upon him only moments ago, when he had crossed the liminal space between wake and slumber: the vision that had hatched within his breast a dreadful, shameful urge to surrender himself to it.

He opened his eyes, and the vision vanished.

'Was it you, Piers, just now?' he asked aloud. But the room was as silent as a grave, and as dark. 'Piers: if it's you, Piers, please come back...'

Lips trembling, the tears finally came.

+

EVERY NIGHT THE shadow of Piers appeared. Unmistakably, yet unrecognisably, him. Dim where Piers had been glowing with life; mute where Piers had been glib; inscrutable where Piers had been, to Edward, an open book. Not a shadow of Piers' former self, but Piers' very shadow. Him and yet not. Piers' double. Piers' – dare he say it? – *ghost*.

Every night it came in its unsettling way, always at the time when Edward was first drifting into sleep, always shaking him violently out of it. Then, as a recollection, it lingered, sometimes for hours, its purpose undisclosed, its motives obscure, silently challenging Edward to impute ones to it. A guessing game sustained by the very futility of its solution.

Edward came to depend on these visits, the eerie sensation he experienced at the sight of the shadow becoming perversely reassuring in its familiarity. And Edward would speak to the shadow, fearful that if he failed to engage it, the one remaining link tying him to Piers would be sundered. Every night, he would speak to it until, exhausted, sleep got the better of him, bringing oblivion.

+

30 June 1312.

Is it you, or am I making you up, Piers?

Why this? Why can't you visit me in my dreams, instead of this? Why can't you come to me as you used to be, and speak to me, Piers?

Isabella is inconsolable. She mourns you almost as much as I do. I left her behind – it will be safer for her in the North. She's still with child.

I don't know where to turn. I feel like an empty shell. The lightest additional pressure will crush me now. Won't you tell me what to do, Piers? If only I could make your eyes out, perhaps they would tell me...

+

6 July 1312.

I couldn't turn Pembroke away. I need all the help I can get. He came back to me offering to forfeit his lands, for failing to keep his promise to me and for putting you in mortal danger. He was in tears. How could I turn away and punish a man who came to me crying for your death? You didn't expect me to do that – did you, Piers?

Is it displeasure in your eyes? If only I could make them out...

+

7 July 1312.

I'll obtain satisfaction for your murder, I swear it upon God's soul! You will be placated.

But you must see that I need allies to do it. There are your own retainers and the few who have never failed me. But I also need Pembroke. And I need Surrey, Piers. I can ill afford turning him away now that, disgusted at Warwick and Lancaster's barbarity, he has come back to me.

You do see that I have no hope of standing against our enemies alone, Piers, don't you? Your eyes are not reproaching me, are they?

+

8 July 1312.

Yesterday, at Swineshead Priory, the conjuror said he could not find you – that you weren't there among the other shadows. As if you hadn't died at all…

Are you alive then, Piers? Can I allow myself to hope that you're not dead? But if Piers Gaveston lives on, then who are you*? How dare you look so much like him? And if you are not he, why do you torment me!*

But everyone assures me you were killed, and that proof of it is in Oxford, where your body lies embalmed at the Dominican Priory.

Why don't you say something? Why won't you let your eyes speak?

+

14 July. Westminster.

Do bonds like ours survive death? Is this how they survive? Shall I see you, like this, every night for the rest of my life? You said you would always come back to me. You promised it often.

Is this what you meant Piers? That you would return as an ashen shadow, staking your claim on me, always at the time between wake and slumber, speechless?

But why are you back, Piers? I see no love in your eyes. I see nothing in your eyes.

Look at me, Piers! Speak to me, Piers. Please...

+

August 1312. Westminster.

'MEDIATORS, PEMBROKE? I sent you to secure the French King's *military* assistance – I need soldiers, not mediators!'

'I'm sorry, Your Grace. King Philip was not willing to lend armed support.'

Many other men would have lowered their eyes at this point, bowed their heads. Not Pembroke: he kept his gaze level with Edward's own accusing one. The black circles, which only ever darkened or lightened, but never disappeared, lent intensity to his eyes. With those eyes, and the hooked nose, he looked like a bird of prey – as distant, and as aristocratic. Edward thought, not for the first time, that under different circumstances – if Piers had never stepped into his life, if Pembroke hadn't been appointed his advisor upon the First Edward's death – he might easily have fallen for the man.

'Seeing that we have already indicated to Gloucester and Richmond that they should mediate the conflict,' said Pembroke, 'I thought it would be acceptable to proceed on the assumption that if we are in no position to wage war, negotiations must begin.'

'So you took the initiative to invite King Philip's clerks to assist in the mediation.'

'Of course, you are at perfect liberty to send them back, Your Grace. But I pray that you should hear me out, first.'

Fingering a plum, Edward returned it to the bowl that had been placed on his table in the King's chamber. He couldn't look at a plum, not to mention put one in his mouth, without his mind going to Piers' cock. While he had been alive, it was amusing. No longer so. Edward gestured for Pembroke to go on.

'Your Grace, if we attack Lancaster and Warwick, the Lord of the March – Lord Clifford – will come to their rescue. Then the border with Scotland will no longer be secured, leaving Bruce free to ravage the North. And it won't be mere temporary raids. Without an army powerful enough to guarantee us swift victory against the Earls, war will be a lengthy affair, giving Bruce a chance to consolidate his power in Northern England. Do you see, Your Grace?'

'You're saying that we can only afford going to war with the Earls if we have at our command an army capable of repelling Bruce at the same time.'

Pembroke nodded. 'Unfortunately, without the support of the King of France, the prospect of bringing this vision to pass has, for now, shrunk virtually to nothing.'

Edward sighed. 'Pembroke, I owe it to the Earl of Cornwall to seek satisfaction for his murder.'

'You forget that I have reasons of my own for desiring revenge, Sire. Lancaster and his allies kidnapped and murdered the Earl of Cornwall knowing full well – I daresay hoping – that your displeasure might destroy me. If you hadn't been so generous, Sire, I'd be reduced to nothing now.'

'Then shouldn't we at least try to make them pay?'

As his gaze fixed absently on the patterned wall-hanging at Pembroke's back, Edward only half listened to the reply, catching mere fragments as they drifted from the Earl's drawn lips: 'The time for that is not yet ripe'.... 'You can't take it upon yourself to sacrifice your Kingdom and your people in a quest for revenge'...

If Pembroke advised that he should wait, he knew he must wait. But how could he bring himself to tell Piers? That day, the thought of Piers' nocturnal visitation was dreadful.

+

November 1312. Windsor.

Isabella delivered a boy. The birth of a healthy boy means, so I'm assured, that my line and Kingship enjoy divine support. Won't you show me for once that you're glad for me, Piers? That you rejoice for my boy?

Do you object to my giving your falcons to Pembroke? You must know how reluctant I've been to part from them. But he has proven himself the most loyal of all my friends. His loyalty, of course, does nothing to mitigate the wrong he did you. Even he knows it's impossible to atone. He hasn't forgiven himself, nor should he. But if I'm to pardon Lancaster and Warwick, as the Dominican Brothers insist, how could I not forgive Pembroke? You understand this, Piers, don't you?

To think that only a few weeks ago the Earls were encamped with their army in Hertfordshire, ready to strike! We would have been at a disadvantage if it had come to a confrontation. Now, I granted them safe-conduct to attend Parliament, but I made it clear that it was only out of sheer necessity. They objected to that: it implied they were murderers and traitors, they said. Well, aren't they? To remind them of that fact was precisely my intention.

Negotiations have now begun in earnest – but don't worry, Piers: I shall never bow to their demand that you should be declared an enemy and a traitor. I may pardon them, but I'll never exculpate them. I swear it, upon God's soul.

+

Late February 1313. Windsor.

I finally recovered them, Piers. All your jewels and your horses, which Lancaster seized in Tynemouth, were restored to me by that cursed brother-in-law of mine, Hereford, and by Lord Clifford.

But Lancaster and Warwick still refuse to endorse the terms of the agreement negotiated in Parliament in December. They no longer insist that the Ordinances be reaffirmed in the peace treaty, but they still delude themselves that I may accede to their demand that you be officially declared an enemy of the Kingdom!

Fancy, until now they had been refusing to return even your jewels and horses other than as the forfeit of a felon's goods to the Crown. Did they really think I would stand for that? I'll never yield on the point that you were always good and loyal. Even if I issue a pardon, I'll never acknowledge the legality of what they did. Their crime is their shame and it will haunt them for the rest of their lives. They will die in the terrible knowledge of it, and the disgrace will cast its shadow on their names long after they have ceased to live, for generations to come. I'll make sure of it.

If I cannot kill them, Piers, I owe you at least this much.

+

Around the middle of May 1313.

IT WASN'T REALLY sunny enough for a ride, and the bluebells were withering, but she would take whatever chance she got. It wasn't every day, since the Earl's death, that her husband's spirits were light enough to offer to spend some leisure time with her. If this overcast, breezy day was good for him, it would be good enough for her.

After racing their horses up and down a hill, they dismounted, left the animals in the custody of their attendants, and took a stroll, alone, along the bank of a chalk stream. The water was very clear, and Edward pointed to the trout swaying in the current. In a matter of days, the mayflies would soon be swaying too, hatching in nebulous profusion to dance their stupefying dance.

'Edward: do you mind this trip of ours to France? It wouldn't be very politic for us to fail to show up at my brothers' knighting, and I can't deny I rather look forward to it... But the timing is hardly ideal, is it?'

'In what way, Isabella?'

She hesitated a moment as a flitting ray of sunshine picked out the turquoise of his eyes, a perfect colour match to the gemstone insets in his gold circlet. They had wedded five years ago, and since then he had only grown more handsome. 'The dispute with the Earls hasn't been resolved yet.'

'But that's just my primary reason for going.'

She looked at him quizzically.

'I've been in two minds about it.'

'About...?' she asked.

'About the dispute. About whether I *want* to resolve it. By nonviolent means, I mean. I still feel that Warwick and Lancaster should die for what they did. What's to gain for the Kingdom if I extend an olive branch to these savages? Don't I insult the Earl of Cornwall's memory when I so much as contemplate reconciliation with his persecutors?'

'But didn't you tell me Pembroke strongly advised that you should avoid war and –'

'Pembroke's advice is sensible; it always is. But is it right, as a matter of principle? Can putting an end to the dispute other than by taking Lancaster's and Warwick's lives be right?'

'But I still don't understand what you'll achieve by going to France.'

'Most likely, I shan't achieve anything. That's a special talent of mine.'

She shut her eyes. She didn't like it when he indulged in self-deprecation, and he knew it.

'Forgive me, Isabella. I'm hoping that if I go to France, your father may be disposed to lend me a hand after all.'

'You mean send over some of his forces to fight for you. But Edward –'

'Yes, I still hope he will. If I plead with him personally. And if we manage to reach an agreement about Aquitaine.'

'But...aren't you worried...what if my father doesn't lend his support *and* your going away scuttles the negotiations – what if the Earls lose their willingness to compromise? What then?'

'On the contrary, Pembroke believes that if I go to France for a time, the effect is likely to be the opposite. The longer we keep the Earls in suspense, the more complete their capitulation in the negotiations is likely to be. Even for someone of Lancaster's means, keeping a standing army is an expensive affair.'

'And what if Pembroke is wrong?'

'If I must face war with the Earls without your father's support, so be it. Whatever Fate brings, at least I shall no longer feel this...shame.' Edward stopped walking and looked away.

Isabella seized his arm. 'Shame?

'At not having attempted to bring satisfaction to the Earl of Cornwall.'

She sighed. 'Edward, I've desired, prayed even, for Lancaster and Warwick's deaths.... But we have a son now. Spending time at the sacred shrines in Canterbury, giving thanks for the blessing of his birth... It made me think. What will an internecine conflict mean for him? I've never known you to favour war when diplomacy remains a viable option. You're wiser than most of your sex in that.' She took his hand. 'The Earl of Cornwall wouldn't have expected you to seek revenge if it means destroying your line and jeopardising your son's chances of succeeding you to the throne of England.'

'I wish I shared your confidence, Isabella. But I'm not sure of anything any longer. I don't know what Piers wants.'

It started drizzling. They sought refuge under the canopy of trees, looking out to the stream in silence. Isabella turned her husband's words in her mind. Had she heard properly? *I don't know what Piers wants.* He spoke of the Earl as if he were still alive. Of course, he might have been speaking figuratively, meaning that it was difficult to know what exactly should be done to do right by the Earl. But the haunted look in the Edward's eyes made her sense that there might be more to his words.

'You said you don't know what the Earl *wants*. What did you mean, Edward?'

Edward sighed. 'I... He appears to me.'

A chill ran down Isabella's spine, even as his words confirmed what she had already started to intuit.

'Forgive me. I shouldn't burden you with –'

'Oh, Edward, you know better than treating me like some contemptible weakling! I *demand* to know. What do you mean he appears to you? Since when?'

He seemed to find it difficult to hold her eyes. 'Very well. I've been seeing him since York. He comes to me at night, before I fall asleep.'

As much as she hoped he was pulling a prank on her – one in very poor taste – she knew he was being perfectly serious. The rain had started making its way through the canopy. It fell less harshly here than out in the open, but the drops that rolled off the wet foliage were bigger, quickly working their way through the sheer material of her veil. One of them landed at the base of her neck. The frigid sensation startled her.

'Every night? His *ghost*?' she asked. Her voice came out very steady, mercifully – incongruous with the horror within her.

He nodded.

She drew a deep breath; her breast was trembling. 'And he says he wants revenge?'

'He says nothing,' whispered Edward, apologetic.

An attendant brought her cape. She took it and dismissed him. Wearing it, she was self-conscious about the green and pink pattern of dog roses gaily trailing over the fabric: it seemed painfully out of place, as if making a mockery of her husband's grief, and of the shadow his revelations had cast on her own mood.

She pulled the hood over her head. 'Does he convey his purpose otherwise?'

He shook his head.

'But...are you sure? Is he...? Is there...? Is it really a ghost you see?'

'His eyes are dull, his colouring spectral. And...'

'And?'

'There's blood. Draining from the stitches, where...the head was rejoined to the body.'

'Oh, Edward!' She turned her back on him, hiding her face in her hands.

'Sorry Isabella. I shouldn't –'

But, shaking her head, she motioned him to be quiet. It occurred to her that one year ago, if he had seen her in distress like this, he would have taken her in his arms. Now, he was standing there wooden, wrapped up in himself. It was as if the Earl's death had shut up something within him.

She drew breath, squared her shoulders, and turned to face him. 'Why didn't you tell me this before? You've been seeing his ghost – for almost a year, you say!'

'You were carrying our son... I couldn't draw you into this.' He paused, then, with sudden urgency, he said, 'Yet, you know, I've never sought to shirk any of it, I've never begged him to leave me in peace...'

His face was wet from the rain. Was he weeping?

'Why on earth not, Edward?'

'How *could* I send him away?'

She sensed his profound despair: it hit her with near physical intensity, like a draught of chilling air breathing out of a cave.

She went to him. 'Edward...'

She laid her hand on his arm. Her touch released his tears, just as the rain let up.

'A cunning man once reproached us – the Earl and me – for our closeness. He said it was unclean.... He said I'd never be rid of him.... And it's all come to pass, you see? The Earl's untimely death, my forlornness, and his shadow coming back to haunt me.... His shadow brings me no solace, Isabella – it should, but it doesn't, and I feel dreadful about it...'

She stroked his back, soaked with rain and shaking with sobs, and told him everything would be all right. But would it? Would anything be all right, ever again? Would it turn out all right for their baby son? In her chamber that night, she prayed to all the Saints in Heaven that it might be so.

But the shadow of Piers continued to visit the King, unbidden, night after night.

Twenty-Two

RELEASE

EDWARD AND ISABELLA were due to sail from Dover on 23 May 1313, to attend the knighting of her brothers in France. Edward was in Canterbury on 20 and 21 May, but instead of going directly to Dover, he quickly retraced his steps, and on 22 May was at Eltham Palace. He had sent a postrider from Canterbury to Westminster, to have certain documents delivered without delay at Eltham, before he himself reached the Palace. The documents concerned Edward's Duchy of Aquitaine, of which King Philip was feudal overlord. The Duchy was to be one of the principal objects of Edward's upcoming discussions with his father-in-law in France. In Canterbury, it had occurred to Edward that he had always taken his advisers' word for his and the French King's respective claims over Aquitaine, without ever personally consulting the relevant documents. This now struck him as unpardonably remiss. King Philip's readiness to provide his military assistance – so that Edward could finally exact revenge from Lancaster and his allies – might well depend on the exact nature of Edward's own claim over Aquitaine. Potentially, therefore, much depended on the content of those documents.

Having arrived at Eltham on the night of 21 May, Edward privately attended to his papers the following morning. He still intended to board the ship on 23 May, despite the relatively long journey between Eltham and Dover. Among other things, leaving on the appointed date was imperative because it meant missing Archbishop Winchelsey's funeral. Nothing could have induced Edward to pay his respects to the man who had excommunicated Piers; having made plans to travel to France on the date of the funeral offered the perfect pretext to miss it.

The King had chosen the smaller, secondary hall to attend to his business. It was a beautiful room. Ecru hangings, with pink rosette and green trefoil decorations, stood out against the sapphire blue of the distempered walls. The furniture was unpainted oak, rubbed smooth with many years of use. Everything bore, unmistakably, Isabella's mark: Edward had made a present of Eltham to her, having acquired it a few years before.

The King had been occupied with the papers for an hour or so, when one of his attendants announced a visitor. Edward sighed, thinking that there were full seventy miles between Eltham and Dover; so far, consulting the documents had left him none the wiser.

'Who is it?' he asked. 'What does he want?'

'He won't say what he wants, Your Grace, only that it's a matter of urgency.'

'And he expects me to receive him?'

The man smirked smugly. 'That's just what I told him, Your Grace.'

'Well?'

'He insisted, Your Grace. He says he is confident you'll receive him when you learn who he is.'

'Does he, now? And who is he, then?'

'A yeoman, Your Grace. From Gascony – so he says. He also…'

'Yes?'

The man looked to the ground, almost apologetic. 'He claims to be your brother, Your Grace.'

'For the love of God, not another lunatic.' But it was bad luck to turn a fool away, and God knew he could use some good fortune with King Philip. He sighed again. 'Show him in.'

A few minutes later, as Edward's eyes took in the stranger, he became immediately aware that the man had an appeal – something perhaps in the way he moved, or the self-confidence his bearing projected – that far exceeded his pleasant, but fairly unremarkable, twenty-something looks. More curiously, Edward had a powerful feeling of *déjà vu,* yet he was positive he had never met the man before. It all made him feel both vaguely unsettled and intrigued. But he pushed these feelings aside, proceeding to treat the stranger as the joker whose role he had obviously come to play.

'Welcome brother,' said Edward. 'Make yourself comfortable. To what do I owe the pleasure of your visit? But perhaps you'd like to tell me your name, first.'

'Your Grace,' said the man genially. He seemed to be about to embrace the King, and Edward found himself wishing that he did so. But the man checked himself at the last moment. 'The name of the man who stands before you is Sir Richard de Neueby.'

'And you say you're from Gascony?'

'Yes, Your Grace.'

Edward's eyes took in the soft features of the other's face and his relatively fair colouring, so unlike Piers'. He knew not all Gascons had to share Piers' darkly handsome looks, but he still had doubts about de Neueby, and made no effort to conceal them. 'But that's not a Gascon's name.'

'Richard de Neueby? No, Your Grace, I suppose it's not.'

'Nor do I hear anything resembling a Gascon cadence. I have some experience of that, you know.'

The stranger looked a little taken aback. 'Cadence, Your Grace? Do Gascons have a very noticeable cadence?'

Edward advanced one step closer. The stranger's face was no more than twenty inches away. Edward stared straight into his eyes. 'Yes, rather. Very appealing. At least it was appealing in the Gascon I knew.' He pulled back and turned towards the window.

'Did this Gascon know you liked his cadence so much, Your Grace?'

'He knew I liked everything about him very much, Sir Richard. Funnily, I don't recall we ever mentioned his cadence. Perhaps he didn't realise he had one. Perhaps I deliberately refrained from telling him.' Edward tried to force back the lump in his throat. Tears – never in his life as frequent and as untimely as in recent months – threatened to make a fool of him. At length, he turned away from the window to face the stranger. 'But back to you: so you admit you're not from Gascony after all. Might you also not actually be my brother?'

De Neueby stood with his legs apart, hands clasped behind his back. 'Oh no, Your Grace, I'm most definitely Gascon. And your brother, too.'

'You must realise you're speaking with the King of England, I suppose, or you wouldn't be Your-Gracing me.... Now, did the father of the current King of England – that would be the former King of England – have fun with Lady de Neueby?'

'I'm afraid I don't know that, Your Grace. Do you think there is some resemblance between Sir Richard de Neueby's face and King Edward's face, Your Grace? If there is, perhaps they do share the same father. It would be an interesting coincidence, to say the least.'

'I thought you had come to explain to me just that.'

The man raised his eyebrows. 'Oh. But I don't know Your Grace. I mean, I do think that the King and Sir Richard are not very much alike; the King is far handsomer.' He grinned. 'But I've no clue as to Lady de Neueby's goings on with the late King Edward prior to her son's birth.'

'Well, that's fair enough – you weren't around then.'

'Admittedly.'

'So let me recap: Richard de Neueby is not a Gascon name; nor have the words escaping your lips tickled my ears with a Gascon inflection. Yet you *are* Gascon. Furthermore, you can't accuse Lady de Neueby's of an improper attachment to my father, the late King... Yet you *are* my brother.'

De Neueby nodded graciously. 'You summed it all up quite nicely, Your Grace.'

'Well, we're agreed on that at least. Now... I've been known for losing my temper for much more trivial matters than a lunatic wasting my time on a very busy day.' Edward sat down at the table. 'Yet, I feel no particular wish to strike you. Puzzling, rather.'

'I very much hope so, Your Grace,' said the other, keeping his peculiar position with feet well apart, hands behind his back, and the chest pushed out – the very picture of self-assurance. 'That you won't strike, I mean. It would be unkind to poor Sir Richard de Neueby's cheek. Is that where you were planning to strike him, Your Grace?' Richard de Neueby grinned. 'Cheek or buttock, he did little to deserve it.'

Edward tried not to smile at the innuendo. 'Yes. Well, sometimes very little is plenty... Was there anything else "poor Sir Richard de Neueby" wanted to say to me, before he is dismissed?'

'I'm afraid I can't be sure, Your Grace.

Edward scratched his cheek. 'Yes, I somehow suspected that.'

'But Your Grace *I* do have something important to say.'

'Oh, you do, after all? Out with it.'

'Would you mind taking Sir Richard de Neueby, Your Grace? Would you mind accepting his...services?'

Taking a weak-brained yeoman into my service? 'There are no openings in the Royal household at the moment, I'm sorry. '

'Oh no, Your Grace. I meant would you *take* Sir Richard de Neueby *now*. Please.'

The stranger started unbuttoning his surcoat. Edward sat watching as he removed it, followed by his tunic and his shirt. Richard de Neueby's body, it turned out, was rather well-made. Edward felt a stirring. He stood. As the stranger got closer, Edward's physical response became more powerful, as did his feeling of *déjà vu*. Before he knew it, Edward was allowing Richard de Neueby's mouth to smother his with kisses, and Richard de Neueby's hand to slip down his, Edward's, hose. The hand found the King's cock: trapped by the fabric, it had started hardening while pointing downwards. Sir Richard disengaged it from the hose, pushing the garment past it, and the shaft bounced upright. At the upward sweep, Sir Richard smiled a smile that was neither coy, nor mischievous; a smile of sheer joy, of promises fulfilled, of all the lustiness of May.

He turned his back to Edward and bent to push down his own hose, revealing hairless buttocks, not very fleshy, white as unbaked bread, and balls, several shades darker, hanging like twin medlars from the base of the fuzzy crack. Edward's heart leapt: approaching the man from behind, he put his hands on Sir Richard's hips, then crossed them over the man's chest, pinching the nipples and drawing the other's warm back against his chest.

Richard de Neueby's laughter resounded like the din of pealing bells. 'You're too tall, Your Grace,' he said, rubbing his lumbar area against Edward. 'We won't get anywhere like this.'

Sir Richard took Edward's hand and led him to a bench. The King sat down, and Sir Richard sat facing him, straddling his legs. Edward offered his cupped hand to Sir Richard's mouth, palm facing upward. Sir Richard understood at once. Edward grinned. When he rubbed the hand, slick with both their spit, between Sir Richard's buttocks, the man jerked his shoulders. His eyes closed, his lips curled in a languid smile. Then Edward pushed inside him, yielding to pleasure as he had not known since his separation from Piers, one year or so ago.

+

THEY HAD PUT their clothes back on and were now sitting a little apart on a different bench, by an open door giving direct access to the Palace grounds. They had made love. He had made love with a stranger, a fraud, a lunatic – one Richard de Neueby. And yet it did not feel like that at all. He almost felt as if he could have complete trust in the soul inhabiting this young body. Suddenly, Edward burst into a deluge of tears.

'What is it, Edward?'

'Oh, it's *Edward* now, is it?' The King smiled between the sobs.

'It's always been Edward,' whispered Sir Richard.

Suddenly, the urge to unburden himself was overwhelming. 'You want to know what's the matter with me, Sir Richard? Well, I lay my heart bare to you. The fact is I had a love, Sir Richard. He was my sworn brother. And he was from Gascony – like you Sir Richard. Indeed, I don't know that the only reason why I agreed to see you today is that you introduced yourself as my Gascon brother. But my love, Sir Richard – it's gone. I lost it. One year ago. And with it, I lost everything.' He swallowed. 'Even the birth of my son hasn't stopped my anguish. And I can't get it back, Sir Richard – I can't get back my love. I can't get back my sworn brother from Gascony, even if he promised he'd always come back for me. There. You know now. Make of it what you will.' He wiped his eyes with his shirt-sleeve.

Sir Richard put a hand on Edward's shoulder. 'But have you *really* lost him, Your Grace?'

Edward looked away – he couldn't bear the pity in the man's eyes. He felt Sir Richard remove his hand from his shoulder. 'I have. Irretrievably. Memories are all I have left of him. Only memories… And…'

'What else, Your Grace?'

'Visions. Every night. Visions of him. Not happy ones – I hardly know him in those visions of mine.'

'Visions, Your Grace?'

Edward turned to face him again. He screwed his face, managing to force back a new onslaught of tears. 'Yes, Sir Richard. Visions... Spectral visions.'

Sir Richard leant over and took his hands. 'Don't trust the shadows, Edward!'

How earnestly he said it! As if Sir Richard knew his grief – every sharp edge, every hard, unyielding facet of it. But how could he?

'I shouldn't trust them?' he asked, half-stupefied.

'No! Shadows are only...shadows.'

'Should I turn my back on the shadows? How can I?'

'Trust that you can, and you will unmake them.' Sir Richard's hands squeezed his. 'What else ails you, Your Grace?'

'I betrayed him. My sworn brother.'

Incongruously, Sir Richard de Neueby's eyes now also filled with tears. His hands let go of Edward's own and rested limply in his lap. 'Haven't you spent every waking hour in the last year mourning for him? I know you have, Your Grace.'

Edward nodded.

'Then how have you betrayed him?'

'I hesitated. I haven't killed his murderers.'

'More death?' The man put a hand on Edward's thigh, and it was all Edward could do to keep from seizing it and bringing it to his lips. 'These are the shadows speaking again. They speak silently – through their silence they insinuate doubt. In that way, they speak of death. Why, it's their favourite subject! You must shush the shadows.'

Edward had not been lying when he said that not even his son's birth had been capable of bringing him comfort during the past twelvemonth. Yet this chance encounter with this holy fool, this Sir Richard de Neueby, was having the most extraordinary effect on him. He could feel the change coming, a soothing sensation gradually washing over him. The King breathed deeply and managed to stymie the flow of tears. At one point Sir Richard's hand

– the one that only moments ago had felt so soothingly warm on Edward's thigh – had returned to the man's own lap. Edward opened his lips as if to say something, but he stopped in his tracks.

'Your Grace?'

'You said I didn't betray my sworn brother from Gascony when I failed to kill his persecutors. But I *have* betrayed him. In another way. Just now. With you, Sir Richard. Or have I? If I have, why doesn't it feel like betrayal?'

Sir Richard smiled and shook his head.

At length, he said, 'You should pay Sir Richard de Neueby for his services, Your Grace. He deserves the King's generosity, if anyone does.'

The request puzzled Edward. He stood and walked to the table, for he didn't want the other to see his confusion. It was obvious Sir Richard should be rewarded; he very much wanted to reward him. Yet there was no adequate compensation for what Sir Richard had given him back: how did one monetise the will to live? Edward sat at the table and took his purse out of a wooden box sitting on it.

But perhaps that was not what he was repaying Sir Richard for. Despite appearances, Sir Richard might be a professional courtesan, trading in carnal pleasure. The soothing words had been thrown in for free. Whores did it all the time, though he couldn't imagine they were normally this successful. Edward hoped the encounter had meant more to Sir Richard than a mercenary exchange; but he couldn't very well deny the man his fee simply because he would have liked the man to have desired him for his own sake.

'Here,' he said, beckoning Sir Richard to come close, and handing him a sum worthy of his reputation for liberality.

Sir Richard took it, nodding his gratitude. 'I had better leave now.'

He bowed, and quickly strode off, out of the open door and into the Palace grounds, before Edward had a chance to think of an excuse to detain him. The payment, of course, had made it infinitely easier to let him go like this. As for that lump in his throat, it would go away soon enough.

A little time after Sir Richard left the hall, Edward realised that a smell – soft and familiar – was lingering in the air. He hadn't been consciously aware of it while the stranger had been in the room; yet, somehow, he now knew that it had enveloped him before Sir Richard left. He walked to the door and looked out into the garden. There must be apothecary's rose bushes planted somewhere near; it was the time of the year when they came into bloom.

+

Oxford, late 1313. The Black Friars' Priory,
where Piers' body lay embalmed.

The Prior had told Edward that having the body on display in the Chapel would be a violation of the spirit – if not the letter – of the principle that excommunicates couldn't be interred in sacred ground. A monk's cell had thus been set aside, specifically for the purpose of accommodating the casket with the body of the late Lord Gaveston.

Looking around the small room, Edward smiled to himself: Piers' embalmed body enjoyed luxuries forbidden to the Brothers in their own cells. From one of the walls hung, at Edward's own direction, one of the tapestries that had been woven for his and Isabella's coronation, displaying the arms of the King and the Earl of Cornwall. Candles were kept constantly burning on a pair of Venetian candelabra supplied by the King. A folding seat, painted red and blue, with bronze feet and a seat in Irish hide, had been installed for the benefit of those whom he was paying to watch over Piers' body and pray for his soul. Quite comfortable too, he thought as he sat on it.

It is done, Piers. Warwick, Lancaster, Hereford, Arundel, and Lord Percy came to Westminster to humbly seek the King's pardon. They came on their knees. The Earls also agreed to supply me with money for the Scottish campaign and admitted to the illegality of coming armed to Parliament. Pembroke was right: if I dragged my feet, they would eventually capitulate.

Warwick and Lancaster ended up accepting the peace agreement on my terms. You know what this means? It means there's no explicit reference in it to you or your retainers as enemies of the King and Kingdom. Nor is there any implicit *reference to your enmity: the Ordinances – the supposed "laws" that you are accused of having broken when you returned to me – are nowhere mentioned in the agreement. This means that the agreement concedes, by implication, that it was never lawful for the Earls to kill you: your exile was never validly ordained to begin with. The terms make it all but explicit that the Earls are the criminals*

– you their victim. Through it all, I was at least always clear that I couldn't deny your goodness and loyalty even in the name of the Kingdom's peace and reconciliation. It was the one certainty I had left amongst a sea of doubts.

My doubts… Sir Richard de Neueby was right: they vanished the moment I was able to unmake the shadows. How could I mistake the shadows for you, Piers? How could I be such an accursed, blundering fool? The shadows hurt me with their silence and their impenetrability: but when did you give me any reason to think that you could ever hurt me? When did you give me any reason to believe that you would ever be anything but an open book for me? I did your memory a wrong in turning it into those shadows. I made that mistake for a whole year, and I'm so sorry for it, Piers – sorrier perhaps than I've ever been for anything.

I ache to behold your face again. If only I could remove the bandaging from your face… But unwrapping it, so the Brothers tell me, would start the process of corruption. Yet they assure me that underneath the waxed cloth it's as if time stood still: that you are as fresh as if you were still alive, scarcely one hour older than the day I last saw you in St Mary's Abbey.

I don't know when I'll be ready to see you buried, Perrot. I've managed to secure the Pope's annulment of your excommunication sentence, so we have permission to inter your body now…but how can I be expected to have you buried, when I feel that doing so might be tantamount to burying my love for you?

+

More than a year later, early January 1315. The Dominican Priory at Langley, where Piers' body had recently been moved to be buried.

At present, the body was on display in the Chapel. The amount of light that filtered through the stained-glass windows was pitiable at this time of year, so candles had been placed liberally on trestles arranged all around the open casket. Edward, having had everyone sent away, was standing next to it, looking down at the bandaged body smothered in dry flowers and aromatic herbs.

Much has happened in the last year, Piers, most of it not good. Pope Clement and King Philip the Fair are dead. Gloucester died in Scotland at twenty-three… and many others besides him, including Lord Clifford – though I can't say I shall miss him *very much.*

Even discounting the death of your brother-in-law Gloucester and my other soldiers, my campaign to relieve the Scottish siege of Stirling Castle was an unmitigated disaster. I'm trying to understand how I offended God, that he would decree that I should suffer such a shameful defeat at Bannockburn. I butchered many Scottish warriors – pointlessly, as it turned out – before Pembroke forcibly dragged me away from the field when all was lost. We had to flee with the enemy at our heels all the way to Dunbar. A humbling experience, to say the least.

Hereford was captured, but I ransomed him for the sake of his wife, my sister Elizabeth. Given his involvement in your murder, I was strongly tempted to leave him at the mercy of the Scots, with the King's compliments... But he was the only Earl – except for Pembroke and Gloucester, of course – who didn't refuse to join me personally in the Scottish campaign. I chose to view his willingness to assist me as an expression of genuine contrition at being involved in your killing. The Black Friars assure me that my ransoming him pleased God, as well as you. I pray that it may be so.

Lancaster, as you might expect, went further than refusing to fight with me in Scotland. While I, with the others, were fighting in Stirling, he took it upon himself to raise an army, ostensibly out of fear that I would march against him to avenge you in the event that I were victorious in Scotland. But believe me, Piers, attacking Lancaster had been the furthest thing from my mind. Even if I can't find it in me to forgive him in my heart for what he did to you, after the peace agreement of one year ago, I had resolved to put any plan of revenge truly and well behind me.

Until now. For through their renewed baseness, Lancaster and Warwick have now willingly forfeited any claim to the continuation of my benevolence. My mind is made up. I'll bide my time, but I shall strike. I shall, after all, avenge your death – even if you don't demand it, Piers. I know now that it will be done for my own sake rather than yours. But it must be done.

At the York Parliament, after my Scottish rout, Lancaster and Warwick were positively crowing. I was glad you were not there to witness it. My cousin Lancaster, in particular, proved himself to be the perfect churl you always saw in him. I felt so ashamed for them, Piers; ashamed at their lowness – almost as much as at my own defeat on the battlefield.

Lancaster kept his army on alert during the Parliamentary proceedings – a serious violation of the spirit of the Earls' commitment never again to come to Parliament in arms. As if that weren't enough, since the York Parliament, the Dog and the Churl have virtually taken complete control of the Royal household, staffing it with their retainers. It's the Ordinances all over again, except worse!

It seems selfish, however, to disturb your sleep with the petty affairs of the living on the very day when you are to be put to rest. Are you surprised, Perrot, that I've finally brought myself to make arrangements for your burial? Nowhere but Langley would do as your resting place. I've been more alive with you by my side than I can ever hope to be again; but if you must rest – and you must – in eternal repose, then let it be at the place closest to my heart, the one that can still stir within me the emotions of the living.

During the battle at Bannockburn, for a moment I had the impression of seeing you fighting in the press, among Gloucester's men. A knight, fighting bravely, moving more nimbly than all his opponents, eclipsing all his companions in sheer deftness...and swiftly avoiding the schiltron that claimed the lives of Gloucester himself and many in his vanguard. My heart leapt at seeing him – at seeing you, *as I had the impression then – saved! Later, I sought out that knight. His name is Sir Roger Damory.*

Sir Roger seems approximately the same age as you – no, he must be somewhat younger than your actual age, for we always successfully passed you off as being only a little older than me... But he's about your height, and his body has the limber athletic build that was so distinctively yours, and that I used to hold so dear. Isabella agrees on the resemblance – and she appears to have taken something of a liking to him. It must be a comfort to her – nearly as much as it is to me, I think – to be around someone whose figure, bearing and motions echo yours. If I must be denied your company, I shall at least treasure an illusory reflection of the real you, Piers.

Sir Roger Damory, then, is due to join my household shortly; whereas you will soon be hidden from sight, Perrot. From my sight. Forever. Can I go through with this? Can I bear to finally see you buried? What would I give to turn back time and make it stand still – always with you, for eternity. Is this what the afterlife has in store for us? I pray that it might. I pray for it every night.

And every day, I miss you dreadfully, Piers. I miss your grin, so liberally given away both in goodwill and in mischief. I miss the musical cadence (you did have one, Perrot) in your turn of phrase. I miss your eyelashes, awnings to the clarity of your eyes. I miss your lithesome, sinewy figure, even as I enjoy a reflection of it in Sir Roger's.

And I miss the smell of your skin, Perrot. I miss that most of all. Does your skin, under the waxed cloth, still smell as sweet? Would that I could lift the layers of fragrance given off by the spices and herbs that have become your second flesh and uncover that light muskiness of yours. Like that day in Eltham, one-and-a-half years ago, when the holy fool, Sir Richard de Neueby, came to visit me, and the apothecary's rose bushes had come into bloom...

+

IT STARTED WITH roses. Or, rather, with their lack.

On the night after Piers' funeral, Edward – his mind still pregnant with memories of his dead lover – told Isabella that she should remind him to visit Eltham in late May or early June, for he wanted very much to admire the apothecary's roses in bloom. Isabella said that the palace grounds were particularly delightful at that time of year, with gillyflowers and dame's violets aplenty; but if it was specifically the roses he wanted to admire, then they should make a trip somewhere else, for she was positive Eltham had never had any. Edward dropped the subject, but when he retired to his chamber, her words were still ringing in his ears.

'My dear, there isn't a single specimen of the apothecary's rose at Eltham.' But how could it be? It was true that, when Edward had stood in the doorway to look out into the garden, after Sir Richard de Neueby's visit one-and-a-half years ago, he had been unable to see any rose bush. It was also true that this had surprised him: for the fragrance to have wafted into the room the way he thought it had, there should have been roses growing rather close to the doorway, yet he hadn't noticed any. And now Isabella had confirmed, without the shadow of a doubt, that there weren't any roses at Eltham, at all.

Yet, that light scent in the air – the musk that he had only ever known Piers' skin to share with the apothecary's rose – had been undeniable on the day of Sir Richard de Neueby's visit at Eltham. As the implication of this first dawned upon him, Edward's heart almost leapt into his throat: Could it be? Did such things really happen?

He breathed deep. The sensible thing was, of course, to dismiss this new inspiration of his – if that's what it was – as wholly outlandish. Hadn't he learnt that his mind could become prey to superstition and betray him? Hadn't he learnt anything from his experience of allowing the shadows to haunt him – shadows that *his own mind*, rent apart by grief, had created and sustained for a whole year? The very shadows that Sir Richard de Neueby had released him from...

But it wasn't as if the alternative explanation, the one he had been telling himself for the last eighteen months or so, was any less fanciful than the idea he had just hit upon. What he had told himself all this time was that Sir Richard de Neueby must be a holy fool. Edward had reasoned that God himself had granted the fool Sir Richard de Neueby his miraculous power to assuage the King's grief; the power to speak truths on matters that he, Sir Richard de Neueby, couldn't possibly have any worldly knowledge of; and, finally, the power to free Edward from the torments of his own grieving mind.

But was this 'holy fool' idea really any less fantastic than the new belief that was, at this very moment, hatching within Edward's breast? If Edward could believe that Sir Richard had been touched by God, why should he disbelieve the alternative explanation – namely, that the effect Sir Richard had had on him hadn't been the work of God at all, but of Piers himself? Edward's mind recalled the attraction he had felt for the stranger who claimed to be his Gascon brother; the queer sense of familiarity; the solace; the feeling of *déjà vu* he experienced in his presence. What could explain all these things better than Piers' spirit having taken residence within the stranger during the brief time of Sir Richard de Neueby's visit? The possibility made Edward almost dizzy with joy.

It all dovetailed perfectly – and it was astonishing that this inspiration hadn't occurred to him before. Wasn't it, after all, as good an explanation as any for Sir Richard's enigmatic talk? Edward couldn't remember every detail of what had passed in speech between them, but he did remember that the stranger had seemed to want to have it both ways: he had said he was Edward's Gascon brother, but he had also seemed to indicate that he was neither Gascon nor Edward's brother. Well, the riddle unravelled itself, if it had been Piers speaking! Piers, in Sir Richard de Neueby's voice, could insist quite truthfully 'I am your Gascon brother', whilst denying, with no less truth, that Sir Richard himself was.

Then Edward recalled the slightly unexpected request, after he and Sir Richard had made love, for a generous recompense. He hadn't seen it coming, considering that it had been Sir Richard himself that, undressing, had practically begged Edward to take him. Now, if this crazed notion was true – the notion that it had been Piers, in Sir Richard's voice, asking Edward to take Sir Richard's body – then the request made perfect sense: Sir Richard had most definitely deserved being paid handsomely for his services. For Edward had then certainly been using Sir Richard's body by making love to it, and Piers himself had been using it, in order to make love to Edward.

Then the final piece of the mosaic fell into place. Shortly after Edward had received news of Piers' death, the conjuror at Swineshead Priory had said – Edward remembered it well – that he couldn't find Piers' soul on the other side. Why, perhaps Piers had never crossed to the other side! Perhaps his soul had stayed on, among the living, so that Piers could fulfil his promise, renewed so frequently, that he'd come back to Edward. And he had chosen to fulfil it at the time when Edward, besieged by shadows, had needed him most.

Edward didn't sleep that night. He couldn't possibly have, for he was delirious with excitement. Piers' soul must, by now, finally be resting in peace: for his promise to Edward had been fulfilled, and Piers' body had been buried at last. This meant, alas, that Sir Richard de Neueby's skin would no longer be redolent of Piers' rose-like musk. But Edward wouldn't pass over the chance to commune again with the man whose body Piers had once favoured as a means of returning to him. Accordingly, he resolved that in the morning he would send one of his agents on what might well turn out to be an impossible quest: namely, to track down a yeoman by the name of Sir Richard de Neueby, about whom little more was known than his having been at Eltham around the end of May in 1313. If nothing else came of it, finding and questioning Sir Richard might at least clear up the matter of whether Edward was slowly losing his mind.

Twenty-Three

HUBRIS

September 1315.

THE KING HAD been holidaying with part of his household in the Fenlands of Cambridgeshire and Norfolk. On a grey and wet afternoon, Edward and a handful of his knights were exploring one of the local waterways on three small rowing boats in parties of two. Edward shared his boat with Sir Roger Damory.

As they rowed, it occurred to Edward that Piers would hardly have been impressed by Edward's choice of locale for holidaying – he had seen too many of Gascony's lush rolling hills, with their backdrop of snow-capped mountains, for that. But, Edward told himself, as an Englishman, he was capable of appropriate responses to the more subdued beauty of his island home. Surely, this boggy, flat, green expanse of grass looked at least a little pretty as it met the dull, grey expanse of sky? He turned the matter in his mind for a moment and then decided to seek Damory's opinion.

'I don't know that I understand such things, Your Grace,' Damory answered. 'But I'm sure that it must be pretty if it pleases you.'

'Does it please *you,* Sir Roger?'

'Well enough, Your Grace.'

'Good. You row well, Sir Roger.'

'Thank you, Your Grace. I'm not as fast as you.'

'But your style is better. You are very adept at most forms of physical activity. And you bear yourself very well.'

'Your Grace, you're too kind.' Damory blushed slightly, or was it just from the exertion of rowing?

Then again, he was the King, and it was only natural that his praise should make people shy, even as they were gratified by it. 'You've been very taciturn, Sir Damory.'

'I'm sorry, Your Grace. Quick with my sword, but not with my tongue.'

'Your reply suggests otherwise. Does it not show you're quick-witted?'

'If it pleases you, Your Grace. But I have not come up with it – my reply, I mean – just now. It's something of a stock line for me. I've been asked to account for my taciturnity before.'

'You're hardly tongue-tied with the fishermen or the craftsmen around here.'

'I'm sorry if I sometimes forget to behave as befits a knight of the Royal household. I mean no insult to you or My Lady the Queen Isabella, who have shown me only goodwill since the death of My Lord the Earl of Gloucester, God rest his soul, at Bannockburn. I'm grateful for it.'

'I didn't mean that at all. Didn't you notice I enjoy mingling with people of lower station, too?'

'Yes, Your Grace, but you're the King. You can do as you will.'

'I wish that were true, Sir Roger. My life is more closely regimented than any of my subjects'. That's just why I feel more at ease spending time with common folks. It makes me forget my station…the demands placed upon it.'

Damory made no reply; Edward realised his rowing companion was at a loss for words. *Sir Roger is right, Piers: he is no conversationalist. He's not you. But I'm the King after all. Sir Roger's allowed to be a little guarded when speaking with the King, is he not? Besides, it's rather endearing.*

'I meant since joining my household, you know,' Edward said.

'Your Grace? Pardon?'

'You've been taciturn since I took you into my household, not just this afternoon. For one thing, you've never approached me – not once – asking for favours of any kind. That, you know, is extremely unusual. But never mind that. You've not told me, Sir Roger, what's *your* reason for befriending commoners.'

'I'm not sure I have one, Your Grace. I've never thought about it.'

'Think about it now, Sir Roger, and when you've thought about it, please tell me.'

Edward smiled, but Damory remained rather serious. *He thinks I am making fun of him, and that I think him dull. I do not, Sir Roger. I don't mind if you say nothing more for the rest of the afternoon. I'm quite happy just looking at you. Your body is so much like Piers'. How well you row, Sir Roger.*

For a while Damory kept hitting the water with the rows, without saying a word. At length, he explained that before King Edward took him into his Court, he had tended to spend time in the company of other knights only when on duty. His limited means had prevented him from sharing in their expensive pastimes, and driven him to consort with men of lesser station.

'That's as good a reason as mine,' Edward said. 'It makes me think… Perhaps when we're alone together, we can think of each other as just two such men – ordinary men. Then we'll feel truly comfortable in each other's company.'

'If it pleases you, Your Grace,' Damory said, but he appeared slightly taken aback. Of course he would, Edward told himself: it wasn't every day the King suggested that you should treat him as an equal.

'Are you cold, Sir Roger?'

'No, Your Grace. It's warm, despite the wet. I've been rowing.'

'Let's stop and have a swim, then. Can you swim?'

Damory arrested his rowing. 'I can, Your Grace.'

They tied the boat to a large willow that had collapsed halfway into the water. They both began undressing. When Damory removed his shirt, Edward couldn't help feeling a thrill at the sight of the sinewy torso, which – like Piers' – tapered precipitously towards his narrow hips.

'Shall we, Your Grace?'

Without waiting for a reply, Damory jumped into the water. Edward wondered if Sir Roger had felt his eyes on him, and if he had been aware of his effect on other parts of Edward's anatomy. Had Sir Roger sought *refuge* in the water – refuge from him? Probably not: here were the other two boats, steering in their direction – that must be the reason why Sir Roger had jumped so suddenly. Edward himself, keen to hide his arousal, dived before they approached.

Later, on their way back, Edward asked Damory if he would like to attend him in his room that night.

'If it pleases you, Your Grace,' Damory said.

His Grace was very pleased indeed.

WHEN DAMORY WAS announced to the King that night, Edward sent away his chamber valets. Sir Roger had changed into a fresh and embroidered tunic – his best, Edward surmised. Nothing too exciting: its cut didn't do justice to Damory's lovely figure. All the same, it was touching he had made a special effort, and the colour brought out the green in Damory's predominantly hazel eyes.

'I'm glad you came, Sir Roger.'

'I'm grateful for the privilege of keeping you company, Your Grace.'

'Didn't we agree we would try to skip the formalities?'

'Yes, Your Grace – if it pleases you.'

Edward laughed. 'But you're hopeless, Sir Roger!'

Damory blushed, and his cheeks seemed to glow in the light from the torches.

Edward walked to the bed and sat down. 'Would you care for some wine?'

'Thank you, Your Gr – I mean, thank you.' Damory hinted at a smile, rather ineffectually.

You really are hopeless, aren't you, Sir Roger? Edward pointed at the pewter ewer and cups on the table. 'Would you like to pour it?'

Damory did as he was bid; one cup in each hand, he walked up to Edward's bed and offered the King one.

Edward patted the mattress, next to where he was sitting. 'Do sit down. What do you think of the wine?'

'I haven't tasted it yet,' said Damory as, with a smooth movement that could have been Piers' very own, he lowered his haunches down on the bed.

He raised the cup to his lips, but Edward, deciding a bold move might be called for, stayed his forearm. 'Would you like to taste it off my lips, Sir Roger?'

Damory swallowed. 'Your Grace?'

'Have you ever kissed a man?'

'Why...yes, on many occasions.'

'I mean for pleasure.'

'For pleasure?'

'Would you like to try? To kiss me?'

'I...'

'Part your lips, Sir Roger, and close your eyes.'

Damory hesitated briefly but did the King's bidding. Edward took the cup out of Damory's hand and set it on the floor. He put his hands on Damory's shoulders and his mouth on Damory's own and nibbled a bit at his lower lip. Then, he started working with his tongue, at first gently, then progressively more daringly. Isabella's praise had made him quite confident about his osculatory skills; he expected he'd soon overcome the man's defences.

When he put his hand on the other man's hose, however, Edward realised he couldn't be more wrong. There was no sign of arousal under the fabric. It took only a fraction of an instant for their afternoon exchange on the boat to quickly flash through his mind. Then, the realisation hit him in all its horror: Damory had not given him the slightest encouragement to make him suppose that he welcomed Edward's erotic interest. He quickly removed his hands and his lips from his guest's body. *A guest!* He had violated a guest. Wasn't there something in the Bible...? He would have to speak to his Confessor!

Meanwhile Lord Damory had opened his eyes and was rubbing the palms of his hands on his thighs, looking rather stiff. 'I'm sorry, Your Grace.'

Damory turned his eyes to the floor. Edward wondered if it was mortification at having failed him, the King, or if Damory was pained to see his own cheeks turn scarlet – Edward could *feel* them turn scarlet. Either motif did Damory credit.

'You've nothing to be sorry about, Sir Roger. I apologise.'

'Your Grace, I'm sure I could get used –'

'You know, Damory, there was a time, when I was young, when I worried about precisely this: that I'd never be able to find a trusted friend or companion, because, as the King's son and future King, people would never feel free to refuse me. No, please don't speak, Sir Roger, not yet. I don't know how I may have changed so much as to presume that you.... As if the people of this Kingdom had not given me sufficient cause to think that I'm not universally liked!' Edward drew breath. 'You're an honest man, Sir Roger. Others in your place would have simply feigned to reciprocate my interest, with an eye to the advantages. You, on the other hand, practically admitted I repel you, but reassured me that, given enough time, you might just get used to that nasty feeling!'

Edward laughed and felt some of his embarrassment lift: mild self-deprecation could help that way.

'I'm not good with words, Your Grace, I told you before, I'm not...I never meant to convey that –'

'Never mind, Sir Roger, your lack of eloquence, your inability to pass lies off as the truth, is your greatest asset – besides your handsome body, that is. But I promise this is the last time I've made the latter an object of unwelcome attention, even in words.'

Damory stood up. 'Your Grace, please don't take offence at my maladroit ways.'

'No offence taken, Sir Roger.'

After all, the fact that you vaguely resemble the murdered man I still love more than anything was hardly a very good reason for wanting to kiss you. But he had to pull himself together, banish the anguished look that thoughts of Piers had, no doubt, left in his eyes.

'Your Grace...'

He smiled. 'Yes, Sir Roger?'

'I think you're a godly ruler and a kind man. You say you're not universally liked. But there are many of your subjects who love you. Including the craftsmen and fishermen I've spoken to.'

'Let's forget about the whole incident.' He passed a hand through his hair, from forehead to nape. 'Only, promise me this: to be always as true to me as you've been today. If you do, I shall make a friend of you. God knows I could use a few more.'

For the first time, a smile curved the whole length of Damory's lips, and lingered there. 'A friend, Your Grace?'

'Yes, Sir Roger. There are advantages to being a King's friend. But I expect you to take my friendship as its own gift, rather than because of the advantages that will come your way. They will come, you know.'

'You do me a great honour, Your Grace.'

'It's you who did yourself honour tonight, Sir Roger.'

They spent the night on a game of chess. When Damory retired, Edward realised his guest had left his tunic on the chair. He had taken it off when the groom had entered to light a fire to dry up the air: the rain had stopped only intermittently during the King's vacation, and everything seemed constantly damp.

Edward summoned the groom again, intending to instruct him to take Sir Damory his tunic. When the boy showed up, however, he ended up sending him away. Alone, Edward took the tunic to the bed and spread it on the quilt. Kneeling on the floor, by the bed, he brought his nose close to the garment and inhaled deeply. He fancied he could detect a faint whiff of man's scent. It might be only his imagination, but it would have to do. Lying on the bed, he started stroking himself – long, languorous movements that seemed the perfect accompaniment to his longing, the barely endurable bittersweetness of it. Then, clutching Damory's tunic against his face, he came.

Early February 1316.

THE HALL IN Lincoln Castle was bustling with people and excitement. Edward and Lord Damory were standing side by side on the dais, surveying the scene. The combination of the fire in the braziers, the candlelight from the cross-shaped wooden chandeliers – hanging from ropes wound around beams in the ceiling – and the wine, liberally dispensed, produced an impression of warmth that might have fooled even Piers. No, not Piers and his intolerance for English cold.

'I think tonight I'll need twice as much wine as usual, Lord Damory.'

Damory signalled to one of the young attendants to bring some wine. 'To celebrate, Your Grace, or because you need cheering up?'

'I've reason for both, it seems. The Queen, my friend, expects a second child.'

'Congratulations, Sire!'

'Thank you. Coupled with the death of the Earl of Warwick last summer, this is indeed cause for celebration. The Kingdom may be righting itself.'

'Indeed. And what's the unhappy news?'

The wine was brought. Edward downed two cupfuls in rapid succession.

'The unhappy news is that the Kingdom is righting itself at my expense, too.'

'Your Grace?'

'I've just agreed that, if Lancaster deigns to show up at Parliament, he should be offered to be appointed Head of my Council.'

'But...why, Your Grace?'

'Because until I'm able to make Lancaster pay, I can't let the country go to the dogs on account of our feud. Or so all my advisors tell me. He's powerful enough to make his will count, anyway, with or without this appointment. And other members of the Council remain broadly loyal to me, so his appointment "will not make a material difference in the balance of power", as Pembroke put it to me. I can't pretend it pleases me, though.'

'But hasn't Lancaster already been more than one week late coming to Parliament –'

Edward lifted his hand to stop him. 'Please don't remind me. He's trying every provocation to make sure I don't forget to privately nurse my hatred for him, even as I'm forced to make a public show of appeasing him. Churl.'

The months that had passed hadn't worked any miracle on Damory's eloquence. He remained quiet – a good listener – but also, so Edward thought, down-to-earth and sensible. Damory had learnt, however, to relax in the King's presence, so that there was now a different quality to his taciturnity, devoid as it was of awkwardness. Damory's awkwardness, of course, had been endearing, but his newly found ease had advantages too. If nothing else, it made it easier for Edward to take him into his confidence and share with him all sorts of indiscretions. Indeed, he had found himself seeking out the knight's company more and more. He didn't delude himself: he knew that one of the reasons why he enjoyed having Sir Roger around was that he continued to find him physically attractive. But he was proud to have been true to his word: he had never importuned Damory again since that night in September.

Damory, for his part, seemed flattered. Edward suspected him of thinking it incongruous that the King should take an interest in him. Let him think what he liked. As long as he remained amiable and true, and gave Edward the impression that he genuinely liked him, Damory would continue to experience the advantages of the King's generosity – both its material and less tangible manifestations.

Tonight, Damory's spirits appeared lighter and his eloquence freer than usual. It must be the wine. Why, occasionally he'd even allow himself to take the lead in the conversation. Edward realised that it made for an overdue change from the usual pattern of Edward unburdening himself and Damory responding either through attentive silences or measured, sparing commentary.

Damory jerked his chin in the direction of a man chatting up three ladies. 'Isn't that Sir Hugh Audley, Your Grace?'

The man was fashionably dressed, in green and red, with long, pointed turnshoes, and flowing brown hair – a little longer than was usual for men to wear.

'Yes, it is. Why do you ask?'

'He's handsome. Those three ladies seem to think so, anyway. Isn't he handsome?'

'I suppose so, Lord Damory. He's all right. A little on the coarse side.'

'Coarse? Isn't he, rather, very suave?'

'Oh, his manners can be quite superb. But I meant that his features are lacking in refinement. Just a smidgen. He gets away with it. But why should that matter to you?'

Edward smiled – he hoped not too lecherously. Lewdness didn't do with Sir Damory.

'I think...he could perhaps be good company for you, Your Grace.'

Edward grinned. 'Good *company*?'

'Why not? It bothers me that I can't satisfy your needs, Your Grace.

You've been celibate long enough.'

Edward put an arm around Damory's shoulders. 'How do you know I'm celibate, now?'

Damory turned his face towards him. 'You spend all your spare time with me, Sire.'

Edward thought that this – their mouths exchanging banter a few inches from each other, the alcohol on their breaths commingling – was as close as he and Sir Roger would ever get to physical communion. He checked the sigh that almost rose to his lips. 'And so you're going to foist me upon poor Sir Hugh?' The notion was certainly amusing.

'I'm sure he wouldn't mind a bit.'

Edward laughed. 'Keeping me *company*?'

Damory's mouth sought his ear and whispered, 'Didn't you know he's inclined that way, Your Grace?'

Edward tried to ignore the thrill of Damory's warm breath blowing into his hear, though his prick had different ideas. 'It never occurred to me.' He let go of his companion's shoulder and, for good measure, he put a half-step between his and Damory's athletic body. 'I like Lord Audley well enough. Better than most of the knights in my household.'

'Despite his *coarseness*?'

'Now, now. I said I like him, Lord Damory.'

Damory curled his lips. 'I thought so.'

'In any case, everyone is inclined to bed the King, Sir Roger – they think it pays off. Well, everyone except you.' *Sadly*.

'I'm sure Sir Hugh Audley would bed you even if you were a pauper, Your Grace.'

This was getting better and better. 'Since when have you taken up match-making, Sir Roger?'

Damory's eyes settled again on Audley. 'I'm indebted to you. That's why.'

'And how can you be so sure about Audley?'

Damory turned to face him. 'He *looks at* you, Your Grace.'

'Does he now?'

Sir Roger's head bobbed enthusiastically up and down. 'More frequently than you return the favour to him. Though you *do* favour him with looks and glances more often than you may be aware of, Your Grace.'

'Well. Perhaps I should start paying a little more attention.'

'Aye, your Grace, methinks you should.'

Edward drank yet another cupful of wine and started studying Audley as closely as their distance allowed. His eye dwelt on the other's rounded arse; the shoulders, slightly sloping, but not unpleasantly so; and the fine column of neck. The man was giving his back to him, and Edward mentally willed him to turn at the count of ten. Audley did so at seventeen. Catching his eye, Edward lifted his cup in salute. Audley's quick smile expanded slowly, eventually reaching what Edward judged to be its full extent. *Half-decent teeth; generous, full lips.* When it came to it, lips seemed more important than teeth. Audley whispered something to his lady friends and made his way across the hall, towards the King. *He's not as pretty as you, Sir Roger, but he will do. He'll do just fine.*

Twenty-Four

ALLIANCES

27 April 1317.

ISABELLA AND LADY Margaret were strolling around the herb garden in the court adjacent to the Royal apartments in Windsor Castle. After the rain, the air was suffused with the apple-like scent of eglantines, newly leafed out.

Isabella linked arms with Piers' widow. Lady Margaret looked very pretty – a little less rotund, perhaps, her cheeks not quite as full as they used to be – but pretty, nonetheless. Her dress was a shade of violet-grey, like the English sky before a heavy shower – Isabella didn't recall skies ever getting violet-grey in France. It suited her, but her veil should have been pristine white, not ecru. Somehow, she never felt entitled to say such things to Lady Margaret. They had more important matters to discuss, anyway.

'HOW DO YOU feel about it?' she asked.

'Pleased enough,' answered Margaret. 'Lord Audley is widely regarded as a catch among the Ladies at Court.'

'Ladies of lesser station than you.'

Margaret smiled, briefly. 'Who isn't, except for you, Your Grace? In any case, he's charming.'

The Queen pursed her lips.

'You don't like my soon-to-be bridegroom, My Lady?'

'I want to make sure you're happy, that's all. Between the two of us, I think the King may have been acting somewhat rashly in arranging Lord Audley's marriage to you. You know that when my husband takes a liking to someone, he can be quite incapable of restraint in advancing their interests. Marriage to you will, of course, be incomparably advantageous to Lord Audley.'

'That's true. It was true of my late husband too – though I grant that the advantage is now of a different magnitude.' Her brother, the late Earl of Gloucester, killed by Scottish schiltrons at Bannockburn, had bequeathed her and her two sisters a fortune. 'You see, Your Grace, the fact that the King himself arranged this second marriage reassures me in going ahead with it. The King's choice of husband served me well the first time. If I could go back, even knowing what was to come, I'd still choose to marry Lord Gaveston.'

Margaret asked herself if she had spoken the truth. Yes, she decided: her marriage to Piers Gaveston had been worth it – even knowing how utterly forlorn and scared she had felt at the news of his death, a few short months after the birth of their daughter Joan.

'But Lord Audley is not the same man as Lord Gaveston,' said the Queen.

Margaret felt her body stiffen; she had to check her impulse to snap in response. God knew how much she had mourned Piers. Of course, as was in her nature, she had nursed her grief largely in private. But nursed it she had, for five years. Should she really castigate herself now if the prospect of a new marriage – marriage to somebody widely regarded as a *beau,* at that – had suddenly filled her with a sense of fresh possibility? The Queen was well-meaning, but, after all, the road to hell was paved with good intentions.

'No, Your Grace, Sir Hugh is not the same man as Lord Gaveston. But I didn't agree to marry him on the basis that he would be.'

The Queen stopped, forcing Margaret to arrest her steps, too. Seeking Margaret's eyes, she said, 'Forgive me, Lady Margaret. I don't know why I'm so upset.'

Margaret felt an urge to atone. 'It's been a difficult few years, Your Grace.'

The Queen nodded. 'I sometimes feel as if the death of the Earl of Cornwall marked a turning point for all of us. Like a harbinger of all the death and misery to follow.'

Margaret pondered this. It was true that since 1312, there had been plenty of death. Not only innumerable, nameless deaths due to the flooding and famine, but also Queen Isabella's father, the King of France, and his first two successors (brother and nephew to the Queen). Even the Pope had died! And, of course her own brother, angel-faced Gloucester, still so young, poor soul.... First her husband and then her brother – and they the best men in the Court.

The Queen said, 'The loss of Lord Gaveston, absolutely ravaged my husband. For a time, I despaired he would never get over it. Then, last year, the King's sister, Lady Elizabeth, died in childbirth. For the first time, I felt frightened of my own mortality, too.'

Margaret's hand covered the Queen's, still tucked under her own arm. 'But with God's help you were delivered safely of your second born. John of Eltham is a beautiful babe.'

They had resumed pacing the garden. The sodden turf squeaked under their feet.

'Yes', said the Queen. 'God willing, John will grow up to be as healthy and strong as his father and brother. Even then, though – after giving birth to John, I mean – my happiness had to be spoilt by Lancaster's refusal to stand as his sponsor.... I've been trying so hard to forgive my uncle for your husband's murder, and to help towards his reconciliation with the King, yet that overbearing bully has been insulting us at every opportunity.'

Margaret had heard that Lancaster even refused to involve himself much with the King's Council, of which he was, supposedly, the Head. She was sure that Lancaster's covert ambition, behind all his talk of 'respecting' the Ordinances and removing the King's 'evil' counsellors, had always been to appropriate power for his own gain. As if he needed any more power, with his five Earldoms.

'But back to you and your wedding,' said the Queen. 'I worry that the King's desire to assist and honour his new associates will bring about new jealousies, strife, and grief.'

Margaret knew who these new associates were: her future husband, Lord Audley; the ever-devoted Lord Damory, shortly due to marry her sister Elizabeth; and the new Steward of the Royal Household, Sir William Montacute, who was witty but intense.

'My Lady, there's no doubt that others will begrudge Lord Damory and Lord Audley their access to the Earl of Gloucester's fortune. A degree of envy and alarm will be inevitable. But that would be the fate of anyone married to Elizabeth, Eleanor, or I.' She observed a speck of orange sparkling against the muted violet of her sleeve – a ladybird crawling over the fabric – and lifted her forearm for the Queen to see. 'We couldn't very well vow ourselves to chastity on that account.'

'Sorry, Lady Margaret, nothing of what I'm trying to say today has come out right.' The Queen coaxed the ladybird on the tip of her index finger, then gently blew on it, and the insect flew off. 'I suppose what I mean is that the King's intentions to elevate Lord Audley and Lord Damory will be plain to everyone, given the timing of the weddings: with the impediment to your succession finally removed, your brother's lands will shortly devolve to the three of you. I worry about the consequences.'

'But what King could be expected not to take an active interest in such matters, My Lady? With his powerful enemies, it's only natural that my uncle would make sure that my brother's lands should pass on to men in which he has complete trust.'

Queen Isabella sighed. 'I suppose you're right. It's bad enough that part of Gloucester's inheritance should end up in the Younger Despenser's claws through your sister Eleanor's right to it. And there's precisely nothing that we can do about it.'

Margaret composed a mental picture of the Younger Despenser: fiery-haired and good-looking in a base, brutish sort of way – which meant not good looking at all, really.

'My brother-in-law does not inspire confidence in you, My Lady?'

The Queen stopped to pick a gillyflower, then brought it to her nose to inhale the spicy scent. She passed it on to Margaret.

'Does he inspire confidence in anyone? The Elder Despenser has always been a staunch ally of my husband's. But the son was always too sensitive to the influence of his late uncle, Warwick. Neither I nor you, I venture to guess, have mourned that traitor's death.'

'My Lady, I can't say I've ever liked my brother-in-law, the Younger Despenser, much. I have, however, felt sympathetic with him over the issue of my brother's inheritance. My widowed sister-in-law's claim that she was pregnant with an heir was always suspect, even before the ludicrous length of time for which she maintained it. It was quite obviously a ploy to keep me, Elizabeth, and Eleanor from our inheritance rights. So, while I never condoned Lord Despenser seizing my late brother's holding, Tornbridge Castle, in protest, I did share Despenser's frustration at seeing his wife Elizabeth defrauded of her rights, and I felt that the King was right not to punish him.'

'Oh, I don't know about that. The King was too lenient, I think. In any case, the accident showed exactly what kind of man Lord Despenser is. Brassy, fierce, mercurial. And I fear his newly-found fortune will only make things worse.'

They had reached the entrance to the hall. The Queen looked at the sun's position in the sky.

'But I've detained you long enough with my worries and forebodings!' she said. 'If you trust that Lord Audley will be good to you, I shall have trust in him too and wish you both every happiness. And I grant that Lord Audley's looks make heads turn. You have pocketed a regular Adonis, if nothing else.'

'Let's hope much else besides, Your Grace.'

What if the Queen was right, though? Had she been rash in consenting to the match? But it was too late to pull back now: she would have to trust her instincts. If only the Queen hadn't managed to make her instincts so hopelessly muddled!

+

1 June 1317.

THE GRAVEYARD SURROUNDING the Church was ominously crowded – not with people, but with evidence of all the dead from recent years. They had gone to their graves in droves, thought Damory. Cross slabs rose as thickly from the domed ground of the graveyard as spines on a hedgehog's back – even if many victims of the famine had never made it to the parish graveyard at all, having been buried in mass graves outside its precincts.

Not that any of this seemed to trouble Lord Audley, particularly. His spirits seemed as unsubdued as ever. Damory tried to check his instinct to censor Audley's jollity. The truth was that he himself had an unhealthy tendency to brood; the likes of Audley, gliding through life blithely, seemingly without a care in the world, could very well teach a prig like him a thing or two.

'How does married life suit you, Lord Audley?' he asked, deciding to take this as an opportunity to practice his hand at light conversation.

Audley put his foot on a slab and propped his elbow on his raised thigh. 'Splendidly, Lord Damory. I daresay, however, that married life will suit both you and me better by year's end, when the lands of the Earldom of Gloucester will *in fact* devolve to our respective wives. I can hardly believe our luck.'

'The King has been extremely generous.'

'And you very cunning.' Audley winked.

Damory immediately frowned and said, 'I take exception to that.' Then, he bit his cheek: there went his efforts at light-heartedness.

'Lord Damory, I'm afraid you'll never convince me that all the favours the King has been granting you – which exceed even those he's been granting *me* – are purely an effect of his desire to reward an entirely *disinterested* friendship on your part. The last time I checked, he made several grants of lands and benefits *at your own request*.'

'And what is that supposed to show, pray?' Damory realised his hand had gone to the hilt of his sword. He made sure to remove it.

Surely, Audley would see that it was normal for friends to do favours for their friends. And if the King's means and generosity exceeded those of other men, the favours he granted would be, by necessity, greater. Wasn't it obvious? Besides, it had been the King himself that had insisted that he,

Damory, must not be shy about requesting favours. Of course, Damory *had wanted* to benefit those on behalf of whom he had then approached the King – but why should this be seen as manipulating King Edward, as Audley very clearly implied? Perhaps he should let Audley know that the favour Audley himself had recently found with the King was largely a fortuitous effect of Damory's own *disinterested* advice to the King about likely outlets for King Edward's erotic needs: what would Audley say then? It hadn't even occurred to Damory that by suggesting Audley as a likely object of the King's amatory pursuits, he could make a useful ally out of Audley. But Audley would never understand this. Damory was struck, not for the first time, by the vast chasm that separated him from the man who was standing right before him, with whom he was about to enter into an alliance of sorts.

Audley had been looking at him in silence. 'Very well, Lord Damory.' He removed his foot from the slab and, straightening his body, proffered his hand. Damory shook it. An unnecessary rift had been averted.

'Still,' Audley said, 'the nature of your ascendance to the King's favour remains a mystery... The nature of mine, on the other hand, must be obvious to anyone. I'm decidedly too handsome to leave observers in any doubt about it.'

'Do you still sleep with the King, then?' asked Lord Damory, thinking he had managed to strike the right note this time: a little bold, by his standards, but it showed he was not a prig after all.

'*Still*? Was I supposed to stop at any point?'

'I mean, since your marriage, of course.'

'Pray, in what universe is *that* supposed to make a difference, Lord Damory?'

'I don't know... I thought –'

Audley laughed amiably. 'Lord Damory! If you keep this act up, you might convince me that you actually *are* as pure as you claim to be! Here's some news for you: I'm far too attached to the material rewards that accompany the King's interest in me to give up sleeping with him unless he tires of me. As you can see, no one can accuse *me* of being anything other than perfectly honest. Besides, the King is very handsome. And he's really quite extraordinarily good at...but I don't suppose the details would mean much to you.'

Audley sat down on the grass. His tone had been a mixture of the mischievous and the benevolently patronising; for a brief moment, Damory wondered if, in failing to respond to the King's kiss almost two years before, he had ended up missing out. A sigh came out of him, unbidden.

Then Audley said, 'If you're unwilling to reveal the secret of your own social ascendance, Lord Damory, perhaps you happen to understand the source of Lord Montacute's?'

Damory looked around: no sign of Montacute's arrival yet. He wondered if the pact of alliance could go ahead in the absence of one of the parties intended to share in it.

Looking down to where Audley was sitting, cross legged, he said, 'Isn't Lord Montacute the King's friend? Hasn't he been in his household for years?'

'But so have I, Lord Damory. Being the King's "friend" – whatever that means – and belonging to his household constitute no special qualification for having influence upon him.'

'Don't they?'

'Certainly not.' Lord Audley paused to reflect. 'I suspect it's his wit. Lord Montacute is awfully clever and *very* amusing. More amusing than me, alas. The King must be sorely missing Lord Gaveston's wit. Clearly, he looked for a substitute in Lord Montacute. You would too, if you had been Lord Gaveston's lover. His company could be quite addictive.'

Damory sat down next to Audley. 'I could never satisfy King Edward's need for witty conversation.'

'No, I think we're agreed on the fact that *that* is not your strongest point. But you have other virtues. You bear yourself well, and you're not terribly bad to look at – though you don't do yourself any favours donning that ancient robe, you know. In any case, I suspect that your appeal, for the King, has to do with virtues, of which you are possessed, that are of a more...spiritual variety, so to speak. Which makes me think...'

Audley paused and Damory raised his eyebrows quizzically.

'Do you think, Lord Damory, that we make up one Gaveston? I mean the three of us – Montacute, you, and I: do you think we add up to one Lord Gaveston?'

'What do you mean, Lord Audley?'

'The sum of our qualities. Montacute has something of Gaveston's wit. You have Gaveston's devotion to the King, his purity of heart.'

Damory felt his face blush.

'You're also a very good soldier, I'm told. Now that leaves me. I'm a decent soldier too. Additionally, let me see...' He stood up. 'Impeccable refinement? Unmatched dapperness? Winsome smile? Good looks? Exquisite arse?' Lord Audley threw a glance over his shoulder at his own backside. 'In fact, it seems to me I contribute rather more than my fair share to this collaborative effort of ours to recreate Sir Piers Gaveston for the King's benefit. Wouldn't you agree, Lord Damory?'

Damory had stopped listening at 'exquisite arse'. Sitting as he still did on the ground, he happened to have as unobstructed a perspective on Audley's backside as he recalled ever enjoying. Realising belatedly that Lord Audley had asked his opinion, he began to say, 'I –'

Audley winked. 'Rhetorical question, you know? Anyway, this theory of mine – isn't it as good an explanation as any for why the three of us are meeting here today to agree on a pact of mutual support – you, Montacute, and I? I confess that the rationale behind it seemed a little obscure to me. But now all is explained: we came into the King's favour at about the same time to satisfy a single need; and we'll all fall out of it simultaneously, too. So we must take care that we don't. And that requires a coordinated effort.'

'Forgive me, but I find it hard to follow you.'

Audley extended his arm to help him to his feet. 'Of course you do. But let me explain: if one of us falls out of favour, the spell will be broken and the other two will necessarily follow suit. The King will lose interest in the illusion, once the illusion is revealed for what it is. The illusion of Sir Gaveston that we, collectively, conjure up for him. Hence the need for us to work together.'

'I can hardly see how that –'

'Never mind,' Audley said, still holding onto Damory's hand, and, now, shaking it left and right to add emphasis to his words. 'I'm convinced I'm onto something. We stand or fall together.'

'If that's true, where does that leave the Elder Despenser? Why is *he* going to join our mutual undertakings?'

Audley let go of his hand. 'You're a pedant, upon my word. In any case,

Lord Despenser, not unlike the rest of us, hates Lancaster. That's reason enough for him to want to make allies out of us. Say, Damory, what is *your* reason for hating Lancaster?'

'I never said I hated him. But I regard the King's enemies as my enemies.'

Lord Audley's eyes affected a loss of patience. 'Why do I *even* ask...?'

Damory wondered if Audley really thought him an unreconstructed bore. 'What's your reason for disliking Lancaster, then, Lord Audley?'

Audley stepped forward towards him, his face a little too close for comfort. '*Disliking* him? I loathe the sight of the man! If Lancaster has his way, it will be the end of us, Lord Damory. Don't you see? To the Earl of Lancaster, we are all "evil counsellors". In confidence, I've come to the conclusion that the Earl is a little barmy. It's the King's favour that marks us out for the Earl's rancour. It's all jealousy: he used to enjoy the King's confidence ages ago; after he lost it, something cracked up here.' Lord Audley tapped his skull. 'So you see, putting Lancaster in his place is a matter of self-preservation for us.'

'I never thought about it that way.'

'Well, you'd better start.'

Montacute and the Elder Despenser crossed the gate into the cemetery. The Elder Despenser motioned them to move to the Church, where they could discuss their alliance away from prying eyes.

There were enough rivalries and conniving in the Court: it seemed to Damory that a pact of mutual support between the men closest to the King was good news, both for them and King Edward. If only the trusted Pembroke could have been included in it.... But Pembroke didn't have much time for them – or, at any rate, not for the three younger men. It was aggrieving to be regarded as some sort of upstart by someone such as Pembroke. But, he reasoned, if that was the price to pay for King's Edward friendship, pay it he must.

Twenty-Five

THE SETTLEMENT

Exactly four months later, on 1 October, Edward, with a portion of his army, was riding by Lancaster's stronghold of Pontefract, south of York. Damory, riding next to the King with Montacute and Audley, could sense the King's tension. Since Gaveston's death, the King and his Court had taken to spending a considerable amount of time in the North of the country, where his presence was made necessary by the continuing Scottish threat and Lancaster's ambitions in the region.

On this occasion, the King had been in York with an army intended to fight against the Scots, but, as on previous occasions, the campaign was aborted. As on previous occasions too, the reasons for this had much to do with the fact that the two threats – the Scots and Lancaster – were mutually reinforcing. The King faced an intractable situation, for any military engagement with Lancaster on the King's part risked being exploited by the Scots and vice-versa. Damory would have hated to be in his shoes.

This time, it had been worse than usual. Securing the support of Lancaster's army in the Scottish campaign had been imperative. Not only, however, did Lancaster fail to provide his assistance, but he also gathered an army of his own and deliberately obstructed the King's progress towards the city. Now, on his return to London by way of Pontefract, the King found he could hardly resist the chance to attack his cousin. The attack would have been as impromptu in its execution as uncertain in its outcome – but who could blame the King? Damory, for one, knew he couldn't: Lancaster had been doing everything he could to try King Edward's patience.

'Your Grace, you must think of what is good for the Realm,' said Pembroke in an attempt to dissuade the King

'I *am* thinking of it.' The King scowled at the sprawling walls of the imposing fortress. 'Ridding the Kingdom of Lancaster will be the greatest service I shall ever have performed for its benefit.'

Pembroke betrayed no emotion as he said, 'We've been labouring very hard to defuse the situation over the past few weeks. Desist from this folly, Your Grace, even if it's the last time you take my advice.'

Edward turned his gaze away from the fortress and looked straight into Pembroke's eyes.

Pembroke said, 'For a whole year, we've devoted our best efforts to finding a solution to your feud with Lancaster, Sire. Please don't throw it all away.'

Audley asked, 'Please remind me, Pembroke, what exactly do you have to show for all your negotiations?'

Of course, though it was unseemly for Audley to address an Earl so freely, Damory thought, didn't Sir Hugh have a point? He decided to speak up.

'With your permission, Pembroke, it's not the *King's* feud with the Earl of Lancaster. The King's enemy is an enemy of the whole Kingdom. It is *our* feud as much as his.'

'Lord Damory is right,' said Montacute. 'Why do we stoop to negotiating with traitors? You won't deny Lancaster is a traitor, Sir Aymer de Valence?'

Montacute's cheeks were flushed. Not even he, for all his eloquence – for he was not only witty, as Audley maintained, but eloquent, clear-minded and strangely intense – not even he could be completely immune to Pembroke's formidably commanding ways. But he had held the Earl's eyes as he spoke. Damory tried to remember if he himself had done the same a moment ago, when addressing the Earl.

Pembroke's eyes flashed darker than ever behind the knitted eyebrows. 'Since when have you three become chief strategists and advisers to the King?'

The Earl's scowl swept from left to right, taking in all three of them in rapid succession. Damory felt like a boy who'd been reprimanded.

'I know more about Lancaster's treachery than anyone, except the King himself,' said Pembroke. 'God knows Lancaster has tried the King's patience long enough to justify King Edward's strike – but it's grossly irresponsible of you to encourage him. The legitimacy of the King's grievances is beyond doubt. But so is the Kingdom's need for peace and stability.' He turned to the King. 'Your Grace, you've already dismissed many of the forces you gathered in the last few weeks. It's true, Pontefract is not heavily guarded right now, but it can easily hold out until reinforcements come to its rescue. The idea that attacking now would secure a swift victory is pure illusion. We'll be dragged into a full-scale conflict that will last many months, and for which we are unprepared. Needless to say, that would be sure to open the door to Scottish invaders.'

They all turned to look at the massive, impregnable-looking keep, lobed like a quatrefoil, towering grey over the motte.

'If not now, then when, Pembroke?' asked the King.

Damory hated to hear the ill-concealed despair in the King's appeal. He understood King Edward's sentiments: every day that passed was another insult to the memory of the late Earl of Cornwall.

'The time will come, Your Grace, trust me. Even Lancaster's former allies are beginning to lose patience. But until you can be sure to quickly overpower the Earl, the country must be stable and governable. Besides, Your Grace, you'll lose the moral high ground if you attack now.'

Damory frowned. 'How so?'

'Because the King has already confirmed a truce with Lancaster – it's already been agreed that all their reciprocal grievances are suspended until the Lincoln Parliament in January. The King can't be seen to renege on his undertakings.'

Audley rolled his eyes – not too brazenly, by his standards – while his fingers tapped his sword hilt. 'Still, the King could do with being seen taking decisive action against traitors.'

'Be quiet now, Lord Audley,' the King said. 'I shall do as Pembroke counsels.'

His voice was sedate; somehow it made him look more handsome, or, perhaps, simply more like Damory's notion of the ideal King. Damory made a mental note to thank the Earl of Pembroke later for stopping them all from acting recklessly.

+

24 November 1317. London.

LOOK FOR SIGNS of Pembroke's distinctive touch in his private room, and you would look in vain. His lodgings – at least these lodgings – were remarkable neither for their austere elegance, nor for being recherché in the sort of understated manner Damory had imagined them to be. Nor, in fact, were they in *any* way remarkable, other than the fact that they *couldn't*, even with some imagination, be described as an extension of Pembroke's persona. Then again, Damory had been summoned, and the man was here, before his eyes; the Earl's solemn intensity sought no sympathetic backdrop.

Pembroke invited him to sit at a rather battered wooden table. The Earl himself took the seat on the opposite side. Staring straight into Damory's eyes, he said, 'I've become convinced that you, at least, genuinely care for the King's well-being.'

This came as a surprise. Damory had never consciously sought Pembroke's regard, but now he suddenly realised that the trust of such a man would be a highly prized possession indeed.

He blushed. 'I want to do what's best. The King considers me his friend. I do want to act in a way worthy of it.'

'Do you trust that I, too, have the King's interests at heart?'

'The King has great faith in you, My Lord. King Edward is a good judge of character.'

Pembroke waved a hand, dismissively. 'I fear the King is too generous and trusting to be a good judge of character. This is why I summoned you. Will you do as I propose, Lord Damory? For the King's benefit?'

‘Anything for the King’s benefit. What is it you propose, My Lord?’

‘You must make an undertaking to me. If you agree, we will formalise your pledge in the form of an indenture.’

‘A pledge – in connection with what?’

‘You must promise this. That as long as my advice to the King is to the Crown’s and Kingdom’s benefit, you will do what is in your power to persuade the King to heed it above that of all others.’

‘Do you mean of Lord Audley and Lord Montacute?’

‘I mean whoever has the King’s ear without deserving it. You must promise that if such people attempt to undermine the King’s confidence in my judgement, you will do what is in your power to thwart them.’

‘But the King already values your counsel above all others.’

‘Except your own, perhaps, Lord Damory. Will you promise?’

‘I promise. Of course I do.’

‘I also want you to promise that you yourself shall not oppose my advice; and that if, in my absence, the King should plan to do anything detrimental to himself, you shall counsel him against it and promptly inform me, so that through our combined efforts, we may dissuade him from it.’

‘I promise.’

‘Then I promise you this, Lord Damory: as long as you do not break your pledge, and as long as my fealty to the King does not require of me a different course of conduct, I shall defend you and keep you against all other men.’

Try as he did, Damory couldn’t dismiss that smile from his lips. Was he going to spoil it all now, by looking too pleased with himself? Would he alienate Pembroke’s goodwill through his own vanity? But Pembroke was smiling in turn. It made him look more earth-bound, and less like a kite.

Early August 1318.

DAMORY TOOK HIS seat, facing the King’s. King Edward looked graver than Damory recalled ever knowing him. Even the King’s choice of clothing had seemed uncharacteristically subdued of late: today, for example, it looked to Damory as if the King's plain tunic was only a little better than his own. No doubt this was due, in part, to the fact that the contents of his own wardrobe had benefitted, in the last few months, both from King Edward's gifts and Lord Audley's advice. But was it possible that Damory's own lack of flamboyancy had rubbed off on the King? He wasn't entirely sure this was a welcome development.

Damory said, 'I discussed the treaty with Pembroke, Your Grace. He says you should accept its terms. This is Lancaster's capitulation. He's politically isolated because of his uncooperativeness. The magnates will not tolerate further delays to the settlement. This is why the terms of the treaty are so advantageous to you – so Pembroke says.'

'Are they all that advantageous, though? A standing Council staffed by men loyal to me, and from which Lancaster is personally excluded – I can see how *that* will be advantageous. But virtually everything else is to be decided at the York Parliament next autumn. And Lancaster's wealth and military power give him substantial bargaining power.'

'Pembroke is sure he will be bought off, as it were, if a suitable financial and territorial settlement is made in his favour.'

The King crossed his arms. 'Concessions that will increase his material power base even further: is there no end to the man's greed?'

'But these concessions, coupled with pressure from the magnates, will convince him to stop challenging the legality of your acts, Your Grace. He'll leave the Ordinances alone once and for all.'

The King sighed. 'Still, Lancaster will insist on the removal of you, as well as Lord Audley and Lord Montacute, from Court. I can guarantee that, Lord Damory. He insists you are all 'evil counsellors', as he once used to claim of the late Earl of Cornwall.'

Damory looked down. 'We've already discussed this, Sire. If that is Lancaster's condition, and if the peace and stability of the Kingdom depend on it, you shouldn't oppose it.'

The King frowned. 'You don't care for our friendship, Sir Roger.'

'I care to deserve it, Your Grace! You've done much to advance my private interests. But I've no intention to let my private interests interfere with the peace of the Kingdom. I promised Pembroke I'd always strive to do what's best for the Crown and the Kingdom. If the condition for peace is that I be sent away from your household, I cannot advise you to keep me with you. I know Lord Montacute and Lord Audley take a different view.'

The King stood up from the chair and went to the window. 'Indeed they do.'

'Then you must ignore their counsel, Your Grace. If the settlement stands or falls on the question of our removal, and Lord Montacute and Lord Audley advise you to reject it, it means that they value their own interests over yours. A reason to ignore their advice.'

'You've become quite the orator, Lord Damory. What a change. You make it sound so simple, too.'

The King's sarcasm hurt him. 'It'll be simpler than you think, Your Grace.' *For you, in the end – though not for me, Sire.*

The King turned away from the window. It seemed to Damory the King looked at him with the expression he used to assume in the early days of their acquaintance – admiring, proprietary, protective.

'Easy, perhaps, to send the others away. But not you, Sir Roger.'

Damory averted his eyes before the lump in his throat settled there and threatened to alter his speech. 'I'm your friend Your Grace. You do me the honour of treating me like one. But I'm no more Lord Gaveston than either Lord Montacute or Lord Audley are.'

He had said it matter-of-factly. That was good. Now let him leave the room quickly, lest he give away his mortification in some other way.

Late 1318. In the King's chamber.

'Is it really necessary though?'

'Lord Audley,' said Edward, smiling.

The tip of his index finger caressed Audley's attractively pouting, full lips. They were lying side by side in bed.

'You're King,' said Audley. 'Can't you just tell them to go stuff themselves?'

Edward thought of what he and Audley had been doing until a moment ago – the smell of lovemaking was still in the air – and smiled at Audley's choice of words. Audley smiled back, and Edward knew the choice had been deliberate.

'I *could* tell them to go stuff themselves. But it's a tactic that never really works. Experience taught me that.'

'Still. Lord Montacute, Lord Damory, and I even agreed to pay Lancaster compensation for our "enmity" towards him. Why can't he just let us be? Why must we be removed from Court?'

'Face-saving. Lancaster's had to give up on virtually all his other political demands: he's determined to cling to this one. Spite towards me is probably another reason. He knows that if he manages to have the three of you sent away, I shall be very disappointed.'

'Why appease him then? Your cousin's a piece of shit, Your Grace, if you don't mind my saying so.'

Lancaster, a piece of shit. He was going to miss Audley.

'Yes, Lancaster's petty motives *would* be a reason not to give in to his demand that you remove yourselves from Court – if only *you* hadn't already given in to it.'

Audley raised his eyebrows. '*I*? I'd never do anything of the sort! It's not up to me. No one gives a fig what *I* think.'

He pulled the blankets down and rested his cheek on Edward's chest. His forefinger started playing with Edward's nipples.

'Oh, but I do, Lord Audley. I care very much what you think. And what you *do*.'

Edward took Audley's hand and put it on his cock.

'If you really did, Your Grace, would you have agreed to send me away?'

Audley's fingers travelled away from Edward's prick, up to the breastbone, and then back, stopping to play about the King's belly button.

'Lord Audley, need I remind you of the confirmation of the grants I made to you?'

'I need no reminder about that,' said Audley sitting up. 'Though I can't say I ever really understood in the first place how anyone – that Commission for the Reform of the King's Household, or whatever it's called – could take it upon themselves to review the grants the King had made. Who do they think they are?'

'Representatives of the magnates of the Realm, Lord Audley. In any case, the point is that, after the review, my grants to you were confirmed.'

'Yes. Thankfully! It would've been outrageous if they hadn't. And frankly, terribly inconvenient.'

Audley resumed his previous position – head resting on the King's chest, hand caressing the King's stomach.

'And am I mistaken in thinking that your grants were confirmed on the condition that you would remove yourself from my Court? And that you agreed to it?'

'But that was put nowhere in writing. As the King, you can simply ignore such details.'

He kissed Edward's breast, and his hand fastened around the King's hardening cock.

'But I don't intend to ignore them. You made your choice.'

Audley turned his deep-set eyes towards Edward's face. 'What do you mean, Your Grace?'

'If you wish to stay, Lord Audley, there may still be a way. Renounce all your grants. As long as you stay in the Court not publicly as my favourite, but as an ordinary knight – the same as you were three years ago – neither Lancaster nor anyone else will object to you. Then we can be together all you like. And keep doing this' – Edward groped Lord Audley unceremoniously between the thighs – 'night and day.'

'That's unfair.'

'Quite.'

'You wouldn't ask me to choose, if you really loved me, Your Grace.'

He started stroking Edward's shaft.

'No, you're right, I probably wouldn't. But then if *you* really loved me, you wouldn't be giving me a reason to confront you with the choice.'

Edward put his own hand over Audley's, and tightened its grip.

Audley sighed. 'Very well. But something tells me you're going to miss my company every bit as badly as I shall miss yours.'

He disengaged his hand and shifted his position to make himself more accessible – one last time – to the King's touch. Edward brushed his fingers between Audley's buttocks: he was going to miss them as much as Audley's irreverence. The crack was still wet and sticky from earlier. Edward pushed his middle finger inside Audley and started stroking himself with his free hand.

When they parted, Lord Audley told Edward that the King would know where to find him if he was ever taken with the desire to see him, and that in any case, he expected the King would want to visit Audley's wife, Lady Margaret, from time to time. Or wouldn't he?

'Goodbye, Lord Audley,' Edward answered, and he kissed the man's lips. It was a chaste kiss, this time, yet he felt his prick stir. A little queer, really, how it seemed to have a mind all its own.

Twenty-Six

NEW BEGINNINGS

Later the same day, Sir Hugh Despenser the Younger entered the King's chamber. He had been wrong thinking he would find the King there. But the King *had* been there shortly before: Hugh could detect a faint smell of lovemaking. (He had a good nose, Hugh.) *No doubt with that interloper, Audley.*

It was beyond him what the King could see in that coxcomb. Of course, he, Hugh, could have fucked Audley and enjoyed it – Audley looked good enough for that. But why did the King insist on treating Audley as if he mattered beyond what he could offer in bed? Hugh wondered about this, albeit only out of curiosity rather than jealousy – the sense of his own superior worth left little time for the latter feeling.

Still, there was no denying that Audley's closeness to the King had been a source of some vexation to Hugh, particularly in connection with the partition of the Earldom of Gloucester's lands between Audley's wife, Lady Margaret, and Hugh's own wife Eleanor. That there should be a partition was inevitable, as both of them, of course, along with Damory's wife, Lady Elizabeth, were sisters to the deceased Earl. But it was frustrating that the

King took Audley's side when, the previous year, Hugh attempted to stake a claim to the portion of Audley's Welsh lands that flanked Hugh's own Lordship of Glamorgan. Hugh would have expected the King to protect Lord Damory's interests from encroachment, but why would he bother for someone like Audley? It was not as if Audley was the only handsome knight from which the King could get pleasure. King Edward's way of thinking could be more than a little perplexing.

So, it was good that Audley – ordered to leave Court – would soon be fading from the picture. Hugh had no doubt that the more physically remote Audley grew from the King, the less his ascendance would be felt. Because Audley was apparently uniquely valuable to the King under the bedclothes, he had enjoyed fairly unrestrained access to the Royal chamber. This had annoyed Hugh to no end, interfering as it did with his control, as Royal Chamberlain, over the flow of ministers, petitioners, Lords, delegates, and even friends and relations, who sought access to the chamber, where much momentous political business was conducted.

The King – no doubt thankful to be spared some of the tediousness that official and sometimes even private business carried with it – had appeared all too willing to let Hugh use his discretion concerning whom to admit to his presence and when. Much to his own surprise, Hugh had found the King's trust in him rather gratifying. This was surprising, because he generally derived no such feeling as *gratification* from the trust or goodwill of others. As a rule, he valued such things exclusively for the advantages they could bring him. This was probably because he never made much of an effort to invite other men's friendship, and, if a man showed some interest in befriending him, he tended to distrust his motives.

Since he could rarely convince himself that other people's goodwill was genuine, he never really felt called upon to reciprocate friendship. The notion that one could value such things as another man's trust or goodwill just for the sort of things that they were had, until now, seemed to him one of those beautiful fantasies weaker people talked themselves into believing, to make their lives tolerable. That he should now find such obvious pleasure in the King's amiability and apparent confidence in him, therefore, was mildly disconcerting.

It was unexpected, too, not only that they had come to such an excellent understanding over the matter of Hugh having strict control over who had access to the chamber, but also, more generally, that King and Chamberlain should now be getting along quite so swimmingly. Despite the fact that his father, the Elder Despenser, had been one of the King's most faithful men since King Edward's accession a decade or so before, the King had always kept his distance from the Younger Despenser until now. This, Hugh supposed, was probably due to him distrusting Hugh's closeness with his deceased uncle, the Earl of Warwick.

Hugh himself could hardly see why his political apprenticeship – for this is how he had conceived of his relationship with Warwick, whom he had never cared for personally – should be held against him. Not that the King had ever ill-used Hugh, or even made it quite obvious that he was suspicious of him. But in a man that could be so excessively demonstrative and so given to rewarding those who pleased him in a manner out of all proportion to their desert, the sparseness and sobriety of the King's dealings with Hugh had been eloquent enough. Proud as Hugh was, his former impression that the King at worst disliked him and at best cared little for him had the effect of suppressing, at the time, any feeling he might otherwise have conceived for King Edward. No sooner had he been appointed Chamberlain, however, than all the former distance and coolness between them had dissipated. They had grown on each other without any effort at all (which was a good thing, for Hugh never tried very hard to get along with anyone).

It helped that Hugh felt powerfully attracted to the King physically – something that, curiously, until recently he'd scarcely been aware of. It must have had something to do with sharing the same living quarters with the King, and, hence, seeing his Royal body in more or less every degree of dress and undress. Hugh also flattered himself that the drawing power the King had over him was not entirely unrequited. Hugh may not have been as dashing as Lord Audley, and certainly not as statuesque as the late Lord Gaveston, but an awareness of his own attractiveness was an integral part of his sense of self-worth. Whether other people could or couldn't appreciate this attractiveness (he suspected most couldn't) generally mattered little. But he knew his own looks had a very definite appeal, and he had reason to suspect the King may belong to the discerning minority that was not altogether insensitive to it.

It would of course be deliciously ironic if he and the King were going to grow as intimate as the King had been with his favourites of yore. The magnates of the Realm had appointed Hugh Chamberlain precisely because he was seen as a safe choice: someone the King was hardly enthused by, and someone whose past political allegiances – via the Earl of Warwick – suggested a lack of antagonism, and possibly even some sympathy, towards Lancaster. Well, if Hugh could fill the space vacated by Lord Audley, Lord Damory, and Lord Montacute, the magnates would all be in for a shock. That would be reason enough for Hugh and the King to become attached to each other. More importantly, their attachment would have the effect of facilitating the fulfilment of Hugh's ambitions.

His own father, the Elder Despenser, had not been very subtle about it: 'The King is a lover of men, son,' he had told him. 'If you have any ambition, you may as well consider...' He hadn't quite completed the sentence, but Hugh had caught his drift. Had he been disgusted by his father's implication that he should offer his body for political and material rewards? Not particularly. Though, perhaps, he hadn't felt aggravated simply because his father had stopped short of turning his implied suggestion into an express expectation. In any case, if his father had implied that Hugh should offer himself to the King, at least he was not advising Hugh to sell himself to someone he believed to be a worthless man: his father's unflinching loyalty to King Edward was obviously based in mutual respect.

Not that any of it mattered a whit, now: for, as it happened, Hugh's growing acquaintance with the King had only stoked the desire that had been kindled by their physical proximity. Hugh needed no particular inducement to offer himself to commune bodily with the King – the pull was already there in the form of a likeable, tall, flaxen-haired man of athletic build, reasonably well-endowed, and only a few years his senior.

Beyond the King's commanding looks, Hugh felt increasingly drawn to Edward's fervour – a trait so lacking in himself, always so impassive and calculating; or that's how Hugh saw himself. 'Fervour' was the best word Hugh had found for describing that quality of the King's which made him express his fondness for those he liked in such a way that left no doubt. It must be rather gratifying to be at the receiving end of so much ardour. Hugh also admired the King's doggedness, his refusal to bow to the demands of the magnates, to compromise other than purely for the sake of form. He respected the King for the grudge he nursed towards his enemies and for his failure to be very successful at dissimulating it.

In short, there was no need for Hugh – even had he been so inclined – to agonise about the ethics of exchanging his body for material and political gain. His body, he was readily willing to give for free – the prospect of lovemaking with the King was appealing enough as to make its fulfilment appear its own reward. If the King's intimacy also won him power and wealth – for which, admittedly, Hugh also felt an intense desire – he was inclined to look upon it as no more than an accident of fortune.

But it was unlike Hugh to spend time rationalising to himself the motives that moved him, let alone talk himself into believing in their purity. What had gotten into him? Should he be worried? No, there was no real cause for concern. He could force himself out of this infatuation if necessary. In the meantime, the novelty of the feeling made rather for a pleasant change. It might well have been the first time that Hugh had conceded that sort of power over himself to anyone – the power to make him mindful of whether or not he 'deserved' (what an absurd word) another man's regard. But he would never let that distract him from what had always been his ambitions. He would see to that.

Meanwhile… Would it be premature, he wondered, to make a pass at the King now? Or should he wait for the actual departure of Lord Audley?

+

HE WAS ABOUT to leave the chamber in search of the King when a groom entered it.

'Do you know where the King is?' asked Hugh.

'Taking a bath.'

Hugh left the room. In the corridor he conveniently bumped into the valet in charge of preparing the King's baths. Hugh decided to follow him from a distance, the embryo of a plan forming in his mind as he did so. The valet directed his steps towards the small storeroom where linen was kept, at the end of the long corridor. He pushed the door open and entered the room. Enough light came through the open door to enable him to reach for the shelves where the clean towels were laid in neat piles. No sooner had he stretched his arm to do so, however, than the door behind him creaked and shut, the latch clicking into place.

'Very amusing. Come on, let me out! The King needs his towels!'

Oh, bother. Hugh opened the door again, smiled benevolently at the bewildered valet, snatched the clean towel from his hand, and shut the door in his face. Click, went the latch. The heavy oak of the door satisfyingly muffled the valet's fresh torrent of protests.

Hugh returned to the King's chamber. There, he instructed the grooms to find the valet in charge of preparing the King's baths, who had mysteriously disappeared. They should inform him that the King would no longer require his services today. He then made for the room where the King always had his baths. The guards, of course, let him through without question, for, as the King's Chamberlain, *he and he alone* (what a satisfying turn of phrase) had unrestricted access to the King's person – though he may have never made use of this privilege quite so boldly before. Hugh opened the door without knocking and shut it behind him.

The King was lying in the tub – a long and thin container crafted by the Royal cooper out of oaken planks. He was giving his back to the door Hugh had just come through. The wave and usual flaxen colour had disappeared from his dripping hair; wet, it had turned straight and honeyed. Four tall wrought-iron candelabra surrounded the tub; the glow from the beeswax candles' flames showed off the steam rising from the surface of the water.

'Here you are.' The King spoke without turning. 'What took you so long?'

'Your Grace.'

The King turned at the unexpected sound of his Chamberlain's voice.

'Your valet had an accident, I'm afraid – nothing serious.'

'Lord Despenser?'

'Yes, Your Grace. I thought that in your valet's absence, you could do with someone else assisting you with your bath. I thought, too, that I'd do as well as anyone else.'

A grin slowly formed on the King's face. 'Did you, now, Lord Despenser? And I suppose the accident that befell my valet has nothing whatsoever to do with you?'

'Nothing at all, except for the fact that I believe I may be the only one knowing he managed to lock himself inside a pantry, Your Grace. Would you like me to let him out?'

'I think we may give him the afternoon off.'

'That was just my thinking, Your Grace. We understand each other so well.'

'And perhaps later you will think of a suitable gift to make it up to him.'

'If that's your wish, Your Grace.'

They regarded each other in silence for a while. Then Hugh walked around the bath tub until he was facing the King. With slow deliberation, he removed first his tunic and then his shirt, dropping them on the floor.

'I take it you're quite happy for me to proceed, Your Grace?'

'You're not generally known for being the kind of man who stops and asks for permission, Lord Despenser. Am I wrong?'

Hugh shrugged. 'But you are King, after all.'

'Pull those accursed hose down, Lord Despenser.'

'Only too glad to do your bidding, Your Grace.'

+

THE YOUNGER DESPENSER unsheathed his legs. Edward was well-acquainted with their shape. Hoses were tight-fitting garments that left little to the imagination, and Despenser's thighs had caught Edward's eye before. A touch too slim, perhaps, for Hugh's well-developed upper body, but athletic; and the overall impression, if one regarded the Chamberlain's body as a whole, was very agreeable, rather resembling a crossbow.

'I knew it,' Edward said.

'Your Grace?'

'Your eyebrows gave you away.'

Despenser arched them. 'My eyebrows?'

'I like the way your eyebrows are so light in colour that they're barely visible against your fair complexion, Lord Despenser. It suits you. But what I mean is that you're ginger all over. From your head, through your eyebrows, and down...well, to your toes.' Edward smiled.

Despenser looked down at his pubic hair. He looked up again at

Edward's face and grinned. Pivoting on his heels so as to give his back to Edward, he grabbed his buttocks and spread them apart, revealing more tangerine-coloured down softening the crack between them. Edward roared with laughter.

Despenser turned around and raised one of the corners of his mouth in a half-smile. 'Have you really been wondering about the colour of my –'

'You must have noticed I've grown somewhat partial to you, Sir Hugh. But come closer, I'm not done inspecting you yet.'

Despenser walked up to him. Edward took the Chamberlain's prick, still soft, in the palm of his hand. It started hardening under both their eyes. Edward kissed the vein that, throbbing, ran down its length.

'Sir Hugh, the water is still warm.'

Despenser lifted his foot to step into the tub but halted mid-motion. He opened his mouth as if to speak, then thought better of it and decided to return his foot on the floor.

Squaring his shoulders, he said, 'You're too large for your own good, Your Grace. Or mine.'

'Too large?'

'There isn't any room in the tub for both of us.'

Edward looked down the length of his body, his knees sticking out of the water. 'You may be right, Sir Hugh.'

Despenser grinned. 'But I needn't really come into the tub at all, Your Grace.'

He raised one leg again and straddled the bath tub like a horse, facing Edward. Then, keeping his legs flexed, he worked his way up until his crotch was a few inches from Edward's face. Edward briefly considered if he should put the Chamberlain in his proper place – at the receiving end of the King's cock, that was. But why spoil a perfect moment?

Sir Hugh's prick was chunkier than Piers', not as exquisite in colouring, slightly leaning to the left, and absurdly enticing – mouth-watering, for that matter – in its own right. Edward wrapped his lips around it, and when, eventually, the warm liquid came pouring out on his tongue, gush upon luscious gush, he spent himself in the tepid bathwater.

Twenty-Seven

HOW TO LOSE A FRIEND

About twenty months later, 19 June 1320.

FINALLY, THOUGHT ISABELLA as she stepped onboard the ship to France, where Edward, as Count of Ponthieu and Duke of Aquitaine, would pay liege homage to the new French King, her brother Philip. Business and a number of contretemps had delayed their departure by months. It was good, finally, to be going back home. She still instinctively thought of France as home. Would that ever change? There was a time when she almost did think of England as home – when everything was going well. But now...all seemed different now.

Of course, to speak truthfully, things had never been going really well in the Kingdom of which, over a decade ago, she had become Queen. The Scottish threat may have, in recent years, gone from bad to worse (last year's failed attempt to recapture Berwick made this all too apparent); but it had always been quite bad to begin with. As to internal troubles, if anything could be singled out as the defining feature of her husband's reign, it was the opposition he had been facing from the English magnates from more or less the first day he had sat upon the throne.

Even so, there had been a time when it had seemed both possible and worthwhile to actively resist all of this, to outwit their enemies. For a long time, she had felt her husband's friends were *her* friends, and his enemies just as much *her* enemies. Why, while the Earl of Cornwall had been alive, fighting and outmanoeuvring their antagonists had even felt galvanising. She had never doubted the uniqueness of the Earl of Cornwall's bond with the King: she had found herself naturally ascribing to it a higher-order value. It had never seriously occurred to her that their bond had not been worth fighting for, or that other concerns might have had a legitimate claim to be weighed against it.

But all that had changed since the Earl's death eight years ago. What was the point of all the strife, now that the reason for it – he whose existence vindicated all the risk and effort in antagonising a whole Realm – had ceased to be? Not that her husband seemed to have much of a choice, she supposed. Some of the magnates refused to be pacified, even when the King did make genuine efforts in that direction. Didn't her uncle Lancaster, for one, prove once again his treachery, first by agreeing to join the campaign to free Berwick and then by withdrawing his forces only a few days into the conflict?

Indeed, there were rumours that it had been Lancaster himself who had revealed to the Scots the whereabouts of her supposedly 'safe' haven during the siege of Berwick. She had managed to escape just in time to York – and then made her way to Nottingham – but it had been a close call. It was rumoured that Lancaster was paid a fair sum by the Scots to give her location away, as well as, more generally, to impede the English attack on Berwick. Whether or not this was true, she didn't doubt that he was entirely capable of using her for political gain.

The same was also true, however, of the very man whom Lancaster himself charged with imperilling her safety during the siege of Berwick – namely, the Younger Despenser. To say that she had failed to warm to her husband's new favourite was understating the case. The Younger Despenser's political alliances had always been extremely suspect – even if, with Lancaster dead-set against him now, the picture seemed to her to have simplified a little. But that was not the root of her concern: after all, there was little evidence to make her doubt that the Younger Despenser was loyal to her husband.

It was Despenser's ambition and ruthlessness that she mistrusted, not his loyalty. Hugh Despenser the Younger wouldn't stop at anything to increase his own power and wealth: certainly not at driving her husband away from her, or even *against* her, if he should find that serviceable to his goals. And if Lord Despenser suspected her intense dislike for him – she had scarcely tried to disguise it – he might well decide that ridding himself of her would simplify his own position vis-à-vis the King, over whom she still retained *some* degree of influence. How could she make sure to guard her own interests and those of her children?

She really couldn't see what Edward saw in the man. For herself, she found him positively repellent. There was something wrong, indecent, about the way he looked. His missing eyebrows...they weren't really missing, but their colour was such a pale reddish blond that it blended with the colour of his skin and gave him a vaguely demonic look. How could her husband consider him a worthy replacement for the Earl of Cornwall?

She had not minded her husband's attachment to Lord Damory – he had always seemed to her honourable and sensible and devoted. Her husband's desire to advance the interests of such a man and to reward him was perfectly understandable – to her, if not to Lancaster and his allies. Yet she feared Damory's influence on the King was declining no less visibly than her own, just at the same time as the Younger Despenser was becoming the apple of her husband's eye. Audley and Montacute, who had left Court at about the same time as Damory, in the end had seemed fairly harmless. Despenser, on the other hand, appeared everything but harmless, and she feared his sway over the King was much greater than that of the others had ever been. What were the Earls and barons thinking when they chose him for the post of Chamberlain?

The Younger Despenser's bad influence on the King had already started to make itself seen. Indeed, if he didn't enjoy the King's unqualified support, how could Despenser have succeeded in making Lady Margaret and Audley agree, only last month, to swap their lordship over Gwynllwg in Wales with the less valuable manors Despenser had offered in exchange for it? It was very aggravating to think that, if the King carried on like that, he – and *she* –

would soon have to endure the enmity of the whole Realm once again. And this time, not on account of a bond in the name of which such endurance was called for, but because of her husband's desire to elevate a man altogether unworthy of his friendship.

Besides, although she had no proof that Lord Despenser had plotted with the Scottish enemy against her during the siege of Berwick, the question remained: would her husband have been so oblivious to the need to properly guarantee her safety if his attention hadn't been monopolised by his new favourite? The Earl of Cornwall wouldn't have allowed the King to neglect the Queen's safety in so cavalier a fashion, she was sure. If she felt resentful – and she did – she believed she was perfectly justified.

+

EDWARD SETTLED ON the vessel's deck. He cast a glance towards Isabella. She looked distracted by her own thoughts. Later, he would have to ask her if anything was the matter – in the past, a trip to France had always lifted her spirits. He looked out to the water. Perhaps it had been a blessing in disguise that the trip had been postponed until now, for the weather was perfect for sailing. Why, the grey waters of the Channel looked almost blue today.

On this day eight years ago, Perrot, your life was taken from you – and from mine own. This voyage across the Channel reminds me of our last few days together – tossed around on a small fishing boat in the German Sea, trying to reach the illusory safety of Scarborough Castle.... I was such a fool. I should've never left you there, nor should I have trusted the honour of the Earls. For a long time, I felt as if I have only half-lived since that fated day. I know it would have been the same for you Piers, if I had died prematurely and left you to toil behind.

And yet, although I hardly thought it possible, that feeling of being unable to savour the intensity of life (except for the intensity of its grief) vanished about eighteen months ago. That's when Sir Hugh Despenser the Younger came into my life – I mean, when he came into it in earnest, Perrot. Who knew I would know such happiness again? With Hugh by my side, I have felt if not the bliss that your companionship regaled me, at least more content than I could ever hope to be since this day eight years ago.

I wonder what you'd make of the Younger Despenser if you were to see him today. We never had much time for him, did we? He has changed, I think – or have I? Do I now see him with different eyes? I find him unaccountably attractive, more so than I've ever found anyone but you. Yet, you could hardly be more different. His green eyes are quite bewitching: I never noticed them before, yet presumably they are the same pair of eyes he has always worn. But it's the uniform, very pale copper of his hair that delights me most. It has an otherworldly quality…

I don't ask you, Piers, whether you feel that I'm betraying you by falling in love with Hugh. In the beginning, I did ask myself that. But even then, there was something contrived about my doubts. It's as if I felt the need to go through the motions of them, while realising all along that knowing I am happy is what would make you happy, and that nothing in my feelings for Hugh dents what I still hold most sacred: my love for you. What I do wonder, sometimes, is whether, had our places been reversed, you could have fallen in love with Hugh, and he with you. Most likely you wouldn't have; but the thought that you might have is very dear to me.

+

8 July 1320. Amiens, France.

SHE PUT DOWN the pewter cup, and an attendant readily refilled it. She and Edward, together with their following, were enjoying a banquet complete with minstrels prior to their return to England in two weeks' time. Garlands festooned the roof of the tent pavilion. The warm weather had made the flowers in them go limp, but the intense blue of the cornflowers remained effective, and it was lovely to dine with the dog roses shedding their petals like rain.

Damory asked, 'Do we have anything in England to compare with the Cathedral in Amiens, Your Grace?'

Isabella was impressed: he really was no longer the taciturn knight of yore. Why, he could even initiate conversation now.

'I think we have plenty that outdo it in the feeling of intimacy they provide, Lord Damory,' Edward answered. 'But none I daresay that compares to its magnificence. We English don't do magnificence. Or we do, but we are not distinguished by it.'

Lord Gaveston: that was *his* turn of phrase, this *his* line of thought. It was touching to hear Edward speak in Gaveston's voice, even after – how long had it been, eight years? She doubted that eight years from now she would be able to think with similar fondness about Despenser's influence on Edward.

'I don't know what all the fuss is about,' said the Younger Despenser, and Isabella guessed the tone of tedium in his voice was pure affectation. 'God only knows why anyone thought it a good idea to build the Cathedral on quite such a large scale. It pains me to think of how much money it must have cost and how much better it could have been spent.'

'Spent on what, for example?' asked Damory.

'A *palace*, for example. If God resides in all the chapels and churches that were ever built for Him, His essence must be spread so thinly that it is pure folly to think He should need any more room than the smallest fraction of each of those sacred buildings. Kings and Lords have much greater use for palaces than God does for churches, let alone vastly outsized cathedrals.'

Though she had seen him trying to conceal the fact, she could tell Edward was amused by his Chamberlain's blasphemy. *How disloyal, dear husband.* Despenser was only saying this to irritate poor Lord Damory. The two men had not been getting along well during their French sojourn with the King – and no wonder, for they were as different as day from night. Edward had told her a couple of times that he was reconsidering the wisdom of inviting Damory alongside Despenser.

'In any case,' said Damory, 'the Cathedral made a wonderfully uplifting setting for the King's payment of liege homage to King Philip. It was truly beautiful, Your Grace.'

Lord Damory was holding his own. Good.

'*Beautiful*?' said Despenser. 'I don't see that at all. Surely, aesthetic imperatives required a reversion of roles. King Edward is far handsomer than his brother-in-law, and the latter infinitely fitter to kneel before him. In fact, the truly beautiful scene was not the payment of liege homage in the Cathedral, but our King's *refusal*, a few days later, to pay the French King the oath of personal fealty the latter had the audacity to demand. That's destined to remain the highlight of this trip. Though, if it had been up to me, I would have reinforced the point by producing my cock out of my hose and pissing all over that Italian brocade robe that the King of France was so ostentatiously displaying for the occasion.'

'Now, now,' Edward said amidst general laughter. 'You forget, it's my wife's brother you're talking about.'

Despenser raised a hand over the crown of his head as if to sprinkle ashes on it – a sign of contrition. Of course, she didn't acknowledge this, just as she hadn't acknowledged his remark about her brother. She had always been good at keeping an even countenance in the face of provocations. It helped that, sitting as she and the Chamberlain did at either side of Edward, their eyes did not have to meet. Not that she felt particularly outraged: the Chamberlain's spewing profanities about her family was the least of her problems with the Younger Despenser. How very deluded Edward was if he failed to realise this.

'Be that as it may,' said Despenser, turning to Edward – and, she presumed – looking straight into his eyes, 'when you put the King of France in his place, you were magnificent, Your Grace.'

Isabella imagined that this public display of a special rapport between the King and Despenser irked Damory no less than her. And unlike her, Damory – poor thing – was sitting in full view of the exchange.

Damory said, 'Yes, you surprised us all, Your Grace.'

Edward turned towards him, for the first time, as far as Isabella could remember, with displeasure. '*Surprised*, Lord Damory? Did you expect me to grovel in submission before the French King?'

'That's not what I meant –'

'Lord Damory,' Despenser said, 'if the best way you can find of employing your newly discovered garrulity is by abusing the King's good graces, you will do us all a favour if you go back to being the tongue-tied knight of yore. *I* certainly liked you better then.'

She saw Edward put a hand on Despenser's forearm, as if to stay him. But the Chamberlain ignored him.

'The King's regard for you is primarily based, so he tells me, on the fact that you're incapable of dissimulation, Lord Damory. I hope the King is wrong on this point, for the views you've just expressed do not do you any credit. You shall apologise to the King at once.'

She hoped Edward would disclaim any need for apologies, but he didn't. Wine – which had been liberally consumed – could make her husband more sensitive to real or imagined insults than when he was sober.

'Of course,' said Lord Damory at last. 'My apologies, Your Grace.'

Lord Damory must be angry at the King for not rising in his defence: she detected a tinge of insincerity in his voice. It hadn't been lost on Edward, either, and she could tell he was saddened. He had never known Damory to be anything other than perfectly honest, and discovering him untrue, even if only a little, even if only once, would be a blow.

But really, Edward had only himself to blame. Lord Damory was a good man: how could her husband not see what Despenser was up to? Damory, she was sure, was simply guilty of not choosing his words carefully. Perhaps, when speaking of being surprised, he had been thinking less of Edward's refusal to pay personal fealty to the French King than about the present accord between Edward and the Younger Despenser. And who could blame him? It was all she could do to bear the spectacle of Edward brushing off, as he was doing right now, the dog rose petals from Despenser's head. And when the Chamberlain's rust-coloured hair got caught in the eagle claws the goldsmith had modelled to hold the pearl on one of Edward's rings, she could have cried at all their fussing.

+

HUGH PASSED HIS fingers through his hair, dishevelled by Edward, and wondered what the look on the Queen's face must be right now. *Sour as a green pomegranate, probably; and with some justification, too.* Sitting as each of them did on Edward's side, he had no way of knowing for sure.

As to any other third parties witnessing his argument with Lord Damory, they were sure to assume that his words were solely calculated to undermine the King's regard for the man. Despite no longer being admitted at Court, Damory was widely perceived to remain his main rival for the King's regard: everyone expected Hugh to feel threatened by him. It was absurd, of course. As if he had anything to fear from Damory! The man was below his notice.

He dropped a strawberry into his mouth and for a moment the startlingly intense flavour eclipsed all else. 'Hautbois strawberries', Edward had told him when they were brought to the table. It was more than a little irksome that the French should enjoy delicacies virtually unknown in England.

Well, let them believe what they will. If they thought his defence of the King was a ploy to alienate Damory from Edward's affections, he would do precisely nothing to dispel that misconception. He could engage in all manner of cheap tactics to discredit his antagonists, if necessary. But on this occasion, he had been genuinely incensed on the King's behalf, and his reprimand of Damory gushed out of his mouth of its own accord – he had little time to think before he caught himself uttering it. It was just as well that no one but the King would ever know this. For one thing, he didn't care for people to realise that he had his own Achilles' heel (he regarded his love for Edward as a weakness, even if it was one he now had no intention to eschew). Besides, the fact that he should be thought generally incapable of noble feelings, somehow made his own love for Edward all the more precious to him.

He wondered if he would be able to procure some plants of hautbois strawberries for his wife Eleanor before they left for England.

Twenty-Eight

UNREST

Late February 1321. Westminster.

HUGH SHARPENED A quill to write a letter as he sat at Edward's table. The King paced the length of the room. It put Hugh in mind of the wild animals Edward used to keep at Langley. He had seen them, many years ago, when they were both little more than children. At the time, Edward used to take virtually no notice of him at all. How far they had come since then…

Edward stopped walking and asked, 'Why does this keep happening?'

Hugh looked up. '"This" being?'

'Why do I always end up with half the Kingdom against me? Why must they always hate everyone I love?'

'You take too much of the credit for yourself.' Hugh put his quill down. The thought that the King might start sobbing right there before him, and on account of him at that, was mildly terrifying. 'It's not as if anyone *liked* me before you started loving me, you know.'

'But at least they did not hate you…. You were made Chamberlain precisely because none of the magnates objected to you!'

'Or because they all did. Since they couldn't agree on someone universally liked, they settled on Sir Hugh Despenser the Younger, who was – and remains – universally disliked.' Hugh shrugged. 'No doubt they counted on your dislike for me too. Fortunately for me, they miscalculated. They must still be wondering at the oddity of it all – the improbability of our match. I certainly do.'

Edward sat down on a chair. 'Do you?'

'Yes, every day. Which shows I'm guilty of not giving my King enough credit for his impeccable taste.' Hugh smiled.

Edward sighed. 'Did I make a mistake ordering my officials to take possession of the Gower peninsula? I wonder if the latest insurrection could have been avoided if I hadn't.'

'Do you regret the order?'

'Not to the extent that it benefits you. But I regret it if it brings you harm.'

'Your intention in making the order was to benefit me, not harm me. Let that be enough. You wanted me to have Gower. Or, rather, you knew I wanted badly to have it, and you wanted to please me. You can't blame yourself for wanting to make me happy – and having Gower will certainly make me happy, in the event you have started having doubts about it.'

Hugh dragged his chair across the floor and sat in front of Edward; leaning forward, he placed his hands on the King's knees.

'Besides, as the King you could hardly have stood watching when Gower was unlawfully appropriated by Lord Mowbray. You *had* to intervene. Mowbray had no greater claim to it than the rest of us to whom his father-in-law promised to sell it. The Earl of Hereford is even rumoured to have paid Lord Braose a consideration towards the land. I mean, if anyone was supposed to have it, I suppose it was he.'

He patted Edward's thigh and leant back in his chair.

'Which should make Hereford mad at Lord Mowbray and delighted to see me taking Gower from him. But he's not: Hereford and Mowbray are on the same side – the Marchers' side – and *against* me, the King.'

'Because, like the other Lords of the Welsh Marches, Hereford realises that you took Gower with the intention of eventually giving it to *me*! My point is that even if your desire had not been to give it to me, you might well have concluded that it was reasonable to take a potentially dangerous bone of contention into Royal hands. So, it's pointless to agonise about whether seizing it for my benefit was a mistake.'

Edward looked doubtful and sighed. It hadn't worked.

'Very well then,' said Hugh, '*perhaps* you wouldn't have bothered taking Gower from Lord Mowbray if you hadn't wanted to give it to me. But, what's done is done. At least now you have a clearer idea of who exactly you can trust. And of those you shouldn't.'

Hugh left his chair and sat down straddling Edward's thighs, facing him.

'You mean, specifically, Lord Damory and Lord Audley, don't you, Hugh?'

Hugh put his hands on Edward's shoulders. 'Look, Edward, I once fucked Audley – metaphorically speaking – when I got Newport out of him in exchange for manors of lesser value. And you let me do it. Given half the opportunity, at one point I wouldn't have minded literally fucking him, either. I certainly don't begrudge you the fact that you did. But it's an understatement to say that I never liked either him or Damory much. Can you blame me? How could I like them, when I saw them as rivals for your favour?'

'Rivals? I thought you always claimed they were below your notice!'

That was true, Hugh supposed. He had claimed that. At one point he may have believed it, too. Well, just because he was uncommonly clear-minded didn't mean he was entirely immune from self-deception.

Edward sighed again. Hugh stood and went to lie down on Edward's bed, face up. He twined his hands behind his head.

Edward said, 'Lord Damory's betrayal pains me very much. I'd never have expected it of him.'

'Why not? He is as interested in Gower as Audley or any of the rest of us who have lordships in the Welsh Marches.'

'Well, if he is, then my favours have corrupted him. I'm allowed to regret that. In any case, even if he wanted Gower, do you think that was sufficient justification for turning against me, his King, and close friend? I've known Lord Damory, and showed him favour, for years – longer than I have loved you. I can't believe he could push all that to one side just because he wanted Gower. He has changed indeed.'

'But Edward, the dispute over Gower simply gave him an excuse.'

'An excuse?'

'A pretext to manifest the change which had already been wrought in his feelings towards you. He wrote you off as his friend months ago, ever since Amiens. Wasn't it obvious? I may be partly to blame. Indeed, I'm entirely to blame. Except that I don't blame myself. There wasn't enough room for both Lord Damory and I by your side. It's that simple.'

'But why couldn't I have kept Lord Damory as a friend, Hugh? He was never more than that.'

'No reason. Some feelings – especially mine, no doubt – have no reason.' He propped himself on his elbows and looked at the King, who was standing by the table. 'I hated Damory – I hate him still. My disliking him is the counterpoint of my love for you. I need no reason to dislike Damory, just as I need none to love you. I think I shall always hate everyone you love – you may as well know it. And eventually I should probably get rid of them one way or another. So you see, Damory did all of us a favour by turning against you. He has simplified things, quite considerably.'

Edward sighed. 'But if you had been in his shoes, *you* wouldn't have betrayed me. I know you couldn't have. Lord Damory's behaviour remains completely inexplicable –'

'You clearly don't know me very well at all, Edward! *Of course* I'd have betrayed you. Your loving another is just what would have turned me against you. Your allowing me to be elbowed out by another – I'd *never* forgive you that! I respect Lord Damory for taking sides against you, even as I go on hating him. I *shall* turn against you the moment you do fall in love with another. Make no mistake about it.'

Edward shook his head. 'Hugh…'

He walked over to the immense bed and embraced his lover. Hugh's body felt stiff in his arms.

He said, 'I'll never love any other living man as well as you. This I can promise you.'

Don't make promises you can't keep, Edward. I am many things, but lovable is not one of them. One day, you'll find out and give me up.

+

1321, August's second quarter. London.

EDWARD HAD DISMISSED the Earls of Surrey, Richmond, and Arundel, who, together with Pembroke, had relayed his enemies' demands. He still couldn't bring himself entirely to trust Surrey and Arundel. Surrey's complicity in Piers' capture counted against him, as did Arundel's participation in Piers' execution, although Edward had pardoned him. And Richmond had always struck him – he always struck everyone – as too indecisive, lacking in conviction. In the Despensers' absence, there was only one man he could fully trust: Pembroke.

Only Pembroke and the Queen were left in the room with him now. And Pembroke was advising that he should bow to the Marchers' requests. Earlier, he had said they were less requests than demands. They *demanded* that he exile both Despensers and that he disinherit them – permanently. They threatened to set fire to the City if he didn't. And they threatened to depose him.

Edward banged his fist on the table, sending the chess set rattling. 'Savages and traitors! And you expect me to submit, Pembroke? I struggle to see how you can do so with a straight face!'

'Your Grace –'

'No, Pembroke, don't Your-Grace me! In the spring, all my attempts to conciliate the Marchers at Gloucester were met with a complete and stubborn lack of cooperation. Should I remind you what Hereford's condition was before he would agree to come to me, the King, and resolve our dispute? He – my own brother-in-law, whom I should've left to rot in captivity, when the Scots did me the favour of seizing him – demanded that I should hand over the Younger Despenser to Lancaster. *Lancaster,* of all people, the very traitor who already murdered the man dearest to my heart. *Lancaster*, the very man who's been orchestrating and fuelling this rebellion from behind the scenes. How could I have acceded to that demand, knowing that I would be consigning Lord Despenser to certain death? Then, when I summoned the Marchers to Parliament in London, so that we could work with the other magnates to address their grievances, what do they do? They deliberately insult me by arriving two weeks late, meanwhile looting and ransacking everything on their way to London – *everything*, Pembroke, not just the manors and lands of the Despensers, against whom alone they allege to have grievances. And now, they descend upon the city *in arms*, forcing their way into it, threatening the lives of the burghers and declaring their intention to strip me of my Kingship! Would you agree this is an accurate account of the situation, Pembroke?'

'Yes, Your Grace, it is,' said Pembroke, although Edward suspected what Pembroke thought, but left unsaid: that his unconditional support of the Younger Despenser was the root cause of all these ills.

'Then what part of the account, pray, would justify my taking the course of action you recommend?'

'None of it, Your Grace. But the epilogue to the events you have just narrated – the epilogue that is sure to follow if you do not do as the rebels ask – *forces* you to accept their terms. You won't be able to save either the Despensers or your Kingship if you don't.'

Edward clenched his jaw. 'That remains to be seen.'

Pembroke didn't sigh, or otherwise betray any sign of impatience.

Holding Edward's gaze, he said, 'As it is, I believe the Marchers are strong enough to defeat us, Your Grace. If I'm wrong, they're certainly strong enough to keep your men engaged until Lancaster sends the rebels reinforcements. We wouldn't stand a chance against the joint forces of the Marchers and Lancaster. These are the harsh realities. They are a reminder, Your Grace, of the need for a King to always find a way of governing with the consent of the magnates – not against them.'

Edward turned away. 'And how am I meant to do that? The moment I pacify one, I have alienated the next. Over and over again, the magnates have proven that they only know unity and accord when they are determined to get rid of the best among them! They make a united front when their intent is to weed out excellence from their midst. Once they have succeeded in doing that, their squabbles start anew, and it's impossible for me to govern with the consent of one, because by doing so, I estrange another. I am weary of it, Pembroke. More so than you can imagine. Governing by consent is impossible in this country – only brute force will do.'

As Edward was speaking, Pembroke had moved around him, quietly but pointedly, so that now they faced each other again. Donning his characteristic black velvet, the Earl gave Edward the feeling of a shadow following him around like a bad conscience.

'Even if you are inclined to take that view, Your Grace, brute force is just what eludes us now.' Aloof, Roman-nosed and impassive, Pembroke continued to stare right into his eyes. 'We do not have it – nowhere near to the same degree as our opponents.'

Isabella – until now sitting in her chair so quietly that Edward had almost forgotten her presence – stood, walked up to the King, kneeled before him, and joined her hands as a suppliant.

'Please, Edward, I beg you. Do you want to see us all imprisoned and slaughtered? Your sons, me – even the baby daughter I have just given birth to? To deny a future to your Royal line? To be deposed and to see my accursed uncle fill the power void? To deliver the country on a silver platter into *his* hands? *Lancaster's* hands?'

Tears started streaming down her cheeks. Pembroke helped her to her feet. Tears on the Queen's face: they took Edward by surprise.

'Please don't cry, my Queen,' he said. 'I'll do what I must.'

He couldn't remember the last time he had seen her cry. When Piers had died, perhaps. She was still little more than a child then. The memory of the young Queen, inconsolable over the death of the Earl of Cornwall, was heart-breaking. He sighed. He must protect her, as well as the city and its burghers. He had to send Hugh away. He had to do it, and he could bring himself to do it. It wouldn't be forever. Hugh was the most resourceful man he'd ever known: together, they'd find a way of bringing him back.

Twenty-Nine

VICTORY

WHILE THE ELDER Despenser left England for the Continent, as demanded by the Marchers, his son only pretended to, secretly spending the month of September at sea off the coastal town of Sandwich, in Kent. Edward, using as a cover a pilgrimage to Canterbury with Isabella, arranged to meet him, first on the nearby island of Thanet, a few miles north of Sandwich, and then further north, in Harwich. It was in the backroom of an inn, in the latter port town, that they were now sitting face to face, on wooden benches. The air smelt of burnt wood, burnt food, beer, and, faintly, of vomit.

Commoners' clothes disguised them both. Piers would have looked incongruous in them – his complexion too good, his nails too smooth, his looks too exotic, his manners too refined. Hugh, however, looked perfectly believable. Eminently fuckable too, thought Edward, but they would have to save that for later.

'The main problem hasn't gone away,' said Edward. 'There may no longer be an immediately impending threat, but the Marchers and Lancaster's forces, united, still outnumber those at our disposal four to one.'

'That needn't matter. If we wait for the day when the forces loyal to you match those of your enemies, we shall wait forever. Every day away from where I belong – in the Court, next to you – is one day too much.' Hugh seized Edward's hand. 'And *you* have waited long enough for your revenge. *Ten years* is long enough.'

Edward pressed his lips together. Hugh was right, of course. He lifted his eyes to look into Hugh's own. Without warning, Hugh leant across the table and reached out to pull Edward's face to his, until their mouths joined. Hugh released him, and Edward, sinking back to his seat, caught his breath.

'Hugh,' he whispered.

'Listen to me: we don't need a massive force to subdue our enemies. If Pembroke insists that we do, he's advising you badly. He's allowing his hatred for me to blind his judgement.'

'Pembroke doesn't hate you.'

'*Everyone* hates me, Edward.'

'I love you.'

Edward lifted a hand to Hugh's cheekbone. He twisted one of his lover's coppery locks between his fingers.

'I know you do. It makes things worse. Those who bask in the King's love are hated by all other men. It's envy, Edward. It's human nature. But that's just what we shall exploit.'

Edward put his elbows on the table. 'Go on.'

'The alliance binding our enemies is fragile. Collectively, they don't stand for anything. They all stand *against* me: that's the one thing that unites them. But in many ways, they also stand against one another. Each has grudges, suspicions, petty jealousies – enough to spare for their own allies, too. So we shall strike first at the least popular members of the alliance – those to whose rescue no one or few will come. Then we will drive a wedge between Lancaster and the Marchers.'

Edward drunk some ale, and pondered Hugh's words. 'I suppose Lancaster and the Marchers' alliance is rather an uneasy one. My cousin's possessions and interests have always been in the North, not in the Welsh Marches.'

'Precisely: how far can his commitment to the Marchers' cause really go? He hates some of the Marchers almost as much as me.'

'Lord Damory and Lord Audley, you mean.'

'Of course. Your former favourites. He detests them precisely on that account.'

The idea that his cousin would conceive a hatred for the men he loved, just because he loved them – albeit no news to Edward – still had the power to pain him.

'Damory's very name,' Hugh said, 'was anathema to him until recently. And Lancaster's not smart enough to let bygones be bygones. If we put pressure on the bonds that keep the anti-royalist alliance together... Before we know, they'll give.' Hugh snapped his fingers.

'But how?'

'You must secure the support of the magnates that have remained faithful to you –Pembroke, Surrey, Kent, Arundel. But once they have pledged their support, it will be necessary to move very decisively. If we do, Lancaster will probably lose his nerve. Despite the matchless army at his command, when have you known him to actually seek a confrontation?'

'Yes. He didn't join in the siege of Stirling, and he left Berwick only a few days into the siege. Nor did he accompany the Marchers south when they broke into London in August.'

'Exactly. Lancaster has little appetite for battle.'

'We are alike in that.'

'You are cousins. But I saw you fight at Bannockburn, Edward.'

'I *lost* at Bannockburn. Quite spectacularly.' Edward looked down. He felt his whole face flush.

Hugh's hand reached out to cover his. 'You may have, but you're no coward. You fought like a lion.'

Edward kept looking at the table. He pressed a finger in the dents of the wood. 'Do you think Lancaster is? A coward?'

Hugh downed his cup of ale and brushed his lips with the back of his hand. 'I think that an army of the Royalist Earls making a compact front with the King's forces will startle him. And if we put our men between him and his allies – if we manage to cut him off from the Marchers' forces in the West and South, I somehow doubt that his northern neighbours will come to his rescue.'

'Going by the same principle that jealousy is part of human nature, you mean?'

'Yes. The most powerful man in the North is bound to be resented by the other northern Lords.'

Edward smiled. 'As much for that fact as for his general vileness, I should think.'

'And once they feel cornered, even Lancaster's retainers may start deserting him. The weaker he becomes, the more defections he will suffer…'

'And we'll win, Hugh!' Edward struck the tabletop with his fist.

'I think so. Of course, there's no guarantee that any of it will work.'

No, there wasn't. But it didn't matter, did it? It must be now or never. Hugh was right. Ten years was long enough.

+

THE NEXT TIME Edward met Hugh, it was at the seafront fortress of Portchester Castle, where the King spent over a week before the middle of October.

'Do you have news of my father?' asked Hugh, sitting down on the flint floor in one of the semi-circular towers evenly spaced out along the walls of the fortress.

They had been doing a round of the outer bailey; the sun was out and, even this late in the year, it might have warmed them, without the fierce wind that brought the scent of the sea.

Edward shook his head and sat down next to him.

'I wonder if he has forgiven me.' Hugh smiled, a little sadly. 'He blames me for his exile. Not altogether unjustly, I suppose.'

'He's always been faithful to the Crown and to me. This must be hard for him. How have you been?'

'So, you finally remember to ask.'

'I didn't get the impression that exchanging niceties was uppermost in your own list of priorities upon seeing me. Not that I minded.'

Edward pressed a fist against Hugh's crotch, and Hugh laughed.

'I told you I'd be fine.' He placed a hand on Edward's thigh. 'I missed you, though.'

Edward savoured the matter-of-fact way in which Hugh said it. Not that Hugh could have said such a thing in any other way.

'Are you saying you've been chaste for the last two or three weeks?' Edward asked, raising a dubious eyebrow.

'Of course I'm not saying anything as absurd as that. I'm a man after all. And the men I have been associating with...'

'Well?'

'They are...you know, *like-minded*.'

'Spare me the details.'

It did occur to Edward that his relationship with Piers had never presented these sorts of difficulties – he couldn't help but be a bit bothered by Hugh's intimacy with other men while he was away from the Court.

'Who are these men?' he asked.

'Pirates.'

A moment's silence.

'Are you out of your mind? I've been known and censored for consorting – and in my case entirely *chastely*, I should add – with builders and ditchers and sailors and rowers... But even I have drawn the line at pirates!'

Hugh shrugged. 'Since I was declared an outlaw and exiled on that basis, I thought I may as well make the most of my newly acquired status. I did, too.'

'What are you trying to say, Hugh?' This whole pirate business had been briefly amusing: no longer so, thought Edward. 'Have you actually gone about robbing ships?'

'I may have given a hand to my associates. No more than a couple of times. It was only two Genoese dromonds. And a merchant ship from Dorset...rumoured to carry provisions for Damory's men.'

'Hugh! You aren't making the task of bringing you back any easier by engaging in acts of piracy, for God's sake!'

'But I'm already back.' He shrugged again. 'I've never left to begin with. You arranged it all, remember? When you put me under the protection of the Cinque Ports.'

'Are you saying this new career as a pirate suits you? That you don't want to come back to Court?'

'I'm simply saying you can't expect me to just sit in one of the Cinque Ports or to leisurely sail up and down the Channel, doing nothing all day and boring myself to distraction, until I'm restored to my rightful position next to you.'

'Hugh, there's a chasm between avoiding boredom and fucking a bunch of pirates while assisting them in robbing foreign ships.'

'Not for me there isn't. Anyway, I didn't ride below the crupper with the whole bunch.' Hugh smirked and stroked Edward's cheek. 'Not quite.'

+

By the time Edward and Hugh were reunited in Lichfield, less than five months later, on 3 March 1322, the Royal party had already counted numerous victories. Among these, was the surrender of Sir Roger Mortimer of Wigmore, one of the Marchers' leaders, who was taken to the Tower of London. In late February, Lancaster's Castle in Kenilworth also fell, and a search of Lancaster's papers revealed correspondence providing evidence of the Earl conniving with the Scots against the English King. Edward ordered the letters to be made public as proof of Lancaster's treason.

It was a cold, late-winter day. It had snowed overnight, unusually heavily considering the time of year. The Despensers' contingent set out from their overnight station at dawn and reached the King's camp in Lichfield around mid-morning. The Royal camp had only just started being dismantled. Edward was never one to rise early, and although the necessities of war had the effect of tempering this habit in him somewhat, they didn't eliminate it.

Hugh's eyes had some difficulty locating the King through the glare of the snow and the general bustle. Then, he saw him: naked except for his hose, the King was rubbing his chest, arms, and armpits with the fresh snow. Hugh smiled at the improbability of it all: not only of a King of England thinking it appropriate to go about his morning toilette like a mere mortal; but also, of Sir Hugh Despenser the Younger desiring, then and there, nothing more than to drink up the joy of watching Edward so occupied, oblivious to the fact that he was being observed by his lover. But today wasn't a day to indulge such desires.

His next move was half calculation, half impulse. He dismounted his horse, walked up to the King and threw himself before him, face down, arms outstretched, prostrated in the snow. As he did so he imagined – with inward approval – the effect of his coppery locks draped on the glistening, frosty carpet. Edward would enjoy his theatrics.

'Lord Despenser!' The King's voice betrayed obvious pleasure at seeing him. 'Pray, what are you doing?'

What indeed? I don't know myself. Perhaps I'm trying to convey to you that if you commanded that I publicly kiss your feet here and now, I would, Your Grace. Go ahead, Edward, ask for it. Issue your command. Do. But he couldn't say that.

'Sire,' he said instead, in a voice loud and clear enough to enable at least the closest tiers of men to hear, 'I surrender myself as a prisoner into your custody. I'm at your mercy. Do with me as you will.'

'Lord Despenser,' replied Edward as loud and as clearly, 'you come before Us a free man, under the protection of Our safe-conduct. The King's justice voided your sentence of exile months ago. You are no outlaw. You are no prisoner. Rise.'

Hugh looked up, otherwise keeping his outstretched position. 'Just a little longer, Your Grace, if you please. I want to show my men – and yours – the proper attitude to their King.'

He winked, and Edward laughed.

'I'm sure they get the idea, Lord Despenser. As to your men... You brought many more than I hoped. Who are they?'

Hugh grinned, and, in a softer tone of voice, answered, 'They're my *like-minded* sea-faring associates, Your Grace. Remember them? They've already proven themselves very useful in battle.'

'I don't doubt it.' Edward crouched down to help Hugh to his feet, seizing him by the shoulders. 'Up now – we don't want you to freeze to the bone and get as stiff as a piece of wood!'

Hugh refused to shift his body.

'On the contrary, Sire,' he whispered when the King's ear had come within sufficiently close range of his mouth. 'The cold snow is conveniently counteracting a certain woodiness induced by the sight of you.'

Edward shook his head. 'It's reassuring I'm still capable of eliciting such lewdness, Hugh, even as you are surrounded by your *friends*.'

Hugh finally rose and embraced the King. When they released each other, Edward led him to a fire, where cabbage soup was boiling – its smell both foul and inviting. While Hugh was drinking his soup, Edward gave directions to his men. His torso was still bare, apparently insensitive to the cold. It made Hugh think that just as long as he could hold onto his greatest desires, the King had a remarkable talent for shutting out much of the unpleasantness that would have been intolerable to many others in his place, driving them to lead prudent and sensible lives. There was nothing arcane, either, in the way in which Edward judged which desires were worth risking the loss of everything – his Crown, his Kingdom, possibly his life. He'd been waging this war to get his love – Hugh – back, and to get back at Lancaster for the loss of his first love, Gaveston.

Gaveston had been accused of bewitching the King, of casting a spell on his heart. Would they say that of him too? He must make sure they would win this war. He owed it to Edward. But he also owed it to Piers Gaveston and Hugh Despenser the Younger – the men who would go down in history as having had King Edward spellbound. Sir Piers Gaveston and Sir Hugh Despenser the Younger: enchanters of Kings' hearts.

Later, in Burton-on-Trent, Hugh insisted with Edward that, as they pursued the rebels, the King's forces must not unfurl the royal banners.

'Sire, you mustn't dignify our opponents by openly declaring war,' said Hugh, 'thereby inviting every subject to take sides, as if there were a prize for the strongest party to walk away with. There's no dispute here to be won through valour and courage. Our opponents are not enemies of war, either to be defeated or to be honourably defeated by. They're mere traitors and common criminals, to be punished and crushed.'

Edward assented, but the cheer that had accompanied him since the morning was gone from his eyes.

+

APPROXIMATELY TEN DAYS later, Roger Damory lay mortally wounded in a bed at Tutbury Priory. He had fought valiantly at Burton-on-Trent but had been left behind by Lancaster and his other allies when, defeated by the King's forces, they had retreated. The Prior showed Edward into the poorly lit room in which Damory lay. His face, spectre-like in its pallor, stood out in the dimness. There was a stench of festering flesh in the room. Edward felt like gagging.

'He will not last long,' said the Prior. 'The wounds run deep.'

'Please leave me,' Edward said, and, controlling his breath so that he didn't draw in more air than absolutely necessary, he walked up to the bed. The wan colouring of Damory's face left little doubt about the fate awaiting him. Apparently unconscious, he already looked much like a corpse. Edward had tried to prepare himself for it, but he winced at the sight. The Brothers had wiped Sir Roger clean, but their attentions had not staved off the corruption of death.

'You betrayed me, Sir Roger. You, who for years used to be my only true comfort. Look what's come of it. Did I not show my love for you? Did I not shower you with gifts and honours – even when you were too shy and unassuming to ask for any? Why did you have to turn against me? How *could* you?'

Damory made no reply. His eyes remained closed. If he was still breathing, it was barely perceptible. For all Edward knew, he might already be dead.

+

I've been waiting for you, Your Grace. I held out for it. Yet now that you're here I'm unable to speak.

The living make mistakes that only the dying can see.... You never stopped loving me, did you? Then why did I feel so betrayed? I truly did, Your Grace. Then again, how could you expect me to take your regard seriously, when you can bestow it so indiscriminately? That you could love one as base as the man who came between us – that's what drove the love out of my heart. Amour propre is the destruction of us all, but only the dying can see the futility of it. Perhaps I should've given myself to you wholly, as that Devil Despenser did; as you once wanted me to. Would things have been different then? But now it's too late to wonder.

The King bent and slowly pulled the bedclothes down, revealing Damory's unclothed body. Damory felt ashamed, less at his nakedness than at the wounds disfiguring both his legs.

'Piers,' the King whispered.

When the King's teardrops landed on Damory's chest, the feeling almost took his breath away, but his body didn't stir. Shortly after, he felt the bedcovers being pulled over him again.

+

'MAY YOU REST in peace,' Edward said and bent down to kiss the wounded man's forehead.

Damory's skin felt cold and lifeless on Edward's lips. Seized by dread, as if death had crawled upon him, Edward turned abruptly away and made for the exit. Hugh was standing in the doorway, leaning against the doorjamb, sulking.

'He's a *traitor*,' he said.

'I know. But I loved him well, once.'

'Come now. We must make haste, to Derby.'

Edward turned one last time and thought he saw tears lining Damory's cheekbones. But the light was bad; he couldn't be sure. Then, Hugh led him away, his hand gripping Edward's arm tight. Hugh pressing his body against his side, smelling of horse and sweat, alive and breathing next to him. Hugh, whose handsome body for once was free – as it had seldom been in the last few days – of his mail shirt. Hugh, demanding his undivided attention.

Thirty

AT LAST, REVENGE

A FEW DAYS later, the Earl of Lancaster was captured and led to his own fortress at Pontefract, in whose keep he was held captive until his trial on 22 March. In the hall – whose furnishings would have been at home in one of the royal palaces – Edward was instructing Pembroke about the trial. The fires were out, and the room was draughty, but cold had never bothered Edward much.

'The indictment against Lancaster,' he said, motioning for Pembroke to take the seat opposite his, 'will list the following charges: the seizure of the jewels and horses in Tynemouth; repeatedly coming armed to Parliament against the King's orders; deceiving the King into granting him His pardon, when the Earl did nothing to deserve it, proving over and over again that he had never any intention to return to Us; impeding Our efforts against the Scots, placing men in Our way to York, and deliberately provoking Us from this very fortress in which we're sitting, five years ago; and, more recently, treacherously negotiating with the Scots to destroy the King and His Kingdom.'

Pembroke's eyebrows, ever so slightly raised, betrayed some perplexity.

'What is it?' Edward asked.

'Your Grace, you made no mention of Lancaster's breach of the Earls' word to you that we, the Earls, would keep Lord Gaveston safe. I would have thought –'

'I'm not punishing my cousin to give satisfaction to the Earl of Cornwall.'

Pembroke's eyebrows went up a further notch. 'You're not, Your Grace?'

'I won't put Lancaster's execution on the late Earl of Cornwall's head. It is *my* own desire and *my* own choice that Lancaster should suffer and be punished for the Earl of Cornwall's murder. There's no particular need for you or anybody else to understand this, Pembroke.'

'Very well, Your Grace.' Pembroke stood, ready to take his leave.

Edward's voice checked him. 'This is why the trial and execution will follow a predetermined pattern.'

'Your Grace?'

'Lancaster executed the Earl of Cornwall without a trial. So he shall not be given an opportunity to respond to his charges.'

'But –'

'None of what I'm going to say is up for negotiation, Pembroke. For once, I elect to do away with your advice. All I ask of you today is to take note of my wishes and see to it that the other judges and the executioner carry them out to the letter.'

Pembroke sat down again. 'Very well, Your Grace.'

'Lancaster will be given no opportunity to respond to his charges. He will be condemned to die the traitor's death – hanging, drawing, and quartering. But I shall commute the sentence to beheading, because, after all, he did grant the Earl of Cornwall the mercy of dying the nobleman's death. Nonetheless, he will suffer the very same indignities that were inflicted upon the Earl of Cornwall.'

Edward wished Pembroke's eyes were not looking at him quite so intently; or, if they must, that they showed some emotion. Even disapproval seemed better than Pembroke's stony silence.

He said, 'Lancaster will be placed on a mule and thus carried to the place of his execution, a hillock a short distance from this very Castle. People shall be present along the road, that they may mock and jeer as seems fit. Finally, lest people think that affording Lancaster the same treatment as he reserved for the Earl of Cornwall means that their life or dignity was of the same value, there will be one difference in the mode of execution.'

'Yes, Your Grace.'

'Rather than by a single stroke of the sword, Lancaster's head shall fall by the axe. The executioner shall see that he chooses an axe that is not *too* sharp. It should take no less than two or three strokes to do the job. Two or three, Pembroke: no more, but no less.'

Did Pembroke shudder? It could be the cold, of course.

'Is everything clear, Pembroke?'

Pembroke nodded. 'It will be done as you command, Your Grace.'

'Leave me now,' said Edward.

It's done, Piers. All will be done just as I described it. Whether or not this is what you want, it's what I want. It won't bring you back, but it will make your murderer wish that he had never sent you to your death. This is your revenge, Piers; but I take sole responsibility for it, before both men and God.

Then the stone mask Edward had been wearing throughout his conversation with the Earl of Pembroke broke down. His mouth started quivering; tears began streaming down his face.

Someone came in, unannounced, through the door which Pembroke had just used to leave. Tears blurred Edward's vision, but even through them, the red of his lover's hair was unmistakable. Hugh walked up to him and sat by his side.

'This is not a day for mourning,' he said. 'It's a day to celebrate.'

Hugh's hand reached up to Edward's jaw, and made Edward's face turn to him. Then, with both his thumbs, he wiped away Edward's tears. Feeling helpless, Edward searched Hugh's eyes. He couldn't read them, but he felt as if Hugh was prey to a strange, all-consuming restlessness.

Pontefract.

ONE. THE AXE falls as the traitor screams. Blood spews as the blade cuts through the flesh at the back of the neck, before its course is arrested by the spine. Edward winces, but keeps his eyes riveted on the macabre spectacle he has so carefully planned. The executioner pulls the blade out and lifts it again, dripping blood over the prisoner's head. Is the traitor still screaming?

Two. Swishing, then a sudden snap. The blade has worked its way through the bone. For a few instants that feel like an eternity, the traitor's body convulses with violent spasms, which send the blood spraying in all directions. Then, all of a sudden, the body falls inert, and the gushing slackens. The pool of blood expands slowly, thickly.

Three. A final time the axe ascends and then descends. A thud, and the head is severed, landing amidst the blood, face down. Blood pours out of the truncated body; dark blood, more black than red. Edward stares impassively, but in the recesses of his mouth, his clenched teeth are fighting against the urge to retch. Viscous blood flows slowly, unstoppable.

The executioner grabs the traitor's head by the hair and, his arm outstretched, he turns it towards Edward, that he may see the face of death on it. And the face of death is...

'PIERS!' EDWARD SCREAMED into the dark, breathless.

He heard a loud thud next to him.

'What is it?' asked Hugh with alarm.

His groom's voice came from behind the door. 'Your Grace?'

'It's nothing,' Edward shouted in response. He turned to Hugh. 'I'm sorry. A bad dream. Did you fall off the bed?'

Hugh sighed. 'Nearly. You almost had me dead with fright.'

Edward put a hand to his own forehead, pulling back the hair sticking to the sweat that had formed on his temples. 'I'm sorry.'

'Don't be. I've grown much too skittish of late. I'm not proud of it.'

Edward heard Hugh get off the bed and feel his way in the dark until he reached the fireplace. He lit a candle by one of the dying embers; the glow lit up his muscular stomach as he returned to bed.

'It's this place,' Hugh said.

Edward looked around the dimly lit room: in the glow of the single candle, the hangings looked discoloured and shabby.

'It's creepy,' said Hugh. 'Do you think the reports are true?'

'What reports?'

'That the spirit of Lancaster performs miracles at his grave and the site of his execution.'

'That's apostasy! Idolaters – peasants worshipping a churl!'

'Yes. I don't know what's happening to me. I'm sorry.'

'Don't, please. Hugh Despenser the Younger doesn't apologise.'

'I'll pull myself together in a moment. Night-time is always the worst.'

Outside, as if on cue, something hooted eerily. They both gasped, even as they recognised it as an owl, and exchanged a quick look, half-ashamed and half-amused at their nervousness.

'I mustn't forget,' said Hugh, 'that I'm by far the richest and most powerful man in the country. Except you, that is. And I must remember that our enemies are defeated, either dead or behind bars.'

'All but the Scots. I suppose it was presumptuous to expect that my lucky streak would continue indefinitely.'

Hugh patted Edward's thigh. 'Is the Queen still sulking?'

'Not as far as I can tell from her letters.' He tried to recollect the content of her latest missive and wondered if it was true.

'I've heard she blames me.'

'You?'

Hugh set the candle on the chair next to his side of the bed, slid down on the mattress, and pulled the quilt up to his neck. 'Apparently, she put it around that the reason why her life was endangered at Tynemouth, while we were fighting the Scots, is that I "deviously convinced you she would be safe there".'

Edward frowned. 'Isabella would never say that. She's perfectly aware of how hard I worked to ensure her safety when the Scots were approaching – and the men I sent in her defence were your very troops. You should know better than to trust rumours.'

'It's not a rumour that she dislikes me, Edward. It's a fact. Anyway, all the Realm is convinced I'm the villain, so you must forgive me if I don't find it very hard to believe that the Queen herself might.'

'Well, you're not exactly a saint,' said Edward. His hand ruffled Hugh's coppery locks.

'I've always believed a man must seize his opportunities when and where he finds them.' He sat up. 'This is my moment. Ours.'

'I know. As long as I don't turn into my father in the process.'

They both instinctively turned to follow a sudden movement beyond the circle of light from the candle. The place badly needed the services of a cat: it was teeming with mice.

'But I fear I may already have,' Edward said.

'It's my turn to castigate you now. I shan't have you all besieged by misgivings and regrets. A King must be a law unto himself. Moral qualms are for lesser men.'

'Now you sound like Hugh Despenser the Younger, at any rate.'

Hugh cocked an eyebrow. 'Is that good or bad?'

'Good. It's all good. I fell in love with the Younger Despenser.'

Edward smiled, hoping the wistfulness he felt wouldn't show. Hugh reached an arm around Edward's shoulder and pulled him close. They stayed like that for a few moments, their temples touching, each seeking the other's trespass on their own breathing space.

Hugh released him. 'Turn around.'

Edward heard Hugh fumble with the flask of almond oil: having secured a generous supply from a merchant introduced to him by his Italian banker, Hugh now always kept some at the ready. Then, Hugh pulled down Edward's linen night braies and was inside him, pounding furiously, and making such a racket that Edward had to reassure the valets behind the shut door that everything was all right. As he addressed them, making an effort to keep his voice steady, he felt himself tighten around Hugh's shaft; and when Hugh resumed his thrusts, pain, searing hot, throttled the tender ring of flesh. Grinding his teeth, angry, he almost thrust his arm back against Hugh's chest to push him away. Only he didn't, and a few moments later, Hugh's pummelling had drawn out Edward's seed as if by magic.

It was February 1323, a year or so since Lancaster's execution.

Thirty-One

THE TRANSIENCE OF TRIUMPH

After spending Christmas 1323 at Kenilworth, Lancaster's former residence, in mid-January 1324, the King and Queen were staying as guests of Hugh and Eleanor Despenser at Hanley Castle, in Worcestershire. This reminded Isabella of the festive season the Royal couple and the Gavestons had spent at Langley fourteen years before, when both Isabella and Lady Margaret had been barely more than children, each smitten with her own impossibly handsome consort (Isabella, in fact, with both Edward and the Earl). She looked back to those times with heart-rending nostalgia.

Isabella never saw Lady Margaret these days. Margaret, of course, was wife to the erstwhile favourite but now imprisoned traitor Lord Audley, captured at Boroughbridge two years before, shortly after Lord Damory's death. Poor Lady Margaret: her first husband murdered as the most hated man of the Realm; and her second now imprisoned as one of the King's worst enemies. Considering that Edward had not taken very kindly to the spouses of the rebel Marchers, it would have been hardly politic for Isabella to seek out Margaret's company. Besides, the rule at Semprigham Priory, where Margaret now lived, didn't make it easy to have regular contact with its residents – not even those who, like her, hadn't taken the veil and were not fully cloistered.

Margaret's sister, Eleanor Despenser – Isabella's present hostess – had acted as her lady-in-waiting for over a decade. Except for her association with her accursed husband – a detail not always easy to overlook – Isabella liked Lady Eleanor well enough, and the King had always particularly favoured her among the de Clare sisters. But Eleanor lacked Margaret's peculiar mixture of reserve, intelligence and quirkiness. Eleanor was much more solid, sensible, and dependable – good qualities in their own right, to be sure, but Isabella missed Margaret.

Of course, any contrast between the two sisters troubled her infinitely less than the chasm between the late Earl of Cornwall, whom she had all but worshipped, and Despenser, Lord of Glamorgan, whom, by now, she very nearly loathed. Her training as Queen meant that she could successfully dissimulate her feelings towards the fiendish creature, but this made the strain of his overbearing presence even worse.

He must be aware of her dislike. All things considered – 'all things' consisting primarily of her husband's infatuation with the Younger Despenser – it was surprising she still retained Edward's regard and, perhaps, even his love. But she worried that any degree of influence she may still have over the King was rapidly waning. Despenser must be working tirelessly behind the scenes to deprive her of it altogether, she was sure. He must have carnal knowledge of the King, too, in the same way that the Earl of Cornwall had had. The thought made her shudder. There could be nothing beautiful and noble in that kind of thing with someone such as Despenser. She had no doubt the man was incapable of love. Besides, he was physically repulsive.

As these thoughts went through her mind, weaving themselves through the weft of powerful feelings that gave them substance, Isabella made sure to make the occasional perfunctory contribution to the conversation in which her husband and the Despensers were engaged. They had been talking about the thirteen-year truce that the Scots had agreed to the previous year; about the new deadline of 1 July that her brother Charles, the new King of France, had granted Edward, as Count of Ponthieu and Duke of Aquitaine, to perform homage to the French King at Amiens; and about the escape of the Marcher leader Roger Mortimer from the Tower the previous August.

The last of these topics of conversation had the power to trouble her husband the most. He had invested considerable resources in attempt to recapture Mortimer, but without success. The rebel was now known to have sought refuge on the Continent. Reports about his whereabouts had been contradictory, but there had been talk of his presence at the French Court itself. No good could come of Mortimer being at large like that. A number of others had fled to the Continent. How long would it take them to re-organise and mobilise their forces against Edward? Could England face another rebellion? Could *she* face it?

She was weary of it, unspeakably so: weary of war, weary of her husband's infatuations, weary of pretending that all was well.

+

Late May 1324.

MARGARET WAS COLLECTING elderflowers to make into cordial. Time spent in the Priory's extensive grounds, attending to light gardening work, always soothed her better than anything. She had found more flower-heads than fit into the hemp sack she had taken with her. Accordingly, she removed her veil to use it to gather the excess ones – an unorthodox move, and one for which she might be mildly reprimanded. Let them try, and she'd let them have a piece of her mind. Her lineage still counted for something, even at Semprigham.

A red admirable butterfly was on the point of landing on her luxuriant cloud of curls (she never plaited her hair under the veil), but the creature thought better of it at the last moment. A memory flashed through her mind, from half a lifetime ago: the time when she and her first husband had rested on a small island dissecting the river Kennet in the King's company before continuing their enforced journey to Bristol and then Ireland.

She had now entered the third decade of her life, and it seemed to her that more than her fair share of history had found its way into her thirty years. She turned to look at hers and Lord Audley's two-year-old daughter – named, like herself, Margaret – sitting on the grass, engrossed in depetalling some daisies. The Queen was right: Hugh Audley was not the same man as Piers Gaveston. Good looks and epigrammatic tongue notwithstanding, Margaret hadn't grown to love him; though neither did she mind him particularly, barring the fact that he was occasionally prone to overdo his affectations of levity. At least she hadn't minded him until he decided to side with the other Marchers and rebel against her uncle, the King.

Sure, she could see why her husband felt that they had been ill-used, when the King allowed her brother-in-law the Younger Despenser to pressure them into entering transactions in land that were of dubious value to them. But it was equally true that the favours her husband had received, in his day, from the King well exceeded the setbacks he suffered at the hands of the Younger Despenser in more recent years. In any case, joining the Marchers' rebellion had been not only a treacherous move, but a foolish one, as her husband's indefinite term of imprisonment now amply demonstrated.

During their life together, Sir Hugh Audley rarely visited her bed. It didn't really displease her. Her second husband was handsome, but somehow she failed to develop for him the kind of attraction that had made her want Piers to make love to her. She was inclined to think that Lord Audley didn't visit the beds of other women, either, despite the fact that he was a notorious flirt. Would she have minded if he had visited them? But the question was academic, now that he was captive and she lived in a nunnery.

Of course, she had pleaded with her uncle to spare Sir Hugh Audley when he appeared set on executing him together with other captured rebels. Quite apart from the fact that if Audley died, she and her inheritance might well be married off to someone much less agreeable than him, she also knew that just because she didn't love him didn't mean she wanted him dead. Margaret was also convinced that although her husband's betrayal must have stung him keenly, King Edward took it for granted that she would plead with him for her husband's life. Indeed, he had probably banked on her appeal even before it came and had decided beforehand that he would grant her wish. The King's affecting, for a while, to want her husband dead was a calculated display of Kingly brawn and austerity at a time when he needed to put to rest rumours that he was an ineffective ruler. She was almost sure of it. She also suspected the King of not being nearly as mad at her as he made himself out to be. Of course, some of his displeasure must be genuine – but then, if she had to be honest with herself, she hadn't been as forthcoming with him as she should have, once she started suspecting her husband of switching sides. And it would have been unusual for a traitor's wife not to have responsibility for her husband's misdeeds laid, at least partially, at her door.

At any rate, she believed that on the whole she remained in King Edward's good graces. Why else, after her husband's capture, would her uncle have discreetly consulted her on the destination to which she would like to retire, and arranged that Parliament should send her there? Her uncle did ordain that she should not be allowed out of the Priory, but being there under guard was also a form of protection for her and the child. It made it difficult for her to find herself caught up in any further plotting – for some of the rebel Marchers and their retainers were still at large, and she'd rather stay well clear of them.

The King hadn't questioned her choice of Sempringham, and she volunteered no explanation, though he appeared a little surprised when she named the Priory, for it wasn't known for the laxness of its rule. But it seemed to her as safe a place as any to raise her second daughter. Without Piers as the father, she couldn't count on the King taking as keen an interest in her well-being as in her first husband's daughter, Joan – who was now living at Amesbury Priory. Besides, she had wanted to atone for her husband's treachery, and retiring to a place such as Semprigham would show her uncle that her desire was genuine. Finally, in the event her husband died in captivity, she thought she would be in a better position to resist the pressure to be married off a third time if she could claim to be settled in the Benedectine ways of contemplative life at Sempringham. If need be, she would take vows.

As she crouched next to her daughter and drew her, protesting, to her breast, Margaret sniffled. She reminded herself that, if the thought of one day returning to her former life felt overwhelming right now, she couldn't rule out that in time she would change her mind. For all she knew, what today felt like repose, tomorrow might well feel like being buried alive. She mustn't make any hasty decisions: if and when she took vows, there would be no turning back.

+

18 September 1324.

'YOU UNDERSTAND THAT it's only until the French King your brother gives up his claims over my dominions in France and instructs your uncle Charles of Valois to withdraw his forces from Gascony,' said Edward to Isabella's back.

She was looking out of the window of her chamber, but he knew she was not taking in the court with the quince tree at its centre, its ripening fruits glistening in the drizzle. From the way her shoulders rose rhythmically with the heaving of her ribcage, he could tell all her attention was strained inward, not outward. She turned towards him, brows knitted, cheeks flushed. She must be beautiful still – he was sure she was – but right now he couldn't see it.

'But why punish *me* for my brother's actions? It's not my fault if King Charles has unilaterally taken the Duchy of Aquitaine and the County of Ponthieu into his hands. In fact, it's *your* fault. Why couldn't you just go to Amiens and pay him homage by the date he set, instead of sending envoys to make excuses and seek a further extension? None of this would have happened.'

She crossed her arms. He sighed. Why was she being so unyielding? What had gone into her?

'You are being unreasonable. It was no one's fault that Pembroke died on the mission, and that the other envoys proved unequal to the task of negotiating with King Charles. I told you, this is not to punish you.'

'It *feels* like a punishment. The allowance you plan to provide me with is much less than the income from the lands that you're about to seize from me.'

'But that's the whole point, can't you see? Your income *must* diminish if my order is to convey to your brother the message that his actions are harming *all* French subjects on English soil.'

'You've already exiled or imprisoned every last one of them, including my attendants, and confiscated their lands – I would have thought you made your point perfectly clear, already. I'm Queen of England before I am a French subject and the sister of the King of France, am I not? Why won't you treat me as such!'

'Well, I'm not proposing to imprison or exile *you*, am I? I told you, the confiscation of your lands is only temporary. You and your household will survive perfectly well on the allowance I am assigning you.'

She snorted. She'd never done so before in his presence; it made him wince.

She said, 'Then why –'

He motioned for her to stop. She clenched her jaw and looked at him askance.

'For the last time, Isabella: I have no choice but to put pressure on your brother before any more of our cities in Aquitaine fall to Valois' forces – it's bad enough to have lost Agen. The King of France must be made to see that his callousness is harming those closest to him. If he acts like a rogue, I *must* retaliate.'

She drew a deep breath. 'Is this Lord Despenser's idea?'

This was getting ludicrous. She may be Queen, but he was the King.

'I've nothing more to say. You are, of course, at perfect liberty to accept or reject the *reasons* for my decision. But either way, you'll have to live with it.'

He turned on his heels and walked out of the Queen's chamber, leaving the door open behind him. He heard Isabella slamming it shut from within. As far as he remembered, this had been the first serious quarrel they'd ever had. He should have been angry at her obstinacy. Instead, he had been unusually self-controlled. He should be worrying that their row might be irreparable, terrified that he might lose her love. Instead, he only felt wistful, like a man who, having already experienced a loss and grieved over it, has nothing left to dread.

Approximately six months later, in early March 1325.
The Tower of London.

As Edward entered his chamber, Hugh turned away from the window. His doublet was a recent acquisition: Italian silk damask with a pattern of golden griffins, facing each other in pairs. Edward thoroughly approved of the symbolism, and of Hugh associating himself with it, for the griffin commingled the lion and the eagle: the most noble of the earth-bound animals, and the most noble of the birds.

A little sunshine had found its way through the window Hugh had unsealed, together with a stray bumblebee. The insect flew about aimlessly for a short while, then appeared to make right for the spot between Hugh's eyebrows, if his eyebrows had been visible, that is. Hugh ducked, quickly, and it flew out.

'I seem to be no more in favour with bees than with Christian folk,' said Hugh.

Edward smiled and sat down on the sheepskin coverlet spread over the wooden bench. 'I made up my mind. The Queen will sail for France on the ninth to negotiate a peace treaty with the King of France.'

'As long as you can trust her,' said Hugh, sounding dubious.

'Of course I can *trust her*. I *do* trust her. She's our best bet. Everybody thinks she should act as a mediator – my counsellors, King Charles, even the Pope. Anyway, what else can I do? The truce in Gascony will soon expire. Either I send Isabella to parley with her brother, or I'll need to lead an army and retake Gascony from the French by force. I thought we were agreed that we should try to avoid war, if at all possible.'

Hugh regarded him, saying nothing. Edward was sure something was on his mind. He had lost weight: it made his cheekbones stand out and his eyes appear larger, which in turn fooled one into thinking their green had become more vivid. Edward felt disloyal for thinking that, a little wasted, he looked more attractive than ever.

'What is it, Hugh?' He extended his arm – an invitation for Hugh to sit next to him – but Hugh shook his head and continued to stand.

'It's just…'

'What?'

'Nothing. Forget it.'

Edward sighed. 'The only thing that worries me is her safety. The French Court teems with our enemies.'

'Yes, but for how long? They'll be on their way here soon enough.'

So that was it. 'Hugh.'

'I know, Edward: the invasion I've been expecting has so far failed to materialise. But the intelligence we've been receiving is reliable. Mortimer is up to something. It's not just the rumours we've heard. His movements and dealings have been extremely suspicious. Your agents have documented them well enough. You can't shut your eyes to it.'

'I don't, but you seemed so certain that he would strike in November –'

'For God's sake, the fact it hasn't happened yet doesn't mean it won't happen at all! Can you blame me for worrying that we might lose everything? Our triumph has never felt so precarious.'

Hugh threw himself on Edward's bed. Edward left the bench to lie down next to him. His hand reached out to Hugh's chin and turned Hugh's face towards him.

'What is it?'

'It's just...I've always known that gaining something is only half the job; after one gets it, one must guard it. But can you believe it never occurred to me that the more complete one's success, the larger the prospect looms of a change in one's fortune?'

Edward pondered. 'You mean, you wish you had thought of this before we triumphed over Lancaster and the Marchers.'

'Perhaps.'

Edward put his arm around Hugh's shoulders and drew him close. 'Would you have advised me not to go to war if you had known how little security we would feel after defeating our enemies?'

'I suppose not.'

'I thought so. And I owe it to you – to your desire to be victorious and to see me victorious – that I finally managed to make Lancaster pay for his crime. If I could go back, I wouldn't change a single thing.'

Hugh put a hand to his head and clenched his fist around the roots of his hair. Edward took his wrist, pulled the hand away, and held it to his own midriff.

'Let's save our worries until the day we can't put them off any longer, Hugh.' He looked into his lover's eyes. 'And you must eat a little more. We can't have you grow all waif-like.'

Thirty-Two

HOW TO LOSE A QUEEN

Isabella's appeals – assisted by the presence of the English army that Edward sent to Aquitaine at the beginning of April – eventually persuaded her brother to conclude a peace treaty. According to it, the County of Ponthieu would return under English control, but Edward would have to give up all his lands in Gascony: most of these would be restored to him only after he travelled to Beauvais to perform homage to King Charles at the end of August.

Five days before the date appointed for performing homage, Edward, on his way to Dover port, stopped at Langdon Abbey. Hoping that his reputation for being as healthy as an ox had never reached the French Court, he bought himself time by writing to the French King that he had fallen ill. The last day of August, after breakfast, he was still at the Abbey, sitting on a turf seat overlooking the herb garden, his ears caressed by the drone of bees. The stems of lavender flowers bent under the insects' weight. Strange how his indecision regarding his next move did not entirely prevent him from enjoying the overblown beauty of the late summer gardens. Perhaps there was some truth in what the Ordainers had once said of him: perhaps it was true that he didn't take the job of governing seriously enough.

He sighed. Those bushes over there, with the blushing hips, were apothecary's rose. He wondered if, when in bloom, the flowers would be crimson or striped, like the one he had offered Piers the last time he saw him alive. Could he have prevented Piers' death if he had been more committed to the work of governing? Could he have willed himself to be? Tears formed at the corner of his eyes. He hastened to dry them when he realised his second-born, John of Eltham, who had just turned nine, was approaching. As he forced his lips into a smile, he wondered what Edward of Windsor – John's elder brother, and heir to the throne of England – might be up to. It had been a good idea to summon both his sons to stay with him at Langdon.

John stood facing him.'Father.'

Edward cleared his voice. 'Hello there.'

'Are you sad, Father?'

He shook his head vigorously. 'No, John. I'm a little worried – that's all.'

'You're worried about going to France?'

'Yes.'

'Why, Father? Are you afraid to drown in the sea?'

'No, John. I like boats. I shall take you out rowing one day – soon.'

The boy was twisting a lavender stem around his finger. 'In the sea?'

'No. On the Thames, perhaps.'

John sat down next to him. His body gave off a faintly earthy smell, rather like hay. It was comforting – like new linen, like Isabella's veils.

'If you like boats, why don't you want to sail to France?'

'I don't like the idea of leaving the Kingdom and my friends behind.'

John pushed his back against the seat and turned his face toward him. 'Because you will miss them?'

Edward put a hand around the boy's shoulders. 'Because of that, and because of what might happen to them if I leave. There are always people ready to cause trouble, you know.'

'Won't my brother stop them? He said you have made him Keeper of the Realm.'

'I have. But Edward is still young.'

John seized the hand Edward had rested on his shoulder. 'Will something happen to us – Edward and I – if you go?'

'Nothing will happen to you.'

'Can't you leave your Chamberlain with us? Isn't he a very strong soldier? Isn't everybody scared of him?'

'He is, John, very strong. But he's in much greater danger than either of you.'

John let go of Edward's hand and scratched his head. 'Why, if he's so strong?'

'Because many people don't like him.'

'Because of his ginger hair?' He giggled mischievously.

'Because he's my best friend. Everyone would like to have the King's love for themselves. They are jealous of those that enjoy it.'

John pondered. 'Your love is putting ginger-man in danger?'

'In a way. Yes, unfortunately it is.'

'Do you love *me*, Father?'

Edward's arm, still circling John's shoulders, pressed the boy to him. 'I do, John, but it's very different. Everyone expects that I should love my sons like my own flesh. No one resents you for my love. They think it's your due. And it is, you know. But they don't like me loving others like that.'

John wriggled out of his father's embrace and stood up. He picked up a stone and threw it at a sparrow. He missed. Before Edward could reprimand him, he asked, 'Do you love ginger-man like us? Like your own flesh?'

'Yes. But don't tell anyone, otherwise people will hate him even more.'

'Not even Edward?' John sat down again.

'You can tell your brother Edward.'

He rested a hand on his son's head. As he started stroking the boy's golden hair, once again he became engrossed with the garden scene.

'Father?'

'Yes, John.'

'Perhaps you could take ginger-man with you to France – to make sure he comes to no harm while you're away?'

'Perhaps. I haven't really decided yet. It's as dangerous for him in France as here. It's dangerous for me too, you know. Many of our enemies are in France. And the French King –'

'My uncle?'

'Yes. Your uncle, the King, might try to arrest us, because he thinks we are responsible for killing *his* uncle.'

'And who's that?'

'The late Earl of Lancaster. He was your mother's and your uncle's uncle. And my cousin. Your cousin too, once removed.'

'Did you and ginger-man kill my cousin-one-reproved? People say ginger-man would be capable of killing anyone at all.'

'Once-removed. We didn't kill the Earl of Lancaster. We captured him, and then I had him executed.'

'Because he was a criminal?'

'Of the worst sort. A murderer and a traitor. The worst that England has ever known.'

'Did you hang and draw and quarter him?' asked John gleefully.

'No. He fell by the axe.'

John looked a trifle disappointed. 'Doesn't my uncle the King of France know my cousin...once...?'

'Once-removed.'

'Yes, him. You said he was a very bad man, Father. Doesn't the King of France know it?'

Edward sighed. 'Perhaps he doesn't want to believe it.'

'Because the Earl of Lancaster was his uncle?'

'Probably, John. It's difficult sometimes to see the faults of those closest to us.'

'Like those we share the same blood with?'

'Yes.'

'And those we love like our own flesh: is it difficult to see their faults too, Father?'

Edward was taken aback. Was this simply the logic of innocence? Or had anyone spoken ill of Hugh in the boy's presence? Could it be – Isabella? Surely, she wouldn't stoop so low? He felt a pang of guilt at doubting her, who had never given him any good reason to.

'Father?'

'Off you go now, John,' he said, with a pat on the boy's back.

+

Three hours or so later Edward and Hugh were lying naked on the bed in the King's chamber at the Abbey. The scent of lavender drifted through the window, drawn out from the bushes by an afternoon shower. It was a simply but beautifully appointed room. Piers would have remarked how the mellow colours of the unpainted oak beams and furniture, the flint of the walls, and the ecru linen of the draperies perfectly set off the precious ornamentation on Edward's folding chairs, trunks, and other furnishings. Hugh, somehow, seemed less likely to make any such comment. He could rough it better than most, if it came to that, but unfinished wood, unplastered walls and undyed fabrics were shabby to him, not quietly beautiful.

'Am I blind to your faults, Hugh?'

'Most likely. I'm certainly blissfully oblivious to my shortcomings, and since you're generally accused of taking my lead in every matter…'

Edward turned to him, making it obvious that his grin was affected. 'I'm sure I don't lack discernment.'

'I'm sure you don't.'

A moment's silence, then Edward asked, 'Do you like Isabella?'

'Where's *that* coming from?'

Edward shrugged.

'I don't mind her particularly. I like her somewhat more than I like most people.'

'You either positively dislike or are completely indifferent to most people, Hugh.'

'Admittedly. You being the notable exception. Since when have you started holding that against me?'

'I don't. But your – *our* – remarkable ability to make enemies is proving itself a liability right now. I still don't know what's best.'

Hugh sighed. 'I do. Keep me at your side. Take me with you to France. The way things have been going, if you leave me behind, they'll have my skin the moment you board the ship.' He turned towards Edward, supporting himself with his elbow. 'In France, we'll be in danger, but at least we'll face it together.'

Edward wondered at Hugh's uncharacteristic intensity.

Then Hugh said, 'There is another way, of course.'

'You mean sending my son Edward of Windsor to pay homage to King

Charles instead of going there myself.'

'Of course. Wasn't that the very plan endorsed by the magnates two weeks ago? We were the first to suggest it last year. Now that the peace treaty is negotiated, you've pulled back. Why?'

'I worry for him.'

'But why? The boy won't be in any danger. Mortimer and our other enemies have no quarrel with *him*. If anything, the risk is that they shall appoint him as their champion. If they plan a rebellion, it's in his name they'll fight it. Far from endangering his safety, if they get hold of him they'll guard him jealously. He is, potentially, their most precious asset.'

'Then sending him to France hardly seems ideal, does it?'

'Granted. But we've run out of options. If Mortimer is intent on launching an attack, he will do so with or without using your son as a figurehead. All things considered, I think sending Edward of Windsor to France is the best thing you can do – if you care not to lose your French lands to King Charles, that is. Personally, I care that you shouldn't lose them.'

I've never even set foot on it, but I shall never consent to losing your motherland, Piers.

'Losing Gascony is out of the question,' Edward said.

Hugh sat up on the bed and stretched his arms.

Edward said, 'He has taken to calling you ginger-man, you know?'

Hugh's nose twitched. 'Who has?'

'John.'

'Of Eltham?'

'Who else?'

'Cheeky little bugger.' Hugh scratched his chin. 'Shows promise, I think.'

'I like it, anyway. Ginger-man.'

Edward's hand reached out to stroke the trail of coppery hairs running from Hugh's navel to the base of his cock. Hugh wasn't Piers, but he was the living man that was dearest to his heart: the thought of losing him was more than he could bear. He was not going to leave him behind as he travelled to France – he had learnt his lesson, the hard way. Yet, if he took Hugh with him, what treachery might lie in wait for them when they landed on the Continent?

+

EDWARD OF WINDSOR – having been appointed Count of Ponthieu and Duke of Aquitaine by his father before his departure for the Continent – performed homage to King Charles for the English dominions in France towards the end of September. The King had not initially worried too much about the fact that both Edward of Windsor and Isabella had been lingering at the French Court after the homage. Even after several weeks had elapsed, he had dismissed his presentiments that the delay did not bode well, choosing to believe Isabella's vague explanations about the reasons why she was being detained in her home country. Before the middle of November, however, one of the King's agents in France reported to Edward that Isabella was considering not returning to England at all.

Edward's first reaction had been disbelief. He had always had complete trust in his wife, or so he told himself. It was simply inconceivable. But the more he pondered the possibility that Isabella may indeed have chosen to desert him, the less outlandish it sounded, and the more indignant he grew. What was Isabella thinking, choosing to stay on in the Court of the man who had been trying to deprive them of their French lands – a Court that, in addition, was practically overrun with their mortal enemies? Wasn't it enough that the English Royal family had been driven to humbling themselves by performing homage to King Charles – who, by her own admission, Isabella found a very difficult man? Why add insult to injury?

Then he remembered how wilfully Isabella resisted his plan to temporarily seize her lands, and how she accused Hugh of being the plan's originator, as if he had deliberately tried to defraud her. That had been very unfair of Isabella, upon his word. His heartbeat accelerated, and droplets of sweat rolled down his ribs – tickling and irritating him. Sure, Hugh pursued his own interest – who didn't? But why should Isabella presume that Hugh would dare do so at her expense? She must hold her husband in very low esteem indeed, if she found it so easy to believe that any self-aggrandising courtier (he knew this was the view she took of Hugh) could get him to swindle his own wife.

He had, then, been right not to restore the Queen's lands to her until she came back. And if this showed, after all, that he had been – despite his erstwhile protestations to the contrary – less than altogether trusting of Isabella's loyalty, didn't her behaviour now vindicate the wisdom of his decision?

A few days after receiving the report of Isabella's inclination to stay in France, Edward, still smarting from what he could not help seeing as outright betrayal, rushed to order that the Queen's income should be terminated with immediate effect. This would teach her, he told himself. But after he had cooled down and talked himself into believing that someone must be conspiring against him, and that they must have affected Isabella's decision, he wondered if he had overreacted. He even felt strangely ashamed. But he couldn't very well reverse the order now and look like a fool. Besides, he shouldn't – if anything was going to bring Isabella around, it would be cutting off all of her revenues.

+

WHEN ISABELLA LEARNT that she had been deprived of all means of support, she was livid. This couldn't be the doing of the husband she knew and loved, who had always been considerate and kind...until that orange-haired fiend had come to interfere in their lives! There was no doubt in her mind that Edward's decision had been instigated by Despenser.

All was lost, then: if her husband was prepared to see her destitute, all must be lost beyond repair. Her eyes brimmed with tears. Then she made the decision which she had been agonising over for the course of so many weeks: she wouldn't – she *couldn't,* now – return to that miserable island across the Channel. Not as long as Despenser remained with the King.

She would make her intentions perfectly plain to the King – for how could she hope that he would see the error of his ways unless the situation was laid before him in its uncanny simplicity? Of course, she knew only too well that her husband would wilfully blind himself to the truth, even if it stared him right in the eye. He had given ample proof of his extraordinary capacity for self-deception in recent years. But no one would be able to say that she hadn't tried.

How wretched the last few years had been. Why had she put up with it? Could she have prevented this outcome if she had been honest with Edward from the start about her mistrust of the Younger Despenser? But her husband's infatuations made him completely impervious to reason. This tendency of his had served him badly enough, even at the time when he had been a good judge of character – when he had been smitten with the likes of the Earl of Cornwall or the late Lord Damory. But, bewitched as he now was by that fiend who was intent on destroying and dishonouring them all, Edward's inability to face the truth could only end in disaster. Well, Isabella and her son were not going to be around when disaster struck.

Thirty-Three

OF LOVE, LOYALTY, AND FAITHFULNESS

2 December 1325.

After dusk had fallen, Edward rowed himself along the Thames, accompanied by a small number of attendants, in order to pay a visit to Eleanor Despenser at Edward's own residence in Sheen. It was relatively mild for the time of year, and Edward enjoyed the exercise.

'Eleanor,' he said to his niece upon entering her room.

Eleanor was lying on the bed, the bedclothes sweeping down on both sides of her heavily pregnant belly. She dismissed the midwife.

Edward kissed her hand. 'How close?'

She smiled at him. 'I believe it may have been a false alarm, Your Grace. The contractions have stopped. You'd think I'd have learnt by now, after carrying so many children. But each pregnancy is different. I'm sorry you ventured out in the cold on my account.'

'It's a mild night. Besides, you know it always gives me great joy to see you.'

It was true. Margaret once told him he had a soft spot for Eleanor, and he recognised the truth in her words. Eleanor had always struck him as a glorified version of Margaret. Taller, more commanding, larger – especially when pregnant, as she had been on and off for much of her adult life. Hugh, despite not stinting on his amatory gifts for Edward, clearly had enough lust to spare for securing the future of his line…

Eleanor was also more confident than Margaret, more dependable, less enigmatic. She was very much Margaret minus the smudges: she was straightforward. If Eleanor had been married to Audley, for example, she would never have hidden her husband's plotting from her King. He was also aware that Eleanor's loyalty to Hugh endeared her to him over and beyond the affection he had always felt for her.

At a different time in his life, Isabella's approval of Piers had similarly sealed Edward's love for her. Oh, Isabella…. Despite his anger and sadness at her insubordination, he missed her terribly. In her absence – and with Hugh himself often away in recent months, doing the round of his Welsh lands and Castles – it was no wonder that Eleanor's company, with her uncomplicated common sense, had felt like a veritable balm.

Eleanor said, 'May I ask where my husband might be?'

He took time, wondering how best to explain. Eleanor burst into laughter.

He decided he'd go for the truth. 'I left him at Westminster. He said that this was no time of day to venture out on the water. Apparently, you've always made giving birth sound so easy, that he stopped worrying ever since you acquitted yourself of delivering your sixth. He said he will be here to check on you in the morning. In the meantime, he sends his warmest regards.'

Eleanor looked well pleased. 'He is naughty, is he not?'

'Very naughty! For one thing – keen correspondent as he is when it comes to attending to business and ordering people about – he doesn't write to *me* nearly as regularly as I would like him to. Certainly not promptly enough to dispel my concerns when false rumours reach me. The news of his supposed death nearly killed me last month!'

'You must excuse him, Uncle. He's quite capable, though, of taking care of himself. Or so I choose to believe. I could hardly spend my life fretting about his safety, considering the risks he takes.'

'And considering the ill-will of his enemies. Why, Eleanor, does your husband meet with so little general favour?'

It was the first time that Edward had addressed this topic openly with Hugh's wife. In recent months, he had had to face the reality of just how much everyone opposed Hugh. He had spent much time and energy defending him from the accusations of his detractors, including Isabella's, though it wasn't obvious that he had accomplished much.

'You know him, Your Grace. He's incapable of ingratiating himself to anyone.'

'He doesn't need to. He is the richest man in the Realm except for me.'

'But even before then – before my husband could suspect that one day he would be basking in your favour, Your Grace – he never really tried to help himself. He never made it his business to court others' benevolence. The concept of being *nice* to people is quite alien to him. Why, whenever he wanted something badly enough, he simply made sure to take it. And I'm afraid that taking has not always meant, for him, to get people to want to give it to him willingly.'

'Do you mind that?'

'I do. But there's honourableness to my husband's ways. He will not flatter. He'll not ask for favours. He is incapable of hypocrisy. And he will not betray, perhaps because he makes almost no one expect his loyalty to begin with.'

'Don't you expect it?'

'I do. He will always look after mine and my children's interests unless we turn against him. He'll secure his children's future. He's attentive to us, in his way. But that's where his loyalty ends.'

Edward understood the implication: Lady Despenser suspected that her husband slept with other women. If he did, Edward was not aware of it.

'Then, again, I look around, and it seems to me that this is more than many women – even women of rank like me – can expect of their husbands.' She paused for a moment. 'Besides, he makes me laugh. And I do think him comely.'

'That he certainly is,' Edward said and immediately worried that he might have shown just a smidgen too much enthusiasm. 'But how about me, Eleanor?'

Eleanor laughed. 'Uncle, you surely needn't have me tell you that you're the handsomest man in the Realm?'

Edward's face flushed as he too laughed. 'I meant whether I'm entitled to expect Lord Despenser's loyalty. Or, which is probably a better question, whether I *can* expect it.'

'My husband loves you, Your Grace,' Eleanor said at length. 'That's all I know. I can't say if it will last – how long. He's never loved anyone before, I don't think. So I have nothing to go by. But he does love you.'

'How can you be sure?'

'Are you not sure about it, uncle?'

He hesitated; then he heard a tweet come from above him and raised his eyes. Dozens of small wooden cages were hanging from the ceiling, accommodating the forty-seven goldfinches he had gifted Eleanor a few weeks ago. The chattering of humans had stirred one of the birds out of its sleep. At this time of year, the birds tended to be quiet even at daytime, but in the spring, the males would start singing in earnest. Then, their liquid, crystalline notes would ring out something like *'Uninquisitively, uninquisitively'*. Uninquisitively: wasn't that the best way to love?

+

LATE MARCH 1326.

Edward. You will agree I've been writing more often recently, and yet there is much I can't write about, let alone tell you face-to-face.

I'm apprehensive about what's to come. You know as much. And I know you share my concerns, despite your remarkable ability to carry on with life as usual even in the darkest of times. I suppose you had many years of training and little choice. You would have ceased living long ago if you hadn't learnt quickly how to stop forebodings of impending doom from crushing you.

I've never feared death, particularly. What's to fear about nothingness? I'm almost sure that's what becomes of us all, though I mostly keep such thoughts to myself and act as if I believe otherwise. I tend to think that confessing and giving to the Church achieve precisely nothing in one's quest for eternal life, but then again, neither can they hurt the prospect of it, can they? Anyway, I've never much feared dissolving into nothingness, though I have always been determined to make the most of my time while I'm around.

Indeed, there have been times when I thought that I'd rather welcome the prospect of turning into nothingness, when my time is nigh. I don't fool myself that I'll be able to keep up this pace of life indefinitely. There will come a time when I'll have to slow down, and it has always seemed to me that life would then become a bore. There are moments when I already feel the tedium of certain pursuits of mine. Yet, I'm so thoroughly embroiled in this life as I have shaped it over the years, that it has taken on a direction of its own – one that claims me even as my own feelings and preferences are shifting. For they have been shifting – starting, I think, from the day you invited me to share your bath with you.

As far as I can remember, my feelings about life and death have always been much the same: that the demands of my own life must be asserted – when sufficiently urgent – even at the cost of inflicting pain or death on others; and that my own death will be the only possible and satisfying conclusion when the imperatives of life have run their course. Until now. For, now, everything has changed. How was I to contemplate such a shift in everything that I believed in, Edward? Should I have seen it coming?

Eleanor once told me that I'm unfeeling, incapable of sympathy. She said it as a matter of fact, without holding it against me – there's rather a lot of me that, I suppose, she must needs accept matter-of-factly. It certainly never occurred to me to take it as a criticism; although the fact that she added that it was 'not my fault' implied her *belief that there was something regrettable about it. It turns out, Edward, we were wrong, Eleanor and I – she in stating that fact about me, and I in believing it. It turns out, I'm not actually unfeeling: realizing that I am not, after all, impervious to falling in love surely negates the certitude of my deadened heart.*

Before you, life had always been a force unto itself to me: one's life requires one to exert oneself in its service, to satisfy its needs. One must take life's needs and demands at face value, or so I felt at the time. What is, for example, the point of resisting the desire to possess, be it either things or people, if one has a way of satisfying it? Wouldn't opposing such desires amount to a denial of life itself – when their stubbornness proves that these desires are themselves the stuff of life? You give them up, and what else is left to push you forward?

But you see, Edward, this is no longer me speaking. It's the older me. Where I only used to see the compelling quality of life's brute force, knowing only of its imperatives, I now see something quite unlike it – and I hardly know what to call it. Value? Meaning? Such notions always used to strike me as redundant and laboured. Life simply is, life demands, life compels: how silly, how futile to dress this truth in metaphysical garb – value and meaning, indeed! That used to be my way of thinking. And yet, being now what I am to you, and thinking of what you are to me... I now feel as if the whole course of my life – every step of the way – was meant to be just the way it was, so as to lead me to you. So that I *should be appointed your Chamberlain (I'd never have been, had I been any more likeable, for the Earls then would have feared my ascendance over you). So that* you *should invite me to step into your bath (it couldn't have happened if I hadn't been placed in your service as Chamberlain). So that* our *lives should become indissolubly joined as they now are: for I told you before that I should never allow you to abandon me.*

Wasn't I meant to love you? And you me – when no one else does, or ever will? How could it be that we met by chance, when you're the one person capable of loving me, and of being loved by me? Do such things happen by coincidence? How can I deny meaning now – knowing this, knowing that it did happen? How could I deny it without hypocrisy? This is why, Edward, for the first time in my life, I feel afraid – there, I said it. I'm afraid that my time will be up all too soon before I've had the opportunity to slow down. For I want *my life to slow down, now. Of course, no one – least of all you – realises the sea of change that has occurred within me. You see me as intent as ever on spurring life forward, on drinking the cup to the dregs – without realising that that's simply me letting myself be carried along with the tide, along the course I pre-determined long ago, when everything was different.*

It took me time to realise what was happening to me. Initially, the euphoria of our mutual infatuation made me feel so reinvigorated. Knowing no better, I channelled this surplus energy into the familiar course I had set myself on many years ago. Only now – when I have it all, now that I have grown fantastically rich and powerful – can I see clearly. Now I'm able to tell the necessary apart from the accidental. The necessary: you and I, together. The accidental: the course I once chose when I thought no alternative was conceivable.

But that course was not meant *to be, not by necessity, I mean. I didn't have to be the King's favourite; the richest man in the country; the one with the power to make or unmake other men's fortunes. The only thing I* had *to be, Edward, was yours. And now I fear that the only thing we were meant to be, we will have been for an instant only.*

I can't think this is going to end well. Now that the Queen has revealed herself as an ally of Mortimer, there's little hope we will come out the winners. Just when the ranks of our enemies increase – both at home and abroad – they have found in the Queen a symbolic bearer of all their grievances against us, to galvanise them into certain rebellion. Now it's not a matter of 'If', it's only a matter of 'When'.

The Pope keeps writing to me to tell me to stand aside and let the Queen resume her proper place, next to the King. But even if that could delay what ultimately must come, and even if it could avert it altogether, I couldn't do it. Now that I've found meaning – or, rather, now that meaning has found me, for I sure never set out on a quest to find it – how can I be expected to give it up?

Thus, Edward, although I could never say all of this out loud to you, or write it in a letter, I'm quite terrified. How else could I respond to the prospect of losing the life that has placed me, albeit all too late, just at your side? The one person in the world who chose the hated Despenser above all others?

+

Mid-June 1326.
Gravesend, where Hamo Hethe, Bishop of Rochester,
had just seen Edward and Hugh off on their way
to London, after they had spent a
couple of days at the Bishop's residence.

HUGH LOOKED UP at the sky: it was overcast. It was muggy, too, and it would take them a few hours to reach the City. Perhaps they could have a swim in the river, later. Edward wouldn't say no to that. For the time being, though, they should just try to enjoy their ride – grey sky, horseflies, and pancake-flat scenery notwithstanding. And being rid of that nagging clergyman: let them enjoy that, too. On a couple of occasions, it had been all Hugh could do not to send the holy man to Hell.

Edward said, 'The Bishop likes you.'

'Edward, yesterday he said that if it came to picking sides publicly, he would stand with the Queen and against whoever stood between her and her marital rights.'

'Remarkable man, isn't he? I thought it very brave of him to say that to my face, when I made my displeasure with Isabella's recent behaviour very clear.'

'Fine, it was brave – but in what world does that suggest he *likes* me? I trust that it didn't escape your attention that he meant *me*, when he referred to "people close to the King who interfere with his relationship with the Queen"?'

'But he's a Bishop, Hugh – of course the sanctity of marriage is uppermost in his mind. The point is he treats you well and fairly.'

'I'm the King's favourite! He couldn't very well do otherwise.'

'He *wouldn't*, Hugh, even if he could.'

'If that's how you choose to look at it, suit yourself. I have my doubts. In any case, that hardly proves he approves of me.'

'Since when have you started caring about the approval of Bishops?'

'I don't. I'm just responding to your preposterous notion that the Bishop likes me.'

'I like you, yet I don't entirely approve of you.'

'But that's just my point. You don't approve of me, but you allow me to get away with murder. Almost literally, in fact. That proves you truly love me. The Bishop doesn't approve of me – of my interposition between you and the Queen, as he puts it – and he makes sure to leave me in no doubt about it. Ergo, he doesn't particularly like me. If he treats me "well and fairly", as you say, he's just being civil – to *you*.'

'Shut up, Hugh. My first love used to think everybody liked him, and my second that nobody does. That's probably because the Earl of Cornwall liked himself, while you secretly dislike yourself.'

'I think I'm reasonably good-looking, actually.'

Edward grinned. 'You're *unreasonably* good-looking, especially out of your clothes. But there's more to liking oneself than thinking one is attractive.'

'So what about you? Do you like yourself?'

'I'm too much and too little like my father for me to like myself. My own son, Edward of Windsor, will make a better King than either me or my father – if he stops being a liar and a traitor, that is. And if he manages not to get killed before he reforms.'

'It may be that Mortimer and his men leave him no other choice, for the time being, but to lie to you and turn his back on you.'

A frown appeared on Edward's brow, and Hugh quickly made up his mind to change the subject: he was, after all, the official reason for Edward of Windsor's and the Queen's refusal to return to England.

'Your daughter Eleanor,' he said, 'was delightful last month at my niece's wedding in Marlborough.'

The furrow on Edward's brow deepened. 'Eleanor is not very much younger than her mother was when I first met her. She looks much like her, too. Again, one hopes she does not take after her in her capacity for betrayal.'

From bad to worse. Hugh's mind raced in search of a new subject of conversation.

He hit on something he thought promising. 'Edward, you said two or three days ago you had a confession to make to me.'

'Did I?'

'Yes, you did. Out with it. This is as good a time as any – we're still a few hours away from London.'

'You won't like it. But, by the same principle you have just stated, if you love me you won't let it come between us.'

Hugh already regretted raising the topic. But he knew Edward had often turned a blind eye to questionable conduct on his part: he had no choice but to return the favour.

He sighed. 'So, what is it?'

'I…. This happened rather a long time ago. It may have been January or February, when I was in Harpley.'

Edward stopped. Hugh waited in silence.

'It's about Sir Oliver de Bordeaux,' Edward said.

At the mention of the attractive Gascon squire in Edward's household, the muscles around Hugh's chest tensed up. Gone, suddenly, his resolutions to keep a cool head, be understanding, and all that. *Fuck it all.*

'Well, then? Did you fuck him?'

'Not exactly. I let him…pleasure me. I…paid him for it.'

'You offered Sir Oliver money to *pleasure* you? You treated one of your squires like a common harlot?'

'No! I paid him afterwards. Payment was not a condition. I think he wanted it. Not the money! I mean that he wanted to give me pleasure. I think! God, I hope so.'

'So if he wanted it, why did you pay him? Don't you think you made enough grants in his favour in the past?'

'The favours he received in the past have nothing to do with this – why do you bring that up? This was the first time we – he…'

'Stuffed his mouth with your cock?'

'Please trust me. It's never happened before. The point is that on this occasion I paid him very handsomely – out of all proportion to the service he rendered. I did so deliberately, so that he could not refuse – refuse *the money*, I mean! I wanted to make it clear to him that I received his service as a one-off gift, that I was giving him a gift in turn, and that that was that. The end of it. I couldn't have him get ideas into his head.'

'Sure. Or into your own, more likely?'

'Yes, perhaps, Hugh.'

Riding side by side, they turned their heads in opposite directions, looking into the distance. After a few minutes, Edward regarded Hugh through the corner of his eye.

'With you in my life,' he said 'there can be no room for others – not as my lovers, not in my bed. I made my choice. If I slip, I must find my own way back to you. This is what I want.'

Hugh was silent for a while. He realised the irony of the situation: Edward was apologising for something Hugh himself had done more than once when apart from Edward – and Edward knew it well. But it was different if Edward did it and if Hugh did it. Both he and Edward recognised the difference. For one thing, physical pleasure devoid of emotional involvement was Hugh's default arrangement – but not Edward's. For another, Hugh ultimately doubted his own worthiness as an object of the other's love; Edward did not.

'Was it hard to have to return to me, Edward? Did you have to make yourself *want* to?'

Edward sighed. 'The difficulty was all in giving up the flattery of feeling desirable to handsome Sir Oliver. Coming back to you was the easy part.'

Hugh's eyes continued to stare into the distance, keeping well clear of Edward's own.

+

THEY WERE MOSTLY silent for the rest of the journey to the City. Once they reached the Palace, they immediately retired to the King's chamber. There were gooseberries in a dish and a bowl filled with the first apothecary's roses of the season. Edward bent over the bowl and inhaled deeply.

'My favourite,' he whispered.

He started munching the gooseberries. Meanwhile, Hugh removed all his travelling clothes. Naked, he walked to the table, cupped his hands around the bunch of roses and lifted them out of the bowl. He carried them over to the bed, where he sat, his legs over the bedclothes and his back against the bed-head. He started stripping the petals and stamens off each rose, tossing the stems on the floor after he had plucked the last petal off each one of them.

Still standing, Edward looked in silence. *What on Earth...? Are you trying to get back at me by ravaging my favourite flowers? Isn't that a little emotionally immature even for you, ginger-man?*

When he was done, Hugh picked up all the petals and stamens in his cupped hands. Edward, half expected him to throw them on the floor too, perhaps tread on them; he wondered what Hugh thought the whole performance would achieve. Instead, Hugh gently scattered the petals and wisps of stamens all around the base of his belly. As he opened his legs a little further and lifted his eyes to Edward – clearly an invitation for him to approach – the petals rolled down his cock and balls.

'You're forgiven now,' Hugh said.

They both burst out laughing.

'Are you coming or not?'

Edward removed all his clothes and sat on his heels facing Hugh, his hands each resting on one of Hugh's raised knees. As he buried his face among the petals nestling in Hugh's crotch, the ambrosial aroma of the flowers blended with a more animal scent. It thrilled him, reminding him of his and Hugh's long horse ride.

His tongue took to teasing thigh, ball, and cock, until Hugh's groans and curling toes signalled his endurance was strained to the breaking point.

'Beg your King to take you into His mouth, Lord Despenser,' said Edward.

'Never. Hugh Despenser isn't one to beg.'

'Suffer the consequences, then.'

Edward resumed his teasing, but Hugh pushed him away with his foot. Grinning, he leant forward and grabbed Edward's shaft. Hugh's hand moved up and down it twice, then pulled, forcing Edward to move his own body up, until Edward's knees were pinned on either side of Hugh's head.

+

As the salt from Edward's flesh assaulted his taste buds, Hugh succumbed to a realisation: whatever the future had in store, it had all been worth it for this. Like a portion of the King's body, this knowledge filled him and, as categorically, wouldn't be disallowed.

Thirty-Four

PURSUED

24 September 1326.
Somewhere in the English Channel, off the Norfolk coast.

ISABELLA'S VEIL FLAPPED in the wind. Impatient, she pulled it off: the weather was ghastly, as usual, and she was hardly likely to get sunstroke. The salt in the air would matt her hair – that was inevitable, annoying, but she'd wash it. People would talk, of course: 'Look at the Queen, with her head uncovered, like some gypsy woman.' But what difference could it make? Considering what she had set about doing, it's not as if she could avoid the charge of overstepping the bounds of propriety. She might as well take full advantage of it and discard, together with blind loyalty to her husband, all unquestioning adherence to meaningless convention.

Did it have to come to this, Edward? Why did you have to drive me to join forces with your enemies – formerly my enemies – and invade the country of which I am anointed Queen? Let it be clear: this is your doing, not mine. You, who first deprived me of my friends and attendants, then of my lands, and finally of the very means of sustenance – reducing me to the status of a beggar at my brother's Court.

The Queen of England was turned away as persona non grata *by her own brother. He claims his honour is at stake if his sister refuses to return to her husband. But how do I dishonour him, simply by trying to safeguard my own honour? And how does he suppose I could return to you after the humiliation you subjected me to? I'm under no illusion that you care to understand any of this. I became invisible to you the moment you set eyes on that brute. A stain on the face of mankind: that's what he is. Do you suppose he loves you, that he's even capable of it? Why, the word 'love' couldn't escape his mouth without defilement! Don't you see that in dealing in obscenity with that abominable creature, you belittle and devalue any goodness you have ever done* us *– the Earl of Cornwall and me?*

If I must die to protest against this iniquity and preserve my honour in the eyes of future generations, so be it. But I'll die fighting. It wasn't difficult, Edward, to find the core of my contingent. In fact, they *found* me. *'They' are your worst enemies, those Marchers whom you punished too harshly, in whose hearts resentment has brewed. Or, perhaps, those you didn't punish harshly enough, permitting them to live and escape – and, now, plot against you. Sir Roger Mortimer is their leader. If my motive in waging this war against you were other than to preserve my honour, I would consider allowing Sir Roger to love me. That I should entertain such a possibility shows how deep into dishonour you, my husband, have already plunged me.*

But there are more on my side, besides Lord Mortimer and the other Marchers. There are also well-trained mercenaries – those that the Count of Hainault has procured in exchange for my consent to the betrothal of his daughter Philippa to our own son Edward of Windsor. Our son, who, as things stand now, is infinitely worthier than you to sit on the throne of England. And there are those men who were formerly your allies but have now turned against you – prime among them, your half-brother, the Earl of Kent.

Your folly, Edward – your compulsion to sponsor the very man who is least worthy of Royal sponsorship – has now turned everyone against you, even those that Despenser's rapacity didn't alienate from you long ago. Am I naïve, then, when I dare hope that, as we march through the country after we have landed, far from being opposed, we shall see our ranks increase? We don't come simply trying our luck. We planned this. We timed this. We know of your present weakness. We know of the losses you suffered one month ago when you sent your ships to Normandy in a show of force against the French King – fancying, in your delusion, that he *is the head of the resistance against you, rather than me. Just because you were devoted to your sister Elizabeth and even ransomed her traitor of a husband, Hereford, from the Scots – just because you are soft-hearted, you imagined my brother would move a single finger to support me. You, who love your own sex beyond measure, are blind to its moving principles. Here's a lesson for you, dear husband: in love and in war, men only have eyes for one another. We women simply figure in their calculations as means, never as ends. My brother, the King of France, scarcely cares a whit more about me than you do.*

Well, this is all about to change. You, and the whole of England, will have to reckon with Queen Isabella and her army – fifteen hundred strong. If I must die in the process, so be it. Better dead as Queen than alive as a starving vagrant, kicked out of the Royal bed by the scheming, orange-haired Despenser. But I tell you, Edward, I don't plan to die. I come not to meet, but to bring death to him who made you unrecognisable to me.

+

Around 10 October 1326. In Gloucester Castle.

EDWARD STOOD BEHIND Hugh, who was looking out a window. He studied the muscles on Hugh's exposed shoulders, and gloried in the lean shapeliness of his bare haunches. They had been on the run for two weeks now. He thought about their current sanctuary, with its massive keep, the tall tower by the main entrance, the River Severn on one side, and a double line of moats on the others. Would it be so bad to be besieged here? There was a physic garden, even a vineyard. The King's chamber, with its adjoining Chapel, was as good as any. Hugh could have the Queen's chamber for his personal use. (That part of the arrangement would be particularly satisfying: on the assumption that word of it reached Isabella.) The Queen's chamber too had its own Chapel. Not that Hugh would have much use for that.

Hugh's voice shook him out of his idle musing. 'Your reign won't go down in history for having been uneventful: there's that at least.'

'I've had to flee before the enemy in the past,' said Edward to Hugh's back. 'This time it's worse, though. Everyone's deserting me. The moment my own wife and son turned against me and started pursuing me like quarry, they gave license to all the Kingdom to do the same.'

'They're not pursuing you. They are after the evil counsellor. The "red fiend".'

Edward hugged Hugh from behind. The sunshine from the window made Hugh's hair look just like copper that had been spun into threads by a magician smith. Even his scalp smelt vaguely metallic. He kissed it and felt his prick, soft, stir faintly as it brushed against the small of Hugh's back.

'Whether they're after you or me makes no difference. I love you like my own flesh. They know you're my life. And they want to take it away from me.'

Edward's forearms girthed Hugh's waist: Hugh covered them with his own hands.

'I would be doing the same, Edward.'

'Stand by me and against the Kingdom – if you were King and our roles reversed? I should hope so.'

'I mean that I wouldn't be letting you get away with it. If I were in the Queen's shoes, and you had chosen another, I wouldn't spare you and your lover either my rage or my revenge. You're the one person in the world that could move me in this way – make me feel utterly betrayed.'

'You punished betrayal in the past.'

'True, but I never minded other people's disloyalty other than as an inconvenience to my ambitions. *Your* betrayal, however, would send me into an exquisite fury. I shouldn't rest until I made you pay for it. So, I bow to the Queen for turning against you, and for wanting me dead. I should despise her if she didn't.'

'You're saying she has every right to want you dead. That's crazy.'

'All I'm saying is that there's integrity to her motives – an un-Christian sort of integrity, but integrity nonetheless. You know it. That's why you cannot bring yourself to declare her a traitor and enemy of the Kingdom.'

'How is all this supposed to make me feel, Hugh?'

Hugh shrugged. 'It's supposed to make you feel better.'

'It's a twisted way of looking at it. You may, after all, be the evil counsellor they accuse you of being.'

He kissed Hugh's neck. Hugh disengaged himself.

He turned to face Edward. 'What's twisted about it? It's her love for you that's driving the Queen to these extreme measures. That's beautiful.'

Edward snorted. He pushed Hugh out of the way and stuck his head out of the window to look at the river, left and right.

Then he turned around. 'Lundy. You said it was our best bet.'

'I think so. If we take a boat from Chepstow, they'll think we're sailing to Ireland. While Mortimer's forces are busy searching there, we could sail back from Lundy, move north and seek protection from the Scots. Or we'll stay put in Lundy and I'll send for my pirate friends. They could help us secure passage to the Continent. Surely you could find someone prepared to offer us protection there.'

Edward sighed. The Scots and pirates: you know something has gone wrong with your rule when they are the people you think of turning to in time of need. But virtually all his God-fearing English friends had turned their backs on him. He could scarcely afford to be picky.

+

EDWARD AND HUGH, with a handful of men, set sail for the isle of Lundy from Chepstow on 20 October. As the boat steered its course between the red cliffs flanking the River Severn, Edward had felt excited and hopeful. Since leaving behind the mouth of the river, however, they had made little progress. A lack of favourable wind was holding them back. After a few days, it became plain that they would be forced to return to the mainland.

Hugh said, 'Impressed as I am by your rowing skills, Edward, – you really do compare favourably with any member of the crew – you won't be able to row us all the way to Lundy. Not with all this cargo.' He flashed a wicked grin in the direction of his confessor. 'Perhaps we should throw Father Bliton overboard.'

'Please don't mind him, Father,' said Edward. 'My Chamberlain has a twisted sense of humour.'

'I count that as one of his *good* qualities,' said the man, as the wind tossed about his head what was left of his sun-bleached hair. Thick-skinned, sunburnt, and deeply wrinkled, Bliton's face looked incongruously at home among mariners. 'It's a miracle this boat has not yet sunk under the weight of his sins.'

Edward grinned.

'It all goes to show,' said Hugh, 'how completely your spiritual guidance has failed me, Father. It seems St. Anne finds you less than compelling too: where is the wind you promised?'

'I never promised the wind itself,' said Bliton. 'I merely promised I would pray to the Saint for her intercession.'

'Much good that did us,' said Hugh.

Edward, meanwhile, had given up rowing. He instructed the small crew of mariners to make for the mainland, towards Cardiff. He could have lashed out, he supposed, at the direction of air and water currents; at Isabella; at Edward of Windsor; at the Fates. His stock of anger, however, seemed no less depleted than their supplies of food and water. Land would mean, if nothing else, a modicum of privacy with Hugh; being out of the drizzle, which was falling frequently enough to cause them discomfort, but not so frequently as to make a difference to their water reserves; and a bath. Or at least it would mean these things unless or until they were captured.

Turning to Hugh, he said, 'I really thought we'd make it.'

They looked at the gulls performing acrobatics all around them, skimming the water's surface, ascending quickly, flying in circles, and dipping again.

Edward asked, 'You know the colony of seabirds on Lundy?'

Hugh nodded. 'The Gannets.'

'They're known as the birds of Ganymede. It always struck me as wrong: that should be the honour of the eagle. Do you know of the rape of Ganymede, Hugh?'

'You may need to refresh my memory.'

'Ganymede was a youth so beautiful that Zeus became infatuated with him. Having turned himself into an eagle, the God swooped down on the youth, carried him off to Mount Olympus, and made him cup-bearer of the Gods.'

Hugh shrugged. 'Clearly, Zeus was smarter than Sir Tristan.'

Edward immediately caught Hugh's meaning: he had given Hugh a richly decorated copy of the romance of *Tristan and Isolde* about three months before.

'Well,' Edward said, 'the fact that the birds of Ganymede – be they gannets or eagles, it doesn't really matter – nest on Lundy, and only Lundy, tickled my fancy. I took it as a sign. I allowed myself to dream. Pointlessly, as it turns out.'

'Dream of what?'

'Of new beginnings. Of giving up the Crown I never asked for. Of a simple life.'

A smirk half-formed on Hugh's lips. 'On Lundy?'

'Why not? I'd make an excellent fisherman.'

'No doubt. There must be no other King in Europe who enjoys buying his own fish, rowing, boating, swimming and all manner of water sports. You could make the transition quite effortlessly. And what role was I supposed to play in this idyllic fantasy of yours, pray?'

'Why, you were going to be Ganymede.'

'And hold your cup?'

'That, or something else. Mostly, you were supposed to be mine. Forever.'

Hugh drew a deep breath and exhaled. 'Lundy as our personal Olympus. I might have grown used to that.'

+

After landing at Cardiff, Edward, Hugh and their small following made their way westwards, to Hugh's fortress of Caerphilly. The stronghold was well-provisioned, but after a few days, the King and Hugh left with a following smaller even than that which had sailed with them from Chepstow, and they travelled further west.

During the first third of November, they divided their time between the Cistercensian Abbey at Margam and the Castle of Neath, within Hugh's own Lordship of Glamorgan, where the news reached them of the hanging of Hugh Despenser the Elder in Bristol. Hugh's father hadn't been a paragon of restraint and self-denial, exactly; but neither had he been more rapacious and self-aggrandising than most powerful English noblemen. Edward felt as much affection for him as Hugh himself did – which was, admittedly, no more than a little. But he felt oppressed by the knowledge that what had merited the man's execution, in Isabella's eyes, wasn't any of a number of misdeeds Despenser may have been guilty of, but the man's unflinching loyalty to the King.

When Hugh and he made the decision to leave the safety of Caerphilly behind them, there was a tacit understanding between them. Edward could sense it. If they committed to barricading themselves within the fortress for the next several months – for that is how long Caerphilly would withstand a siege – there could only be one outcome: their eventual capitulation when the siege succeeded. The thought was unbearable to both Edward and Hugh. Much better, for now at least, to be out in the open, ride, be on the move. He could hardly expect Hugh, ever the man of action, to lock himself up in a Castle and patiently await his doom. As for himself, physical activity and the outdoors always kept his spirits up. They could, after all, *return* to Caerphilly before Mortimer's forces arrived for them – if the monks' prayers at Margam, the negotiations between his spokesmen and Mortimer, or, ultimately, Divine Providence brought about no material change in their prospects by then.

It was possible, Edward acknowledged, that all of this riding back and forth from Castle to Abbey merely gave them the *illusion* of accomplishing something. Were they labouring under a notion that they could indefinitely put off the moment when they would have to decide on their next move? Perhaps, leaving Caerphilly behind signified no more than their determination to walk to their deaths now, to make themselves an easy target for the enemy, rather than prolong the agony. Perhaps so. Edward knew only one thing for sure: he had learnt his lesson when he lost Piers and wouldn't make the same mistake again. He'd never leave Hugh behind. They would either manage to escape together, or they would be caught together and face their fate.

By mid-November, their enemies were already in South Wales, tracking their scent trail. At that point, Edward and Hugh, who were again guests of the Cistercensian monks at Margam Abbey, paid lip-service to the conclusion that the only sensible course of action was now to repair to Caerphilly. Yet, it struck Edward that Hugh was no more in a hurry to return to the safety of the fortress than he himself was. Making this moment last – the one in which the impossible remained a possibility – rather than taking definite steps toward prolonging their self-preservation seemed the priority in both their minds.

Edward was aware of a certain disjunction in his and Hugh's mental life at this time. On the one hand, there were the non-verbal ways in which they communicated to each other faith in the impossible prospect of a future life together (they couldn't be called the 'silent ways', because prime among them was erotic activity, and Hugh was never very silent then). On the other hand, there were the verbal ways in which they both spoke as if knowing that fate would catch up with them shortly. Hugh would become uncharacteristically talkative then, and a queer exaltation sparkled in the greenness of his eyes.

'If we don't make it to Caerphilly,' Hugh said early one afternoon in one of the Abbey's cloisters, 'I only hope my son will do himself honour in holding it against Mortimer as long as possible, and that neither he nor Eleanor will come to harm because of me.'

At the centre of the cloister was a well, and they were looking straight into it, each speaking to the reflection of the other's face, their elbows resting on the stonework that surrounded the water hole.

'Isabella has always been on good terms with Eleanor. I think she will not allow Mortimer to harm either her or Huchon.'

'I hope you're right. Either way, Edward, my own death sentence has already been written. Now, listen to me: as far as you're concerned, they capture me, I'm dead. Do you understand me?'

Edward sighed. It hardly bore thinking about. He lifted his eyes to look directly at Hugh, but his lover continued to keep his riveted on the bottom of the well. 'What are you trying to say, Hugh?'

'I'm saying you must give me up – give up any thought of me – as soon as we are separated. It'll be easier for both of us that way. I must be as good as dead to you as soon as I'm out of your sight. I certainly plan to think of myself as a corpse the moment they lay their hands on me.'

Edward returned his eyes to the water hole. Hugh's logic seemed fantastical, but Edward knew Hugh would be angry if he tried to change subject. 'How are you going to do that?'

'Will-power. And I'll refuse any food or drink. With any luck, I'll be either dead, or at least half-dead, before they get around to executing me. If not, I'll at least have entered into the right mood and walking to the scaffold will be a mere formality. But you must do your part: don't make me cling to life when I seek oblivion.'

Edward's eyes filled with tears. They fell to the bottom of the well, causing diminutive ripples. For a moment their reflections were distorted. 'If that's what you want.'

'That's just what I want.' Hugh shook his head and their eyes finally met. 'Don't cry.' He cupped his hand around Edward's jaw. 'Don't you realise that this is the perfect finale?'

'Perfect?'

'Yes, Edward: A whole Realm after the Younger Despenser because the King loved him beyond measure, wouldn't give him up, preferred him to his Kingdom, and loved him better than Queen Isabella herself, one thousand times over. Hounded by everyone, because he had King Edward spellbound.'

Edward wiped his tears with his fingers. 'What's perfect about that? It's just as John said: my love is killing you, just as it killed another before you.'

'Death will come, one way or another. Much better for it to come through love that is extravagant, delirious, and distracted than otherwise. What greater tribute could you have paid me?'

Hugh kissed Edward on the mouth, apparently caring nothing that two monks had been casting inquisitive glances in their direction from the opposite side of the cloistered quadrangle.

'Your love has every right to kill me, Edward. Do you hear? Every right to take away what it gave me in the first place. Did I live before you made me yours? If I did, it was an incomparably different form of living. Life to me used to be like an itch that won't go away. Real, undeniable, yet senseless. I scratched and lived. I despised any notion that life could be anything more than that. Then you came along. At first, I resisted you – what you, without ever asking me, demanded that I should be. Well, my efforts were pitiful!' He grinned. 'But the likes of me, Edward, aren't meant for this. We break under the strain.'

Edward put a hand on Hugh's mouth, willing him to hush. The fingertips of his other hand traced the outline of Hugh's eyebrows, all but invisible to the eye, yet distinctly present to the touch. Hugh let him do so for a few moments, then his hands seized Edward's wrists and pulled the King's hands away.

'One last thing. They'll strip me naked before they hang me. You know that's how it's done. When they do – stop crying, Edward, please – when they do, be sure not to take your eyes off my prick.'

This was getting absurd. Had Hugh gone out of his mind? Edward put a hand to Hugh's forehead.

'I'm not raving, Edward. I mean it. A man who's hanged will go stiff there, most times. It's not a myth – I've seen it with my own eyes. With any luck I'll be one of those that spurt some seed too. That too happens, from time to time. It will be my farewell gift to you.' Hugh grinned again. 'Promise, Edward. When the time comes, I don't want you to look at my face.'

Edward could find nothing to say. Hugh frowned, with a barely perceptible twitch of his right lip and nostril.

'Will you promise, then?'

'If that's what you want,' Edward said and wiped away the tears with the back of his hand.

+

THE FOLLOWING DAY, Edward and Hugh were betrayed by one of the monks. Led into an ambush, they were captured by a party led by Henry of Lancaster – brother to the late Thomas, Earl of Lancaster – in the valley of Pant-y-Brad, about twenty miles east of Margam Abbey, and half that distance from Caerphilly.

As they saw their captors approach, neither man put up any resistance. They simply looked at each other, and Hugh fastened his arms around Edward, his lips pressed to Edward's neck. He said nothing and thought of nothing, only feeling and smelling the dampness of Edward's clothes – it had been raining and thundering on and off all day. They stood in each other's arms, perfectly still, for a few moments only; then the 'red fiend' was dragged away.

He was dead: dead to Edward, and dead to the world. Dead. But it wasn't that easy. *How can I begin to embrace death, Edward, when your taste is still with me?* The tip of his tongue reached out to lick the bitter and salt that had rubbed off Edward's neck when his lips had sunk into it, and tears gathered under Hugh's closed eyelids. But it was all right, no one would notice: it was getting dark, and it had just started raining again.

It was the first and last time Hugh Despenser had wept since the time when he was a very small boy.

+

EDWARD AND HUGH were led through the gully of Pant-y-Brad to nearby Llantrisant Castle to spend the night. Their captors took care to keep them well apart, not only overnight in the Castle itself, but also on their way there.

Edward, riding behind in the rain, could just about make out the outline of Hugh's shoulders in the rapidly dimming daylight, but Hugh didn't turn once to look back at him. He was being true to his word. *As of this moment, he's dead to the world.* Edward straightened his back as he gulped back the tears. Before he knew it, even his lover's blurred silhouette had vanished: somehow, he had missed the moment when Hugh disappeared through the gate of the Castle.

Thirty-Five

BLOODLUST AND MERCY

ON THE MORNING of 17 November, Edward woke up to realise he had been granted the mercy of a deep, dreamless sleep. Henry of Lancaster seemed determined to show him every reasonable courtesy under the circumstances. Not for the first time, Edward thanked God that his captor bore no more than a passing resemblance to his dead brother, either in appearance or manner.

Sir Henry informed him that Hugh had already been removed from Llantrisant Castle. He was being escorted to Hereford – approximately sixty miles north-east of Llantrisant – where the Queen and Mortimer were stationed. Edward snorted when he learnt that Isabella and her ally were staying with Bishop Orleton – as vile a traitor as any.

Edward would be taken in the same general direction as Hugh, but only for about two-thirds of the distance to Hereford, until they reached Sir Henry's own Monmouth Castle. For the time being, the King was to remain there in Sir Henry's custody.

+

A FEW DAYS later, Isabella, Mortimer and Bishop Orleton were debating, at Orleton's Hereford residence, what should be done with Despenser.

It had been a difficult few days for Isabella. Orleton might be a valuable ally and liberal with his hospitality, but she couldn't bring herself to like him. She dreaded his touch – whether it was his hand resting on her forearm during conversation, or his finger drawing a cross on her brow after the sacrament of confession. If, during her recent stay on the Continent, she had often felt that she was not being given her due, Orleton went to the opposite extreme: he was ingratiating to an intolerable extent. Though he was not an especially plain man, his sycophantic ways blighted his presence in a way that made her want to cringe.

As for Mortimer, their victory had emboldened him in ways that made her worry about the future – for her and her son Edward. Mortimer continued to treat her with tact, but he seemed less and less ready to defer to her judgment. Of course, he had understood that she needed his support and was likely to give it for the foreseeable future, even doing so without rubbing it in her face. But she sensed too that he was not unaware of his effect on her: he realised, somehow, that she was drawn to his staying power. He wasn't as well-made as Edward or Damory, let alone Lord Gaveston. But just as Orleton had a way of looking uglier than he was, so Mortimer's confidence made you forget his unremarkable looks. She had started doubting her motives and second-guessing herself: it was unsettling and irritating.

Since news of her husband's capture and reports about his dejection and quiet resignation had reached her, her resentment towards Edward had started to subside. Whatever blame for her husband's estrangement she had previously allotted to Edward himself was now redirected, rightly or wrongly, entirely towards the Younger Despenser. She was now more inclined than not to think of Edward as a victim of his own naïveté, generosity, eagerness, as well as of Despenser's ruthless manipulation of these weaknesses in the King. Thus, if her indignation with her husband had started mellowing a little, her spite for Despenser had only increased. She fully realised the hatred was eating away at her, but she couldn't let go of it.

The fact that, much to her disconcertment, the Chamberlain's capture had failed to make her feel the sense of triumph she had anticipated only augmented her anger. Why, as an unjustly dispossessed Queen and wife, was God denying her the consolation of taking pleasure in her own victory? Perhaps, she told herself, she sensed that her victory would remain precarious until the Younger Despenser was blotted out of existence. For as long as he remained alive, she would be unable to rejoice in the righting of all her wrongs.

Happily, they all agreed – Mortimer, Orleton and she – that Despenser should be put to death, and that any trial preceding the execution would be a mere formality. It was only fair that the man who had taken the life of a Queen from her should pay with his own life. The disagreement was about the place of execution. She had her heart set on London. Only if staged in London would the execution attract maximum publicity and fully mark both the triumph of justice and the inauguration of a better time for the Kingdom. It was, therefore, both unexpected and disappointing when Mortimer informed her that there wasn't enough time. Despenser's self-imposed fast was taking its toll: he would die any day now, and he certainly wouldn't last until he was removed to London. He had to be executed immediately, in Hereford. Orleton agreed that natural death would be entirely unbecoming for the man who had seduced the King and defiled the Crown. The Angels wept tears of blood at the thought of the Younger Despenser's sins: he had proven himself such an obdurate sinner that only through the most severe and exemplary punishment would he stand a chance of truly repenting in his heart, and of being spared much worse torments in the afterlife. As a matter of Christian duty, as much as for the sake of justice, he absolutely must be put to death now before he starved himself to it: the execution had to be at Hereford.

Isabella relented. 'Let it be done, then, as soon as possible.'

'In that case, we must immediately send for Sir Henry of Lancaster in Monmouth,' said Mortimer. 'It was agreed that he should be given the satisfaction of attending the execution of the man most instrumental in the murder of his brother.'

'Sir Henry must be instructed to bring the King,' Orleton said.

She frowned at him. '"Must"? I fail to see the necessity of it. You speak with so much fervour, Bishop, that one could be forgiven for thinking you own life depended on it.'

The Bishop shut his eyes and hung his head, revealing a bald patch that had, so far, escaped her notice. Then his neck straightened, his lids opened wide, and his eyes stared straight into hers, sparkling with earnestness.

Speaking too fast, he said, 'My Lady, with your permission, King Edward shouldn't be denied the moral schooling that attending the execution will provide. We've been rightly maintaining that the Younger Despenser corrupted the King and his judgement, but we cannot entirely exculpate the King. If King Edward had not utterly cast the love of God and of his most beautiful Queen from his heart, the Devil, in the form of Lord Despenser, never would have had any power over him. We don't do the King any favours by sparing him: he must witness Despenser's punishment if he is to turn away from the Devil.'

'Won't that make a saint of the King in the eyes of the people?' asked Mortimer.

Orleton considered. 'Just because the King's spiritual edification requires that he see justice being done to the man he wrongly favoured, doesn't mean King Edward himself should be seen by anyone. He could be kept in a pavilion nearby and be made to look through a net, or some other such arrangement.'

Something in Isabella revolted at the idea. 'Surely news of Despenser's death will be a sufficient lesson for the King?'

'My Lady,' said the Bishop, 'the King's tyranny was bound up with his unnatural love for this man. What better way to persuade the King to return to God than by making him bear witness to the righteousness of God's Hand administering – through us, His willing instruments – frightful torments on the felon Despenser?

Suddenly, she felt she couldn't bear it any longer. 'You decide that between yourselves, then.'

Feeling weary and empty, she made for the door and went out into the gardens of the Bishop's palace. Stopping by a large stone bowl filled with rainwater – clearly a former baptismal font – she looked at her own reflection. The hardened mouth, the lifeless eyes, and the ashen colouring made her wince. The silk and silver thread trimming around her neckline seemed only to magnify, by dint of contrast, the dullness of her countenance. *You'd think I was the one who was defeated, captured, and about to be condemned. Is this the part where I'm supposed to burst into a demented laugh, break down under the strain of the enormity of my actions?*

She quickly retraced her steps and pushed open the door to the room where the others were having their discussion. Mortimer and Orleton turned their faces towards her in surprise.

'It will all be done in the way the Bishop recommended.'

+

THE SCAFFOLD WAS unusually high and conspicuous, for the edification of the many. It had been erected in Hereford's Market Place, in a spot in full view of what would be the King's vantage point – the upper floor room of a building overlooking the square. The King was escorted there on 24 November, several hours before the time of Despenser's execution, and remained there under guard. Bishop Orleton did give some thought to stratagems that would ensure the King would actually watch the spectacle, rather than turn away from it when the time came; but he balked at putting them into effect. As a result, the two burly guards watching King Edward inside the room in which he had been confined – there were six more stationed outside the door and a whole garrison occupying the building as a whole – were given only a few generic instructions. They should make sure the King would not leave the room; they mustn't obstruct the view from the window; and if the King attempted to address the crowds from the window, they must stop him.

+

EDWARD, IN ANY case, required no coercion to be made to watch Hugh's execution. Even if what he saw would haunt him forever, devotion to Hugh demanded that Edward share in his pain.

The wait during the hours when, out of Edward's sight, Hugh's trial was being conducted at the other end of the large Market Place was excruciating. Edward spent it in prayer, asking God to forgive Hugh's sins and accept him into Heaven.

Now and again, he would overhear people's glee as they exchanged stories about the prisoner: 'He was paraded naked through the town's streets before being led to his trial'... 'He looked in a sorry state indeed: skin clinging to his ribs; cracked, scaly lips'...'Apparently, he's touched no water for over a week'...'Did you see the chafing around his forehead?'...'I heard that a wreath of stinging nettles was placed on his head at the time of his capture, and has been refreshed daily'... Eventually, the roars of the crowd signalled the moment when the trial concluded and the condemned was being led to the scaffold. Edward rushed to the window. Hugh, still some distance away, had been tied to a litter and was now being dragged by four horses towards the gallows.

'Excuse me, Your Grace.'

Edward winced at the feeling of someone's touch on his shoulder. He collected himself and turned. A rough-faced guard held out a palm offering a small lump of a whitish substance.

'With permission, you should put it in your ears, Your Grace. It's beeswax.' The guard winked and said, in a lower voice, 'I pinched a candle from the Bishop's palace earlier today – I trust you don't mind, Your Grace?' He gave Edward a knowing look. 'Your Grace, it will be better if you put it in your ears. You shouldn't have to listen to Lord Desp – to this unholy crowd, I mean.'

Half-stupefied, Edward surrendered to the kindness in the guard's voice. He took the wax, warm and soft from the guard's kneading, broke the lump into two, and sealed his ears. As he turned again to the window, the litter drew close to the gallows and stopped. Hugh was untied and stripped of his clothes; Edward's tears couldn't entirely blind him to the cuts that had been etched all over his lover's body. Then, several men gathered around the condemned. As they drew back again, Hugh re-emerged with the noose around his neck. He appeared unable to stand. Faint from lack of food and water, Edward thought with gratitude, wiping away the tears. Hugh had done it just as he had planned: walking to the scaffold half-dead.

Edward instinctively shut his eyes as they started hoisting his lover up the gallows, but immediately forced them open again: he wouldn't let squeamishness stop him from sharing Hugh's torments. The apparent lifelessness of Hugh's limp body as the rope pulled it up the wooden structure broke Edward's heart; but he still thanked God for being spared the spectacle of twisting torso and convulsing limbs.

He wanted desperately to search Hugh's eyes, when his promise came back to him: he wasn't allowed to look into Hugh's face. As his gaze took in the body he had held close so often in the last four years – and yet, as he now felt with an unbearable pang of regret, not nearly often enough – he realised the red etchings criss-crossing the white skin were biblically-inspired inscriptions. Sickened, again he turned away from the scene; and once more, drying his eyes, he returned them to it.

Finally, as Hugh was being pulled higher and higher, slowly but surely what Hugh had said would happen did happen. Just as, out of Edward's sight, the noose around Hugh's neck must be stopping the blood from draining away from the beloved face, make it puffy and unrecognisable; so too, by some mysterious laws of physics and anatomy, whatever life was left in the white, cadaverous body seemed to decant to the base of Hugh's abdomen, and the higher Hugh went with every new pull of the rope, the higher his prick soared, until it was pointing to the heavens. It was like a miracle, and for a moment, Edward forgot everything: there were no more trials or executions, no sins and crimes to atone for, no trumped-up charges, no bloodshed, no bloodlust. Only Hugh's manhood – grand and reaching for the sky.

The reverie lasted no more than a few moments. Then, what Hugh had said *might* happen – what he had *hoped* would happen – happened too, and Edward snapped out of his stupor. Did Edward dream of it, or had the fluid actually flown? How was it possible, if Hugh had refused to drink anything from the time of his capture? And even if the seed *had* spurted out, had the scaffold been close enough to the window for Edward to even see it? But these doubts only came later. At the time of the event – or the event he imagined – Edward only knew, if for an instant, of Hugh's full triumph as he spent himself over the taunting crowds. They who had lusted for blood and death, they were dealt the sap of life.

Hugh didn't die by hanging. Edward knew he was never intended to. Before he exhaled his last, Hugh was lowered to the ground and his face repeatedly slapped until he revived. Then he was tied to a ladder. The ladder was made to stand against the building opposite the one occupied by Edward; and when Hugh ended up at a height more or less level with Edward's eyes, the King knew it had all been carefully planned.

The moment during which Edward had vicariously experienced Hugh's triumph swiftly passed. Everything in Edward by now was shattered, except his resolve to keep watching, to make Hugh's pain his own. A man climbed up the ladder, brandishing a butcher's knife. When he reached the condemned, he took hold of his balls and semi-erect cock and, to Edward's complete horror, sliced them off at the base. Mechanically, Edward's gaze followed the man's bloody hand as it waved Hugh's bodily parts at the jubilant crowd. *I won't look at your face, Hugh, I'll not fail you, not like I did Piers! Not you too, Hugh...* Edward stopped breathing while his eyes went on to track the arc traced by Hugh's severed genitals as they bounced off the man's hand and landed into the pyre that had been lit near the foot of the ladder. For the rest of the execution, Edward kept his eyes firmly on the innermost area of the blazing fire, scarcely aware that the sizzling and sputtering increased after something else – he knew not what – was thrown into the pyre.

Later, his urge to punish himself through intimate knowledge of every least detail of Hugh's ordeal forced Sir Henry to give an account of what his eyes had missed. After the castration, the blood had flown thickly down Hugh's thighs, drenching his calves and dripping from his toes. The executioner had then cut open Hugh's belly and, with slow deliberation, pulled out his entrails to the tune of his victim's screams. Finally, after feeding the entrails to the flames, the man had plunged the blade under Hugh's breastbone and snuffed out both the voice and the life of Hugh Despenser the Younger by carving out his heart. The false heart of a traitor, it was said. But Edward knew that Hugh's heart had been many things – too often unmoved, perhaps – but never false, and quite incapable of treachery.

HUGH WAS DEAD. The candle wax sealing Edward's ears had prevented any sound from alerting him to the exact moment when it had happened. Nor had Edward received any visual cues of Hugh's demise. For he never shifted his gaze from the flames once they had accepted the parts of Hugh's body with which the people suspected the King to have had an improper familiarity, and on which he had promised Hugh he would keep his eyes riveted. Yet, without either hearing or seeing, Edward sensed that his lover was dead the very moment Hugh had ceased breathing.

Edward knew then how the script would continue a moment's hence. Out of his eyesight's range, Hugh's corpse would be – was being – pulled down the ladder, decapitated, and quartered. His head would later be shown off on a spike on London Bridge, whereas the four quarters of the Kingdom would each receive one of the quarters of Hugh's body, to be put on public display. Carlisle, for the North-West, would get Hugh's left arm and the left-hand half of the torso; York, for the North-East, would get the right; Dover, for the South-East, would get the right leg and hip; and Bristol, for the South-West, would get the left. Even after the butchery was over and the crowds, satiated, had left, Edward religiously kept his eyes on the billowing flames until not just the fire, but his whole world, had turned to embers.

+

THE GUARDS SAID they had been instructed to keep him under watch until Sir Henry of Lancaster came to collect him. They would then escort them both to their lodgings for the night, though Edward already knew that sleep wouldn't come. Sir Henry, in whose custody Edward officially remained, would subsequently take his precious charge to Kenilworth, as impregnable a fortress as any in England. It was a curious twist of fate – but also one that afforded Edward a bittersweet comfort – that he should spend the remainder of his life, so he imagined, a stone's throw from the place where Piers had been executed.

Indeed, to all the unmitigated horror of the last few hours, another small mercy had also followed – a sign, to Edward, that God at least had not forsaken him. After he had pulled away from the window, exhausted and rent apart by grief, he had sat on the floor, arms crossed, elbows on his lifted knees, his forehead resting on his forearms. He wasn't sure how long he had been in that position when a light pressure applied to his arm made him lift his head. The guard's mouth gaped and closed without emitting any sound, leaving Edward bewildered. Then he remembered to remove the wax from his ears and handed it back to the man.

'I got it, Your Grace,' whispered the guard, extracting a parcel out of his surcoat.

The man opened the parcel – it was a large piece of folded canvas – to reveal four or five handfuls of ash and cinders. Edward looked at him, trying to focus, but his thoughts were blurred.

'Lord Despenser's heart, Your Grace, I'm sure I got it – it's bound to be mixed up in there. The executioner flung it into the fire.'

Edward's eyes – their lashes still matted from weeping – filled up with tears again. He took the parcel from the man's hands and drew it to his heart.

'Why?' he asked, realising the pointlessness of the question even as he was uttering it.

'You're still King, Your Grace. My King.' The guard smiled shyly and looked away. 'Besides, I too love another.'

Edward blessed him. Then he removed a ring from his finger and slipped it into the man's palm. It was a narrow gold band, into which was set a small but perfect garnet: an early gift from Isabella.

Thirty-Six

A KING'S CAPTIVITY

Edward had jumped to conclusions when he assumed that he would spend the rest of his days, and ultimately die, in close proximity to the place where death was visited upon Piers. Sir Henry's custody of the King at Kenilworth turned out to be merely a temporary arrangement. In January, Edward was formally deposed, and his first-born was crowned the Third Edward. But the boy was still under the age of majority, and the new de facto ruler of England was Mortimer. When, at the beginning of April 1327, Edward's guardianship was transferred to Lord Berkeley and Sir John Maltravers at Berkeley Castle, it was obvious to Edward that Mortimer was worried. In the wrong hands, Edward's custody could be used to whip up opposition to Mortimer's rule; clearly, Mortimer didn't trust Sir Henry.

Even with all the time that, in his relative solitude at Kenilworth, Edward devoted to morbidly dwelling on Hugh's death and even imagining – and sometimes desiring – his own, he was left with plenty of waking hours to reflect on the relationship between Isabella and Mortimer. As Edward pictured it, Mortimer's control over Isabella – and his own son? – must be a mixture of need, personal charm, and veiled threats.

To begin with, need. Surely Isabella acted impulsively, without realising that, by striking an alliance with Mortimer, she was embroiling herself in something that she would later find impossible to extricate herself from. Could she really have wanted her own husband deposed? Didn't the situation, quite simply, get out of her hands? But since it came to this, to his own deposition, how could Isabella be expected to handle it alone? During and after the invasion, her grievances as a wronged wife and Queen had lent legitimacy to Mortimer's cause. But wasn't the situation, now, quite the opposite? Edward knew what the magnates and commoners were like. Soon enough, they would feel dissatisfied and turn against the figurehead of power, the Queen, and would start heaping the blame upon her shoulders. She couldn't afford to lose any allies: she would need to hold onto his party for better or worse.

Secondly, personal charm. Piers himself, many years ago, stated that Sir Roger Mortimer had an aura about him. It was true, though he was hardly what you'd call handsome. That Mortimer might be a traitor who deserved death – which he certainly was – did not change that fact. While Edward might not always be trusted to be an impartial judge of the virtues and defects of his own lovers, he had never found it very difficult to recognise that his enemies – with the notable exception of Thomas of Lancaster, he supposed – were not necessarily bereft of *all* good qualities.

Third, threats. Edward didn't doubt that Mortimer's hunger for power made the Queen herself fair game in his eyes. If Mortimer restrained himself, it was not because of any scruples, but because it happened to be expedient to him. Hadn't it been rumoured that, when he was still on the Continent with Isabella, he threatened her with death if she returned to the King? Edward didn't go so far as to imagine that Isabella's choices were simply coerced out of her by Mortimer. He knew her mettle too well for that. But he had loved her enough – and he knew that *she* loved him enough – to find it hard to believe that the favour she showed Mortimer was purely spontaneous.

The queer thing was that although Edward had every reason to loathe Mortimer as intensely as he once hated Lancaster, he found himself, for reasons that remained quite inscrutable to him, caring very little about the man. Mortimer figured into his thoughts not in his own right, but simply because when he thought of Isabella or the Third Edward, Mortimer necessarily came up. Edward had been nursing his rancour against Lancaster for a decade. Hugh – so he said – even admired him for it. But what would Hugh say now, if he saw him so unconcerned about Mortimer as to scarcely intend him as an independent object of his musings, let alone plot revenge against him?

This wasn't purely out of a sense of the impossibility of revenge in his present situation. After all, he had heard rumours that some of his former friends were mobilising, with the goal of delivering him from captivity and restoring him to power. Perhaps nothing would come of it; but, although he had never entirely felt in his element in the political world, he had been in it long enough to know that the tables could turn very quickly on Mortimer. Edward's relative indifference to Mortimer and his fate, then, was not born out of a pragmatic realisation that revenge was completely out of his hands – for it wasn't. Nor was it a result of a newly-conquered wisdom. Edward hadn't learnt to practice Christ-like forgiveness and wish good upon his enemies, as the Dominican Friars kept encouraging him to do with respect to Piers' persecutors.

Perhaps, the source of his indifference to Mortimer was this: when he finally avenged himself on Lancaster, he found that his bitterness at the Earls' murder of Piers was not significantly assuaged. Perhaps, he had learnt that if he let a grudge eat away at him, revenge could never replenish the part of himself that he had fed to his hatred. Perhaps, he had also learnt that the dead don't demand that the living should avenge them, nor even that they hate their persecutors.

Sir Richard de Neueby (Edward was still inclined to think that Piers' soul had been inhabiting the stranger's body during his visit at Eltham in 1313) had told him precisely that. 'Don't trust the shadows,' he had warned Edward – the shadows that had made Edward think that Piers demanded to be avenged. And didn't Hugh, in his own way, absolve Edward not only of the need to hate Isabella – 'If you had preferred another to me I would have turned against you too,' he had said – but even Mortimer himself? Didn't Hugh tell him that death, *this death,* would be the perfect consummation of their bond? That it would seal his own triumph forever – timeless and incontrovertible proof that the King loved him, Sir Hugh Despenser the Younger, better than the Queen, the Crown, and the entire Kingdom?

Didn't Hugh look drunk with a queer exaltation as he explained it all to him?

Whatever the reason, Mortimer and his fate – except insofar as they had a bearing on questions concerning Edward's wife and the new King – simply failed to hold Edward's interest. In any case, Edward's current priorities were concerns of an intimate rather than a political nature. First was the matter of Hugh's remains. Apart from the loss of Hugh himself, what pained Edward most during his months of captivity in Kenilworth was the fate of his lover's body parts. To be in possession of the ashes of those parts that had been consigned to the flames was an unspeakable consolation. But whenever he thought of Hugh's head on a spike on London Bridge and his other parts scattered around the Kingdom, defiled by birds, oozing foul-smelling humours, and arousing disgust in passers-by, he was filled with both indignation and heartbreak. The thought of Hugh's wife, Eleanor, having to witness that spectacle, if and when she was released from the Tower, was particularly painful. Although his friends didn't have unrestrained or unsupervised access to him, he was still able to receive visitors. He asked a few of the most trusted among them to intercede with his son, the King, so that when the time came – when the King was in a position to decide such matters for himself – he should, out of love for his own father, have Hugh's remains collected and given proper burial.

The second matter of concern to Edward was his own fate. He had not opposed, but neither had he formally approved, his own deposition. He could scarcely bring himself, of course, to endorse the decisions of a Parliament that, never having been summoned by him in the first place, had no right to take such a momentous step against England's anointed Sovereign. Nor, even if it had been he who summoned the Parliament that stripped him of the Crown, could he have accepted the articles of deposition. That he could and should have ruled better, he had always been prepared to concede; but he had enough pride left in him to be indignant at the charge that he was guilty of deliberate cruelty and of forsaking his subjects. Even so, resistance to the deposition, given his present condition of captivity, would have been futile. He was also weary – unspeakably weary – of the task of government.

He knew he had never been drawn to political business. He was able to carry the burden if it came with the capacity to make the men he loved exalted above all others. That capacity, of course, was still attached to the Crown. But Edward – his introspection went at least that far – now belatedly appreciated the perils of injudicious uses of that capacity. At the same time, he kept feeling that any *judicious* use of it would have, for him, defeated the point and thrill of having it in the first place. Most important, however, was the absence of the condition that made the capacity valuable to him. That condition was, of course, the existence of a loved one. Hugh, like Piers before him, had been taken away from him forever.

It seemed impossible that there could be another man whom he would love as much as his two dead lovers. Piers and Hugh could not have been more different. It seemed to him as if they occupied the opposite ends of a spectrum comprising all other potential lovers, with the consequence that he could only conceive of anyone other than Hugh or Piers as a necessarily diluted or compromised version of the two vivid originals. Even assuming that there could ever be another man for him in the future, it had taken him almost seven years after Piers' death to fall in love again, this time with Hugh. He would be lucky if it took him only another seven years to find his next lover. And in seven years' time, he would be practically an old man. So, no, there really was no point in clinging to Royal power, since those that he would want to honour by using it had been forever taken away from him, and no one would come after them.

But if Edward had accepted the loss of the Crown, and even bowed to the inevitability of a life in which love would henceforth be known to him only by the pain of its absence, it hardly followed that he would be content with leading a life of captivity, no matter how decently his captors treated him. The very fact that he wondered about the possibility of future love showed to him his own inability to come to terms with the permanence of his current captivity. Even during the dreary winter months he spent at Kenilworth, which hardly invited outdoor pursuits, Edward – so used to vigorous exercise, riding for many miles a day – sometimes felt as if his confinement would drive him insane. Because of this, he welcomed news of his transfer to Berkeley Castle with all his heart. It was due to take place on 3 April 1327. If anything, he only regretted that Berkeley was a mere seventy miles away.

Thirty-Seven

RECLAIMING HIS FREEDOM

Avignon, at some point during the early 1330s.

THE POPE AND his Curia had taken over a whole section of the Dominicans' monastery. Edward wondered how the Dominicans felt about it; then he remembered that he himself had always expected hospitality from any Abbey he visited, sometimes without any notice at all. Even so, he dared say that he'd never descended en masse upon them in quite the same way the Pope had on the Black Friars of Avignon – let alone established himself in his hosts' premises indefinitely. Yes, he had been a little more considerate than that, in his day.

'And what happened after the transfer to Berkeley Castle, My Lord?' asked Manuele Fieschi, notary in the Pontificial Chancery.

The man's diminutive frame had an annoyingly distracting habit of disappearing among the folds of the beautiful damask robe he was wearing. It was a little like speaking to a disembodied wraith; except that Fieschi's eyes, glancing at him from across the table at which they were both sitting, were much too lively for a ghost.

'I stayed in Berkeley until the end of the summer of 1327, or thereabouts,' Edward said, intertwining his fingers and resting his hands on the tablecloth. He was a little ashamed at the dirt under his fingernails, but it was too late. He judged the cloth must be a silk and linen blend, for what else, other than silk, would lend the linen such lustre? Not that such details were supposed to matter much to him any longer, of course.

It occurred to him that his present appearance must look odd to Fieschi. Apart from his humble travelling clothes, his hair and beard were much longer than when Fieschi had visited him in England some years before, and their blondness was sun-bleached a shade or two lighter, like someone who spends virtually all his time outdoors. Which was more or less an accurate description of what he had been up to since his escape to the Continent.

'My custodians, Lord Berkeley and Lord Maltravers, treated me well enough, but the prospect of a life, however comfortable, in captivity caused me much distress.'

'Naturally,' said Fieschi, refilling his cup with the smoothest, most delicious wine he ever remembered drinking.

'Thankfully, not all my friends had forsaken me. While many prelates and barons had voted to deprive me of the Crown, there were as many, I understood, who wanted me to resume wearing it. Attempts were made to free me.'

'Is that how you left Berkeley Castle?'

'No. One of the attempts almost succeeded, but I was recaptured. Mortimer, however, feared that my supporters sooner or later would have their way, and he secretly sent two knights to kill me.'

'He did,' said Monsignor Fieschi. Edward chose not to take the man's excitement personally. 'And who were they?'

'My attendant, who alerted me to the plot, told me they were Thomas Gurney – the man whom Lord Berkeley had recently appointed as my co-custodian – and Simon Bereford. But I never saw them.'

'What happened?'

'Before they arrived at Berkeley Castle, I managed to break free from my prison, disguised in my attendant's clothes.'

Fieschi raised his eyebrows, whose perfect arch, Edward thought, must excite the jealousy of many a noblewoman. 'How, My Lord?'

'Luck. My disguise fooled the Castle's guards. They were fewer than usual that day.'

Actually, it was Lord Berkeley himself who had arranged for the Castle to be semi-deserted that day, so as to facilitate my escape. No doubt Gurney had sought his collaboration in the plot to kill me, and Lord Berkeley couldn't bring himself to be an accessory to regicide, especially if he was in any doubt about the legality of my deposition. In retrospect, I may have helped myself on that account when I once said to him, after the failed attempt at freeing me from Berkeley Castle, that I believed myself still King, not only in my heart of hearts, but also in God's eyes. Perhaps, too, Lord Berkeley had no personal ill-will towards me, which shows a noble disposition, considering that I once had him imprisoned when he laid waste to half the country with the other rebel Marchers and forced me to exile Hugh. Be that as it may, I shan't tell you any of this, Monsignor Fieschi, for when you report this to my son, the King – as you are bound to do – there is no reason to implicate Lord Berkeley either one way or the other in the affair.

'And then?' asked Fieschi.

'When I reached the gate, I hit the porter on the head. He'd been asleep. I used his keys to let myself out.'

Fieschi's mouth gaped. 'Did you *kill* him?'

'Probably. To save my life, you understand. I've come to suspect that the knights charged with killing me may have produced the porter's body instead of my own at Gloucester for the funeral of Edward of Caernarfon, formerly King of England – who, as you know, was generally reported to have died of natural causes. The porter was unusually tall, like me.'

'Too convenient a coincidence to pass over.'

'That's what I think. Also, Kings' hearts are generally removed from the body: I suppose the porter's heart may have been sent to Queen Isabella, as evidence of my death – evidence intended for Mortimer, I mean.'

I confess that in my weaker moments, I can't resist thinking that it would serve you right, Isabella, to be buried clutching a casket containing an impostor's heart; but at other times, especially when I think of the letters and gifts you sent me while I was a prisoner at Berkeley, I find the idea dismal. If only one good thing is to come out of the story I'm revealing to Monsignor Fieschi, let it be that you're not unwittingly subjected to that final indignity, Isabella.

'And where did you go when you left Berkeley, My Lord?'

'To Corfe Castle, on the south coast. My attendant accompanied me.'

'Why there, of all places?'

'At my attendant's suggestion. He knew the Castle's constable would give me refuge.'

No need for you to know, Monsignor, that my other keeper, Lord Maltravers, had been at Corfe some weeks before, at Lord Berkeley's instigation, precisely to arrange a safe haven for me there in case of need, with a whole Castle garrison sworn to secrecy. I owe it to my former appointed guardians – Lord Berkeley and Lord Maltravers – to keep them free of any suspicion that they either participated in my killing, or indeed that they saved my life, which they most certainly did. The times are still sufficiently volatile and turbulent that being suspected of either saving me or murdering me could easily turn out to be fatal to them at some point in the near future.

'And who was the constable at Corfe, who was so faithful to you?' asked Fieschi.

Edward bit his lip. 'Thomas.... I forget the rest of his name just now.'

That was close. The name of the Royalist Constable at Corfe Castle will have to be 'Thomas' for you, Monsignor. I'm not going to tell you it was Lord Maltravers himself. Even with Mortimer now executed, men formerly sympathetic to him could seize power again from my son; and if they learnt about the true identity of my helper, Lord Maltravers would be in trouble.

'Who was his Lord, if I may ask – since you do not recall his name?'

'That was Lord Maltravers – Sir Thomas was his deputy. But Lord Maltravers never knew I was hiding there. Sir Thomas kept me well-hidden.'

Fieschi dabbed his forehead with an exquisitely embroidered handkerchief. 'Incredible. For how long?'

'Until word went about that I was not dead after all. Then, in late 1329 –'

'So you were at Corfe two whole years.'

'Yes, I was. In 1329, the Earl of Kent, my half-brother, who switched sides more often than I can count, but who died for me in the end, learnt of my whereabouts and wrote to me of his intention to rescue me. But his letter was intercepted by one of Mortimer's agents, who had by then been installed in the Castle. Which also meant that it was becoming increasingly difficult for the constable, Sir Thomas, to hide my presence there. So, at his advice, I fled to Ireland. That was shortly after Kent had been executed.'

'In the spring of 1330, then,' said Fieschi.

'You're well-informed about our island's tumultuous politics.'

Fieschi shrugged. 'And then, My Lord? Don't leave me in suspense.'

'I was in Ireland nine months. Then, with Mortimer once and for all removed from the scene, courtesy of the new King, my son,' – *the boy is finally coming into his own, isn't he?* – 'I decided I could afford briefly returning to England. One last time. In the habits of an eremitic monk, just to be on the safe side.'

'Did you visit the King – your son, I mean?'

'No. I sailed directly to Sandwich.'

Because – if you want to know, Monsignor – Sandwich is both very close to Canterbury, where I met my first love, and pregnant of memories of my second. Indeed, it was Hugh's pirate friends that, from Sandwich, escorted me to the Continent. I wonder what you'd make of that if I told you, Monsignor.

'A long voyage from Ireland to the south-east coast of England.'

'Fairly long. To cut a long story short: from Sandwich, I went to Sluys and from there, I came here, passing through Normandy and Languedoc. The details of my itinerary would be tedious to recount.'

'All on foot, My Lord?'

'Naturally. Hermits don't ride horses.'

Fieschi pursed his lips, and Edward half expected him to whistle in admiration. But the Monsignor checked himself at the last moment.

'Indeed. And where will you go next?'

'I've not decided yet. Gascony is the one place I'd really like to visit.'

I wish I could visit your native land, Piers, if only to see the spring pastures blanketed with poet's daffodils.... You said that one day you'd show them to me, but God saw fit that you shouldn't keep your promise.

'But, what with Gascony having remained in English hands, it may be the least safe place for you to be, My Lord.'

'Indeed. In any case, for the time being, I rather hope to prevail upon you to secure me an audience with the Pontiff, and that he will be kind enough to grant a former King, fallen on hard times, his hospitality.'

Edward looked around the richly appointed room: was he simply no longer used to luxury, or was the Papal Curia more magnificent than any King's palace?

'I'm sure the Pontiff will be delighted to have you as His Guest, My Lord. I cannot formally guarantee it until I've spoken to him, but – informally – consider it arranged.'

'I'm very obliged to you, Monsignor.'

'Don't mention it. For what it's worth, I think you were ill-used. Very much so.'

'Thank you. Though I must admit, I've done my share of ill-using. The last few years have afforded me, if nothing else, at least enough time to realise that.'

They were both silent for a while.

'And... You do not desire to be restored to Kingship, My Lord?'

'To tell the truth, I find my present situation not entirely uncongenial, Monsignor. At least it is...restful. After all I've gone through...you understand.' Edward felt a lump forming in his throat. He swallowed. 'You needn't write that down, Monsignor.'

Thirty-Eight

BECOMING A MAN

AT THE END of June 1336, John of Eltham, Earl of Cornwall (the first to enjoy the title since Piers Gaveston), took a break from the Scottish campaign in which, as a commander not yet twenty years of age, he had distinguished himself, so it was rumoured, as much for valour as ruthlessness. His brother, King Edward III, was still in Scotland. He had sent John to Northampton to lead the Parliament of 28 June.

Castle Rising, the Dowager Queen Isabella's preferred place of residence when not travelling either on pilgrimages or visits, was only a few hours away by horse from Northampton. John acted on impulse when he decided to visit her. They rarely saw each other. He was soon due to return and rejoin his brother in Scotland and.... Well, one never knew what might happen to a soldier.

+

THE SIGHT OF her son, as he ambled confidently through the doorway into the Castle hall, startled Isabella. Tall, his brow wide and sun-kissed, wavy flaxen hair bouncing on his shoulders, and eyes clear and blue – he looked for all the world just like his father when she had first met him almost thirty years ago. Was this the reason why she had chosen to see so little of him in recent years? Had the growing resemblance put her off, frightened her?

He approached to kiss her. 'Good morning, Mother.'

'Good *afternoon*, John.'

'Oh yes. I suppose it is. I woke up rather late.'

'It runs in the family.'

Isabella smiled faintly as she recalled her husband's sleeping habits. She asked her attendants to leave and offered her son some refreshments.

+

'To WHAT DO I owe the pleasure, John?'

'Nothing in particular. Do I need a reason to visit my mother?'

She wore no veil, in the Italian fashion, with her lush, tightly packed tresses coiled behind her temples. Streaks of silver highlighted the interwoven strands of hair. She looked beautiful, more youthful than he had expected; he felt unreasonably proud.

'You look very well, Mother.'

'So do you,' she said, taking him in briefly, with eyes that made him feel slightly uneasy. She quickly looked away. 'Shouldn't you be telling me your brother Edward sends me his regards, or something of the sort?'

'Edward doesn't know I'm here.' He paused. 'What is it? Why won't you look at me?'

She turned towards him. 'Don't be silly.'

'I'm not a monster. If you heard rumours about me.... War is war. And I haven't been nearly as beastly as some of the tales paint me.'

She laughed, without joy. 'I heard the tales. So what? Even if I believed them, it's not as if I would be one to speak, would I? I've been beastly myself. In my day. You probably take after me. In that at least.'

'Meaning?'

'Meaning that you are the spitting image of your father, John of Eltham. And that's why I can't bear to look at you, if you want to know.'

'Do you still hate him, then?'

'I've never hated him.' She turned to look at him again, the tip of her thumb between her teeth, and this time she held his gaze. 'Never.'

'Forgive me…if I find that difficult to believe. Your actions imply otherwise.'

'John, you're not yet twenty. You cannot possibly understand.'

'Try me. For a while, everyone's favourite line about me was how precocious I was. You know, slaughtering all those Scots, and I was only seventeen.'

She sighed.

'If you didn't hate my father, why did you have him killed?'

Sharply, she said, 'Are you out of your mind? It wasn't me who had your father killed.'

'You ruled the country with the man who did. For three whole years after he did it. What's the difference?'

'There's a sea of difference. How do you suppose I was to rid myself of Mortimer, until your brother delivered me of him?'

'You tell *me*, Mother. I thought you pretty capable when it came to ridding yourself of unwanted men.'

'Just as I said. You can't – or won't – understand.' She paused and drew a deep breath. 'Once I made the mistake of allying myself with Mortimer, that was the point of no return. I had to keep going.'

'Did you also *have* to bankrupt the Kingdom with him?'

'Who says I did?' she asked, defensively.

'Edward. I mean, the King. And the official records of your incomes and expenses.'

'John…I can't explain it. After the invasion... It's as if I didn't know what I was doing. I was raging mad at your father, and drunk with my victory over the Despensers, and I resented Mortimer for not going away and for helping me become what I'd become. I hated myself. Nothing seemed to matter anymore. I don't expect you to understand. To really understand, you'd have to have lived through it.'

'Didn't I? Live through it?'

She closed her eyes and put a hand to her forehead, looking weary. 'Have you come here to ask me to account for my past?'

'Perhaps. It hadn't occurred to me when I decided to visit you.'

'Go on then. Since we started.'

He considered, briefly. 'Why did you hate my father?'

'I never hated him,' she said with ill-disguised impatience.

'Oh yes? For years you poisoned our minds – Edward's and mine – against him.'

'You've become quite the perfect specimen of your class, John, haven't you?'

What could she mean by that?

'*Men*,' she clarified.

He shrugged.

She shook her head. 'I hardly ever saw you after the invasion, John. How on earth could I have *poisoned* your mind?'

'You allowed those around me to slander him at will. Do you have any idea – I was ten, Mother... You didn't save me from them.'

He crossed his arms and lowered his eyes to disguise the tears that were perilously close to welling in them. He knew he was like his father in this – his brother Edward had said he was always a little too prone to emotional outbursts.

'It looks like you managed to save yourself,' she said.

He swallowed. At least her coldness managed to stop his tears in their tracks: she looked as relieved as he was at the realisation.

'And so did he, you know? He saved himself.'

'Edward, you mean.'

'Yes, Edward. But Edward the father, not the son.'

She looked alarmed. 'What are you saying, John?'

'I'm saying that my father never died at Berkeley Castle.'

Her upper lip twitched. John would have a bit of explaining to do to his brother Edward, who had pointedly instructed him not to talk about the matter with anyone. But John would worry about that later.

'What do you mean? They *saw* the body.'

'They did, but did you? I certainly didn't. Those who did, I'm told, only saw something wrapped from head to toes in the bandages of the embalmer. It could have been anyone, really – or a wooden effigy, like the one that was placed on top of the coffin. Father fled and saved himself.'

'Who says, John?' She had kept a steady voice, but the vestiges of tears started gathering in the corners of her eyes.

'Edward recently got a letter from someone at the papal Curia. Someone important, dependable. Someone who couldn't know certain details, unless Father himself had told him.'

'Who?' The word came out sounding like a puff.

'Sorry Mother, I'm not at liberty to say. I'll already be in trouble with Edward for telling you as much as I have.'

'Where is he now? Your father?'

She shook his arm. It was the first time in years she had initiated bodily contact of any kind with him. He shrugged her off, gently though.

'I'm not at liberty to say.'

'John!'

'I don't actually know, Mother! Edward refuses to tell me. He thinks that if he told me, I'd go to him.' His voice almost broke. 'I would, too.'

His mother had taken to pacing up and down the room. Then she stopped, took a deep breath and told him to follow her outside.

The grounds looked overgrown. The vibrant green of a few weeks ago had given way to a duller shade, and the foliage of the shrubs had grown rather too abundant and thick, their maturity already hinting at the decline that was to come as summer progressed into autumn. It made John wonder if it was possible for people also to grow too much, too worldly, and thereby lose too much of...of whatever childhood was blessed with.

'I never hated your father,' she said, this time quite without anger – indeed, with a tinge of feeling in her voice. 'I loved him. More than I've ever loved anyone. More than he was capable of loving me.'

'There was enough love in Father's heart to suffice both you and Lord Despenser, Mother.'

She was taken aback; he noticed but went on.

'You really didn't need to have him killed – let alone imprison his wife for two years in the Tower.'

+

'You knew?' she asked. It was extraordinary, she thought, that the Younger Despenser's name had been uttered in her presence without her flesh crawling.

'That you imprisoned Lady Eleanor? She was my keeper. I was with her in the Tower when she surrendered, don't you recall? She'd been like a mother to me.'

A task I so spectacularly failed at – why don't you add that, John, since it's clearly what this is all about? But she wasn't going to say that.

'I meant if you knew about Despenser.'

'That you wanted him dead? Of course I knew, Mother – I was ten, not stupid.'

'No. I mean, did you know that your father loved him? *Loved* him, John!' She had raised her voice.

He took time to reply. '"*Like his own flesh*". Father told me himself. His very words.'

Isabella closed her eyes and, raising her chin a little, she swallowed.

'My brother and I were quite terrified of him, you know.'

She took a few moments to collect herself. 'You were?'

'Deliciously terrified. Behind his back, I used to call him "ginger-man". A form of exorcism, I suppose.' He smiled. 'Then one day, he spoilt it all. He approached me and told me very seriously: "I hear that you call me 'ginger-man', John of Eltham." He put his hand inside his robe. I was sure he would draw out his dagger and slay me on the spot, and it frightened me out of my wits. Instead, he took out a gingerbread loaf, in the shape of a man. "Ginger-man!" He handed it to me with a bow. And I started receiving gingerbread men every week. I think Lady Eleanor Despenser had them baked and delivered at his instigation. After that, it was hard to keep up the pretence that he struck dread in my heart. Not that I had to keep it up for very long. A few months later, he was dead, his head impaled and rotting on London Bridge. Poor ginger-man.'

Listening to this account of her son's relationship with Despenser made Isabella think with horror of the fate of Huchon, the Younger Despenser's eldest son, who had been holding his father's Castle of Caerphilly against hers and Mortimer's siege, having been left there by Edward and Despenser in the days before their capture. In her folly, she had at first insisted that Huchon should be executed, though she had later consented that he should be 'merely' imprisoned for life. Thankfully, her son Edward had seen fit to free him after seizing power from Mortimer.

John was saying something about redcurrants, his mouth stuffed with them. She found, quite suddenly, that a weight had been lifted off her chest.

'You look like a child.' She hinted at a smile. 'A very big one.'

'A moment ago, you said I was a paragon of manhood, or something.'

'I said that you'd become a perfect representative of your class. Which is subtly different, you know? And I didn't mean it as a compliment, particularly. So I suggest you should take my rediscovered awareness of your childlike attributes and run with it, John of Eltham.'

He looked at the position of the sun. 'I think that's just what I'll do, Mother.'

He kneeled before her and, looking up, offered her his lips, slightly reddened by the fruit, for her to kiss; she had to close her eyes as she reached down to press her mouth against his, because the resemblance was too much.

He rose to his feet and made immediate arrangements to leave.

Thirty-Nine

REVERIE

Approximately two months earlier,
deep in the hills of south-western Lombardy, in Italy.

EDWARD HAD SPENT an hour fixing some wooden supports in the Abbey vineyards. He unrolled the sleeves of his woollen tunic to cover his faintly tanning forearms, and put the scapular back on. It was the same length as those donned by the monks, but he was so much taller than them, that the hem only reached down to his knees. Tunic and scapular had become his habitual attire since settling at the hermitage of St Alberto di Butrio. The name translated to St Albert of the Ravine, a reference to the limestone gorge above which the Abbey rose, sitting on a wooded outcrop overlooking a creek. When swelled by winter rains, the creek tumbled precipitously down the gorge, but at this time of year, it had already started shrinking, soon to dry up altogether.

He was now wandering the adjoining forest – the one on the hill immediately to the south of the Abbey, which was mainly chestnuts, rather than the forbidding pine forest to the north. He was on the lookout for unfurling shoots of wild asparagus. The harvest had been underway for more than a month.

Was he getting on in years, or did this winter seem to have lasted longer than usual? It was a general source of amusement at the hermitage that, even by the standards of men well used to the rigours of monastic life, 'the English gentleman' seemed completely insensitive to cold; yet, he had become less and less patient with drawn-out winter weather. So much for the simple life making one tolerant of adversities. In any case, he was fairly sure that, in previous years, by the beginning of May, the tree canopies were already verdant, whilst this year, the leaves had only just started to unfurl – the tender greens and ambers of the bursting buds bejewelling the branches. Be-*jewelling*. How interesting that, as appreciative of fineries as he had been in the past, he now didn't miss them in the slightest. Perhaps living a monk's life – or a life among monks, to be more accurate – did bring with it some wisdom, after all.

He reached a familiar clump of wild asparagus, which he had already despoiled – or rather, *pruned* – one week ago. New shoots had already taken the place of those he had removed. Was the plant's growing power inexhaustible? He took a few more shoots but left some to fully develop into stems: he felt that that level of doggedness, even in a plant, should be rewarded.

The wild anemones carpeting the forest floor in patches were very pretty. They too looked like jewels. He wondered if the poet's daffodils – which Piers had wanted to show him so badly – were jewel-like too. He had said they studded the mountain meadows of the Pyrenees at this time of year…

No, Edward didn't miss his jewels. But he missed other things from his former life. Falconry, for one – there were all sorts of hawks, kites, and eagles regularly visiting the hills here. And beautiful horses, and riding all day, and his hounds. He missed those, too. Hounds were far too expensive to keep at the hermitage. One would have thought they could have been trained to earn their own keep by catching enough rabbits, mice, and partridges to survive on. But somehow, it didn't quite work like that.

He wondered if his sons King Edward and John of Eltham were as fond of luxuries as he had been. Did he feel a pang of regret at realising that he had genuinely no idea? Perhaps they had the same passion as him for riding and outdoor pursuits. Did the Third Edward also try his hand at thatching and digging ditches, as he himself once had? Probably not. His own proficiency at these 'improper' pastimes had been held against him; and, from what he could tell from the irregular news he received, his son seemed much more sensible than his father had ever been and much more sensitive to the need to make a good impression as a ruler. He wondered whom the Third Edward might have inherited these qualities from. Like himself, Isabella could not have been said to possess an abundance of these virtues either, to be perfectly frank. That, perhaps, is why they had gotten along so well. Until the last few years, when it all went wrong, somehow.

He still puzzled over the question of *exactly* how. She had resented it when he had sent her French retinue away and seized her lands. But why had she insisted on blaming Hugh for it? Why had everyone else, too? Blaming Hugh – and Piers before him – had of course been something of a national pastime in the 1320s. And, as a self-fulfilling prophecy, it had seemed to make Hugh only more implacable and unapologetic in pursuing his own, but mostly Edward's, self-interest. Even now, as he thought about Hugh's unyielding fierceness, he could feel a stirring between his thighs. St Francis of Assisi was said to have thrown himself on the snow once when he woke up feeling lustful. There was no snow in sight, though. He supposed he would have to live with his own arousal whenever he thought of Hugh's wildness – until next winter, at any rate.

As his hands worked on another well-provisioned asparagus clump, he chuckled to himself. Hadn't Hugh theatrically prostrated himself in the snow before him when they had met in Lichfield after his return from so-called 'exile'? Hadn't he made some mildly lewd joke on that occasion, too, for Edward's ears only? Something about the cold from the snow putting out his arousal? Fancy Hugh and St Francis hitting on the same idea. Hugh and St Francis: not the most likely of analogies. *I miss you, Hugh. Ten years later, I still miss you every day. Sometimes, like today, I miss you so badly I could die.* He sat with his back against a holly oak and, covering his face with his hands, he pressed his palms against his eyes in an attempt to stymie the tears.

He couldn't forgive Isabella for Hugh's death. She had been widely known to have wanted him dead. Why, Edward had even heard rumours of her banqueting with Mortimer under a specially constructed canopy while enjoying Hugh's grisly ordeal! But Edward had always refused to believe that she could stoop so low. Indeed, the more he thought about it, the more he found it hard to believe that Isabella had even insisted on Hugh's death sentence. She may have wanted him dead, but there was a difference between wanting and doing, was there not? And yet something was clear: she hadn't stopped his execution.

Edward still believed that once Isabella had made the mistake of striking an alliance with Mortimer, she had gotten involved in something that had rapidly grown out of her control. That she had then made the most of the situation, whatever it had turned out to be, was simply proof of how resourceful and astute she was. But precisely because she was so resourceful and shrewd, it defied belief that she had lacked the power to stop Hugh's execution; so why hadn't she? It seemed all the more unconscionable, as Edward was sure that she must have exerted herself on other occasions to soften some of the excesses in Mortimer's regime. He was fairly certain, for example, that Isabella had been the one to spare those who had taken part in Sir Henry of Lancaster's failed attempt to topple Mortimer (before Edward of Windsor led his successful coup against the tyrant).

Learning that his former favourite, Audley, had partaken in Henry of Lancaster's plot against Mortimer had been a source of considerable satisfaction to Edward. Audley, having suffered imprisonment at Edward's hand (for siding with Mortimer and the other rebel Marchers in the early 1320s), and having been freed by Mortimer following Edward and Hugh's capture, had later betrayed Mortimer himself! How deliciously ironic. Audley was now even rumoured to be a trusted official in the Third Edward's service. Possibly, then, Audley would still prove himself a reasonably good deal for Margaret, who had left Sempringham Priory and resumed living with him a decade or so ago. Edward could only hope for the sake of Margaret that, along with his former talent for picking the losing side in any dispute, Audley hadn't also lost his looks.

But back to Hugh. It was plain to Edward that after their invasion, Mortimer had needed Isabella as much as she had needed him. That Isabella had not used her power to stay the execution was more than Edward could forgive. He had not stopped loving her, not entirely, but one could love and yet not forgive.

Hugh had told Edward he must remember that he, Hugh, would have done the same had Edward chosen the Queen over him. Sure, he believed Hugh could kill in cold blood. But could Hugh *really* have had Isabella killed, knowing the pain he would have inflicted on Edward? For all his confidence, Hugh couldn't possibly have known what he would have done if their roles had been reversed. No one could. And in this reality, it was Isabella that had Hugh killed (a crime of omission, if not commission). She hadn't completely eradicated Edward's love for her in the process, but she had managed to blight her husband's days for the rest of his life; and perhaps she had destroyed her own prospects of living in happiness too. Edward would never know for sure.

He still thought of Isabella, but his emotional commitment to her had been slowly petering out since he had put more and more physical distance between them. His memories of her had become memories of a past that was waning, and his thoughts of her receded further and further into the background of his mind – except, that is, at moments like these.

Edward stood up – his tears by now had dried – and he resumed his quest for the prized asparagus shoots. Had Monsignor Fieschi conveyed the story of his escape to his son the King yet? It was thanks to Fieschi that Edward had found his new Italian home. Surely, by now Fieschi must have told King Edward of his father's fate and whereabouts. Yet, the Third Edward had made no attempt to contact him. Had his son disbelieved the story? And if he hadn't, what did he plan to do with the body of the impostor who had been buried instead of his father in Gloucester Cathedral?

Arrangements for the proper disposition of bodily remains, for some reason, were always uppermost in Edward's mind, including arrangements pertaining to his own body when the time came. To this end, he had received permission to build his own grave on the Abbey grounds. He had been slowly hewing the grave into the stone in an arched alcove in the west-facing wing of the cloister. It was hard work, but he preferred it to being buried in the Abbey's old cemetery, which was the destiny of all the Brothers at the hermitage. He was penitent; he had learnt, or was learning, all about humility. But he had been King once (though, he conceded, not a very good one). If it was his lot to die in the obscurity of these Italian hills, he had no objection; it had, after all, been his choice; but he wanted his remains to at least lie in the cloister. When the rays of the setting sun flooded it, the grave – looking out as it did towards the open valley, with the hills arranged around it like an amphitheatre – would be as regal a resting place as any.

Yes, the western cloister suited him as well as anywhere. Well, anywhere except Langley, but he had long ago given up hope of being laid to rest next to Piers. Next to both Piers and Hugh, he should say. For when he had set foot on English soil for the last time, five years ago, he had been able to see the White Friars in Sandwich and had secretly charged one of them with taking the ashes of Hugh's heart to the Black Friars in Langley. He had instructed the White Friar to ask permission from the Brothers at Langley to bury the ashes at the foot of the apothecary's rose bushes in the herb garden. He had no reason to doubt that the Brothers at Langley had consented to this arrangement – the Dominican Order had remained loyal to him after his deposition. He had given much thought as to how to best dispose of Hugh's ashes, and it had seemed to him that it could only be at Langley. He was not sure – even if it could have been arranged – that Piers and Hugh would have appreciated sharing the same tomb. But he thought neither would object to Hugh's ashes resting under the rose bushes.

It had been a great comfort when he had learnt that, not long after Mortimer's execution, the Third Edward had allowed Hugh's bodily parts to be collected from the four corners of the Realm and given decent burial at Tewkesbury. Wasn't it the best proof that the Third Edward was destined to be a godly King, after all?

He could no longer spend vast amounts of money having Dominicans all around England pray for his deceased lover as he had done for Piers. But he lived in a monastic community whose motto was '*ora et labora*', and he was living by it as best he could. Therefore, he spent virtually all the time he didn't devote to physical work attending service or in personal prayer, adding up to many hours per day. There was no shortage of spiritual work going towards interceding with God for the salvation of Hugh's soul, even if it all stemmed from Edward's goodwill alone. But that – to be honoured and loved by one rather than the many – had always been Hugh's lot. Edward could never have fallen in love with him if Hugh had been either self-deprecating or delusional rather than lucid when he claimed that no one liked him. It was quite true: one man alone had truly loved Hugh; but then, at least he had been loved madly, and by a King no less.

+

EDWARD RETIRED FOR the night. It would be only a few hours before he would wake up for the Night Vigils – the prayers to be completed before daybreak. He often thought of Piers when he went to bed. They had been notorious for rising late, which meant, among other things, that on many days they missed the only sunny hours that the miserly English weather afforded them. He had often wondered, when young, why sunshine insisted on showing up at the most unholy hours of the early morning, never to be seen again for the rest of the day. It was more than a little ironic that, now that he had taught himself to get up well before the crack of dawn, he lived in a part of the world where he could count on consistent sunshine for most of the day and most of the time. It robbed him of half the reason for forcing himself to get up early.

But he would soldier on. Hugh needed his praying, didn't he? The Night Vigils were particularly good for that. Besides, at this time of year at least, waking up in the middle of the night afforded him the pleasure of listening to nightingales. He sighed. When, as King, he had happened to be up in the middle of the night, the pleasures he had received had not usually come from listening to nocturnal warblers; they had proceeded from the warm human body lying next to him, or over him, or under him…

He recalled his attraction to Priories and Abbeys when he had been still a boy and not yet King. (He remembered the time he had insisted with his father on staying a whole week alone at Edmund St Bury's before the Scottish campaign of 1299.) That attraction – he now realised – had been partly based on the hunch that monastic life fostered a special kind of love among Brothers: a kind of brotherly love that did not entirely rule out, and perhaps invited, certain forms of bodily intimacy. Well, whether or not he had been right in this hunch back then, it seemed clear that nothing of the kind went on in this Benedictine community that had become his home in the Italian Apennines. Silence, during the short hours of sleep, was strictly observed, as far as he was aware. If the Brothers occasionally sought solace in each other's arms, he had certainly not been privy to any of it.

Did he mind? He would be lying to himself if he claimed that he didn't. It had been ten years since he had been held by another man. At fifty-two (he had recently had his birthday) his body, what with his physical work and the regimented routines of monastic life, seemed to him more vigorous than ever. And the inhabitants of this country had more than their fair share of beautiful faces. Why, some were even endowed with eyes trimmed with eyelashes nearly as long as Piers'.

And yet...he must remind himself that he had not left England, travelled half of Europe and settled in this secluded mountain retreat to rediscover love; he had come to save his life, to put it in order, to find the peace and tranquillity that had always eluded him. Most of all, he had come to secure salvation for Hugh's soul. His beloved Hugh, who, despite confessing more frequently than anyone Edward knew, had once implied that only nothingness awaits us on the other side. Besides, Edward now had an additional reason to remain at St Alberto: namely, the need to be out of his son's way. By all accounts, the Third Edward appeared to be doing perfectly well as King without his father's example close at hand.

So it didn't matter. It didn't matter that he felt as if he had hardly aged. It didn't matter that he had vaguely unchristian dreams about one of the novices that had recently joined the community. It didn't matter that at Mass he might get distracted from pious thoughts by the curve of a neck and shoulder; or by the knowledge that one of the most handsome among the Brothers might be sitting right next to him, perhaps close enough for his thigh to unwittingly brush against Edward's own. And it didn't matter that memories of Piers' prick, or Hugh's thighs, would flash suddenly through his mind at the most inopportune times. None of it mattered. He was at the hermitage to seek salvation, not love. And he had to try and go to sleep now, anyway.

THE FOLLOWING DAY, during the hour of afternoon rest that followed the noon repast, Edward was standing in the shade of the cloistered garden, gazing at the apothecary's rose shrubs. It had been a joy to find that they belonged in the gardens of St Alberto just like they did in virtually all Abbeys in England. Soon, the bright crimson rosebuds would smother the bushes – he looked forward to the spectacle. Judging from the buzzing in the air, the bees kept by the monks were as impatient as him.

He was absorbed in these thoughts when he realised that someone was approaching. To his surprise, it was the very novice who, of late, had taken to occupying his dreams with embarrassing frequency. The novice was carrying a bunch of white flowers and coming towards the area of the cloister in which Edward was standing. Edward looked to his left and right: no one else around, so the novice must be coming for him. *With flowers?* Edward allowed his heart to leap – just a little.

'*Per te.*' These are for you.

He had been very matter-of-fact. He didn't quite have the attitude of someone performing an act of kindness, let alone someone in love. But perhaps he was inexperienced, a little embarrassed?

Edward extended his arm to take hold of the flowers. '*Molte grazie*', he said with a charmed smile.

He was a little rusty himself when it came to courtship: becoming momentarily engrossed with the flowers seemed as good a next move as any. He had never seen the likes of them. Each had six petals, slightly twisted, arranged to look rather like a star, and of the most dazzling white imaginable. At the centre of each flower was a small corona, a tiny, ruffled disc with a bright orange outer rim, a yellow middle band, and a green eye. The foliage was a glaucous green. But the most extraordinary thing about them was the scent – heady, sweet, and spicy. Edward was quite enraptured.

In his tottering Italian, he asked, '*Cosa sono?*' What are they?

As he raised his eyes and nose from the bunch of flowers, he realised, much to his puzzlement, that the novice had already turned on his heels and had been about to leave.

'*Cosa?*' asked the young man, turning around again. Pardon?

'*I fiori: cosa sono?*' The flowers: what are they?

'*E che ne so? Non li ho mica raccolti io.*' How am I to know? I didn't pick them.

Edward felt foolish. He thought he understood but didn't have full confidence in his command of the language and decided to double check.

'*Non sono...da te?*' They are not from you?

He was sure he hadn't phrased the question correctly. The lad must think him a dotty old man. How old was he anyway – half Edward's own age?

'*Nossignore.*'

Edward gestured impatiently, as if to ask, Who are they from, then? At least he had fully mastered the Italian art of gesticulation, if not the linguistic knowledge that was supposed to go with it.

The novice shrugged. '*E' venuto uno che ha detto di darli all'inglese.*' A man came and said to give them to the Englishman.

'*Dov'è?*' And where is this man?

'*Se n'è andato, credo.*' He left, I think.

'*Ma chi era?*' But who was it?

The novice shrugged again, impatiently, signalling to Edward that he had not the foggiest notion. This second shrug also had the most curious effect on Edward's interest in the novice, which he had foolishly conceived over the past few weeks. Namely, the last shred of such interest – which had miraculously managed to survive their conversation thus far – had now been utterly destroyed.

'Thanks for nothing,' Edward would have liked to reply. He didn't, partly because by now he was supposed to know better than to let such trivialities annoy him, but mostly, because he was not sure how to formulate the sentence properly in Italian. *Grazie per niente?* Or: *Grazie di niente?* The thought that the novice might fail to understand if he picked the wrong option, and that he, Edward, would then have to try to explain, struck him as absolutely frightful. As the novice walked away, Edward automatically brought the bouquet back to his nose once more to inhale the bewitching, potent scent.

'Ass,' he said, thinking of that discourteous cretin of a novice.

Then, with the big strides his stature made him capable of, he hurried through the main building of the small monastic complex and exited it from the opposite end. The main gate of the Abbey opened onto the only road connecting the hermitage to the rest of the world. He might still be able to overtake his mysterious visitor and come back in time for the Ninth Hour's prayer, unless the visitor had taken one of the paths winding through the forest – in which case, Edward's chances of finding him would be remote.

Edward had first walked down that road two years ago, when he had approached the Abbey grounds for the first time. At the time, he had been struck by how, as he got closer and closer to the hermitage, the birds started singing, and his progress miraculously got cooler and cooler, providing relief from the sweltering Italian summer heat... He was now about to walk this same road in the opposite direction. Absorbed in reminiscing, he almost missed the silhouette, ever so slightly familiar, of someone sitting in a clearing in the woods, near the Abbey's gate. From the bank of the hill, the man was looking out to the undulating horizon, his back to the road and to Edward. He wore a tight-fitting doublet that showed off his square shoulders and well-shaped torso. The plain material, lacking either embroidery or ornamentation, did not suggest high social status, but it was a beautiful shade of cloudy blue-green, rather like the teal of the waters lapping the Cornish coast. The man seemed to sense Edward's approach: he turned and looked up. A little aged, but Edward had seen his soft English features before, although he found himself struggling to place him.

'Still damselfly-like,' the man said, a little shyly, as Edward came within earshot. 'Your eyes, I mean.'

Vaguely disconcerted, Edward, narrowed his gaze. A brief pause. Expectancy on both sides, bridging the gap between them.

Then the stranger spoke again. 'Well, what do you think, Your Grace?'

'Think?' Edward's voice broke, as his lips quivered in recognition.

'Why, of the poet's daffodils, brother.'

And a silken smile enveloped the lips of Sir Richard de Neueby.

Afterword

This is a work of fiction, but much of it is grounded in historical research. Apart from reading a number of 14th century chronicles, I have relied on contemporary historical studies, including: Maddicott's *Thomas of Lancaster;* Philips' *Aymer de Valance* and *Edward II;* Hamilton's *Piers Gaveston;* Haines' *King Edward II;* and Chaplais' *Piers Gaveston*. By far the most important historical work that has inspired and shaped the book, however, is the body of research carried out by Kathryn Warner – not only her two biographies *Edward II* and *Isabella of France*, but also her website *edwardthesecond.blogspot.co.uk* (a veritable treasure trove).

I cannot claim that the work is entirely free of historical errors, but the chronology of events in the novel is, as far as I'm aware, all correct. Much of what the novel narrates in fictional form did happen, and it happened at the places indicated in the book. To my knowledge, whatever I invented is compatible with the historical record. This doesn't necessarily mean, of course, that things went the way I imagined they did – only that we have no evidence that they didn't.

Not just the major events, but also many of the secondary details in the book are true to historical fact, at least as far as historians have been able to reconstruct it. Thus, Edward was tall, wide-browed, and wavy-haired; he did like swimming and rowing and speaking to commoners; Piers was regarded as dashing; Isabella was thought uncommonly fair (and liked apples); Edward did give Eleanor forty-seven goldfinches, just as he gave Piers tapestries and quilts to take with him on his first exile; Isabella and Edward did board separate ships on their way to England after their marriage; Edward did wear black and green at his coronation; Piers is reported to have assigned those nicknames to the Earls; Hugh really prostrated himself before Edward in the snow; the monks at St Mary's were notorious for their incontinence; Edward did give Hugh the manuscript of *Tristan and Isolde*; Edward III was conceived at Lent; etc. On the other hand, we know nothing about what Hugh or Margaret looked like, nor do we know whether Edward loved the apothecary's rose or Piers the poet's daffodil. Having Langton nicknamed Lan-goat by Piers was my own idea too. And so on.

We don't know how Piers and Edward first met, so their first encounter in Canterbury and their first love tryst in Carlisle in 1299 are invented. There are some clues suggesting Edward and Piers may have entered into a sworn brotherhood compact, but there's no hard evidence. Piers is reported to have been roughly contemporary to Edward in age, but the findings of recent research communicated to Kathryn Warner suggest he was quite a bit older. I think that a difference in age makes more credible Edward being smitten with Piers at first sight, which by all accounts he was. But the novel also suggests an explanation for why Piers came to be believed to be much closer in age to Edward than he really was – namely Edward's and Piers' deliberate deception on that point.

Isabella's adventure in the secret passage at Berwick is made up. Its purpose is to provide some insight into the reasons why I imagine her to have endorsed Piers and Edward's relationship. As Kathryn Warner has demonstrated, although we have evidence that Isabella objected to Hugh, there is none, and indeed no reason to suppose, that she disliked Piers. That virtually all fictional and non-fictional accounts of the times of Edward II assume otherwise tells more about their authors' preferences and bias (and frankly, their lack of imagination) than about Isabella herself.

The true reasons why Edward's father punished his son and sent Piers and Gilbert de Clare away from Edward's household in 1305 remain unclear. A trespass on someone's forest, as indicated in the *Annales Londonienses*, is a possible explanation. Most historians seem to assume it was Edward trespassing upon Langton's land rather than vice-versa. I followed Haines in assuming the opposite. I embroidered on this trespass by imagining that, during it, Langton witnessed Edward fellating Piers. I did so for dramatic (and erotic) effect, but also because it seemed as likely a reason as any to account for the King's disproportionate response.

Historians still puzzle over what exactly caused the King to exile Piers to Gascony in 1307. The chronicler Walter of Guisborough reports that the cause of the exile was Edward asking Langton to intercede with his father so that Piers could be granted Ponthieu. But how can it be so, historians ask, if Edward and Langton appear not to have been on good terms at the time? And why were the terms of the exile so lenient, if it is true that the First Edward went into such a fury as to pull the Prince's hair out with his own hands? I solved this puzzle by supposing that Langton learnt through a spy about Edward's intentions regarding Ponthieu and that he reported these intentions to the King of his own accord. I accounted for the generous terms of Piers' exile as a ploy on the King and Langton's part to get the Prince and his Companion to comply.

The crime I impute to Langton, however, (namely, his attempting to have Piers murdered at sea) is completely invented. The real Langton – a bishop, but also a shrewd statesman apparently entirely at home in the cutthroat world of politics and temporal power – may or may not have been capable of murderous plots. If he wasn't, I beg his pardon for making a villain of his literary namesake in this book.

As for the King making a scene and pulling Edward's hair out, it seemed improbable that Edward, physically commanding as he was, would meekly submit to such treatment. So I assumed that the King *threatened* to pull his son's hair out, and then not on the occasion of Piers' first exile (when the King had good reasons to avoid antagonising his son), but on the occasion of their earlier quarrel in 1305. After all, what could be more natural than a chronicler getting the two altercations mixed up and misreporting a threat of violence for an actually violent deed? Besides, making Edward's hair significant to his 1305 rather than his 1307 quarrel with his father provided me with an explanatory device to make sense of the King's decision, in 1305, to send Gilbert de Clare away from Edward's Court alongside Piers.

Historians also puzzle over what may have happened to cause a sudden, irreparable rift between Edward and his cousin Lancaster in November 1308. I assumed that by this time Lancaster was already disaffected with the King; what was new in November 1308 was simply that Lancaster gave himself away. Thus, I also made Lancaster the real instigator of the anti-Gaveston meeting of the Earls in February of the same year.

There's no record that Edward saw Piers off on his third exile; but as Kathryn Warner pointed out, this seems out of character. Thus, I imagined he did see Piers off, albeit secretly. Piers' reason for returning so quickly from his third exile is a matter for speculation; I have speculated that physical illness was at the root of it.

There's no evidence that Edward and Piers met at St Mary's after parting at Scarborough Castle, though they may well have. I simply couldn't bear not letting them see each other one last time. We are told that Piers' decapitated body was retrieved by cobblers or Dominican Friars, though without any additional detail.

Although 14th century chronicles sometimes expatiate on supernatural events, none speak of Edward being haunted by Piers' ghost. Edward did see a conjuror at Swineshead Priory not long after learning of Piers' death. But it's anyone's guess whether it was a conjuror of spirits (as I assume), or one dealing in other tricks. The cunning man episode is also made up, though Edward is likely to have passed by the mill on the river Kennet when accompanying Piers to Bristol for his second exile. The purpose of the cunning man incident is, of course, to lay the groundwork for the King's subsequent haunting. (Incidentally, there seems to be evidence going back to the early modern age of local folklore about a cunning man or woman in the area; I saw no good reason why the tradition couldn't have originated a few centuries earlier).

Edward really was visited by one Richard de Neueby at Eltham, who claimed to be his Gascon brother despite his non-Gascon sounding name. Surprisingly, De Neueby was paid good money after his visit (which was not the typical fate of people making outlandish claims of being related to Royalty). I came up with an explanation for the incident that would of course be entirely out of place in a history book. Happily, it is perfectly at home in a work of fiction. Oliver de Bordeaux is also a true historical figure, and Edward did pay him for something (unspecified) he did when the King sat by his bed! This information, as myriad other details about minor events in Edward's life, is only available to us thanks to Kathryn Warner's painstaking research.

We don't really know the exact nature of the relationship between Edward and Damory, or Edward and Audley, or Edward and Montacute (nor do we know what these favourites looked like). It's obvious, however, that Edward liked them very much. I imagined Edward's relationship with Damory to have been platonic and his relationship with Audley to have been almost purely sexual. For all we know, it might have been the other way around. There is no record of Hugh and Damory falling out at Amiens: it was a device of mine to account for Damory's later betrayal of Edward.

To paraphrase Jane Austen, Hugh Despenser the Younger may well be a hero that no one but me will like. Hugh is an enigmatic figure. All those intrigued by him will be delighted to hear of Kathryn Warner's biography (still forthcoming at the time of writing): *Hugh Despenser the Younger & Edward II: Downfall of a King's Favourite*. This is the first ever biography of the Younger Despenser.

We don't know if Hugh had sex with the pirates in whose exploits he partook (pleasing though the thought may be), or with other men besides Edward. Strictly speaking, we don't know that Hugh – and for that matter Piers – had shaken the sheets with Edward, either (though it defies belief to suppose they didn't).

There is evidence of Edward liking Margaret's sister, Eleanor, a great deal. The reality of Margaret's confinement at Sempringham Priory may well have been less rosy than I paint it. Then again, it's not necessarily the case that it was. Indeed, the real, historical Edward may have been nicer than my fictional Edward: the nastiest thing the King does in the novel (that is, his order that the blade due to sever Lancaster's head be on the dull side) is my own invention.

We don't know what was in Hugh and Edward's minds when they left Caerphilly: I think my psychological account is as good a guess as any. Thankfully, there is no evidence that Orleton made Edward attend Hugh's gruesome execution. Conversely, there's none that he didn't. We know, however, that Orleton was no shrinking violet when it came to destroying Edward's kingship and reputation: he has the dubious distinction of being the first person ever recorded as having accused Edward of being a sodomite (in 1326).

Needless to say, perhaps, there is also no report of Hugh getting an erection, let alone ejaculating, during his hanging. Hugh being no less a favourite of mine than of Edward's, however, I wanted him to have a triumph of sorts over the crowds that had come to gloat over his murder.

The meeting between John and Isabella at Castle Rising is pure invention. John died a few months later in Scotland. I wish he hadn't, and that I could write a novel about him.

Finally, we don't know what really happened to Edward after he was transferred to Berkeley. Conventional historiography has him murdered there in 1327, but there is significant evidence that instead he may have secretly made his way to Italy. If he did, it is difficult to know exactly who enabled his escape. I supposed Maltravers and Berkeley were responsible for thwarting Mortimer's planned regicide, but it's possible that Mortimer was less of a villain than I think he was. In other words, it may have been he and Isabella who masterminded the whole thing – Edward's pretended death, his secret custody at Corfe, and his subsequent escape to the Continent. By far the best analysis of the evidence for and against Edward's survival after 1327 is in Kathryn Warner's myth-busting book *Long Live the King*.

Quite naturally, being Italian and loving Edward, I found irresistible the hypothesis of his having escaped death at Berkeley and having sought refuge in Italy. Equally naturally, many British historians, eager to own the King's death (and, apparently, liking him less than I do), want to believe he died at Berkeley Castle. Happily, there's no more evidence that he did, than of his escape to Lombardy.

I want to thank Steve Berman at Lethe Press, who liked the novel enough to want to publish it, showed me where my writing technique was lacking and generally gave the project his personal attention. Solana Warner did some brilliant (and sensitive) editorial work. Mai Sato's and Martha-Marie Kleinhans' feedback helped me improve the content by demanding more space for Isabella, more descriptions, and – in Martha-Marie's case – more sex! Samar Habib's careful reading assisted me in countless ways, including by curbing my enthusiasm for the past perfect tense. Thanks to Kathryn Warner I avoided some blunders in my use of medieval honorifics; any remaining errors, of course, are mine. Other readers of early drafts who deserve my thanks for their encouragement are Gloria Bona, Luciana Gottardi, Thomas Tapmeier, and, of course, my muse – Hideki Kojima.

Aleardo Zanghellini
August 2018

About the Author

Aleardo Zanghellini is Professor of Law and Social Theory at Reading Law School. His work is interdisciplinary in nature and regularly appears in leading international journals. Much of it is in the field of law and sexuality, but he also interrogates general concepts and principles of political morality that are of interest to political philosophers and public lawyers. His 2015 book, The Sexual Constitution of Political Authority, is an analysis of the erotic dimensions of state power. It argues that the disavowal of male same-sex desire has been, and partly remains, central to mainstream understandings of political authority. *The Spellbinders* is his first novel.